I0583895

Praise for The Judas Line, Book 2

"A fast-paced book which does not lack for history or adventure. The inclusion of death and destruction are a given and it is good that there is a lot of humour instilled throughout. I would say that if you're a fan of Jim Butcher's *Dresden Files*, you will enjoy Mark Everett Stone's work. Recommended."

—*Michelle Herbert, Fantasy Book Review*

"Evil does not die so easily. *The Judas Line* is a novel following Jude Oliver and the long family line that lies behind him, specializing in assassination, using the artifact known as the silver. Jude Oliver must find the origins and stories of his family to be able to end the Silver's legacy for good, with only a single Catholic priest by his side. Blending paranormal and biblical ideas, *The Judas Line* is a riveting thriller that should prove hard to put down."

—*Midwest Book Review*

★ "This delightful Catholicism-infused quest fantasy stars a likable and original duo. Fr. Michael Engle, a pragmatic Catholic priest, and Jude, who has a considerably more uncertain relationship with God, are unlikely friends, but when a blood-covered Jude runs into Mike's church asking for help, Mike listens to him, believes him, and joins him on a quest to find the Holy Grail, which Jude hopes will help him destroy a legendary and dangerous family heirloom. Along the way they encounter Cain, the Norse gods (drinking and watching *Bridge over the River Kwai*), and a Valkyrie with the requisite 'chainmail-covered pillowy breasts.' When Mephistopheles shows up, Jude manages to label him an Arch-Fiend of Hell without irony and without irritating the reader. Stone's depiction of magic is realistic and intelligent and his treatment of Catholicism refreshingly informed and three-dimensional. Even the obligatory near-apocalyptic ending is coherent, surprising, and exciting."

—*Publishers Weekly*

The Judas Revelation

The Judas Revelation

THE JUDAS LINE CHRONICLES, BOOK 3

MARK EVERETT STONE

CAMEL
PRESS
Kenmore, WA

CAMEL PRESS

A Camel Press book published by Epicenter Press

Epicenter Press
6524 NE 181st St.
Suite 2
Kenmore, WA 98028

For more information go to:
www.Camelpress.com
www.Coffeetownpress.com
www. Epicenterpress.com
www.markeverettstone.wixsite.com/mysite-1

All rights reserved. No part of this book may be reproduced or transmitted in any form or by any means, electronic or mechanical, including photocopying, recording, or any information storage and retrieval system, without permission in writing from the publisher.

This is a work of fiction. Names, characters, places, brands, media, and incidents are either the product of the author's imagination or are used fictitiously.

Cover design by Sabrina Sun
Interior and cover production by Scott Book and Melissa Vail Coffman

The Judas Revelation
Copyright © 2020 by Mark Everett Stone

ISBN: 978-1-60381-284-9 (Trade Paper)
ISBN: 978-1-60381-285-6 (eBook)

Printed in the United States of America

Acknowledgments

⁓

I WOULD LIKE TO THANK ALL MY fans who clamored for sequels, I hope it lives up to your expectations. I would also like to acknowledge my beta-readers and friends for their suggestions and Jennifer McCord at Camel Press for her extraordinary patience with me.

This one is for Mom and Dad

THE BOOK OF

MICHAEL

THE BOOK OF

ISHMAEL

CHAPTER ONE
NEW OLD ENEMIES

H E HAD AN UGLY CURL TO his lips. More than a sneer, yet much less than a smile. It conveyed all manner of wickedness, depths of depravity no man could ever plumb and a total disregard for anything but himself. It spoke volumes of his self-indulgence, the lengths to which he would go to achieve his goals. Looking at it made my stomach clench in nausea. All in all, a lot conveyed by a twist of flesh controlled by a sphincter muscle.

"You think these cuffs can hold me?" asked the sneering man, handsome as the devil despite the ugliness of his mouth. A long lock of jet black hair curled over an eye as blue as glacial ice, a stark contrast to his swarthy skin. Thick, gleaming steel manacles encircled each wrist with even thicker chains joining them behind his back as he knelt on the floor. His legs were similarly bound, with a half-inch steel cable connecting the shackles, but he held himself regally despite the undignified posture and the rather scruffy, loose green surgical scrubs draped over his lean form. He was so sure of his superiority that you'd think he *planned* to be in the little ten-by-ten cell, that it was all part of some clever and bold con.

"If you could break them, you would have." The speaker stood over the man, massive arms crossed in front of an equally massive chest, an overlarge Taser clipped to a wide brown belt. A face like a shelf of granite stared down, expressionless and cold. I could practically sense his desire to use the specially modified Taser on the kneeling man.

"When you play with fire, mortal ..."

"You get burned," I finished as I opened the door into the cell. I had been listening and watching covertly for a while and I knew my cue when I heard it. The cell smelled like burnt dust, the kind of reek that wafts from heater registers on the first cold day of autumn. It made my nose twitch.

The kneeling man snorted. "Of course, you were peeping. I expected as much such."

Mouth barely moving, the big man said, "Sir, you should not be here. This one is dangerous."

I nodded slightly, rubbing my nose. "It's okay, Milo, he can't overcome the will of God."

"The will of God?" The kneeling man laughed. "You think you know God's will? Does He chatter in your ear, sweet nothings to get you hard in the middle of night?" The sneer was back in full force, contorting his face into something other than human. "I know God, you febrile human, you mewing cunny, and let me tell you … He is a sadist. A self-absorbed, self-indulgent father too enamored of His overly convoluted games, His precious destinies, to give a good flying fuck about His children."

As the man spoke, Milo grew whiter and whiter with rage, his huge muscles clenching and unclenching, and I set a comforting hand on one granite shoulder. The cloth of his black t-shirt was stretched tight to the breaking point. "Easy, there. Just words, Milo." My voice was gentle, calm.

Muscles under my palm slowly relaxed. "Yes sir." Softly, like the breath of a dying man. "Thank you, sir."

"No sirs here, Milo."

"Okay."

"Aww, isn't that nice, two men all queer for each other."

Once again Milo tensed but eased up as I squeezed his shoulder. "Very funny, Hermes," I drawled. "Remember you are a prisoner here." Smiling grimly, I waved a hand at the inch-thick iron bars that comprised one wall of the cell. I took a knee, moving my face closer to the prisoner. The concrete floor was cold through the fabric of my jeans. "Cooperate and you will be treated fairly."

"Fairly? What do humans know of fair? I am *ageless*. I have seen all that is fair and unfair and let me tell you, mortal man, I am unimpressed. You should be at my feet pleading for your life if you know what's good for you. My wrath will last *eons*. I can keep you suffering until the stars burn out."

I leaned in close and Hermes recoiled. A familiar warmth suffused my flesh, like hot oil sliding through my veins and I knew the power of the Lord was upon me. It had been a while and I basked in the feel of the Almighty's love and sweet regard. My voice lashed out in a command I could not control. "*Behave, Hermiel.*"

The room shook slightly as the shock of my voice, filled with awful power, rippled outward in a wave that curdled the air. Hermes/Hermiel paled, finally showing some emotion besides disdain: Fear. Buckets and buckets of naked fear, something I reckoned he hadn't dealt with in a long, long time. "It's *you*," he breathed.

And like that, the feeling left, leaving me upon the verge of tears. Words are weak things to covey what I felt but Imagine that you're a child in the back seat of a car and your parents are in the front, driving and talking quietly. It's dark and warm and you're tired, but totally content in the knowledge that nothing bad can happen because you are loved, that your mother and father will get you home safe and sound and you begin to drift off into slumber absolutely sure in your parent's infallibility. That total, wholehearted belief and comfort, the innocence that lasts only a few years before life strips it away. Imagine that suffusing your body, caressing, loving.

Then take it away in an instant.

That's how I felt. I wanted to weep, to tear at my hair and clothes, but instead I lowered my voice to a whisper. "Now, Hermiel." The name given to me, his true name, the Harbinger of Floods, a former Cherubim of the Host. "You will tell me what I want to know, do you understand?"

Defiance crept into his eyes, but the fear returned when I lifted a finger. Ah … he was afraid of my touch. Afraid that if I placed a single finger against his cheek he would be consigned back to Hell. Silly, really. I didn't have to touch him at all.

Hermes nodded. "Okay."

THE BOOK OF

HERMIEL

CHAPTER ONE
WIGHTS IN NIGHT SATIN

WHAT CAN I TELL YOU? Humans are, to my kind, mayflies. Their brief lives a flicker upon my awareness before suddenly extinguishing themselves in all manner of creative ways. However, I do find some pleasure interacting with them. Chocolate, for example. That has to be their best invention by far. Forget the cure for polio or smallpox, or flight for that matter, they pale in comparison to the creamy, dark sweetness of pure milk chocolate. The Finns pretty much have a lock on the best, with the Swiss a close second.

Sex is another thing I dig that seems to be a particular human obsession. Even more so than chocolate, which only proves my point about their inferiority and complete lack of judgement.

Now mixing sex and chocolate only seemed natural, didn't it? I recommend Fazer Weiner Nugat if you have the patience to unwrap the little rectangles of heaven from their foils, but a Teuscher chocolate bar will do in a pinch.

The woman was good, limber and hungry and she made a valiant effort at satiating my chocolate/sex desires, but, being merely human, couldn't. Good time though. Last time I truly enjoyed a shag was that Russian noble, Catherine in 1768. Now *that* was a feisty one. Great between the sheets and gave mean head.

I stared out from my Miami Beach penthouse at the ocean, a dark mass a couple dozen stories below. The wine-dark waves always called to me, a tug at my deepest essence, a muscle spasm just behind my heart. They haunted me, those waters, and I couldn't bear to live far from the gentle sound of their surging. Part of my nature. I used to be the Harbinger of Floods for a reason.

"Come back to bed, Harry," the woman murmured, not quite awake.

White sheets were tangled around her shapely legs and her long honey hair lay in tangles over the silk pillowcases. A satisfied smile was pasted to her pretty face with its spray of light freckles. "We can cuddle some. Maybe do more than cuddle."

"Why?" I lit a clove cigarette with a disposable lighter and drew the aromatic smoke deep into my lungs. "I'm done."

"Done?"

"Done. Finished. End of story." Another drag. Damn, it felt good. I so loved the aromatic smokes; too bad they were banned the US. "Get out."

"Wha-?"

"Get the fuck outta here, Janice."

"Jackie!"

"Whatfucking ever. Take a hike. There's a few twenties on the dresser under the Tiffany lamp if you need cab fare, but fuck off, will ya?"

She started get all indignant, working herself up to a good scream, but one icy look quelled her right quick and she shut up and began worming into her slinky short party dress the color of steam, covering the leftover streaks of chocolate. The dress stuck to her like a coat of paint, emphasizing her ass and tits. Pretty damn nice, a body built for porn.

"You're such an asshole," she hissed right before the door to the penthouse slammed shut.

Not the first time I'd been called that and I was pretty sure it wouldn't be the last. My smile felt wicked as I relived the night's fucking, the thrusting and grunting and licking and I almost wished she would've stayed. Almost. Chicks like her are a dime a dozen. Well, maybe a quarter. Fifty cents tops.

The clove smoke filled my nostrils, pungent and pleasant and I decided on some beer to accompany the flavor. A good Belgium dark. Fortunately for me, my valet made sure to stock nothing but the best and plenty of it. Stony may not be much to look at with his burn scarred features from his run-in with in IED in Kabul, but he was loyal because I brought him the man who stole his face, an insurgent bomb maker named Tariq who took a goodly long while to die. What he did to the bomber rivaled anything I saw in the Rebellion. When Stony was through, the remaining bits and pieces were dumped overboard about five miles from shore and I had a servant for life. The human capacity for revenge is amazing. I hoped Lucifer was taking notes.

Still naked from my all-night fuckfest, I popped the top off a Vander Ghiste Oud Bruin and took a long pull from the dark bottle, standing in the light of the open fridge. Damn, those Belgium bastards could brew. Don't get me wrong, I love a good mead, but there's something about a good brew after a hard night's fucking that just plain *satisfies*.

I looked around at my penthouse apartment with its marble floor and polished ammolite countertops, the semi-precious stone throwing rainbows even in the dim light of the kitchen. The throw rugs were of brown alpaca so soft it felt like you were walking on clouds and the sheets on the bed satin, so white as to nearly blind the eye. Everything I owned was the best, made by the best and finer than kings and potentates could imagine, which was only my due as a god.

That may be stretching things, I admit. I am a fallen angel, a Cherubim on the outs with Daddy dearest. Simplicity itself to clothe myself in a deific mantle. Hermes, messenger, god of athletes and thieves. Suited me just fine. Zoriel and Postial pandered to warriors and such under their greater god hats, but the fun was down in the dirt where you could really fuck with the mortals. Besides, as strong as they were, they lacked in the old IQ department. I've met oxen with more going on between the ears.

Why did I choose to work with those two and their less than stellar-witted brethren, to become a lesser god of the Greeks? Easy, less work and more pay, so to speak. And why did I choose the Greeks to lord over? The choice was simple, they were a passionate, vibrant, quarrelsome, warlike, stubborn, and foolhardy people. It seemed like every emotion they had burned brighter in them than in others. Mayflies, but ones that knew how to *party*. And let me say this, those Greek women back then were horny as fuck and loved to please a randy god who deigned to show up with an incredibly epic boner.

Ping!

Ah, a call. I picked up my tablet from its charging plate on my nightstand and laid my thumb on the upper left-hand corner of the screen. It glowed green for a moment as it analyzed my print, then the display came to life showing me a face I thought gone the way of the Dodo. It appeared against a black background.

"Fuck me," I laughed. "Here I thought you were buried face down, so you could see where you were going, Burke."

Burke Deschamps, son of the none too lamented Julian Deschamps, asshole extraordinaire and head of the Family, the direct descendants of Judas Iscariot. And through him, Lucifer Morningsar, my ex-boss, the great rebel rabble-rouser himself. Not that I talked to the wingless wonder anymore. I said goodbye to him after the Rebellion when Dad, Mike and the other choirboys threw us all out of the upstairs loft and I wanted nothing to do with his whole Antichrist-taking-over-the-whole-fucking-world-bringing-about-the-Trials-and-Tribulations nonsense, initiating The Apocalypse. Or Armageddon or whatever the fuck you want to call it. Lucifer is strong and shit, but like most of Dad's kids, he's heavy on the brawn and light on the brains.

Forget *The Omen* where Damien Thorne is protected by infernal forces and people died in seriously creepy and fucked-up ways, that was the movies.

Real life is far more stupid and sloppy than what you see on film. Lucifer's been trying the End Times routine for centuries to no avail because all his descendants proved far too human, too fragile to be the vessel he needed. That's the price you pay for relying on mortals.

There was one who fit the bill, an anointed child, Julien's son Olivier, the one "destined" to be the antichrist (or Redeemer, to use their silly lingo). The brat turned his back on his diabolical family, stole the Silver and the Codex and pulled a Houdini. That's how Burke got himself a case of dead, by fucking with the one guy who was as powerful, if not more so, than he was. Boy, didn't Olivier exit him from this reality quickly, a fact the Family tried to keep quiet, but couldn't from me because of my sheer awesomeness. Looking at his mug begged the question, "How did you duplicate Jesus' favorite party trick?" I gave him a glimpse of my angelic teeth, all straight and blindingly white.

Burke's perfect olive skin flushed slightly, which was an improvement because in the old days he would've blown a gasket in three seconds flat. Before death Burke had magic to spare and superb physical skills but hovered barely above a Chihuahua emotionally. Maybe death turned out to be a learning experience. Not that I would know. "And, of course, it is good to see you again, Hermiel," he drawled.

Yeah, he sure knew my name. Not surprising considering his boss. And the fact that the Family had used my services on and off again for the past two-thousand years. Our history together is a long and profitable one, although when you work with assholes you need to get used to the stink.

I squinted at his smug face. Slightly large nose, deep brown eyes that were almost black and short, very thick coal-dark hair and caterpillar eyebrows that threatened to join in the middle. Some acting lessons and he could have his own TV show, like *The Bloodsucker Journals*. "Seriously, how come you're alive? Word is Olivier punched your ticket but good and burned your body to ash. Unless you're twins, that is, and in that case, I'll call you Beck, so I can tell the difference."

"Ha-ha, Hermiel."

"All right don't get your panties twisted. I know you're just dying (get it, *dying*) for me to ask why you called, but I'm rather bored and fucked out right now, so I'll just hang up, so I can get some shut-eye." Technically, being an angel and all, I didn't need to sleep, but I liked to. If I wasn't so industrious I would graduate to lazy in a heartbeat.

A flash of annoyance marred his features. "I want to hire you and your usual team of cutthroats."

Of course. A job. Usually I worked alone because humans tend to fuck things up, but there were a few hand-picked mercenaries I used because of their reliability, discretion and an above-the-elite skill set. When they weren't working for me they could be found in some Middle Eastern shithole giving lead poisoning to insurgents and offering the US government plausible deniability. They called themselves the Wights.

Mortals, so clever with names.

"You must want someone executively dead, Burke. Who is it? Head of state? Celebrity? Or perhaps Gordon Ramsay, I always hated that fucker."

Annoyance crawled across his face. I was getting to him … I love that shit. "Your target is the new leader of the Templars."

The Knights goddamn Templars. Pain in the Deschamps hemorrhoids for centuries and sworn enemies of the Sicarii, that ancient order of assassins also founded by Judas Iscariot. For the Deschamps, it was the Family business, killing people on the sly and you'd think they'd have plenty of wetboys and wetgirls to take out the Knights. Perhaps they were on vacation to Satanic Disneyland. I mean, c'mon, they practically *invented* assassination here on Earth. I said as much to Burke, but he wasn't having any of it.

"The new leader is something not seen in a long time, Hermiel," he retorted, swallowing his irritation. "He's a prophet, a real one."

For the first time in decades I felt a thread of fear sliding through my guts and I hated it. I suddenly knew Burke's target.

Six months ago, the fallen Seraphim Atheniel, a rebel angel who took the form and aspect of the Greek Goddess Athena, disappeared from the face of the earth and I felt it. A clarion call buffeting my mind as divine forgiveness flooded down from Heaven, from the Pearlescent Throne, and touched a spot far away. France, I think. The forgiveness took the form of a shaft of light that only those without earthly scales over their eyes could see. I didn't need to see it, and I didn't want to see it. The sound that wasn't a sound alerted me and that was enough. The fact that I could *feel* the forgiveness from the penthouse as well as Athena's enthusiastic acceptance of it, her glad cry that rippled around the world was bad enough. I knew deep in my bones that all the fallen, all those who assumed the mantles of various deities across the world felt Atheniel's exultance, too. The flavor of her angelic essence, as recognizable as an oft-gazed at picture, could not be mistaken.

Most of us were content with our lot, or so I assumed because I don't hobnob with my brothers and sisters anymore and they pretty much felt the same way, except for those lazy bastards of the Norse pantheon. Odin, Thor and the rest of the lot were so swept up in self-pity and reliving glory days with that pathetic excuse for entertainment that was called the Valhalla Club, that it made me sick. So, what if we fallen had lost most of our powers over the centuries, becoming weaker and frailer? We were still a fuckload lot stronger than human beings by a long shot and basically immortal if we didn't get chopped into slurry with a Cuisinart. Even lost limbs grew back over time and who didn't love *that* happy crap?

But a feeling one of our own earning forgiveness and reentry into the First World took me down a peg or two, reminded me again of what I lost and the hurt of it. I guarantee you that the others felt the same way.

"Burke, you absolute dickhead," I ground out, suddenly feeling as if my teeth were too big for my mouth, "a Prophet with a capital P? One of Dad's personal pets? *Are you out of your fucking mind?*"

I took a calming breath trying to stifle the fear that washed through my veins like ice water. "Listen," I continued a bit more evenly. "What makes you think a fallen angel is going to risk being stuffed back into Hell by a person with divine power at their fingertips." It would be like being touched by Dad himself. My skin began to itch. "Sure, given enough time, I am plenty sly enough to escape Lucifer's basement apartment, but do you really think that I'm going to risk it? No way, no thanks no how, no soup for you, come back one year."

"One-hundred million dollars."

There are many benefits to being immortal, one of them is plenty of time to amass a serious fortune. In truth, I didn't need to work, I had plenty of cash to last the next dozen millennia, so one-hundred million dollars was no great incentive. I said as much.

"Half a billion, then."

Half a billion, shmaf a billion. Still not any great reason to risk my angelic self being thrust down into the cellar. My mouth opened, and I felt an epic takedown of all of Burke's arguments lay thick on my tongue when my teeth suddenly snapped shut.

An idea. An Idea. An IDEA. A lightbulb-over-the-head, come-here-Watson-I-need-you sort of idea. Of their own accord my lips slipped upward in a smile so deliciously wicked that Burke's image recoiled in alarm. When an angel smiles like that, run as far and as fast as you can because savage things are a-brewing.

"By the Patron, stop grinning like that!" Burke snarled, hiding his fear well, but to my angelic eyes I could see the emotion running deep under his skin.

Patron. What a laugh. It was as if the Deschamps were afraid to call him by his correct name ... Lucifer. Perhaps Lucy didn't like to be reminded of his former station in life. For the rest of the fallen, though, we couldn't help but have our noses rubbed in it. Dad's glory was all around ... in the sunrise, the ocean currents, the mountains thrusting at the sky. Everywhere. I guess in Hell there wasn't anything of Dad's to bother his snobby senses.

"Burke, my lad, I will do this thing for you," I laughed, still smiling hideously.

He was less than comforted. "What do you want?"

"Something I know you, and only you, can provide."

Had he been a lesser man he would have broken out in a cold sweat. As it was, he narrowed his dark eyes and barked. "What?"

"I want the third Passion Nail, the one you anti-choirboys call Ablewand."

His face paled to parchment.

"In advance," I added.

CHAPTER TWO
EVERY THORN HAS A ROSE

———— ❧ ————

ABLEWAND. STUPID NAME FOR A RELIC. I flipped the dagger end over end, testing its balance, marveling at its crudity. No edge, the shaft was square cross-section, tapering to a needle point. No shine, just a simple, rough iron shaft. The head of the nail had been inserted into a five-inch iron hilt with equally crude two-inch cross guard that held the blade firm. The balance was about what you'd think … terrible.

When Daddy's little boy was nailed to the cross on Golgotha, the Romans, ever efficient and thrifty, used three long nails to hammer through his wrists and feet, tying his arms and ankles to the sturdy wood. The worst punishment they could devise and possibly the longest, most lingering death a person could suffer aside from cancer. Those nails, slick with junior's blood became powerful relics, like the grail and the spear.

What most people don't know is that relics aren't made by touching something holy or being used for holy works, but because of the importance they hold in historic events. The Crucifixion was one of the most significant events in all human existence. One which proved to be turning point in mankind's destiny, because of that significance, because of the power of the moment, items connected to that moment were imbued with abilities beyond human understanding. Look at the Ark of the Covenant, aside from any face melting properties it might have, the army holding that relic could conquer the world.

The Holocaust created quite a few relics that are thankfully lost to man, or at least I hope they are. Hell has nothing on the tortures man inflicts upon himself and what he creates from such misery. Hitler's 7.65mm Walther PPK, the pistol with which he committed suicide, could shoot a bullet through a three-foot brick and mortar wall from five miles away with unfailing accuracy. That's just *one* facet of what it could do. Imagine a serial killer getting hold of that sucker.

It took a serious amount of cajoling to secure Ablewand, but I knew I had Burke on the ropes because he wanted one of Dad's finger-puppets killed. He hemmed and hawed and tried to lie but lying to an angel is futile. We always spot lies and, in the end, Burke agreed to my terms. Along with Ablewand, I'd receive all the details needed on one Michael Engle, Dad's newest Prophet, priest and former Army Ranger.

That was some fucked-up shit right there. A real, live GI Joe who got himself all religified. An incongruous turn of events, a war hero turned priest. Just goes to show that even Dad has a fucked-up sense of humor.

One hand caressing Ablewand, I once again considered Burke, Mr. Back from The Dead himself.

"Now that you've met my price," I'd said a couple days later once negotiations were done, "how about telling me your secret. How are you still alive?"

The pleased look in his eye made me want to smash his face right through the tablet. I knew I could either ask for Ablewand or the secret and no secret could compare with such a relic. "Suffer," he said a trifle smugly.

Dangerous ground to tread when dealing with a fallen. Sure, he was a bad ass, but I saw the birth of stars and the galaxies burst into life. I was there at Lucifer's side when he ripped the wings from our enemies and feasted on their flesh. I saw the towers of Heaven burn and a rain of angelic blood over the Fields of Silver. What had he ever done besides get his ass handed to him? Come back from the dead? Pales in comparison, let me tell you.

"Tell you what, Burke lad, why don't you give me a hint. A little one to mull over for a while. You know it'll drive me crazy trying to make sense of it." And like that, I had him. As intelligent (for humans) the Family might be, they were pathetically easy to manipulate.

He was definitely the kind of kid who enjoyed pulling the wings off of flies and the thought of me staying up nights trying to puzzle out his secret would amuse him no end.

"I'll tell you this, Hermes, this has been in the works for a hundred years."

Not much, but I'd expected that. "That it?"

An enigmatic smile answered me. I could live with that.

Once again, my fingers caressed Ablewand's hilt. This new Prophet, this priest, might be one of Dad's new choir boys, but now I possessed a relic that might keep me safe, or safer than without. I slid the dagger into the worn leather sheath it came with, blackened and cracked with age, and tied to the outside of my right thigh with a loop of leather cord. It looked a bit strange attached to my faded jeans, but I wanted the relic close and easy to draw.

A day later, I exited a rental Caddy and trotted across the street keeping out of the direct light of the streetlamps toward the five-story glass and steel monstrosity that today's foolhardy thought of as modern architecture. They could damn well sit on it and rotate, in my opinion. Back in the day people used to give a damn about craftsmanship when it came to buildings. Columns and gargoyles and hand-carved touches that gave a structure *class*. Most of what you see today looks like Frank Lloyd Wright had a massive brain fart.

On the outskirts of Atlanta, immediately south of the 85 near the Hartsfield-Jackson Atlanta International Airport, under the racket of airplanes taking off and landing, stood this ugly office building. The glass, tinted so dark that it looked to drink up the ambient light, gave no clue as to what lay inside. I knew that glass was not only virtually bulletproof, but soundproof as well, offering both protection and a measure of fucking privacy. Only those who needed to know knew what went on behind the only entrance to the place.

A set of glass double doors opened before I reached the ten-foot mark thanks to some hidden cameras. "Hello sir," said a mild, tenor voice.

Devan Marquan looked like the poster boy for tough guys. Black … excuse me, *African American* … heavily muscled with long arms and even longer legs under a lean torso that looked hard enough to break bricks against. A thick ridge of scar tissue ran across his forehead above his thunderous brows. The product of a knife fight in Tangiers, or so he said. Knowing Devan, it might have come from a jealous husband … or wife.

The leader of the Wights smirked. "Saw you on the camera. You were sitting in that Caddy for a long time."

"Is the team here?"

"Of course. You came at the right time," he answered, holding the doors open wide. "It's initiation night."

The inside of the building opened wide, hollow except for the last two stories, which were given over to offices. Mercenary work paid well enough that the Wights were able to hire a couple of secretaries … excuse me *receptionists* … as psychotic as they were. Rhonda and Mark took care of all the finances and made sure the bills got paid, the right palms greased. When you routinely delivered on your assignments you earned the right to the fucking spectacular fees the government was willing to pay.

Uncle Sam might be a right bastard, but he's a *rich* right bastard and that's all that mattered to the Wights.

While most people thought mercenaries had all the integrity of a rabid weasels, this particular crew, especially Devan, always kept to a contract, which made them desired by countries both large and small. Although only the larger ones could easily afford their rates. Half in advance and half upon completion. The smaller governments reneged often, which usually led to the assassination of the entire executive branch. Simplistic solutions like that usually meant that others would not fail to live up to their end.

Professionalism, integrity and ethics, the core qualities of the team. Yes, I said ethics because even though there were those who could afford the Wights, Devon never took contracts from rich dickheads who only wanted to oppress others, which means their clientele was smaller than you'd think. They especially avoided typical Third World countries whose dictators' main idea of fun was using chemical weapons on whatever local tribe or political group whose beliefs were considered bad form, just to see how much twitching they could do before dying.

The Wights were mercenaries, not assholes.

"Initiation night, eh?" The large space that used to be the first three stories of the building had been converted into the NRA's wet dream, a complete training room dedicated to armed mayhem. Remember when I said soundproof and bulletproof? That was to protect the outside world from what happened inside.

On most days you'd see a target range and an obstacle course, not to mention mats where some serious Krav Maga was practiced. Everything had been shoved out of the way, the Nautilus equipment, the free weights, what have you. Only the climbing wall remained where it stood, mostly because moving it would be a pain in the ass.

In the center of that big space, surrounded by load-bearing columns, were the large, blue wrestling mats, scuffed and torn and oft-mended with duct tape. The subject of the initiation stood with arms akimbo, balanced lightly on the balls of his feet.

Devan nodded. "Yep. New guy. Name Thorn."

"Tell me his name isn't Damien." Wouldn't that be apt? The Wights stood on the mats near the rookie, obviously waiting for my arrival, the man with the job and the money.

Devan gave a short bark of laughter. "Wendell. Goes by Whip."

Wendell? No wonder he had a nickname. "Who died?"

You see, when a Wight came home in a body bag, Devan hired a new one and subjected the person to a rigorous screening process. After that, the fun began.

Eyes flickering to mine, Devan said, "Lance."

Lance. Nicknamed Thermal Lance for no good reason because it sounded cool. "Aw, I liked him." Truthfully, I couldn't care, but it always paid to be nice to the help.

"Took a bullet between the ears in Kabul." Devan sighed. "Poor bastard. Just finished paying his widows' the death benefits."

I was surprised he died considering there wasn't much between his ears to damage. Still, he had just enough brains to join a polygamous cult and had himself a bevy of very young and willing wives who dug scars. Very Old Testament type of marriage arrangement that the overly religious thought archaic and rather silly. However, show them a homosexual and suddenly, they practically vomit bible verses at you.

And some called *me* perverse.

The Wights didn't need so much room. It wasn't necessary to move everything out of the way, but Devan possessed a flair for the dramatic. Overhead a spotlight shone on Mr. Thorn, who tried to look nonchalant, but failed spectacularly.

Lean hipped and wiry instead of heavily muscled, he looked more like a young circus acrobat than an exquisitely trained killer of men. I noted a trickle of sweat run down his cheek.

Wights turned at the sound of our footsteps and I greeted them warmly with hugs and backslaps. Always good to make the hired help think you actually cared, especially if you wanted them to do something potentially fatal. They were a fine bunch of rogues and I knew I could trust them all to do the necessary thing within their capacity for abrupt violence.

The Wights:

Devan, J.P. Goetz, Llamar Norman, John Schoenhauser, Anne Richman (the only woman, but don't think she was at a disadvantage … she could outfight, out drink and out fuck any ten men), Adam Kroenig and William Oshman.

And the Thorn kid, of course.

Every single fucking one of them former military, top of their game, the elite of the elite, from SEALs to Rangers to Force Recon to Delta. Any single one of them could rip a budding nation in half or prop it up for life.

"Big man," said J.P., a large man himself at six-two, but as a former god and Cherubim I wore flesh that hit six-five and was much better looking, of course. "Good to see you. Always a party when you're around."

Anne's homely face looked almost pretty as she rubbed her hands together and said, "We get *paid*, too."

Affirmatives all around. Devan clapped his hands. "All right, you apes, let's get the initiation completed, before the kid falls over from being bored to fucking death." Instead of bored, though, Thorn looked a little green around the gills.

My smile must have unnerved him somewhat because even under the harsh glare of the spotlight I could see his face pale further. I loved initiations … one of the few times besides fucking that I actually enjoyed interacting with mortals.

Llamar went first. "This is a pin I got when I made Eagle Scout," he said, holding up the silvery oval badge with its image of a spread winged eagle. I snorted. He might have stolen it because he was no more Eagle Scout than I was a Labradoodle.

Snake fast, he slammed the badge into Thorn's chest pin first, driving it deep into the muscle, then gave it a good, hard slap. I gave the kid credit, he didn't even grunt as blood seeped through his white cotton T-shirt.

Anne held hers up, a small gold rectangle with two short prongs on the back. "This is my very first piece of flair I earned from Whiskey Jack Crow's restaurant as a server from way back in the day." Both prongs slammed hard into the kid's bicep and her fist hammered the cheap flair deep as it could go.

Then the rest. By the time it was J.P.'s turn, the kid's shirt looked like it was used to mop up a slaughterhouse, with rivulets sliding over sweating skin and around old scar tissue. By the time Devon finished him off on the right pectoral with the skull-and-crossbones pin of the Wights, the waist of his jeans was soaked all the way down to the crack of his ass.

And still not a peep.

Devon smiled as he laid in the last punch, driving the pin home. "Good job, Whip. You passed."

The team whooped and hollered and even I threw the kid a golf clap. As he began to remove the pins from his bloody body, I held up a hand. "Wait it minute."

All celebration stopped abruptly, and I found myself at the center of a ring of eyes. I held up a fist. "You know who I am, Thorn?"

Hazel eyes met mine and shied away. "Yessir. You're Harry, the guy who originally formed the Wights. You get us jobs and sometimes join us when you want."

"Exactly." I moved in close and held my fist under his nose. "I don't much like the nickname 'Whip'. Sounds fucking stupid." Concentrating on my hand, I used a bit of my angelic essence. Not a lot, just a fraction because I didn't have that much to spare. My fingertips tingled, feeling like hot feathers were caressing the skin. Back in the day when I was a god, I spent my power recklessly, with abandon. Ah, youth. The older I get, the stingier I get with the angelic essence, although sometimes I tend to be careless with it when overly emotional. In that sense I was a lot like the clever monkeys that surrounded me.

"This is your new nickname," I said, holding up a shining silver pin.

Thorn looked at the pin, eyes puzzled. "A rose, sir?"

Devan laughed, the first to get it.

"That's right." I slammed the pin home in the center of his chest. The spike was less than a centimeter long, but I knew it *hurt*.

This time he grunted. Score one for me.

CHAPTER THREE
KNIFE WORKS

～

A FULL MOON BLAZED IN THE SKY bright enough to read by, which didn't help our situation any, but we Wights had something the Templars lacked.

Me.

I caressed Ablewand's hilt, finding comfort in the cold iron. Even though it looked rough it somehow felt silky and a little soft. Perhaps I was imagining things.

Devan's voice slid through the earwig. *"Green two in position."*

"Green Three in position."

"Green Four in position." And so on until Rose chimed in with "Green Eight in position."

That left me, Green One. "Okay boys and girls. Ready to rock and roll on my mark. Remember, this is not an exfil, but a termination of a terrorist cell led by a religious fanatic who thinks he's a priest doing God's work. Take no chances, take no prisoners. Remember, Green Six, jam their comms when I give the signal." Ours would remain open, leaving them deaf, but not us.

Multiple 'yessirs' later and I gave the go head to take down the farmhouse.

Ten miles outside of Council Bluffs, Iowa, there was a little place called Lewis Township, a cluster of homes that could barely be called a village. At the edge lay a small ten-acre spread encompassing a terraced hill, a small orchard, barn, two sheds and a maple tree old enough to have seen the incorporation of Iowa as a state.

Nestled next to curve in a small road stood a goodly-sized house shaded under the maple which was our target.

Burke supplied the intel and I followed it to this little slice of suburban

Americana in the middle of the country. It wasn't hard to understand. Who would want to hide out in Iowa? Its greatest metropolis is Des Moines with a population of little over two-hundred thousand people. I had to hand it to Engle, he knew how to jump into a hole and pull it in after him.

As the team slid shadow-like across grass, ditch and trees toward the handful of sentries we could see with our night vision goggles, I wondered why Burke didn't just bomb the fuck out of the house and be done with it. Perhaps he wanted confirmation that priesty boy was dead instead a bag of random pieces parts for DNA analysis. Either way, I wasn't about to underestimate one of Dad's boy toys. He always chose the clever ones. Let me tell you, that Moses guy outmaneuvered Ramses three ways to Sunday and the Pharaoh didn't even know what hit him. All things being fair, Ramses wasn't the brightest bulb in the fridge, if you know what I mean. Spent more time fucking his concubines than governing, but, hey, that's what inbreeding does to a family.

A guard, green and ghostly in my sight, stood just beside the front door, half concealed behind a large rhododendron bush. I let loose couple of rounds from my suppressed HK MP7A1, a great SMG capable of killing 950 morons a minute.

The guard died without a sound, brains and blood decorating the taupe wall behind him.

"Green One in position."

"Green Two in position." And so on until …

Harsh barking came from the barn that stood about twenty meters from the house, the sound bouncing from the tin roof lending the gunshots a deeper resonance.

"Fuck. Green One, this is Green Six, Green Eight is down. Repeat, Green Eight is down."

So much for Rose. It looked like there would be a new initiation soon.

"Team, full breach now, now, now!" The time for subtlety was long gone. We had to hit warp speed before Engle could rub the sleep sand from his eyes.

My fingers dug into a thigh pocket of my loose black pants and pulled out cube of plastic explosive the size of a Vegas die. Mashing it against the front door lock, I inserted a detonator and stood back a few feet as the five-second timer wound down to zero.

Crumph! The sound pushed against my face as I raced forward moving almost as fast the pressure wave itself. Bits of debris floated in midair, bouncing off my speeding body as I pushed through into what looked like the living room. A wide-open space with a guard in the center, seemingly frozen in the act of firing a shotgun the size of a potato cannon.

Oh, in case you're wondering, I was in full Hermes mode. You know, the whole Messenger of the Gods thing, going so super fucking fast that mortals couldn't hardly see me. Cost a bit more of my angelic power, what was left of my divine essence, but I really didn't feel like getting my guts shot out. Not that it would necessarily kill me, but who wants to go through pain and the dry-cleaning bills?

Anyway, the guard, a gaunt-looking woman with enormously hollow cheeks, barely had time to blink before Ablewand took her in the left eye. There was a momentary resistance, then a comforting *give* as it slid all the way to the hilt. I dropped my speed as blood and fluid splashed against my fist.

One second. Then two. Then the *rush*.

A momentary tingle through my fingers, a tickle like fleas trapped in my glove, then a staggering warmth so intense I thought my sleeve would burst into flame. That warmth raced up to my shoulder and neck and hit my brain with the force of a baseball bat slugging a home run in the World Series. For a moment, just a fraction of a second, all went yellow and white as my brain lit up with such an orgasmic flow of energy I nearly came in my pants right there. I contained myself, forcing the energy down, down, down deep into the pit of my stomach where it set up shop as a slow burn.

Better than coke, better than heroin or oxy or ecstasy. Better than a wild night of fucking with a double-jointed, nymphomaniacal acrobat on steroids. A flow of pure energy as the spark of divine grace that inhabited the woman became mine as her soul departed the rough clay of her body. Not much by Cherubim standards, but more than I had possessed in a long, long time. Not since the time of Charlemagne had I felt so fucking *alive*.

"Wow," I breathed, reveling in the sensation of a power previously diminished.

A dark figure appeared at the back door, so quiet that I barely heard the squeak of his rubber-soled boots. *"Green One, I have eyes on you. Are you okay, boss?"*

Almost absently I dropped the corpse, feeling the blade slide free from the skull. *"All good, Green Two."*

"Top floor secure, Green One."

That left the basement. Green Three should have had the basement secure by now.

"Green Three, you copy."

Nothing.

"Come in, Green Three."

"Green One, Green Six here. Door to basement open. No sign of Green Three. Going in."

"Negative Green Six. Wait for the team."

No answer.

"Green Six?"

Still no answer.

Shit.

"Shit." I removed my goggles and rubbed my eyes. According to the blueprints on file with the city of Council Bluffs, the stairs to the basement were behind a door next to the kitchen. I could see it from where I stood. Repositioning my goggles, I held a finger to my lips and Devan nodded once. All quiet from now on until the threats were neutralized.

Maybe I should have used more angelic energy to speed myself up now that I had some to spare, but I was like an addict finding a stash ... I desperately wanted it to last as long as possible, taking just the smallest hits necessary to keep the buzz going.

Green Two took the doorknob and yanked the door open, ducking to the side as a flurry of bullets creased the air where his head had been. Snarling, I yanked a pin from a frag grenade, counted to two and lobbed it down the steps, not bothering to yell 'fire in the hole'.

"Are you crazy?" Devan hissed, too startled by my action to use comms.

"You think Green Two and Six are alive?"

Boom!

The sound hit hard and fast, bouncing up the stairwell and smacking me hard all along my body like getting hit with a wet mattress. It jiggled my guts like a sack of water balloons.

Frowning furiously, but shutting up all the same, Devan spun toward the doorway and unloaded a full clip from his SMG. *"Clear."*

I let him take point. The bottom five steps were covered in slick decorative bits and pieces of the guard who took the full force of the blast, his shredded body barely recognizable as human. Only the boots looked whole.

There was a good reason for the carnage ... the door the man had been guarding was not only locked, but made of reinforced steel, heavy enough to withstand the blast and localize it to the small landing. A deliberate sacrificial move by the man and a testament to his dedication.

A quick test showed that the door remained not only unharmed except for some minor shrapnel dents but locked as well. Somehow, I thought that one of my little shape-charges would prove an exercise in futility.

"Now what, Green One?" There was some snark in the voice.

Attitude? Really? From Devan? Of all the cheeky little talking monkeys jabbering at me throughout the ages it turned out the one I thought most loyal was giving me a bit of sarcasm in the middle of an op. That shit had to end, and I mean right *now*.

Using a slight bit of the essence I channeled through Ablewand, I gave myself a daunting aspect. Not a physical change, exactly, more like an air of menace and fear that usually brought mortals to heel.

"Do we have a problem, Green Two?' I drawled softly, making sure my comm was off. "Now of all times?"

A wave of malice like the acrid stink of burning tires emanated from my pores and Devan Marquan recoiled, breaking out in a rash of fear sweat that gratified me immensely. "No sir," he stammered, properly cowed like a good mortal.

I swear, good help is so fucking hard to find.

Every now and then, when I was wearing my god hat, a mortal got too big for their britches, or in the olden days, their *exomis* or *chiton*, I'd have to lay the smack down and turn them into a tree, or a frog or something squishy. I made it showy, with all sorts of witnesses so the others would pass the word along that you did *not* fuck with the gods. I mean, there was this one time when a kid named Ptalemon stuck out his tongue during my annual festival, the Hermaea in Pheneos. and right there and then I transformed him into a goat. Served the little fucker right, bleating and baa-ing in terror while his mom, a fat wench with bad skin, screamed her ass off in terror. After that, the parents kept their snot-nosed brats at home in fear that I might turn one into a sheep and try to milk it. Left the kid all goat-y until the next festival, then turned him back as an act of benevolence. The kid was never quite right in the head after that. I know, I checked often.

Contemplating a replacement for my number two (I mean, really, folks, things get out of hand once the mortals think they can talk out of the side of their mouths at you. When that happens, buy some lime and a dig a hole in a swamp, because shit's about to get ugly), I placed my hand against the steel door and closed my eyes. A trickle of warmth flowed from my fingertips into the door and I felt the locking mechanism. Just as I prepared to use some telekinetics, the lock gave a soft *click* and the door swung in under the slight pressure of my fingertips.

My SMG rose, ready to spray into the dark hallway, but it was empty. The only thing there was another door at the end of a ten-foot hallway.

"Please proceed alone, sir, and leave the weapon behind."

Gods don't jump out of their skin, but even a fallen angel can be startled when disembodied voices come from nowhere.

Except this wasn't nowhere, it was a recessed speaker camouflaged in the ceiling. Clever monkeys.

"And if I don't?" I felt Devan stiffen. "Just asking."

"Then the explosives in this building will detonate and you will die. You're fast, but not faster than an electric signal. Tell your men to stand down and wait."

Shit. Someone had eyes on me. "Mr. Engle, I presume."

"Good guess."

Playing for time seemed like the wise course of action. Besides, I didn't want to face one of Dad's boys alone. Not that I was afraid. Nope, not me. "Seems foolish to hand myself over."

"I just want to talk."

"I want to kill you."

"Is that a no on my invitation."

Devan was looking at me with an expression I've never seen before. Thinly veiled disgust. He knew I was stalling, but what's worse, he knew I was afraid.

He had to go, no question, but I'd make a quick, two to the back of the skull execution style. No pain. Least I could do for the past few years of loyal service.

With a grin that felt far too forced, I handed over the SMG to Devan and walked down the hall, trying to act all nonchalant and shit, but irritated that a human might see the slight tremble in my hand. Ablewand slid into my palm and I reached for the other door. It opened before I could touch the knob.

"Come on in," said the voice from the overhead speaker. "Make yourself comfortable."

"What about the two team members sent through the basement door."

"Unconscious, unharmed."

"And they are hostage for my good behavior?"

"No, they will be released no matter what."

"Color me doubtful."

"We are not the Deschamps Family. We have morals and work for a higher, more noble purpose."

That's all a matter of perspective, but I still entered the room.

Not very big, basically a cube of dark gray poured concrete illuminated by a bare bulb in the ceiling, but large enough that the man sitting in the corner on a cheap folding chair with a gun pointed my way could get a shot off before I could reach him. Assuming I didn't speed up, that is.

"Mr. Engle, I presume?" I asked, gripping Ablewand tightly and reaching for some divine energy. He sure looked like the photo of the man Burke had supplied, although a little more gaunt, like he missed the last twenty or thirty meals.

He was a big man, shoulders wide and forearms like a longshoreman, wearing black on black, with black sneakers and a button-down shirt topped with a clerical collar. A bushy handlebar mustache bristled on his face underneath a severe flattop buzz cut. His blue eyes twinkled as he said, "It is Father Engle."

I was about to ask him about the location of my missing two teammates but realized I didn't give a goodly fuck. Instead I merely nodded and let the power flow through my veins, soaking my tissues with incalculably warm and wonderful energy.

That all came to a crashing halt when he continued with, "But I am not Father Engle."

What?

The hand without a gun came into view, clutching what looked to be a silvery cylinder of metal, his thumb over a deep red button on one end. He pressed it.

The world slowed down drastically, but even moving at speeds that would shred mortal tissues like wet crepe paper wasn't fast enough stop the door from closing with a soft *thump*. My fist left a dent in the steel right before I turned to the man, frozen in the middle of a shit-eating grin and I thrust outward.

Ablewand took him in the throat, entering easily as if sliding into a sheath of butter and the tip spurted out of his neck as the hilt, thrust with nearly all my angelic strength, hit him hard enough to crunch cartilage.

He died without knowing I killed him.

I would have felt self-satisfied, almost delirious with joy as the divine spark of him flowed along the wand into my hand, but the clouds of white gas entering the room from overhead vents thrust me violently into unconsciousness.

THE BOOK OF

MICHAEL continued

Chapter Two
An Apt Punishment

―――⌇⌇―――

HERMIEL GROUND TO A HALT. THE story had spilled from him like water from a broken jug … in a rush without stopping until dry. Now he knelt there, breathing hard, dark hair lank and matted with sweat. Gone was the arrogance of an angel who would be a god. Only the fear remained written large on his face, etched deep into once-flawless skin. I can't say I felt sorry for the man. He chose the road he wished to walk, like we all do and could only blame himself upon the reaching this destination.

Head down, he mumbled, "You must be the Prophet, then."

"I don't call myself that," I replied. "Really not one for prophecy."

"Then what do you call yourself?"

My laughter cut through suddenly and he jerked his head up. "Mike. I call myself Mike."

The angel searched my face for a long moment. "You don't look like your picture. Younger somehow, with longer hair and no mustache."

My fingers touched my upper lip. I'd worn that mustache for over twenty years. Grew it after I came stateside from Iraq after the first Gulf War. "How foolish would I have to be to not change my looks, considering that the Family wants me dead?"

That earned me a tired nod. Apparently Hermiel the fallen angel was finally afflicted with a sense of defeat. Not surprising considering the power of the Lord had put some serious fear into him. "Stupid me. Who was that mortal … the one in the basement?"

A pang shot through me and the small, mean part of my soul that we humans must strive day and night to defeat wanted to leave him in ignorance, but that thought was not worthy.

"All the Templars are volunteers, devout believers in God from all faiths: Catholic, Protestant, Judaic, and Muslim. All have been shown His glory. Those poor men in that house were all very ill, dying. It was their wish to sacrifice themselves for the sake of their families, for the sake of mankind, to the greater good. They knew that the Templars would take care of their immediate kin … so they could die at peace. They deserved no less."

"A trap then."

"Of course. Although I half expected the Family to send a drone like the one they used to attack Cain." The investigation into that incident rolled some big heads in the military, despite protestations that they had been hacked and that it was not their fault. It had been a calculated guess on my part that that option was no longer viable for the foreseeable future, which left a surgical strike. I'd hoped for some Dagger Men, a one or two-Word magus. A fallen angel was more than I expected. Lucky me. Not so lucky for the men the Wights killed, though.

Still, their families would receive benefits and I would personally see to it that their kids received scholarships to the university of their choice.

"Cain?" Hermiel raised a perfect eyebrow. "That fucker still breathing? I figured some enterprising Sicarius would have punched his ticket by now."

I shook my head. "We needed intel."

"By 'we' you mean the Templars."

"Of course. And thank you very much, by the way. It is appreciated."

His laughter was a broken thing, sounding of regret and torn metal. "I have no loyalty to Burke and the rest of the satanic Brady Bunch. Those fuckers." More shredded laughter. "Should never have taken the job. Too fucking greedy."

That brought up another point. "Ablewand. You got greedy for a relic." A souvenir from Christ. "Do you know about any others?"

Hermiel shook his head. "Nah. Only the Nails. Three … Ablewand, Stoneshear and Denial and I only know about those because of Atheniel … Athena. I guess you've already met her." Hermiel's eyes bored into mine, filled with some dark emotion. I felt my skin pebble. "Don't ask me about the other two," he continued when I refused to reply. "I can't tell you what I don't know. I got lucky with Ablewand because of a Sicarius I tortured for giggles back in the 18th Century, but something tells me I won't see it again. Fucking shame."

Lecturing the angel on the use of such a holy relic for selfish reasons was like trying the teach the Aryan Brotherhood about the Torah, so I didn't waste my breath. Instead, I studied the fallen for a while as he stared at me in a sort of halfhearted defiance. I could tell he wanted to reach down into a great well of anger and frustration, but defeat had robbed him of the motivation to do so.

What to do? "Hermiel, what do you think I should do with you?" I don't know why I asked, it just felt right that I did.

The angel was as surprised as I. "Fuck. If it was me I'd put a bullet through my head and be done with it."

Not my style and by his sad little grin, he thought so too. I shook my head and knelt in front of him. "Hermiel, Harbinger of Storms, do you repent your participation in the Rebellion against the Throne and seek the Lord's forgiveness?"

"Fuck no."

Thought so. "Why haven't you asked about the Wights?"

A look of genuine puzzlement crossed his face. "Why?"

And there lay the true answer, naked and bold as you please. He was still wrapped up in his selfishness and sense of superiority. Humans were so far beneath him that deigning to worry about them never crossed his mind. We were there to serve his needs, his pleasure. Temporary dalliances while he frittered his immortality away in boredom and hedonistic excess.

Forgiveness comes only to those who truly seek it.

So, the real question remained: what to do with the fallen? Killing Hermiel would only send him to Hell and would Lucifer be able to hold onto him? Fallen angels only stayed with Lucifer because they wanted to, because they really had nowhere else to go to nurse their hate and resentment. Except for those like Minerva, Hermes and others who assumed the mantles of false gods, so they taste a fraction of the majesty they had lost.

"Okay, angel," I said, raising a finger. "Here's the plan."

He recoiled, eyes hard on the digit that hovered a few inches from his nose.

"Sending you to Hell seems counterproductive and holding you prisoner is not something we do. We're not set up for such things considering we are constantly on the move. This leads me to a creative idea, assuming the Lord finds it pleasing to His sense of justice."

Now he was sweating, his eyes wide, but he kept his voice even and full of arrogance as he said, "Do what you want, I don't care anymore."

A lie. I could feel it as it slithered into my ears. Bold and delivered with heaps of cockiness, but a lie just the same. All right, time to see if the Lord would countenance my plan.

It had to start with a prayer. Which one, though? It hit me as soon as I contemplated the situation and I felt the assurance of the Lord flow through me.

The Prayer of Absolution, words so stunning in their purity that they often took my breath away, but not now, not at this time. This prayer was the correct one, one that grants forgiveness as well as a measure of understanding. I only hoped that Hermiel could see what was coming as a gift rather than divine punishment.

"God the Father of mercies, through the death and resurrection of your son, you have reconciled the world to yourself and sent the Holy Spirit among us for the forgiveness of sins. Through the ministry of the church, may God grant you pardon and peace. I absolve you of your sins, in the name of the Father, and of the Son and of the Holy Spirit. Amen."

Once again, the warm and glorious power of the Lord gripped me, creating of me a vessel for His will. As the Glory filled my tissues, Hermiel began to scream, a rending, deep, throat splitting howl of terror and hate that pierced my ears like ice picks.

Mercifully, it lasted only a short time. After the last echoes of the scream faded, Hermiel looked at me with fear blasted eyes. "You've condemned me, priest. Turned me into a freak." The chains pulled at him, and it took all he had not to be slapped flat on the floor.

"What I did to you is give you a gift." Not that he would see it that way. Not by a long shot. Instead he would consider it a curse.

His next words proved my supposition. "You've *cursed* me!" he screamed, hate distorting his face. "I'm mortal now. *Human.*" The word was flung at me like a piece of offal, intended as an insult.

I had to laugh. "Welcome to mortality, Hermiel. Now if you die unrepentant, Lucifer will have you forever."

God is sometimes cruel, but not unnecessarily so.

CHAPTER THREE
BEING THE BOSS SUCKS

M ILO GAVE ME THAT LOOK, the one I've been getting for the past few months since I took over the Templars. Part adoration, part worship, all reverent.

I hated it.

Shortly after assuming the mantle of leadership I killed the Oracle, the Family's soothsaying prisoner. This man, this good, kindly man, was blackmailed into grudging cooperation with the Sicarii. You see, while they had him, they were also monitoring his wife and children and if he didn't cooperate...dire consequence would ensue.

As an Oracle, the information he provided was often cryptic or misleading, something common to seers, it seemed. A double-edged sword. When I encountered him in his remote cabin in Switzerland, he asked me to kill him. It was the one option he had that would ensure his family's safety because his oracular capabilities were hereditary. The Sicarii would have to keep his children alive and well to see which one would become the next Oracle. If he came with me, joined the Templars, his family would be killed before we could dial a phone to warn them.

So, I killed him, a mercy bullet to the brain and in that I felt only a small amount of guilt. No, the real guilt and shame came from learning that the Oracle, that good and pious man, was in fact the direct descendant of Christ.

I took the life of quite possibly the holiest of men and that chewed at my soul. No matter that it was necessary, or requested by the man himself, it hurt worse than anything I'd ever felt, even the death of my best friend, Morgan Heart. Or Jude Oliver. Olivier Deschamps. The man who was to be the Antichrist.

Funny how life unfolds. I'd read scholarly accounts of possible identity of the Beast and the most recent theories are that the Antichrist John of Patmos wrote about was, in fact, Emperor Nero. Boy, did they get that one wrong. No, Olivier Deschamps was to be the unholy vessel for Lucifer on this earth, a man strong enough to contain the Devil's evil and channel it to shackle the world. To remake it according to Morningstar's infernal design.

Saved by an angel, offered a choice between good and evil. Olivier Deschamps chose neither, opting instead to hide out in Omaha, Nebraska. That's when I met him, a young man filled with troubling thoughts … naive, yet experienced, ignorant, yet filled with such knowledge that it forever altered how I viewed the world.

He died as Morgan Heart, the man he became. He could have chosen power and life and glory, defeating his enemies and bringing the Family down, but he chose to save me and the wanderer Cain instead. He chose good over evil. Love over vengeance.

That changed everything.

Forget about fundamentalist thinkers who say that Revelations will happen as it is written. That's bunk. I believe God gives us what is probable, what will happen if we don't find our better angels, but Morgan found his and thus Revelation was confounded.

For now.

Lucifer, like God, plays the long game, hedging his bets while he attempts to rig the outcome, so there still could be an Antichrist in the making, but that too depended on the actions of the Templars and those willing to confound the Deschamps family.

I opened the door to my office. A temporary one filled with a single desk, a lamp, a tablet computer and five burner phones. Because of the massive resources the Sicarii have at their disposal, remaining in one location is not viable, not if we wanted to keep breathing. Fortunately, in the last six months the Family has managed to piss off the right people, people with the kind of resources the Templars sorely needed.

People like Cain. Yes, *that* Cain. A viciously wealthy man, possibly the wealthiest in the world and the greatest living magus of all time. With his wealth and resources, we were able to recruit believers, true believers in the Lord to fight the forces and evil. With his help we were able to contact another man who enabled us to grow even larger. The Pope. Yep, that Pope, the one in Vatican. How cool was that?

Usually the Family had its fingers deep in the Vatican pie, but this humble man, elected without consent of the Sicarii, changed everything. We were able to offer utterly loyal bodyguards, the cream of the Swiss Guards vetted by us, and he was able to put us in touch with those members of the military elite whose faith was beyond question. From there the Templars expanded to each continent, growing from a handful of men and women to nearly a hundred. All ready to die for the cause at the drop of a hat. That doesn't sound like much, but when you work against the most powerful Family in the world with a dirty hand in every government, recruiting even that much was a major feat.

In the Army I was used to leading men into dangerous situations, even saw combat in Desert Storm, but this was different. Now I'm a priest, a servant of God, a man of peace thrown into a war that's been raging since the dawn of time. Back in the day I took my orders and did my best to carry them out, but now I'm the one giving the orders, orders that send young men to kill or die.

Like the poor guards at the house in Iowa. Of course, I knew they were likely to die, which is why I recruited terminal patients. People with cancer and such to take a bullet in exchange for the surety of their family's continued well-being. Six physically fit, yet dying, people. Six spouses, twenty-five children and assorted pets. People of faith, volunteers from all walks of life. They deserved a better death, but at least their passing was for the greatest cause of all.

That logic never sat well with me. It hurt, the brutal choices, but in the long run I would rather send those at the end of their lives to die rather than the young with so much life still ahead.

Wiping a tear, I sat at my desk in my uncomfortable chair and put my elbows on the surface, rubbing my face and forcing grief down deep. I would pay for that later, most likely in an epic weep-fest, but right now I needed to be hard and strong and keep the sorrow at bay. Business today, crying tomorrow.

Milo entered, closing the door softly behind. "Done, sir."

I raised my head and studied my right-hand man's hard face. "Thank you, Milo. And our new member of humanity?"

His granite face broke into a smile, which was almost as horrifying as his scowl. "Sleeping like a baby. In a few hours he will be dropped off in Toronto with fifty Loonies in his pocket and Spice Girls T-shirt."

I tried not to laugh, but the absurdity of it all split right through me. After a few moments Milo joined in and we guffawed until our sides hurt and I hit the floor with a resounding *thump*.

Gasping, I said, "Thanks, Milo. I needed that." The thought of Hermiel the former fallen angel lost in Canada in an old Spice Girls concert T-shirt and a hangdog look on his face tickled me three shades of pink. It provided a much-needed lift to an otherwise lousy day.

"You're welcome sir." Milo gathered himself quick and became grave. "But did we actually learn anything?"

Did we? These traps for the Sicarii assassins, their infamous SS teams, had been increasingly harder and harder to set. The first few worked like a charm, resulting in the capture of a couple of the Dagger Men and the eradication of three full teams. The intel proved valuable, encryption codes, recent activities and such and it was surprising how willing the servants of evil would talk given the choice between a bullet to the brain or freedom. Those we captured couldn't go back to Sicarii for fear of repercussions, so we gave them a few hundred dollars and dropped them off in the city of their choice. A win-win.

However, this was the first time the Sicarii, elite assassins all, farmed out a job. Looks like the higher ups were getting nervous.

"We received confirmation that Burke is, indeed, alive," I replied over steepled fingers. "At first, I thought it all guff, smoke and mirrors to put us on guard." When I first heard it my hair about stood on end. "And we also learned it's because of some project a hundred years in the making, that's new." I shook my head. "No, this is big. Morgan killed Burke, slit his throat and burned the body along with his house. Burke is ash and dust and, yet, somehow still alive. That's serious intel."

"What does it mean?"

My lips thinned. "Somehow the Deschamps have learned how to bring back the dead."

Chewing his lower lip and shaking his head, Milo left without another word. As for me, I leaned back in that uncomfortable chair with my hands behind my head and stared at the ugly fluorescents above.

Sioux Falls South Dakota was one of those towns people have heard of but never visit unless they attended Augustana University. A perfect place to lay low while I coordinated efforts of the Templars in our never-ending war against the Family Deschamps, the head of the snake that is the Sicarii.

The Devil's descendants.

Cyber raids on assets, physical raids on known Sicarii training camps and schools, although I drew the line at attacking their children despite the fact they learned the delicate art of murder as soon as they could walk. But if we could disrupt the teaching, force the Sicarii to suspend training for a while, then that was victory enough for me.

Some of the Templars were all for destroying the *entire* Family, root and branch, but what were we fighting for if we killed children? It's been pointed out to me that many would have no problem putting a bullet into the skull of baby Hitler if given a chance, but that's sophistry of the basest sort. As a child, Adolf Hitler had not made the decisions that led to his rise, had led to the Holocaust, which was as much a product of those other power brokers of the Third Reich as well.

No, given a time machine and the wherewithal, I would have tried to reason with young Adolf, minister to him and show him the glory of the Lord. That's the correct answer for that problem. Truth be told, that's the go-to answer for us priestly types anyway.

I shot a tired grin at the lights above, deliberately procrastinating. There were reports to read and plans to make and research to do, things to keep a middle-aged man hopping. I was tired. The constant moving from place to place, the worry and the threat of imminent death was enough to wear down even the strongest of men. I needed a distraction.

God must have heard because at that moment my tablet emitted a gentle chime. Apparently, I had email. I closed my eyes ... the Lord had ways of answering a plea that was at odds to what one really wants.

"What now?" I muttered, tapping the email icon on the tablet. An unknown address. I ran virus countermeasures and a security scan for snifferware, programs that, while not technically viruses, merely noted the IP addresses of the computer receiving the email once opened then erased themselves. Nothing.

A large blot of gibberish met my eyes. Encryption, one I recognized. It was our latest and greatest. After opening the decrypt software, the nonsense resolved a letter addressed to me. Pages and pages of email.

My eyes grew wide as I read ...

THE BOOK OF CAIN

(and Maggie)

Chapter One
Scream a Little Scream for Me

"**L**ET ME BET THE FIRST TO put this on the record: This was a Bad Idea!" Maggie ducked just as a string of bullets passed through the space where her head had been. She cursed and removed the empty clip from her Agram 2000, reloading from a thigh pouch in one, swift, practiced motion. She enjoyed the compact weapon, light and durable and able to shoot a lot of bad guys in a very short amount of time.

Cain grinned behind his dark glacier sunglasses, teeth shining whitely. "Although the execution of our assault leaves much to be desired in efficiency, the thought behind it remains hale and true. It comes to me now that we should have had the foresight not to tarry at the local publican's. Allowing our Sicarii nemesis to receive heretofore unknown reinforcements, thus jeopardizing our well-crafted plan." Not that he minded tarrying. Good liquor was one of his favorite weaknesses, of which he had a few.

"It was you who wanted to 'tarry' at that fucking bar!" Maggie reached over the little cubicle wall and let out a burst from the little Croatian SMG. She wasn't trying to hit anyone, just buying some time so her one-time master could come up with a plan to keep their hides in one piece. *Screw the mission,* she thought. *I want to live!* Although she realized that hanging out with Cain on dangerous missions didn't lend itself to longevity. Perhaps she should have stayed in the Valhalla Club back in New York City? She shook her head. Nah, a decree of death still hung over her head there. What's a girl to do in times like these?

"Need I remind you that establishment is the sole purveyor of Glenlivet Nadurra Peated single malt Scotch? Do you possess the faculty for reasoning to comprehend the magnitude of that accomplishment? Did not the slow yet wonderful ethyl alcohol fire not titillate your senses? Rightwise, did not the delicate earthiness finish lightly at the back of your tongue? Dare I wax rhapsodically on the craftsmanship of the pot distillation process of the barley mash that lent such complex notes to the ambrosial bliss of the libation?"

"I prefer mead, if you must know!" A short pause as several more rounds stitched the cubicle walls, rending them into so much expensive confetti. "Scotch tastes like dirt to me."

That set in the air for a while as Cain reloaded his Interdynamic MP-9, a rugged little submachine gun crafted of inexpensive polymer and stamped steel parts. He racked a clip and studied his former apprentice. "Did you say 'dirt'?" Could his ears have been playing tricks? Dirt? Where were the people with discernment?

A ratcheting *boom* shook the office building and a hole the size of grapefruit appeared above Maggie's head, swishing her long blond hair around. She cursed and screamed, "Yes, dirt! Now do *something*! I'm about to be perforated here."

"Shield cannot stand long against such gunfire and, if my sensitive aural passages prove to be as acute as my memory, yon round that nearly reduced your height by six inches emanated from a .50 caliber weapon of American design. More than one strike from such a weapon would ruin the efficacy of the spell." He gave her a pitying look. "Were I a perceptive member of the Sicarii clan, should there be such a thing, I would find it quite necessary to eliminate from this planet a person with such a leathern palate to regard the greatest drink known as tasting of mere soil. No wonder they find it just to employ a mighty weapon."

Maggie's face became a study in outrage. "You have got to be fucking *kidding* me right now!" She closed her eyes and started counting to ten.

Badoom! Her count was interrupted as another large hole appeared an inch from her nose, the bullet tearing away the cheap pressboard of the cubicle wall easily before punching its way through the opposite wall next to Cain's right elbow.

Before the woody bits fell to the floor, a Word slipped from Cain's mouth and the big man gathered himself and *leapt*.

The average ceiling height of a modern office is nine feet. In his socks, Cain stood close to seven. Somehow, he managed to sail over the four-foot cubicles, then across *thirty feet* through the five-foot space between cubicle walls and ceiling without banging his head. As he flew, the Swedish SMG chattered noisily, 9mm rounds shredding the man carrying the 50 caliber into red ruin. Before his feet touched the floor, he shouted a Word with as much effort as his throat and indomitable will could bear. To Cain, the magic smelled of fresh cut roses, one of the more pleasant odors of magic in his repertoire.

The three men standing there dressed in black, M4s clutched in their hands, staggered back, two of them dropping their assault rifles. The third, however, did not. Instead, he raised his weapon, finger tightening on the trigger.

Not good. Cain braced himself for the end, surprisingly calm and knowing full well that the 5.56mm NATO rounds would move faster than he could utilize one his Words. His ridiculously long life began to flash in front of his eyes and he knew he wouldn't reach the Trojan War before a bullet deposited his brain across the wall.

Gore erupted from the shooter's throat, followed by a sharp crack and a growled "fuck". The man dropped like a puppet with cut strings and bled his life onto the blue carpet. Before he stopped twitching, Maggie was there, jammed Agram left behind and hatchet in hand. One of the black clad men drew a long K-bar and prepared to meet two-hundred pounds of screaming Valkyrie wannabe. The other drew his own knife and lunged at Cain before the immortal son of Adam could reload.

Maggie screamed, a bark of noise that pierced the air like the hatchet that swung down at incredible speed. It was a good scream, one of her best and she felt very proud at its sheer volume, but the man merely leaned back, the hatchet missing his nose by a fraction and then lunged forward, slicing. The razor-sharp blade cut easily through Kevlar, but skittered away, deflected by the shining chain mesh that lay beneath the ballistic fabric. His eyes widened a fraction behind his balaclava. Good thing titanium armor was light as well as durable.

A large fist slammed forward, knocking the knife to the side followed by the hatchet which impacted the center of the man's chest with a muffled *clang*. He cocked his head to the side at her look of surprise and thrust three times, faster than one could blink, the K-bar slicing a line of fire across knuckles, hip and drawing blood across Maggie's temple. The large woman jumped back, snarling.

No fair! The bad guys should *not* wear armor too. "&$^." The Word spat from her mouth in a snarl of anger.

The man jumped back, obviously confused behind his mask. What happened next almost tore his sanity to pieces.

Grace, one of the few Words available and her personal favorite. Preternatural clarity of physical self, elegance of movement and balance, not the spiritual kind that Mike had in spades, although that would be cool, too.

Suddenly Maggie was everywhere, hatchet flashing, clanging against chest armor. Blunt end, sharp end, it didn't matter, the weapon was all over the place, unavoidable. Her adversary tried to keep up, tried to stab and slash at her like before, but she was never where he thrust, every move he made anticipated until frustration and pain took his edge and she delivered one right to his forehead.

Skull splitting with a loathsome *crack*, the man dropped spewing blood and brains, leaving Maggie panting over the corpse. *I need to work out more. Maybe after a pint of cider ale.*

"Quit fucking around," Maggie grunted at Cain as her lungs pumped furiously. "Finish him already."

"Always one to remove the sport from a wonderful fight." Cain, grappling with his opponent, broke the man's wrist, then lifted him screaming into the air. That scream was cut off by the floor as Cain slammed him down once, then twice. He looked at the body, admiring his handiwork. Not the pain he caused, just the victory over a worthwhile opponent. Whoever the Sicarius used to be, he showed himself to be damn good with a knife, although not as good as a man with thousands of years of practice. Heck, Cain was the one that showed the Apache how to knife fight but look how that worked out ... instead of gracing him a fine name like Raven, they called him Coyote. Not very nice considering that he never thought of himself as the trickster sort.

"I must confess, former apprentice of mine, to a level of disappointment at the use of magic in this contest of martial skills to gain advantage. Most distressing."

Maggie kicked the corpse at her feet. "I don't have millennia of experience like you do. A girl's gotta use what's available to get the job done. Besides, you started it." Rifling through pockets, she found nothing to garner her interest. "No ID." She ripped of the balaclava after levering the hatchet free of the skull. Pink and red studded the metal. Fair hair and freckles met her eyes. "Young. Damn Sicarii ... using kids to do their dirty work. Has Mike really been paring their numbers down that much?"

Cain knelt by the man he'd so easily defeated. "You would know the answer to that query had you chosen to remain with the Templar community proper instead of gallivanting around the world with your former master." He stared at the body. Everyone looked young to him these days, even the most wrinkled octogenarian. "There is here a hint of an odor of piscine foulness that emanates from the region of Amsterdam." Removing the still-living assailant's balaclava, Cain discovered him to be older, with graying hair and deep lines around his nose and mouth. "Odd."

"What is?"

The downed man let out a piteous moan and opened eyes in a bleary attempt to focus, but he shut them tight in pain. He drew a ragged breath and coughed out bloody spittle.

Cain grinned in delight. It looked as it would be profitable evening after all. "If I am not mistaken, my good fellow, and in all modesty, I never am about such things, you are slowly dying of a lung punctured by the jagged splinters of a broken rib. By all accounts a tedious and quite agonizing manner of death." Cain ran a hand along the man's face, forcing one eye open. "So, I offer you a proposal I think you will discover most agreeable: find yourself loquacious and divulge all to our waiting shell-like ears and you will be most properly rewarded with your life or perish slowly on the floor of this rather tedious office building."

No answer, as the man was too busying coughing up blood and groaning piteously. *Typical of those who wish to prove themselves difficult.* Cain let slip with a small Healing, just enough to ease the man's pain a bit and enjoyed the smell of summer grass.

The man suddenly stopped coughing and some of the tension bled from his face. "Better. That's better."

"So, he speaks." Maggie was not impressed. She wanted a pint and an inch-thick burger with a side of gravy fries. Nothing like a firefight to build a good appetite.

"Use your powers of observation if they have not atrophied due to disuse."

Just like Cain, use fifty words when five would do. She reckoned that being an immortal he had the time to waste on a few thousand words. He should know that mortals couldn't wait around for him to ask the time of day or order a Philly cheesesteak. "What we have here is some ugly old dude. So?"

"So?" Cain shook his head. *Kids today.* "Then allow me to offer up an interrogative statement used to test knowledge: In our various dealings with the Sicarii, have you ever laid your cornflower blue eyes upon a Dagger Man, or woman for that matter, I am not sexist by any measure, with hair the color of iron?"

A cold chill raised goose pimples on Maggie's skin. "No, never. Every damn one of them were in their twenties or thirties."

Smiling like the Cheshire Cat, Cain gestured toward the injured man. "Despite his somewhat aged appearance he showed himself a most capable combatant. His level of skill actually forced sweat to my skin, something I have not encountered in quite some time." Although that chap Odysseus put up a good fight during the Trojan War. *Actually, put a hole in my tender hide with that bloody long spear of his. T*hat was a simpler time without bullets and bombs. The good old days. "I, too, have never encountered such a phenomenon. To my vast and reputable knowledge, as the Sicarii age, assuming they live long enough to form follicles of gray, they are moved in positions of mentorship for the youthfully evil. Therefore, ergo, in conclusion and thusly, this simple man of considerable knife-wielding skill, is *not* a Dagger Man."

"Then what the hell is he?" Maggie held up a hand. "Nix that, I don't have time for you to formulate a properly lengthy line of inquiry." She knelt at the wounded man's side and took his strong jaw in one hand, giving it enough of a squeeze to get his attention. "You in there, old man? Good. Listen up, you are going to tell us all about who you are and what you are doing here, and we promise, cross our hearts and all that, to let you live with all limbs intact." Another squeeze and he grunted in pain. "Consider that a pretty please with cherry on top."

"Uh ... ow!"

"'Uh' is not an adequate response, Mr. Tall Gray and Ugly." She laid a hand against his chest and pressed lightly. He screamed as if his guts were being ripped out through his nose. "I suggest you start talking, I really don't like doing this."

After a moment the man stopped screaming and gulped for air. "Okay, okay! We're Dark Forest!" Tears began to form at the corners of the man's eyes. "Hired last week to catch you guys. Our employer gave us a picture of him." He pointed at Cain, who merely stared back blandly. "Told us to be ready for a call with a location. Four hours ago, we received a call, told you were here in Salem, Oregon." Shuddering, he drew a ragged breath which resulted in more bloody coughing. "We flew here in time to receive a call that you were in the Bull & Barley drinking your asses off. We tailed you here and decided this was a good a location to ambush you." *Cough, cough.* "Bad move on our part."

Cain snorted. "Dark Forest?"

"Merc group usually works for the US government when they don't want to be 'officially' involved in an operation. Specializes in wet work." Maggie crossed her arms and narrowed her eyes.

"Assassinations."

"That's what wet work means." To the man. "Did your employer tell you who we are?"

"Some terrorist cell fixing to blow up the capitol building." The man licked his lips. "Can you patch me up now?"

"One moment, my good sell-sword." Cain leaned in. "Did you happen to imbibe anything before initiating hostilities? An efficacious potion, perhaps?"

"How did you know?"

Cain nodded and used a Healing. The mercenary breathed in deeply, face filling with wonder just before Cain uttered another. Eyes filling with confusion, the mercenary asked, "Who are you?" just as Maggie clocked him soundly on the jaw.

She shook her throbbing hand. Hitting people made her feel good but having a solid pair of padded gloves would have been better. "A Forgetting, I assume."

"Of course."

"What did they drink? That potion you asked about?"

"I used Force to end this charade quickly and without further loss of life. The entirety of my will and considerable vocal strength was employed, however these miscreants seemed virtually unaffected." Face hard behind his sunglasses, he continued, "Two were merely divested of their weapons while the third, through force of strength or will, managed to cling to that which came a hairsbreadth of ending my rather long and tedious existence. It seems that the Sicarii have learned a lesson concerning the usefulness of Botanical Magic, one so rudely taught during our escapades in the Big Apple. It is well for us that my spell reduced the efficacy of their potions or I would have needed to have killed him rather employ a simple Forgetting."

Maggie had spent quite some time with Cain, far more time than most. Two years was the maximum any could withstand the Curse, the Mark of Cain that forced the immortal to wander the Earth in loneliness. A tailor-made damnation for the murder of his brother millennia ago. Sure, he'd take apprentices now and again, Maggie had been one, but never for long, never for more than two years.

For some reason she had been able to not only be his apprentice for two years but join forces with him a couple years after the incident in New York. Since then she felt no desire to leave his side. It was as if her purpose in life eclipsed the curse that marked his eyes.

After New York, after losing Morgan Heart (or Jude Oliver, whatever. It didn't matter, there was something special about him, not just his *Vampire Diaries* good looks), she wandered aimlessly. No longer welcome with the society called The Valhalla Club run by those fallen angels who had assumed the mantles of the Norse Gods, and unsure of her place in the world, she had traveled the United States and most of Europe looking for something. Anything.

Then she found the Templars. Here was a group that had real *purpose*. A group in need of fierce warriors like her, people who didn't fit in, people out of time, out of place in the modern world. Throwbacks. Misfits.

Believers.

She believed, that's for sure. When she was a young woman still full of dreams of becoming a kick-ass cop, she saw her first elemental, a fire sprite no larger than a dime. I danced in a campfire, a little blaze her father started so they could roast marshmallows while camping at Whiskeytown Lake in California.

Her father couldn't see it, neither could her brother or her mother, but she could, dancing and cavorting among the burning twigs and she quickly learned never to inform her parents, who, after the first time, took her to see Dr. Ekelund to have her head professionally shrunken. To avoid further psychiatric sessions, she kept her mouth shut and her eyes open.

Sighing, Maggie stood and massaged her bruised knuckles. "Let's do what needs to be done and leave before the cops arrive."

"Do you not wish to learn the reason the Sicarii supplied these sell-swords potions to deflect hostile magic? Such a thing has never been done."

"Don't you get it, Cain? Morgan used Botanical Magic against the Family and they got their precious asses handed to them." She chuckled grimly. "And Mike has been bloodying their noses bad for the past few months. I reckon the Family has lost a good fifty, sixty Dagger Men to the Templars. Now, to let the next batch of assassins ripen, they're hiring mercs to take us out. Giving them potions to help them do it. No, this new leader they've got is a heck of a lot smarter than Blaine and he's using outside resources to conserve what he can of the Sicarii."

"That, dear Maggie, is a succinct and apt description of the conclusion I have reached. It warms the cockles of my heart to know that all the time and effort I invested in your training has resulted in such a fruitful mind."

"Yeah, yeah. I bet you say that to all the psychopathic girls with an axe fetish." She coughed into her fist. "Get what you wanted to get and let's go. Leave the merc to the cops, let him explain the bullet holes."

CHAPTER TWO
THE DEVIL IN THE DETAILS

CONNECTIONS WERE MADE. Signals were encrypted, then decrypted and a few seconds passed before a face appeared on the tablet computer. Long and lean, slightly big nose, olive skin and curly black hair cut neat in CEO chic.

"Well, well, well, if it isn't the endless man himself." The teeth that flashed on the screen seemed impossibly white. "How are you doing, old boy? Still wandering the earth in search of forgiveness that will never come? You must realize that your false god talks a good game about the subject, but never seems to offer it much to those he has a hard-on for."

Something about the man made Cain sit up straight and pay attention. The face was so familiar. It ate at him a bit, but he didn't force it, recollection would come in its own time and not before. He learned that lesson a long time ago. "Do I see before me the very person who now rests his precious fundament upon the very seat of power once claimed by Mr. Blaine Deschamps himself? You would have me to believe that my call has been anticipated and therefore you waited by your communication device with baited breath to converse with the one and only Cain? You flatter beyond words."

"And so, with the words. Always so wordy, Cain. Living so long, never changing."

Beside him, Maggie stiffened, mouth drawing into a bloodless slash. Although Cain was the most powerful man on earth, she bridled at the disrespect shown.

"I feel I should know the face that greets me with such disdain as to harden the most valiant and generous heart."

In the upper left-hand corner of the tablet numbers flashed: *11%*.

Dark eyes narrowed. "Really? You don't remember me? That hurts." Teeth flashed, more a snarl of a predator than a smile. "Although it was twenty-five years ago, it pains me to think I didn't leave an impression."

Air left Cain's lungs in a rush. *It cannot be.*

"Oh good, you do remember," Burke laughed. "Here I was worried you forgot."

There had been many a time during the long years that Cain felt himself at a loss for words, surprised and discomfited. The birth of his first child, Enoch, for one. A good boy, not deserving of the stain of his infamous father. That relationship hadn't ended well. Despite his surprise, he kept his best poker face firmly affixed, merely stroking his lower lip as he considered Burke calmly. How could such a thing be? *Oh well, the sun often shines down upon a new thing*, Cain thought, inhaling deeply through his nose and calming his body. "If my prodigious memory does not fail, you were a precocious, yet highly obnoxious, little boy standing at your older sibling's side who mocked my attire and called me a doddering old fool with delusions of grandeur."

22%.

Burkes eyes practically twinkled with glee. "Ahh, a test to prove I am who you think me to be. Very well." He held up a finger. "One, it was not a sibling, but my father, Julian." Another finger joined the first. "Two, I did indeed mock you, but I called you 'an out-of-time failure who is as irrelevant today as he was when the failed god chose his brother over him.' End quote. Oh, and then Julian commanded Boris his bodyguard to see to my discipline for speaking out of turn. He backhanded me hard against the mouth and I spat out three baby teeth."

Cold skittered down Cain's back causing his muscles to twitch involuntarily. How could this be? The man was *dead*. Obviously not, though, he was sitting right there on the opposite side of the tablet. "Young Olivier Deschamps is said to have ended your miserable existence, erasing you from the world with cleansing fire. It flies in the face of reason to see you amongst the living as your lord and master possesses no ability to bestow life unto the dead and ashen. Indeed, it seems perhaps young Olivier was without reason, afflicted by some peculiar malady that rendered him susceptible to hallucination and flights of fancy."

Before he finished speaking Burke shook his head. "No, I was dead."

"Then would you mind relating unto me the circumstances which find you on this side of the veil?"

"It didn't take."

"That is the totality of the situation? I certainly do not credit such a thing."

"Look, as much as I love to hear you take all day to ask a simple question, and believe me, it's a thrill, let us conduct business. You're still alive, so you must have done away with my mercenaries. This brings me to the salient point of the conversation."

"Do tell." Gone was any mirth in Cain's voice. Instead it contained a cold sharpness like a freshly honed knife. Apparently, his call had been anticipated, and one thing he absolutely *hated* was being predictable. Other people were allowed that sin, but not him. So, he set his teeth and waited. Out of the corner of his eye he saw Maggie take a small whetstone and begin sharpening her hatchet. She only did that when she had some serious need to bury it into a convenient forehead.

48%.

"I have concluded, considering your vast wealth and magical ability, that wasting Sicarii resources on you is counterproductive." Burke leaned into the camera, face filling the entire screen. "You have time and again destroyed every person sent to kill you and that cannot be tolerated. That is why I hired mercenaries. I will continue to do so … in vast numbers. The only thing I waste is money while keeping my Dagger Men intact."

"Go on."

"I plan on placing a bounty on your head. Ten million dollars."

Caine blinked in surprise. That was new. He enjoyed new things, but this not so much.

Burke smiled like a snake regarding a mouse. "You have so covered yourself in cutouts, stand-ins, and complex legal paper that hardly anyone knows what you look like. Even the CFOs of your many companies have never met you. This will make it much easier for me to label you as a terrorist. By this time next month, your face will be everywhere any everyone will be after your and the bounty on your head."

"Unless?"

"Yes, old man, there is an unless. You must sign a new set of Accords." Burke held up a hand. "The same as the previous you've signed with all the Family heads, no changes."

Of course, since Blaine Deschamps violated the first set of Accords (of course an argument could be made that Cain was the first to infringe upon the centuries old agreement by aiding Morgan Heart in attacking a Family stronghold in New York City). War raged between Cain and the Deschamps, resulting in the death of a few dozen Sicarii and an apprentice of whom Cain was fond.

THE THOUGHT OF LINCOLN, THAT STURDY, *good* boy whose only fault was having him as a master sent a flood of familiar rage through him. Anger … his oldest companion, his greatest curse. Not jealousy, although that emotion helped feed the fury that led him to kill his brother, not arrogance, but pure, unadulterated anger. The poison of his life. Anger led him to pick up that rock and anger fueled his muscles when he swung it. In the darkest parts of the night, when not even the fingernail moon shone in the sky, when the world lay still and silent under the stars, he still heard the impact of rock on bone, the dull *crunch* of the skull shattering and the jolt that traveled up his arm to the shoulder. After all this time, anger, the old curse he was born with, was something he could control, could harness to his steely will and use. It no longer drove him, the anger at self, the man he used to be, the man he feared he still was.

"Your desire is for me to capitulate to your extortion and agree to bow out of the current conflict, so you may best use what resources that remain to defeat the Knights Templar and secure once again your primacy in this world?"

Burke nodded. "That sounds correct."

"Go fuck yourself."

That took some of the starch out of Burke's shorts. "That's a mistake," he growled.

"The fact that you tender this offer merely provides proof that your organization has suffered and continues to do so quite magnificently. The monster that is your Family finds itself bleeding, cut by the Templar razor and will continue to bleed and does not need the likes of me salting the wounds."

73%.

"Is that a no?"

"Most definitely."

82%.

Dark eyes bored into Cain's. "Consider this offer carefully, old man. You will not get another."

88%.

"Goodbye, Burke." Cain terminated the connection before the counter could reach ninety. "We must be away," he said abruptly, smashing the tablet against the table before stomping on the pieces.

"Are you nuts!" Maggie cried, pocketing the whetstone away. "We nearly got killed at that office building for that!" Her blood pressure threatened to explode a vein or two in her skull. First his insistence on drinking single-malt scotch, then that ambush at the building Cain owned because 'residing therein is a necessary component of our current confrontation with villains dire.' Or some such. When he emerged from the top floor office carrying only the tablet, she felt the need to vent some serious rage, but knew he had his mysterious ways. Still, he was so *aggravating*!

"This tablet contraption," Cain replied. *Smash, smash, stomp, stomp.* "Is the most advanced communications device ever created." *Stomp.* "They are absent serial numbers and geo-locator chips, a feat that in today's society is quite prodigious, to say the least. Only a dozen or so remain in existence and have a combined value equal to twenty Bugatti Chiron." *Smash*. "Although I am prone to excess verbosity and exaggeration, I assure you that estimate leans toward the conservative. It is only because of vast wealth and the ability to utilize that wealth to sway others to look in the opposite direction during manufacture that I possess those tablets at all. There are so few because you can only spend so much before it attracts the notice of those not in your employ."

Maggie was feeling frustrated enough to add to the carnage by swinging the hatchet down on a particularly stubborn bit of detritus. It gave with a satisfying *crunch*. She enjoyed it so much that she did it again. "Then why the fuck did you break it?"

"You realize your language has deteriorated mightily since departing my tutelage."

I will not kill him. No future in it. "Call it a natural degradation. How about answering the question?"

"I destroyed that valuable device because the counter in the corner reached the eightieth percentile, an indication of the powerful intrusive measures the Family utilizes to locate a perspective target for assassination. Once the percentages increase above seventy, the tablet cannot be employed again. They have the scent, so to speak, of this particular device and can swiftly locate it within moments." Cain nudged a sparkle of glass with the toe of his sneaker. SO much money down the drain. "Since the news of that villain Blaine's death, I desired to understand the identity of the puppet master, however I did not expect to see a dead man."

Morgan Heart's journal had become required reading for the Templars, if only so they could truly understand the enormity of the forces arrayed against them. Mike also wanted them to understand that even those thought lost to evil could come back to God's grace. It was always about choice. *There's always a choice, although it might be a hard one.* Somehow, she doubted Burke would choose his way from Lucifer's clutches.

"Dead or not," she said, holstering her hatchet and checking her more modern weapons. "It's time to leave this place." A modest apartment complex, nice but not too clean or swanky to attract notice. Cain had assured her that he owned it and still maintained a two-bedroom on the fifth floor they could hole up in while they planned their next attack on the Family.

"Relax, my former apprentice. The Family considers this apartment far too low rent for a man of my advanced tastes. I sincerely doubt they will cast their eyes to this humble locale."

With a roar, the floor beneath Maggie gave way in a flume of dust and flame and she dropped from sight.

CHAPTER THREE
UNFORTUNATE SON

———∞———

SMOKE AND HEAT AND THE IRRESISTIBLE pull of gravity held Maggie tight and she fell, the floor in pieces around her, pacing her descent and she knew she was dead, knew that if she didn't arrest her fall, she'd break her legs like matchsticks. Those that waited would pick her off like a wounded deer and that would be it for the wannabe Valkyrie, the woman who spat in the face of the Valhalla Club and that just would not do.

She screamed a Word.

Female magi were rare, perhaps one percent of all magi were women and considering the scarcity of Word slingers, that meant what emerged thirty feet below into a burning second story apartment took the Sicarii there by surprise.

Seven feet of Valkyrie clad in shining chrome armor bearing an axe the size of Cadillac hub cap in one hand and a Sig Sauer P232 380ACP in the other emerged from the smoke. Wings of raven black fluttered behind her and her eyes burned with cold blue fire behind a chrome Viking helmet.

The Sig spat once, killing the first of the Sicarii, taking him in the throat and the axe, long-handled and razor sharp, blurred forward to shear into bone of another, destroying both eyes and tearing the top of his head off.

An Uzi barked, and a line of holes appeared in the shining chest plate, knocking the Valkyrie off her feet as she screamed a Word that the last Sicarii knew well. Healing ... to him it smelled of lemons. He knew the large woman would be whole once again and fired, empting the clip at the seemingly stunned Valkyrie. Before he could reload, the woman was on her feet in a stunning display of dexterity and grace, emptying her little automatic point blank at the assassin.

All five rounds hit, tattooing his chest and throwing him backward to rebound off the living room wall in a haze of sharp pain. Bruised ribs, possibly broken. He barely had time to mumble his own Healing before the giant axe came for him.

He ducked, and the weapon buried itself in drywall. He threw one, two, three quick jabs and was surprised to feel not burnished chrome, but fabric that gave under his fist.

"Aspect," he grinned, naming the spell. "Clever girl."

The Valkyrie's form blurred, the chrome armor melted into ballistic cloth and titanium chain mesh. The giant axe became her hatchet, although bloodied and decorated with brains. What was once a Valkyrie, giant and imposing, turned into Maggie, not as big, but imposing nonetheless.

No answer, she merely swung the hatchet and the Sicarius ducked, shouting Pain with every bit of breath in his newly healed chest.

Maggie nearly doubled over, but for her, pain, even magically induced, was an old friend and she rode the wave of nerve flensing agony like a surfer, above, over, and ultimately past as the magic subsided. You didn't become a Valhalla Club champion fighting with axe and shield against hordes of snarling misogynists without enduring a fair share of hurt. She answered the Sicarius' look of surprise with a hastily muttered Word: Grace and got down to some serious business.

Only ... the Sicarius, a youngish man she doubted needed to shave more than twice a week, was damn good at his job, too. She spun, leg sweeping low, but he jumped easily, gracefully as well, but not magically so. Her hatchet glided over his head as his knife scored across the ballistic cloth of her side, exposing the mesh underneath. Back and forth, hatchet verses long knife.

Pain blossomed above her eye as the knife bit. Damn, this kid was *good*. Quite possibly the best she ever faced, save Cain, who was in a class all by himself. Blood trickled into her eye before she could mutter a Healing.

"Strength," grunted the Dagger Man, grinning. That Word, to the normal person, would slide in and out of their ears leaving nothing behind, no trace, no impression, but Maggie understood. He grinned like a shark sizing up a plump little seal.

"Strength," she replied, using the same Word. To her it smelled like hot tar.

The Dagger Man frowned, but his discomfiture didn't last. Snarling, he jumped at Maggie, whose Grace allowed her to avoid his grasp. Mostly.

With a shout of victory, he snagged her left arm in his right hand. Before she could pull free his left trapped her right. All hands were in use, holding their opposites, vying to abruptly end the conflict.

This guy is half snake! Maggie grimaced, then gripped him back, her hatchet inches from his face, his knife inches from hers and they both struggled to gain primacy, to use their weapons to destroy the other and they both *squeezed*, Strength-enhanced muscles causing bones to groan alarmingly and it turned out to be contest of who was naturally stronger, the Sicarius who was a young, tall, virile man with a lifetime of assassination training, or the woman who was used to hacking people to bits with an axe few could even lift because Strength didn't grant people the same amount of power, evening the playing field, it only enhanced what was naturally there and each combatant strived to overcome the other, to kill before the spell wore off and millimeter by millimeter Maggie proved the stronger, her hatchet coming fractionally closer to the now terrified Dagger Man and sweat broke out on both their faces as they strained, tissues nearly tearing themselves apart, shaking, trembling and the hatchet, edge razor sharp, touched the Sicarius' lip and he screamed Strength, but it didn't help because he was maxed out already, Maggie was naturally stronger and he made a move out of desperation, lashing out with a kick, going for the knee, to collapse bone and cartilage, but he lost his leverage and Maggie freed her right hand and *slammed* the heel of that hand against the back of the hatchet which shattered teeth and cleaved tongue, slicing through cheeks before exiting the back of the Dagger Man's head in rush of blood.

"There," she growled as the top half of his skull separated from the rest, plopping down onto the floor.

She turned around, exhausted from fighting, from slowing her fall floor by floor with nebulous wings created by Aspect, from just about everything that happened in the last 48 hours. Smoke stung her eyes and her body began to tremble, her muscles rebelling somewhat as Strength slowly leeched from her. Suddenly from came the sound of an explosion and the apartment building shook.

"Now what?"

MAGGIE DISAPPEARED INTO THE HOLE IN the floor and Cain immediately saw the tiny fire elemental that created it, eating through joists and plywood so quickly that not even he could have seen it coming. And he hadn't.

As the smoke billowed upward and the tiny intelligent sparks chewed across the edges of the hole, enlarging it, time slowed as Cain's mind went into overdrive. Thousands of wars and countless battles honed his intellect to computer-like speeds during times of stress, weighing odds and probabilities before his heart beat twice. The air elemental outside would prevent attack from the sky, the earth would swallow anyone who dared tunnel and water protected the sewer, but he had neglected fire, which was a mistake.

Hopefully it is not my last.

Where would the attack come from? Not an RPG like before when caught unawares. Not from the floor. Where?

The walls.

He was in the air as split second before the bullets intersected at the space he just vacated. Hip brushing atop the granite counter into the small kitchen, careening off the oven to crack the heat-resistant glass and hitting the floor with enough force to bruise elbow and knee, Cain managed to put his MP-9 in hand.

Granite chips flew along with splinters of oak and shards of glass as bullets ripped through the small kitchen, tearing a $20,000 remodel to flinders. He figured it had to be Sicarii because they acted with cool efficiency, one firing while the other reloaded.

No taunting, no calling out, they were all professionals. Why try to cajole or entreat a victim who was far too aware of their mission? The question that rankled him, however, was how did they find him and so quickly?

For a moment he worried about Maggie but realized that divide and conquer was the strategy and they hoped, but didn't expect, that he would rush to her defense, opening himself up to their bullets.

"#*$," muttered Cain, going for Strength.

Nothing.

One more time then. ""#*$."

Again, nothing. His stomach performed a slow roll as realized there was only one thing that could block Word Magic. One terrible thing.

Blood Magic.

The cost of such a thing was death … the death of an innocent. Usually the death of an infant because such pure blood provided the strongest magic. That thought awakened the fury within him, but instead of bursting free from cover he channeled the rage along old familiar lines. He didn't live this long fighting year in and out against the Sicarii without having a few tricks up his ancient sleeves.

From a thigh pocket of his rugged cargo pants he took a small, dull green sphere about the size of an American half-dollar coin affixed to an even smaller rectangular box. He twisted the box until he heard a dull *click*, silently counted to two, then tossed it over the granite counter into the living room just as a round from one of the gunman nicked his arm. He ducked, ignoring the wound and covering his head with his arms.

One of the great things about being obscenely wealthy is the ability to create new and intensely dangerous ways to commit the same old mayhem. Cain spent a considerable sum to create a mundane, yet hideously lethal, device as compact as his extremely well- paid scientists could manage: a grenade.

Octanitrocubane is comprised of a cube of carbon atoms with oxygen and nitrogen groups (NO_2) attached to each atom. The detonation velocity of this compound is roughly 10,100 meters-per-second, making it the fastest known explosive. Small amounts were created in laboratory conditions, but not enough to clearly test as a viable explosive compound.

That is until Cain committed his considerable resources to the problem ... and he just threw the result into the small living room.

With a roar like the mother of all lighting strikes, it detonated inches from the hole Maggie had fallen through. The blast tore into the cabinet he was hiding behind, tearing it apart, ripping it into a hail of splinters that imbedded themselves into Cain's exposed flesh. Granite countertop rained down in bruising chunks while the sound wave pummeled his ears, rendering them insensate.

After a few moments, in the quiet aftermath of the explosion, Cain shrugged off the rubble coating him, pulling large splinters from his hands. *That was ... energetic. Perhaps smaller next time. If the good Lord sees fit to grant me a next time.* Groaning, he stood on trembling legs, ears muffled in silence and staggered into the next room to survey the damage.

What was left of his attackers could have been spooned into a coffee jar. Judging by how much was impacted into what was left of the drywall and ceiling, there would be room left over for Burke's ashes, should he ever catch up to the new leader of the Sicarii.

Amid the red smears he uttered a Healing, bits of granite and wood popping from his skin as his flesh suddenly, very energetically began to knit. As he stood there, the warmth of the spell suffusing his skin, a sudden heat surrounded him, crisping his beard and his long, curly hair.

"*What are you doing?*" he demanded, casting his eyes to the floor where a large fire elemental, the kind referred to as a Burn, rose from the floor, a pillar of sentient flame, a tornado of reds, golds and oranges.

"*The agreement is made,*" said the Burn in the crackling Language of Fire. "*You defeated my summoner, so you must be eaten.*" It loomed, spitting sparks and Cain blinked, eyes drying from the heat.

He knew there was no negotiating with elementals after an agreement had been made, it was one of the first things any magus worth their salt learned. Cain had two choices and both sucked.

"*Come!*" he cried in a different Language, full of vowels and whistling. "*Protect me!*"

The Burn struck.

Cain was awash in liquid fire, hotter than he could have imagined. Every nerve was alight as skin boiled away and the fat underneath melted. When his mouth opened fire rushed into consume his tongue and shatter his teeth, but a Word emerged, carried on waves of an agony so great it pushed him to his knees.

Healing.

Instantly his tongue started to reform, the tissues of his lungs, seared by flame, became whole and vibrant again, just long enough for him to scream another Healing as his eyes burst from their sockets, boiling liquid cascading down his cheeks. Healing … and again … Healing, Healing, Healing.

Consumed and regenerating, a cycle of life and death, fire and magic as superheated air entered lungs, destroyed lungs the same moment they healed, over and over again pain unending, unendurable. When you've lived for over *fifty-thousand years* and have access to magic, no pain is really new. In fact, it becomes something relied upon because when everything, everyone, around you dies or fades or simply disappears, pain is always there. An old companion that will never leave as long as the heart beats and the blood flows. Sometimes pain was the only thing that reminds you that you live, that defines living.

So, for Cain, the unendurable was endurable and thanks to his curse, the agony that would have rendered others mad didn't affect his horrible, terrible sanity, forced upon him by a vengeful god for a crime thought to be inexcusable.

It wasn't murder, the first murder, the first fratricide that angered God so, but the first lie told by man. 'I know not. Am I my brother's keeper?' Thanks to Morgan Heart, that simple, basic fact had been laid bare before his unbelieving eyes and he at last saw the depths of his misconception. In a universe where life continues after the death of the body, lying to God is the greater evil because it insulted the Almighty as well as showed a tremendous amount of arrogance and pride. Hubris.

Lucifer's Sin.

All this and more went through Cain's mind as he burned alive and healed over and over again for what felt like hours. This he reckoned fundamentalist Christians must think was what Hell looked and felt like. He had second-hand knowledge (first-hand knowledge came from Wotanael, who posed as the god Odin for the Norse. He spent the first three millennia after the Rebellion in Hell trying *not* get Lucifer's attention while planning his escape). Hell wasn't the burning realm of pain and suffering. No, Hell was knowing you were out of God's sight, alone, lost and utterly miserable. Wotanael seemed agitated about it, swearing he would rather be dragged to Heaven by his tongue than go back.

For Cain, this Hell lasted for only a few moments … or thirty Words of Healing … before he was knocked to the floor by a buffeting force.

"You shall not have him."

It was the Gale, the great air elemental he summoned earlier to protect him from airborne assault, coming to his call, to his defense against the Burn.

"You cannot stop me," countered the pillar of fire, having been tossed aside by the larger elemental. *"The more you blow, I more I eat."*

Skin ... he had skin again, knitting itself over pink muscle and ivory fat. Darkness receded as his eyes slowly grew whole and he kept muttering Healing, continually, as the Gale and the Burn twisted together to form a funnel of fire. A tornado of destruction that consumed wood, plaster and wiring within moments. Hot wind raged through the apartment, fed by the air streaming in from the broken windows. He could once again feel the heat as nerve endings mended. It covered him like water, like a burning blanket, but it did no harm because the Gale was too strong for the Burn. It moved the fire elemental away from its summoner, saving him.

Cain could see and now that his nerves, once charred, regained their ability to send outraged signals to his brain. He could finally believe that life still clung to him, that death would not come this night. The relief was almost tangible.

"Get rid of that Burn," screamed Cain through newly formed teeth and lips. "Get the woman ... save us both."

Almost contemptuously the tornado *flexed*, and the Burn was thrown through the broken window, torn by winds too strong to resist, and fell to the parking lot below where it began consuming a Ford Focus.

"Get the girl," mumbled Cain after another Healing. "Downstairs."

The elemental flowed through the hole in the floor. "Fire will return. It cannot fly, but it will eat this building to get to you."

"Hurry, then."

Within seconds air exploded from the hole in the floor, Maggie in its invisible embrace. Cain felt himself lifted, carried on strong yet gentle winds, winds that tore the roof from the building and carried the two tired and hurting humans to safety.

CHAPTER FOUR
THE MIGHTY FINN

———◈———

"**Y**OU REALIZE I'M NOT COMPLAINING."

Cain looked askance at his former protégé. A week had passed since that night at the apartment complex. The Gale had gone back for survivors, but by the time it returned, the place was ash and smoke. A Burn is an effective destroyer, erasing everything of value at the sight. Even the nails had been reduced to rivulets of slag.

From there the two traveled via Gale to St. Paul, Minnesota, to one of the hundreds of safe houses owned by one of his many shell corporations, cut-outs that distanced him from investigation. A journey that took a better part of a day at a high enough altitude not to be seen from the ground.

During the flight Cain had been only semi-conscious thanks to the first case of Backlash experienced since the Anarchy, the unrest in England circa 1135 AD. Magic was not some infinite well of power, the Law of Conservation of Energy would not be denied. It was channeled through the magus and, if abused, caused increasing amounts of damage to the wielder's body, very possibly culminating in death.

"That sucked big time," Maggie said after they settled in. Cain recovered enough to eat a breakfast big enough to sate a dozen lumberjacks. She poured coffee, which he insisted on brewing using a French press. It smelled more than wonderful, and she thought that's what Heaven must smell like ... fresh brewed coffee. "Now what? We go back to Mike, back to the Templars? That'd be my play."

Extra crispy bacon slid down Cain's throat as he considered his answer carefully. He followed the bacon with coffee, extra cream. Real cream, not the fake stuff that comes in the plastic bottles located next to the Maxwell

House in the coffee aisle at your local grocery store. No, it was light cream with 18% fat and it eased the bitterness of the caffeine with just the right hint of sweetness. Like Maggie, his idea of Heaven definitely included coffee.

"We could indeed do the very thing which you propose," he said once the last bit of bacon surfed its way into his tummy on a creamy wave of coffee. "And perhaps that would be the wisest course of action, one that would enhance our priestly friend's struggle against the Family infernal. However, that does not strike me as the *correct* course of action at this juncture."

Maggie sat, a sinking feeling in her gut. For the past six months they had been waging their own war against the Sicarii, attacking them on two fronts, forcing the Dagger Men to chase after shadows. Now it seemed this Burke fella found a way to counter that by hiring outside the Family for the first time in their existence. *And it's far too effective,* she thought. *We got our asses handed to us.* "What then?"

Cain mulled over a croissant shining with buttery goodness. "Before the ascendancy of young Burke to the Sicarii throne the use of Botanical Magic was considered beneath the Dagger Men, a kind of bastard magic, if you will." The croissant disappeared in two large bites. "It is of some concern that he now employs such magic with greater frequency and allows his minions to employ tools of Blood Magic."

Before the Gale transported them from the apartment complex, Cain had seen the remains of runestones, small polished, dun-colored rocks carrying the remains of blood runes. Portable magic nullifiers ruined by the blast of the grenade. If Botanical Magic was considered a bastard science by the Sicarii, then Blood Magic would be thought of at the prodigal son ... practiced only by the Family elite. The fact that mere Dagger Men, Family though they were, possessed such things meant that Burke felt it necessary to throw out centuries of tradition in the name of expedience. And necessity.

"I'm not gonna like our next step, am I?"

"Understand that for the past two millennia the Family has ossified, layers of its members lying in geologic strata, immobile. That is, until outside influences induced pressure to crack the Family rock, crumbling it, reforming it to unfamiliar yet more stable positions. You, me, Michael and the Templars are the pressures put upon the Sicarii and they have risen to the challenge by shattering old memes within the Family culture and erecting new ones that beforehand would have seemed repellent. Burke is the instrument of this change, rising to the occasion evidencing adaptability and perhaps a kind of contempt for older, more acceptable ways. This sets him apart from other Family heads, such as Julian, who would never stoop to ways contrary to historical norms and this alarms me to a great degree.

"I have been harmed more by Burke's actions than any other in recorded history. He is as intelligent as he is ruthless and how he discovered us at the apartment, much less readied an SS team to assist our journey into afterlife is beyond my comprehension. Therefore, we must with all due haste resort to methods that I find personally rather distasteful."

Get the point, Maggie gestured with one hand while taking a large swig of coffee. She had a feeling she'd need the caffeine sooner rather than later. She snagged a surviving piece of bacon from his plate and chowed it down in one bite.

"We must get away to another land, a country almost halfway around the globe in an effort to enlist a person I am most loathe to entreat. However, to quote the old chestnut, desperate times call for desperate measures and we seem to find ourselves quite desperate. As rich as my accountants inform me to be, the Family is nearly so, and they hold the greater numbers, bolstered by those willing mercenaries who have no qualm in accepting their coin."

Okay, this shit was getting real. "Where are we going?"

After dabbing his lips with a napkin, Cain took off his wraparound shades, exposing his wolf-like blue/white eyes and stared into hers. "Nepal."

SINCE BOARDING A PLANE, EVEN A privately owned one, meant airports and airports meant CCTV and facial recognition software and facial recognition software meant Family interference, which meant international travel by other means. That meant an air elemental. A Gale.

"You realize I'm not complaining."

Cain sighed, the sound carrying quite nicely considering they rested in the arms...? Stomach? Hands? Of a large Gale, which protected them from the thin atmosphere of fifty-thousand feet and kept winds from tearing the breath from their lungs. A little cubby of silence in the amorphous being that over 99.9% of the population couldn't see. The only thing the Gale couldn't protect the two from was the below freezing temperatures that ate through their heavy winter clothes. So cold, in fact, that when Maggie spit, it froze with a soft *crack* before it passed six feet. She imagined little spit pebbles plinking softly into the Mediterranean Sea far below. *Plit, plit, plit,* goes the spit.

"It comes to mind," Cain said through his balaclava, which smelled like stale breath and snot. "That your ability not to complain sounds remarkably like that which you say it is not."

The dawn light failed to warm Maggie's eyes and the skin around them felt dead ... numb. It seemed amazing, this flight without an airplane, carried by a being only a magus could see, yet faster than an airplane. No stops for fuel or the deplaning of old passengers and the embarking of new. Despite the dawn, the ground and water far below remained a mass of darkness, only a faint glinting separating soil from sea.

"The cold eats right through you." Her voice carried easily, clearly in the undisturbed air of their safe bubble in the belly of the Gale. "I've never felt anything like this before. Never this cold, even in Minnesota."

What could he say? The cold bit him as well, even though the balaclava, his long underwear, snow pants, flannel shirt and doubly-padded extreme weather parka. He checked his watch, special made, ruggedized to withstand the freezing temperature. Two more hours, give or take ten minutes.

"It will become colder, my dear. Far colder than you can conceive, beyond the capacity of your imagination."

"Just who are we going to see?" He hadn't told her. Refused to tell her. This didn't stop her from asking time and again.

Cain gave his stock answer. "The father of darkness."

NEPAL. SANDWICHED BETWEEN CHINA AND INDIA, it boasts the Ganges plains in the south and the rugged mountains in the north. Winters can be brutal, the summers placid, almost perfect. It is also home of the Mahalangur, a mountain range whose most famous resident is Mount Everest. In fact, the international border between Nepal and China lays across Everest's exact summit point. To the Nepalese, the mountain is Sagarmāthā, the Forehead in the Sky.

The Forehead wasn't the destination. Too many people that time of year, people who paid the big bucks to trek to the summit of the world's tallest mountain. People in the best shape of their lives, with lungpower and stamina to climb to an altitude so high that they would slowly begin to die. Base camps teeming with people celebrating their lives, starry-eyed dreamers willing to die to reach a goal, willing to risk freezing or falling or succumbing to heat delusion. Adrenaline junkies who needed shots of the stuff to survive. The mountain is patient and despite all precautions there would be death … eventually. The mountain always receives its due, a sacrifice of flesh, always voluntary, always fresh.

Fifteen or so miles from Everest the Gale set down in a narrow valley devoid of trees, but with a stream and short spring grass. Bushes dotted the landscape adding to the bucolic vision of an impossibly blue sky, blindingly white snow atop thrusting peaks and greens so intense one could almost taste it on the tip of the tongue.

The sole inhabitant of that valley waited next to a blue and white tent, smiling whitely as the Gale spun downward with its burden. Details began to form as the two magi neared the ground … bushy blond beard, broad shoulders declaring considerable strength and classic Scandinavian features.

Maggie's stomach performed a slow roll as her spiraling descent grew quicker and quicker, threatening to send her lunch down ahead of her. She clutched her backpack firmly in her arms and closed her eyes. It helped, a bit. *Where's the Dramamine when you need it?*

"Master!' cried the man in heavily accented English. Maggie opened her eyes as her feet touched the grass in time to see Cain sweep the man up in a big bear hug.

It took a moment for her eyes to adjust, for her mind to accept the scale of what she was seeing. Cain was big, extremely tall, yet lanky, built like a basketball player. He said his father, Adam, was a giant in comparison to modern man, as were most people in that day. He said he was the shortest in the family, his brothers Abel and Seth stood several inches taller than he, as did his mother.

This man made Cain look tiny. Heck, he made a professional wrestler look like an anemic child. Maggie reckoned, as the two men tried to squeeze the pulp out of each other, that he stood a few inches shorter than Cain and was near twice as broad, not an ounce of that was flab. Muscles as hard as river rock writhed beneath his tight-fitting clothes from nonexistent neck to calves like cantaloupes. Blue eyes like lamps shone from his face, joy evident as he laughed and laughed and laughed, fists pounding Cain's back.

There was something wrong, she saw. It wasn't a big tell, a slight tic around his right eye, the cornflower blue orb shuttering open and closed at odd intervals.

The Curse.

She knew the Curse placed upon Cain's head by God forced him to wander the earth for all eternity, its presence made manifest by the blue/white eyes of a wolf. Two years, a simple timeline, but for Cain a crucial one. It was the longest possible span of time a person could stand to be around him before the Curse really kicked in. For some unknown reason it never affected her, not that she complained.

Others had told her it started with a tingly, itching sensation, that unnerving feeling that someone walked over your grave. Before too long standing near him gave the willies, made one jumpy. Maggie had seen a woman named Allison, one of his many former apprentices, who started slightly every time he spoke. Cain repeatedly told her to leave, but she wouldn't, she was addicted to the magic, the near inexhaustible font of knowledge he represented, and she did her best to brave the Curse for as long as possible.

One month after the two-year limit she ran, gripped by an unknown terror she couldn't control. Maggie never heard from her since. She hoped the woman, little, mousy with kind smile, found some peace and learned to live without the source of knowledge she so craved.

This big man, however, looked to be a few days from running screaming, heading for the hills and not stopping until he was hip deep in water.

"You look to be as hale as I have ever beheld you to be!" cried Cain, laughing all the while, big booming bursts of noise like tiny claps of thunder. "Truly your prodigious strength has increased tenfold."

A pair of sunglasses quickly hid blue eyes when the two men disengaged. This wasn't lost on Cain, but you couldn't tell by his expression. "Ekki, come meet your counterpart in the fairer sex. A great warrior and magus like yourself with a penchant for the dramatic that exhibits in Valkyrie-esque feats of legerdemain."

"Pleasure to meet you," said Maggie, shaking the big man's hand. There was a lot of mustard in his grip. "Ekki … interesting name."

More teeth shone through the blond beard. He had a nice smile. Nice enough to start a tickle behind her tummy. *Beware, Maggie. You still have a long way to go and a vendetta to complete.* Still, he looked a handful in the sack. "It's Finnish, like me." He had the kind of flat, indescribable accent most Europeans develop from learning English from a young age.

"Ekki was one of my most talented protégés, a six Word magus of not inconsiderable talent in Botanical Magic."

She whistled. Six Words! Maggie turned to Cain. "Why here?"

"Elementals won't go near where we have to go, some agreement they made centuries ago. They are very close-mouthed about it," said Ekki, putting in two cents worth. He looked to the mountains to the northwest. "I arrived shortly before you and haven't been able to whistle up a single elemental, which is quite unusual." His smile left as quickly as it appeared. "Why do you need me, Cain? Understand that I am happy take your call and assist in whatever capacity I can, but why me?"

"We are on a quest most perilous and it may come to pass that extra muscle will carry the day. As a six Word magus possessing the musculature of two strong men, I find in you more than ample strength to aid our pursuit."

"Really?"

Cain nodded. "Really, really. Besides, no one else was available."

Ekki's laugh was rueful. "That's what I thought." A smartphone made an appearance, looking absurdly tiny his enormous, gloved hand. "I have downloaded all maps of the area. There is no village like the one you described. I checked."

Cain smiled, this time without humor. "No cartographer has ever laid pen to parchment to impart the location to where we must depart." The sun glinted off his wraparounds. "It is high, not overly so, but enough to dissuade casual travelers."

Sun far overhead and the grass emerald beneath their feet, the two shouldered the backpacks and followed the Finn, who seemed happy to put his back to Cain. They made for a peak, some two hours walk away, shrouded in mists despite the crystal of the sky. Despite his earlier ebullience, Ekki made no attempt at conversation and Maggie reckoned that he was feeling enough of the Curse to curb his tongue.

As for Cain, he knew this symphony of discomfort well, it was something he had lived with, agonized over, for fifty-thousand years. However, the brown rings around his blue/white irises, appearing after that affair in New York City with Morgan Heart, gave him some hope that redemption would come sooner rather than later. For the first time in as long as he could remember hope stirred behind his heart.

Hope, he thought. An emotion fraught with boundless possibilities and perils. How could it not be the last to escape behind the teeming evils that resided in Pandora's Box. Every time he took a new protégé there was hope, but time eventually aged and withered that hope, rendering it dust and sorrow.

Fifty thousand years on the planet would put the ordinary person around the bend, that or cause their brains to seize, but not Cain. The Curse saw to that, keeping his mind sharp and his recollections perfect, but it couldn't diminish his sense of hope, no matter how grim life became. Because to an immortal, everything happens in a blink.

Blink ... your child is born.

Blink ... you bury that child.

Blink ... you just buried the grandkids, great-grandkids, buried for centuries and left them in the dirt under your feet. *Blink, blink, blink.*

If you asked Cain about immortality, how cool it was, how you could see the world from every point of view and learn all its mysteries, he'd tell you the one, true thing about forever. The truest, most precious bit of knowledge ever to be conceived in the entire short history of mankind.

Immortality sucks.

Die, he would say, when it's your turn. Don't shirk from what happens next because it will be new, it will be different, and it won't happen in a blink. *I carry my Hell with me,* he pondered, smelling wildflowers on the breeze. *On shoulders unbowed by age.*

Hope, that fickle bitch, whispered in his ear about redemption, all because of the man who could have been the Antichrist introduced him to a very good man, a priest and prophet of the Lord.

The Antichrist and a priest walk into a bar ...

It just goes to show that life has a way of surprising anyone, even an immortal. Take Ekki, for example. In 1999 a movie called *Fight Club* became a cult hit thanks to superb acting, unapologetic themes and moral ambiguity of its main character played by Edward Norton. Thanks to this film, real-life fight clubs sprang up all over the world and that's where Cain discovered the Finn.

Cain partook of the fighting, although the matches ended quickly. Not a single person could stand against uncounted centuries of martial experience and his prodigious strength. That didn't stop him from attending the clubs and placing a friendly wager or two. Some would call such a thing immoral, but to a person who lived long enough to see slavery go from an accepted practice to reviled and outlawed everywhere, only the laws of God really mattered. The laws of men were far too influenced by whimsy.

Between apprentices, Cain took to having small air elementals, called sprites, whirl above his head in a complicated dance of airy joy. Those who could see the hidden, those with the capability of becoming a magus, would see the elementals and then Cain could take on a new apprentice, someone to share his joy of the secret world, the world of magic.

On the fourth floor of a parking garage, ostensibly closed for maintenance, lay a fight club, a group of youngish men in various stages of fitness from obese to rail thin, convening the in exultation of being men. Like those tribal support groups where men go to redefine their masculinity by playing drums or hunting with spears, these men chose to define their archetype by beating the crap out of each other in an orgy of ebullient violence.

That night the action wasn't very good. The fighters, slick with blood and sweat, seemed more tentative than aggressive. They threw half-hearted punches and grappled without passion, but that didn't stop the betting, which continued unabated. All those who attended fought, even those who bet.

As per usual, he fought as soon as he could, ending the fight by submission with as little pain as possible and always wearing his sunglasses, which lent him a sinister air. After the first day he became their Everest, their mountain to climb, but he only fought one per night, even though there were challenges aplenty. Rumor circulated among the men that he was the inspiration for Tyler Durden, the anti-hero of the movie.

That amused him no end.

On that night of tepid punches and kicks, a new arrival added some much-needed spice to the proceeding, a big man with a big, blond beard who towered over the others there like the god Thor among the citizens of Midgard. *Although*, thought Cain, staring through his wraparounds at the big man. *Thor would have been drunk.*

"We have a new member here," said the man who accompanied the blond behemoth, a guy named Phil, a regular. "He's from Finland and I vouch for him. His name's Ekki." He pronounced it Ehk-key. "First night, have to fight."

"First night, have to fight." A chorus with all the solemnity of a hymn. He was instantly accepted … after all, they were men, brothers in genial brutality. Clapping their hands, the men made a circle and the Finn entered, removing his shirt. His chest was thick with blond curls. Muscles rippled smoothly under that hair, filled with damaging potential.

Quiet descended. While it wasn't unusual for members in good standing to bring new recruits to the club, very few of them looked so ... impressive. The club was chock full of men who measured themselves by their fists, but they sure weren't suicidal enough to risk the giant knuckles of the Finn who stood there like a behemoth among hamsters. There was bravery aplenty, but it was heavily laden with pragmatism.

It became so quiet in the garage, in fact, that it seemed to Cain that his ears were smothered in cotton. Even the sound of breathing failed to reach him and just as it stretched to the breaking point, the noise of a couple dozen tendons and vertebrae twisting slithered through the air. All heads swiveled his way and forty-eight eyes slapped against his skin.

As for Ekki, he wasn't staring at Cain, but at a point a foot above his head, eyes slightly wide and dreamy.

But of course. How very interesting ... "Well, gentleman," he murmured. "As courage has fled to parts unknown, and for reasons that are self-evident to those with sufficient ocular capacity, it behooves me to set my thews to the task at hand." He removed his T-shirt.

Ekki suddenly focused on Cain, body quivering with earnest anticipation and he crouched slightly, turning his body to the side to present a smaller target, although that was difficult to do considering his size. He raised scarred fists the size of country hams.

Unlike the others, this one had more than a modicum of skill at the art of unarmed combat. Cain swiveled his head, listening to his vertebrae pop. *There is a strong possibility he will have a chance to lay a hand upon me. How fun.* Blood rushed to skin, flushing it with excitement. For too long he had been the best and no one could stand against him and likely no one ever would. The thought of an actual fight where he could break a sweat brought a glad smile to his long face.

The Finn's eyes darted from Cain's face to the space above his head. He seemed distracted, so Cain fist flashed forward, popping him lightly on the nose, which began to bleed.

Thwack! So fast. Cain's head whipped around, neck muscles creaking in protest and his check becoming numb after the initial quickfire shot of pain. For a big man, the Finn was fast, and it felt like getting hit by a sledgehammer wrapped in several layers of beef. The image of the Finn rippled as tears formed but didn't fall and blood filled his mouth from where his teeth cut into his cheek.

"Marvelous," he crooned, wiping away with the back of his hand a trickle of blood that escaped his lips. "Excellent."

Most men would have recoiled from the smile pasted on his face, but not

Ekki. The Finn grinned and set to.

Cain blocked a jab that would have crushed his jaw and lashed out with a vicious back knuckle that took Ekki over right eye which was answered by an elbow. It took him hard in the side and his ribs groaned alarmingly as hot agony ripped through his liver, but he sucked it up, took it because he knew pain well, his old friend. In some ways it was comforting because it reminded him that he could still feel, that life hadn't put a callous on his soul, something perilously easy for an exceedingly long time on earth. He used that pain to throw three quick jabs that felt like hitting a granite plinth and may as well have been for all the damage it did. The Finn just took it on the chin and threw a dizzying flurry of kicks and punches that backed Cain up, forcing him to the edge of the circle where hands pushed him back in.

Smiling wider, Ekki grew more confident and brash with his attacks, landing a couple with such resounding *smacks* that the crowd *ooh*ed in appreciation. Grinning through the pain, Cain gave a little whistle, a terse command in the Language of Air.

The sprites wizzed furiously above his hair, spiraling up and down in a dizzying dance that dazzled the eye and Ekki's grew wide in amazement, his face a mask of wonder that turned into pain then went slack after two hammering blows from Cain's fist took him in the left cheek and right eye. The lights went out for the big Finn and the cold concrete became his mattress as his slack body hit hard with a meaty *slap*.

I thought as much. Cain knelt next to the unconscious man as the rest of the club cheered. "What shall we do with you, my good lad?" he muttered under his breath as he checked the Finn's injuries. Nothing much, but the blond man was going to hurt when he woke. "What drove you to heights of madness that you would seek out and join such a gaggle of misfits, eh?"

Ekki groaned.

"Perhaps you flirted with lady madness because your blue eyes beheld sights no one else could? Is that the seed of your self-destructive behavior, young man? The hidden world layered beneath this one?"

As for me, it certainly provides an entertaining fashion to pass a Saturday night.

"CAIN? EARTH TO CAIN! WE'RE HERE."

He jerked his head up, images of Chicago tattering in the winds of reality. The three of them stood near a collection of crude stone and wood houses at the foot of the mist-shrouded mountain, surrounded by a group of Nepalese men of varying ages, all armed with firearms pointed in their direction.

"How very nice indeed," Cain smiled, "to have cause to send us a greeting party."

CHAPTER SIX
HI, JUDE

───⌇───

A MAN WITH MORE SALT THAN PEPPER in his hair, brown face seamed by decades of hard weather and sun, barked out a question filled with liquid consonants, jabbing an ancient, but obviously well maintained, Lee-Enfield rifle at the trio. Like the rest of the men, he wore gray trousers and a dark shirt, of good quality but oft mended.

"Anyone wanna hazard a guess at what he's jabbering on about?" Maggie eyed the rifle warily. *I am way too fucking young to die here.*

"I believe he's speaking Newari," said Ekki, hands raised. "But I don't know the language, maybe one or two words."

"Why you here?" asked the man in broken English.

"Do me the courtesy of allowing me to speak on our behalf." Cain took a slow step forward, hands raised. He spoke to the man with the rifle. "We are here to see the big man," he said in Newari. Maggie rolled her eyes. Of course, he would speak this language in the ass end of nowhere. And somehow be much more succinct, at that. "We mean no harm."

The circle of men closed, the threat of death hung thick in the air. "I'm the big man," replied the obvious leader of the bunch. "Leave now and you will leave alive."

"How the fuck to do you know Newari?" asked Maggie.

Cain raised an eyebrow. "Really?"

She had the grace to look sheepish, eying the Lee-Enfield. "Oh, right."

Cain turned to the leader, "You and I know different. Tell your boss that Cain is here, and I am owed a debt. I am here to collect."

The leader considered this for a long moment then nudged the man next to him with an elbow. "Deliver the message." He said to Cain, "I hope for your sake you're telling the truth."

During this brief conversation Ekki stood with his head down, eyes hidden behind dark sunglasses. Maggie saw that his cheek was twitching, a furious accompaniment to the facial tic next to his eye. *Uh-oh.* "Cain ..." she began.

He didn't bother to turn around. "I see it." To the leader, "My large companion can no longer abide and would like to take his leave from your charming little village. I give the utmost assurances that you and yours will never lay eyes upon his face again."

The Lee-Enfield lowered a tad. "What's wrong with him?"

"Poor lad, he suffers from a mild constitution, being of such a delicate nature and is not able to long tolerate the rarified air of the heights. He makes his home by the sea where the salt breeze is most soothing to his tired nerves." Cain glanced at Ekki and felt an old familiar pang. Another one gone, following uncounted other apprentices who came before.

Laughter filled the air as the hard, Nepalese men barked their mirth, but the motley variety of handguns, rifles, and brutal looking long, curved knives called *kukri* never wavered. These were men used to shooing outsiders away. "You tell your friend he can leave and make sure he never returns." The leader's smile creased his weathered face, but never reached his eyes.

The two watched Ekki almost disappear down the shoulder of the mountain, relief evident in the lines of his body and the speed of his descent. So big, so powerful in form and magic yet unable to withstand the Curse. No one was.

Except Maggie, of course.

The two waited in the circle of men among weapons unwavering, the owners carrying faces of stone. If it hadn't been for the fact that she had five Words, Maggie would have been afraid. Not of death, but of dying without being able to fight back. Hacking bodies with an axe, warrior to warrior brought home the thought, the feeling, of imminent death, but at least there was a chance to fight back, a chance not to die by the other's hand. In the middle of a circle of enemies armed with guns, even though most of the weapons looked to be from the early part of the last century, made her feel more vulnerable than she had in a while.

She didn't like that feeling one bit.

It burned uncomfortably, but she bore it while she waited for the return of the messenger. He returned quickly according to her watch, although her gut told her it had taken forever. The young man whispered to the leader whose eyes widened. A quick bark had the other men lowering their weapons. "Come," beckoned the leader, voice now at a near whisper.

At last. Cain nodded to the man and followed as he led the way up the mountain through the village that clung to the rocky slop like a barnacle to the belly of a ship.

Rough, whitewashed walls of stone, thatched roofs met the eye, only a couple of the houses stood over two stories, most lining the narrow road made from the bones of the mountain. Cain had been to Nepal several times, and while this was in no way the meanest of the villages he had visited, it certainly ranked among the smallest, with only a dozen or so houses. Its inhabitants didn't let size matter, hanging colorful awnings of orange and red over the windows and the people here wore simple, clean clothes that were well cared for. Their boots had a sturdy, man-made look to them that people in European countries and the States would pay an arm and a leg for. A tiny, tidy place, but prosperous nonetheless.

The road, more of a glorified path, ran up the side of the mountain and the group, led by the older Nepalese leader, put the village behind them. Soon enough the path steepened, and Maggie began to get a workout better than at any trendy gym, her thighs at first burning pleasantly, then with more serious heat as the grade became steeper.

Getting old, she huffed silently, her backpack an unrelenting anchor on her back, the straps digging through her thick coat into her shoulders.

"Hurry up," the aging leader commanded, waving his hands. If he was discomfited by the slope he didn't show it, nor did the other men who traipsed along as if it were flat ground. No hands strayed near the holstered or sheathed weapons, but Maggie knew that if she tired anything they'd spill blood faster than she could blink.

Around boulders the size of houses and down gentle slopes covered in grass so green it hurt the eye, the smell of wildflowers in the air, but eventually, despite the downslopes, they always resumed climbing toward the tree line. Closer and closer they came to the fog, or cloud or mist that covered the upper reaches of the mountain, shrouding its summit from prying eyes. As far as Maggie could tell, the mists churned sluggishly, slowly, but never drifted lower or left the mountain despite the mounting wind that bit through her heavy winter clothes.

Before her legs gave out completely and the oxygen grew too thin, the path ended at a cave mouth that glared blackly at the group. Its smooth regularity told Cain that it was less a natural opening than an adit to some forgotten mine.

"Enter," said the leader, gesturing toward the opening. "When you return, if you do, I will escort you back the way you came."

"That's it?" asked Maggie after Cain translated. "You're not afraid we'll try something?"

That brought a smile. "Yes, try. You try good," he answered in his halting

English, teeth gleaming whitely. "You try so I go home and sleep. Good."

Wonderful. Cain graced her with a rueful grin and they entered the cave.

Like most of the mines in the 19ᵗʰ century, it was low and square and braced every couple dozen feet by trusses made of what looked like fossilized wood. The tunnel sloped gently down and smelled of dust and the faint tang of curry, a strange combination that tickled both their noses. What made the whole situation even more eerie were the LED lights on every brace. The kind found at the local hardware store, the size of a hockey puck with adhesive on the back so they would stick to almost any surface. They gave off a hard light that didn't illuminate much, just a six-by-six patch, enough for someone to follow without bumping their head against a crossbeam or trip over a stone.

Maggie thought the place had the air of a bad horror show, the kind that comes on late night on Saturdays under the heading of *Creature Feature* or *Terror Tales.* As for Cain, he thought it was needlessly spare, or evidenced a severe lack of showmanship.

Now Houdini, there was a showman.

A minute or so of slow walking brought them to a door made of a wood frame with hide stretched across. It still had hair sticking to the surface, long and thick like a yak and it smelled faintly of oil and piss.

Running her fingers through the soft hair, Maggie said, "A door? In a *cave*?" For some reason she kept the words to a whisper, like the tunnel was sanctified ground and needed to be shown proper reverence.

The door opened inward, revealing a slight form in a yellow silk kimono decorated with purple orchids. It was a woman, slender, yet tall, with high cheekbones and dusky skin. Her hair was long, black as pitch with a few streaks of soft silver running through. Her smile was wry, with a hint of self-deprecation. She looked as elegant as a queen standing there holding an electric Coleman lantern in one hand, as if she ruled this domain and answering the door was a part-time job on weekends.

Her eyes met Maggie's quite frankly, appraising, but narrowed once she caught sight of Cain hunched in the tunnel beyond, the ceiling too low for his height. "Shit. I hoped it was just a joke," she remarked in perfect English. Maggie was sure it was for her sake. She had the feeling that the woman spoke dozens of languages fluently.

Cain tossed her a smile dialed up to eleven. "Greetings, madam, allow me to perform the introductions. This fine young lady standing fully clothed in the finest cold weather and accompaniments is the great and good warrior maiden Margaret Kirk, wielder of axes most terrible and sharp." He placed a hand to his chest. "If you still retain memory—"

"I remember quite well. I am not senile yet," finished the woman in exasperation. "Windbag who uses fifty words when only ten will do. Come in, come in. I suppose we have much to talk about." She moved back to let them in.

Spacious despite a relatively low ceiling and made comfortable by a plethora of throw rugs that once clothed local animals of all varieties: tiger, leopard, fox and wolf to name a few. More hides decorated the walls, softening the stone and providing an accompaniment to the paintings mounted there.

Maggie was no great art lover, but she was sure the smaller one in the far corner, lit also by an electric Coleman lantern was a Picasso and the one above a couch made entirely of large pillows on a wood frame was a Van Gogh. The rest of the large room was appointed with sturdy looking hand carved chairs and a dining table. Maggie assumed that one of the two passageways from this chamber led to a kitchen and she felt her stomach start to rumble at the thought of food. She removed her parka, surprised at how warm it was in the cave/room and wondered if there was a space heater chugging away somewhere.

"Sit," said the woman, gesturing toward the couch. "I'd serve tea, perhaps some biscuits, but you're not staying that long." She sat in a chair that looked more like a teacup made of red, orange and yellow cotton. Oddly enough it looked very comfortable.

"Talk." Before Cain could speak, she held up a hand. "Be succinct. I know it is difficult for you but try."

Cain looked like he was counting to ten but held his temper. *What I do for the good of the world. I certainly am not receiving adequate compensation for my efforts.* "We needed to see you."

"Why?"

"The children are being naughty."

She blinked. "Is that news?"

"*Extremely* naughty."

"Do tell. Remember, succinct."

"They have violated the Accords, used a drone in an attempt to kill me, and hired mercenaries to do same. Mercenaries they supplied with Botanical Magic and Blood Magic."

"You are shitting me!" The vulgarity exploded from her mouth like a shotgun blast. For a split-second Maggie saw something ugly and mean beneath that beautiful, regal exterior, gone so quickly that she almost thought she hadn't seen it at all.

"I shit you not." Cain crossed his arms. "This is the truth. While I have many peccadillos, I am not in the habit of lying." He grinned. "Not often, anyway."

"Shit, shit, shit, shit, *shit!*" swore the woman, anger marring her fine features. "There are rules for a *reason*." She stood. "Stay where you are." In a swirl and whisper of silk she disappeared into one of the passageways.

Cain seemed satisfied, crossing his arms and leaning back. It was a tribute to that craftsmanship of the couch that it didn't creak alarmingly under his weight. "That ought to do it."

"What?" Instead of leaning back, contenting herself to wait, Maggie stood, filled with nervous energy despite her fatigue from travel and the altitude. "Will you tell me what the fuck is going on now? Who is that lady? Where is she going and who is she going to? Can I get some damn food before my stomach eats my liver for lunch? I am so fucking sick of granola bars." She began to pace, reminding Cain of a Bengal tiger.

"I suspect our hostess is digesting the intelligence supplied. I further posit because of her haste that the help the we came to enlist will be forthcoming. As for the nature of that help, I will let her explain as it is her story and right to do so."

Wonderfuckingful, she thought, trying not to think about an extra-thick pastrami sandwich from the Carnegie Deli, served with a dill pickle and chips. She could almost taste the rye bread and the tang of the spicy brown mustard was a vivid memory on her tongue. *Stop it!*

What could she say? Trying to out stubborn Cain was like trying to out stubborn a marble statue.

Only a few minutes passed, but it felt like hours to Maggie, before the woman returned wearing a heavy parka like those the others wore and sporting an olive-green duffel almost as tall as she was. Her long black hair was pulled back in a severe bun. An enormous curved knife, a kukri big enough to decapitate, rode along the outside of her left thigh.

Cain rose to his feet. "Have you come to the same conclusion as I? I take it from your dress aid will be forthcoming."

Smiling, the woman shook her head. "For one with such keen intellect, you should know the answer."

He narrowed his eyes. "These days I prefer a straight yea or nay."

The woman pursed her lips. "I know we have stood on opposites sides in the past but trust me when I say I am on the side of the angels this time." A long pause as she adjusted the kukri. "I knew this was coming when the Silver was destroyed."

"How do you know *that*?" Maggie blurted, sensing danger and readying a Word.

Calmly, the woman met her eyes. "I felt it. They were mine, after all."

It took a moment, but the realization dawned. *Holy shit!* For the first time in ages her mind went blank as the woman laughed at her discomfiture.

"That would mean ... mean ... mean ...." Maggie felt all sorts of strange and unable to piece together a coherent thought.

"What your boss here has known, but has not informed you, is that I am the person he came here for." The woman crossed her arms, face still alight with laughter. "I felt the destruction of the Silver because I created it. I am the founder of the Sicarii and the Family you have been fighting all these years. I am Judas Iscariot."

THE BOOK OF

MICHAEL continued

Chapter Four
Surprise Surprise

———∿∿———

I HOPE YOU HAVE ENJOYED THIS NARRATIVE, Michael. Read the postscript to the story I'd just finished. It was incumbent upon me to include young Maggie's viewpoint and thus she helped me put pen to paper, or more accurately, fingers to keyboard. It is a wish of mine that you found the story written in third person satisfactory because the world has seen many a moon since I attempted storytelling of any note. I am sure that young Morgan Heart regaled you with my first attempt, the results of which were highly unusual.

And here this part of our story finds its end. You will no doubt receive more to this tale, but it is time for another to take up the task. Farwell and I hope to lay my startling eyes upon you once more in the future.

With my warmest wishes,

Cain

P.S.

Maggie sends her heartfelt regards as well.

I LOWERED THE TABLET. Wow.

Judas. I mean, *Judas*. The first Anti-Christ, the Founder.

Mind well and truly boggled.

Looking outside I wish I hadn't. The part of Buffalo, New York, I currently inhabited would look better with a coat of paint after being bulldozed to the ground. Miles of industrial parks under a washed-out night sky. I knew deep down in my gut that America needed places like this, places for storage and such, but it still hurt to look at, all the self-inflicted ugliness.

Three cities, three days of long-distance management of the Templars, giving orders on a site in the Dark Web, that part of the Internet not accessed by normal search engines. Our chatroom was designated by a web address consisting of a slew of numbers and special characters and you needed a password to log on, one approved by me. Despite these security measures, everything was heavily encrypted. The Sicarii had some world-class programmers out there, but fortunately we had better.

Thank the Lord.

From the time I first received Cain's story until now, during those long three days, seventeen Templars died, all by the action of mercenaries employed by the Sicarii. Five in Great Britain, nine blown to bits by a car bomb in Florence and the last three the victims of a group of snipers. We inflicted terrible losses on the Family and it sure looked like they were replying in kind. What had started as a low-key war in the shadows was swiftly spiraling out to the edges of public perception. What a mess. What made things worse, far worse in my opinion, is that the Family didn't care about collateral damage. Those Templar fatalities were accompanied by dozens of civilian casualties.

One of the first things I let the Templars know when I assumed the leadership role that was thrust upon me was my zero-tolerance rule for collateral damage. Absolutely none, not *ever*. Violation of this rule was grounds for dismissal from the Templars. Nothing justified the death of innocents, even if it meant killing Burke Deschamps himself and every high-ranking member of his infernal family.

As I looked up, searching for the stars behind some thin, washed out clouds bleached with light pollution, I silently prayed to the Almighty for a sign, something to point me to what my next steps should be. Little black rectangles floated far up, rubbing the bellies of the thin clouds as I considered the following rather pressing issues:

1. Burke was back. In spades. A clone? Or an infernal sort of resurrection, his soul spat out of Hell to burden our planet?
2. Mercenaries everywhere taking aim at the Templars. The Deschamps had virtually unlimited resources to hire every mercenary on the planet and that put a cold wind in my shorts. It was only Burke's desire to keep everything out of the public eye that the Templars weren't swamped by hundreds of mercenaries at once.
3. Too many dead. Even with the influx from the Vatican, the best of the best joining us, seventeen deaths put a sizable dent in our ranks.
4. Lack of intel on how to hit Burke where it hurt. Thanks to Cain we had a huge amount of funding, but the Family was too financially entrenched to hurt that way. Heck, they owned entire countries. How do hurt something so big?
5. How did Burke keep finding our people now that the Oracle was dead? Was there another one? Until we neutralized his source of intelligence, there were big, indelible neon targets on all our backs.

I'm no big drinker, but right then I needed to feel the pleasant burn of a good Kentucky sour mash down my throat. Fortunately, I had a bottle of my good friend Jack D. in the bottom drawer of my desk. Just as my hand reached for the drawer a lightning shot of adrenalin raced through my body causing every muscle to contract at once as something finally registered through my fatigue and a metric ton of strange dumped in my lap.

Black rectangles above?

Parachutes!

My palm slammed into the alarm button set next to the office door, the first step. The second was to scream at the top of my lungs, heard over the sudden blare of the klaxon, "Incoming!"

I'm always armed, two at the hip for a cross draw, one .22 in an ankle holster and an M4 for when it hits the fan, like now. Carbine at the ready, I pushed through the door to see Milo charging toward me full tilt.

"Paratroopers, everybody out," I barked, no longer a priest, but a commander of soldiers.

We raced down the hall toward the back of the building, two more men joining us, Paul and Gabriel. I always traveled with a retinue of bodyguards, anywhere from one to eight and if I'd had any say in the matter, there wouldn't be any, but in this matter the Templars wouldn't listen.

Under Milo's huge fist the steel exit door burst open, just in time for use to see our cars, a brace of GMC SUVs, explode in balls of fire, the heat wash knocking us back into the building.

"RPG," gasped Milo through the cotton that enveloped my ears. The explosion felt like being hit with a ton of pillows moving at mach 2.

The world tilted and whirled, and I flailed at the wall, trying to stop the spinning. Back when I was a drinking man I used to close my eyes to stop the bed-spins, but it never worked. That didn't stop me from closing them now and what do you know, the planet slowed down a touch, enough for me to regain my equilibrium and lurch to my feet. The M4 was outside where I dropped it, but a quick crossdraw saw my palms filled with a pair of .45 ACPs.

Stumbling my way toward the doorway, I arrived in time to see two men thud down onto the back parking lot in a flutter of parachute silk carrying the smoking tubes of RPG launchers. As their feet hit asphalt, the tubes hit as well, their hands becoming busy with AK-47s and I knew there was only a split second before they regained their balance from landing and turned me into the clerical version of Swiss cheese.

My revolvers barked, spitting out death and the first man fell in a spray of blood and tissue, but the second recovered enough to raise his weapon and a noise like the end of days thundered in my ear, a heat bloom against my cheek as hot gasses expanded, an ice pick of pain piercing my ear drum and the second man screamed as his stomach suddenly sprouted a hole that spilled guts onto a handicapped parking spot, splattering fluids.

I yelped as the pain from my ear blossomed behind my eyeballs and a familiar sticky warmth flowed down my neck.

Milo, he'd shot at the second man with that big hand cannon of his, the blast close enough to set my ear bleeding. A large hand grabbed my arm and pulled me into the hallway while the other closed the rear door, but not before I saw half a dozen more men float down from the sky, rifles pointing our way.

From behind the door came the sound of firing and the heavy steel suddenly dimpled crazily, the sound of rounds loud in the hall and we sprinted the other way, knowing full well that others covered the front of the building.

I was in full army mode now, though, years of training taking over my frontal lobe, analyzing data, forming strategies and considering odds with the speed of a supercomputer. Bad guys, lots of bad guys … we were surrounded, and they had firepower, a whole lot of it if those RPGs were any clue. Fortunately for the Templars, it pays to be paranoid, and to have rich friends like Cain.

"Garage, now!" I yelled through the fuzz in my ear. I've never been temporarily (I sincerely hoped) deaf before. Not that it mattered because Milo and Paul nodded while Gabriel brought up the rear.

Sure, we had (and I mean *had* because now they were heaps of smoking, twisted metal) SUVs, appropriately armored, but due to the recent developments regarding mercenary activities, I decided on redundancy.

We were located at the end of a business strip mall in the industrial park, sharing a wall space with firm that sold PVC piping for all needs, separated by drywall and two-by-fours. Thing was, that company, called Rally's Plastic, was a front, one of Cain's many cut-outs and existed only on paper, the office space was empty.

Except for the car.

Milo and Paul kicked through the breakaway wall to Rally's, the drywall shattering into powder under the force of their size thirteens. Yesterday Gabriel had removed the two-by-fours and touched up, creating an emergency exit of sorts.

Still in the building, though and we had to go. Rally's boasted a floor to ceiling window wall, painted black so no one could look in and see the place was virtually empty except for the Subaru STI parked inside.

The little white car, so innocuous at first glance, held a whole herd of horses under the hood and all-wheel drive. Perfect for when you have a need for speed and boy was I ever needing.

Shaking plaster dust out of our hair, we jumped in the little vehicle, the weight of four big men straining the suspension, but it was modified to handle the load … and so much more.

Me behind the driver's seat, I plunged the key into the ignition just as …
Boom!

Fire erupted from the office space we just vacated, filling the escape hole and singing the paint job, peppering the car with bits of debris that did no real damage except to Cain's insurance company. The car rocked as the pressure wave tried to toss it about, but we were already in motion as I slammed the stick shift into first gear and jammed my foot on the accelerator.

In the movies cars at speed break through anything. This is a heaping load of bulldirt because most cars will turn into steel spaghetti when driving through plate glass reinforced with an aluminum frame. People tend to think of aluminum as the metal that their soda-pops come in, all bendy and such, but at appropriate thickness, it is far less so. Besides creating the escape hole to Rally's store front, Gabriel had also cut through the aluminum frame in a dozen places for such an emergency. Paranoia, remember?

I absolutely trust in God, but I'm pretty sure he trusts in me to take care of my own issues and to only call on him for the heavy stuff, like the Apocalypse.

The front grill rammed through the safety glass, the wall exploding outward in the twinkly shower of popcorn glass that crunched heavily under the smoking tires. We were jounced in our seats as the car juddered over the four-inch lip of the storefront and we raced through the front parking lot like a gazelle across the savannah. Rubber squealed as I drove the engine to redline. Before I could swerve … no, I apologize, that would be a lie … I *wanted* to hit the man pointing at AK straight at my head, rounds *spanging* off of UL level 10 bullet resistant glass, glass strong enough to repel a .50 cal … for a short time.

God bless Cain and his deep pockets. The Templars sure couldn't afford such extravagant military-grade protection.

The body went *splat*, curving around the reinforced bumper, the shooter's head hitting the hood and cracking open like a coconut thrown from a skyscraper, splattering the windshield. The wipers were up to the task.

Mourn later, I though sadly, *pray later* as I threw the car into second gear, whipping out of the parking lot and into the street. More rounds stuttered against the body of the car, but that, too, was bullet resistant. We left the mercs in the rear view.

"These look like Somalis!" Milo thundered from the back seat. "Why are there Somalis attacking us?"

Good question. How did they get AKs? Never mind … in the US you could get practically anything if you had the money. I shifted into third and went for triple digits on the speedometer.

"The real question is how the Family got mercs so fast in the first place.

We've only been here thirty-six hours." Paul's voice was calm as the windless ocean and as deep. Gabriel merely grunted not being so big on words.

That was a good question and I started to think on it when I remembered one very important detail. *Idiot!* I almost cursed but restrained myself. Getting harder and harder to watch my mouth with the pressures mounting up lately. My left hand spun the wheel and the little Subaru protested violently as I cut a hard U-turn in the middle of street, tires smoking as I yanked hard on the emergency brake. My body wanted to keep heading north, but my seatbelt was having none of it. The other three almost squealed in surprise but managed to maintain a professional military composure.

To the look I knew Milo was throwing my way I growled, "Forgot the Codex."

"Leave it," came the reply as the car completed the U.

Yeah, right. "Not on your life, not on mine." First gear again and by the streetlights I could see black tire marks on the pavement. I didn't turn on the headlights because that would just let the enemy know I was coming back.

The *Codex Infernales,* the Sicarii Bible, their history. Most of had been translated for me by Morgan. Most, not all. In it was the story of how Judas Iscariot went from guerilla fighter to betrayer of Christ. It was also the repository of knowledge concerning Blood Magic, the horrible practice of sacrificing the lives of the pure for magic. Necromancy by any other name. As far as I know, it was a Deschamps family tradition *not* to copy the Codex, instead keep its secrets within the inner circle of the family.

Letting it fall back into Burke's hands was not an option.

The Subaru was a quick, eager beast, champing at the bit with all its four-hundred fifty horses under the hood and I let it have its head, racing back toward the offices. My hands felt slick on the wheel as my eyes scanned for hostiles.

From the back seat came the sound of quiet prayer, barely heard over whirr of tires and the high-pitched squeal of twin turbos. At this point, we could use all the help we could get.

The screaming of the engine was announcement enough as we neared the parking lot and the windshield began to *spang* with the hail of hundreds of bullets, but I didn't slow, instead I shifted back into third and jumped the curb.

"Paul," I yelled as a Somali, no more than a kid with eyes as big as saucers, tried to jump out of the way.

Thump! The car shuddered as the left front bumper took him in the hip, no doubt shattering every bone there and his scream was mercifully cut short as he collided with the building head first.

Bulletproof windows don't roll down ... too thick, but the doors were able to open and as I spun the car at another shooter (*splatter*) Paul opened his, the door flying wide as centrifugal force took it, cutting loose with a TEC-9, the little SMG chattering noisily. Blood carnations blossomed on two more shooters before I completed the spin, the door slamming shut.

We were alone in the front parking lot. But not for long. No time to waste, I yelled, "Milo, with me, you two stay!" and exited, my pistols out in time to catch another young Somali as he appeared in the broken window front of Rally's.

Blam! Both bucked in my hands, the reports simultaneous. The Somali sagged, lifeless.

Knowing Milo had my back I raced to our store front and swung the door open.

The bullet meant for my head missed by a country mile, but I still heard a meaty thud. Milo grunted.

No time, only reflex and the .45s barked, blood sprayed and a Somali fighter, an older man with white in his hair fell and I ran down the hall. Milo would either live or die, but the Codex had to be saved and our lives were nothing compared to that. As that thought raced through my mind, two more Somalis burst into the hallway from the back and we hit the deck and ate carpeting just in time to avoid their first rounds. We retuned fire from a prone position as bullets swarmed over my head and the two antagonists danced as they died, arterial blood fountaining. I felt something hot and wet hit my face, but I was already on my feet and didn't even bother with the knob on the next door on the right. My blood was up, my muscles were primed for violence, my shoulder hitting wood so hard the door sprang inward, the lock plate just pieces of shrapnel imbedding in far wall. I reached my desk, opening the bottom drawer and there it was, the old wooden box that contained the Codex and it was in my hands instead of my .45s. Back into the hallway, the taste of blood in my mouth, the coppery smell of death flooding the place.

My feet hit the parking lot a second before more bullets shredded the air where I had been, and I made it to car, flinging the box at Gabriel as more men in parachutes descended.

One was perhaps a bit smarter, he didn't fire his RPG before he hit the ground. He raised the weapon as his parachute fluttered to the pavement behind him.

"Go, Father," said Gabriel, jumping out of the car. "GO!"

My heart lodged itself in my throat and, God help me, I shifted into first, burning enough rubber to momentarily obscure Gabriel as he fired on the Somali aiming the RPG, nearly cutting him in half.

Cry for him later, I thought as the STI screamed across the parking lot and it took all of me not to race back because Rangers leave no one behind, it's part of the Creed: 'I will never leave a fallen comrade to fall into the hands of the enemy and under no circumstances will I ever embarrass my country.' But I wasn't only a Ranger, I wasn't only a priest in the Catholic Church, I was the leader of the Knights Templar, that ancient order dedicated to combating the Sicarii wherever they are, and I had a sacred duty. Gabriel chose to sacrifice himself for me, for the Codex, for God and, despite my feelings, my desire to head back and attempt a rescue, I had to honor his choice because it this fight was all about choice. The choices we make, our free will to choose between Good and Evil. *Timshel.* Thou mayest.

It felt like ashes in my eyes.

One last mercenary tried to stop us, angling his 'chute down and firing wildly but the car hit him at forty mph and I drug him under for a couple of blocks, the STI jouncing and shuddering, until what was left rolled free.

My voice came out hard and brittle, "Milo, call that man of Cain's, tell him we need a plane at the airport." There was blood in my mouth from where I chewed my lower lip in frustration.

His faith in me shone from his eyes as he answered, "Where to, Father?"

"England first. I'll decide later. It's time we upped the ante on the Sicarii."

"Amen to that."

"Dear Lord Jesus and Mary, Mother of God, hold all these brave souls in the palm of your hand, comfort them and their families. Send angels of protection, love, and comfort to all the service men and women still at war, bring them home safely and comfort their families. We ask all our prayers in Jesus' name. Amen."

A prayer for a fallen soldier. The best I could do, but it felt right, and I learned long ago to trust my instincts in such matters. I think Gabriel would have liked it.

The rest of the group solemnly muttered 'amen' and dropped each other's hands. With reverent eyes they looked at me, at peace knowing that Gabriel's soul was well tended to. While it rankled them some that his body lay out of reach, the flesh was of lesser concern than the soul. I stood shakily from where I knelt, floor unsteady due to the turbulent winds outside.

Nodding, I sat down on the kidskin seat of the private jet provided by one of Cain's many corporations and opened a small bar. Bourbon met my eyes; Pappy Van Winkle and I eagerly pour two fingers. Not a big drinker, I did have a few shots now and again. I didn't let alcohol become my crutch, but I could see how it could be so. The happy numbness of a good buzz, the warm cottony feeling …

"Skip to my lou, my darlin," I crooned softy after a sip.

"Father?"

"Nothing, Milo," I replied. Darn but that was good bourbon. Just the right bite, the right amount of heat. It settled comfortably in my tummy. "I am reminded of the last plane trip I took east across the Atlantic." Unlike that trip, we traveled in disguise from top to bottom. Although once one the plane and out of sight from prying cameras we reverted to normal clothing, which, upon landing, would be sacrificed for disguises once again. "That last time was with Minerva."

Minerva. A fallen angel who once posed as the goddess Athena. As a favor to Cain she saved me from a serial killer sent by the Family. While we didn't grow close during our time together, we did develop a mutual respect for one another.

After the incident at Notre Dame (no worries, I hear the contractors fixed the place as good as new) and before I killed the Oracle, the hand of God came upon me, filling me with His divine glory. I put Minerva to the question of forgiveness and I saw that in her heart she was repentant, sorrowful for her sins of rebellion and cloaking herself as a false god. For the first time she asked to be forgiven and God granted her His mercy. She disappeared, translated to Heaven and that's the last I saw of her.

I often wonder if she looks down upon me and thinks kind thoughts even though I have waded through a river of blood to be where I am now. A priest, a shepherd of Christ, a representative of the New Testament which dealt with God's love and the sacrifice of His child. I also represented the Old Testament, which dealt with much sterner stuff, such as His wrath and His discipline and His rules for a righteous life.

It was hard reconciling these two aspects of my teaching, the shepherd and the warrior, but as usual I looked to the Bible for my answer. Wasn't David a shepherd? Didn't he arise and kill Goliath. The Bible is full of devout men who killed in God's name. That eased my conscience somewhat, but Christ taught the way of peace, but then again, he only had to deal with the Romans, I had the Family. What they would do to me would make the Crucifixion look like a holiday retreat at Club Med.

"You know, Milo, with Burke showing up and hiring all these mercs, it's going to be the biggest mess of the century."

Wait …

What was that …? Something about … the thought snagged my mind, an irritation that wouldn't go away nor did I want it to. Century … century … what was with that word?

Lightbulb over the head time. My skin goose pimpled and I jackknifed out of my seat and raced toward the back of the plane. The box, the old box with the Codex.

"Father?"

Morgan's translation met my fingers and I began to scan the pages. "In here somewhere," I muttered. My skin felt hot. "Where are you?"

More urgently. "Father?"

"Milo," I said, mind traveling a million directions at once. "I have an idea. I think it's time we hit the Deschamps harder than ever before." I could feel a smile crease my face.

"Thank the Lord, Father. It's about fucking time."

I guffawed, but my eyes never quit searching the papers and a few moments later my tablet *dinged*.

A new email. My eyes nearly bugged out of their sockets when I saw the subject line and for the first time since being ordained I cursed.

"Shit just got real, Milo."

THE BOOK OF

JUDAS

CHAPTER ONE
JEALOUSY

———— ∿ ————

T HE KNIFE FLASHED FORWARD, and the keen edge cut deep. Blood sprayed and coated my face, thick and rich and it tasted good. Dead man bleeding at my feet, I turned to my children. They watched avidly, eyes gleaming wetly. I had their undivided attention, which was a good thing, although young Simon looked too close at the pooling blood. Too interested in death by far.

I recognized the beginning of that sickness, had seen it before countless times with the Sicarii in Judea and put down like animals those who evidenced it because the sickness spread like rot until they couldn't be trusted. Rabid dogs. Madmen.

"Never be distracted by your opponent," I said, pacing back and forth avoiding the red puddle, the cold floor hard against my feet. "He will try to throw sand in your eyes, trick you and you must be wary of such things."

Wait. Scrap that. Ancient history and not relevant. From what I understand you know the story, received it from the Devil's mouth, so to speak. My many-times great grandchild Olivier.

Cain said I should tell you my story, but it is a long one and I am unsure where to begin. It would cover so much ground and the flight from Kathmandu is not long enough.

Ah, I have it! I will tell you the snippets you do not know, fill in the blanks so you will have a greater understanding of Judas Iscariot. Some things which have not been written in the Family history, which is called the Codex. I wish I had burned that a long time ago, and scattered the ashes to the four winds, but hindsight is perfect, of course.

Now the name. I grew up Judah, an adopted son of Simon Iscariot, the founder of the Sicarii, those Judean rebels who fought Roman rule. From him

I learned to slink in the dark, the subtle thrust of the knife that leads to a quick kill and how to disappear. By my early teens I eclipsed my father in the art of murder and had over two dozen Roman kills by the time I was fifteen.

I thought my actions correct and just. While Roman law stated that all would be treated equally, the reality was quite different. Many a Judean woman felt the violating touch of a Roman soldier without the justice that should have followed. So much for Roman law. We Judeans had our own law and it came at the edge of a knife.

By sixteen, I led the Sicarii, my father deferring to my leadership because I met with success after success. Even though the Romans killed five Judeans for every Roman death, we considered our war well waged.

Then came Yeshua, or the more commonly referred to name: Joshua. Whom you, of course being a Catholic priest, know by his Greek name, Jesus.

I won't bore you with the details save to say that he captivated me. By his very presence I received a measure of nourishment and, dare I say, hope. One look in his penetrating brown eyes and I was caught in the net of his personality, of his wisdom and holiness. Within a matter of hours, I became one of his followers.

It did not take long for the jealousy to set in like a cancer.

I do not mean I was jealous of Joshua, far from it. No, I was jealous of the former prostitute he took as his wife. Does this surprise you? It shouldn't. In a time when most were married before their sixteenth birthday, to think that he would keep himself from a woman is ludicrous. Phillip wrote about it, but his account never made into the Book, which was a shame because it would have ended many an acrimonious argument regarding Joshua's life.

How he loved Mary, his one and only and I felt such wrath at the attention paid to her. I do not mean I wanted Joshua in a sexual way, I prefer women and still do, but when his loving eyes look deep in your soul you crave his regard more and more. Spiritual heroin and I was hopelessly addicted, so very fervent for a word from his lips and a kind look, but though he treated all with great love, obviously more was spared for Mary. My greed for that attention consumed me.

In such fertile ground does sin grow.

Even when he sent the twelve out to minister for him, with the power of healing and to see unclean spirits, that fundamental need for him was not sated because of our distance from one another. I wanted to always be close to him.

It was in Hazor, a small town a couple of days walk from the sea of Galilee where I ministered to the sick and the poor, bringing Joshua's words to those in need, that my life changed. I often slept on the floor of mean little huts or with the animals in their pens. This time I slept in an abandoned house, barely three walls and a ragged roof, but it held out the wind well enough.

Come to me my son.

The words trickled directly into my mind, waking me from a deep slumber. "What?" My voice was thick and heavy with sleep. Heavy cloth rasped against my naked skin. "Who's there?"

It is I, your Father.

Sweetness laced the voice, but underneath there seemed to be a thicker layer of offal, yet it was powerful, seductive. My knees hit the floor so hard the skin and I bent my head in prayer. "Oh, my Lord God, I am not worthy to receive you."

Shhh … come now, My son. I am here at your time of greatest travail to render aid.

"Travail? Aid, my Lord?" What was he talking about? Keeping my head down, I snuck a look around. All was dark, and the flickering of stars shone through the window.

Your ache for the man Joshua. I know it consumes you and I have heard the cries of your heart for am I not your Father?

Sudden sweat slicked my skin. "My Lord, what do you wish of me?"

Only to inform you of Joshua's heart, which has turned from you.

My own muscle turned to ice in my chest, radiating cold to my limbs. "Wha-? How? Why?" I squeaked.

Joshua is wary of you; of the violence you have practiced by killing Romans in My name. This has turned his heart from you and he considers you a devil. So, he has told Simon Peter, so he believes.

I gasped. I shuddered. I cried bitter tears that fell like rain. A hot flush blossomed on my cheeks and swept to the nape of my neck, quickly traveling through my body, dispelling the cold. Instead of ice, my heart now burned as an ember and I felt an emotion I thought only reserved for the Roman rapists … Hate.

It is so fine, the line between love and hate and how easy it is to cross. In fact, the two emotions often blur together like two different colors of paint smearing on a brush. That hate unmanned me and I fell from my knees, crawling on my belly on the floor, the wooden planks, worn smooth by countless feet, becoming wet with snot and tears.

"Oh why, oh why," I cried. "Why would he do such a thing."

It is hard, My child. After all, you took Roman lives for Me, performing holy actions at My behest and I am well pleased with you. Joshua has made a mistake, turning his heart because of his love for the woman from Magdala. This is a flaw.

"But is he not Your son, bearer of Your miracles? I have seen them. He has healed the sick, straightened the legs of the crippled."

You are My son, Judas. One of many and a finer one there has not been. I am well pleased with your actions and your heart. I have decided it is your time to represent Me in the fullness of My power and glory.

From misery and hate to exultation in an instant. The Lord said I was His son! I was to be chosen! However, ... "What of Joshua, my Lord? Does he not carry Your standard?"

Worry not about Joshua. I am displeased with him and will exalt you. If you are willing to bear the burden.

Of course, there was no doubt. Like the legend of Atlas, I would bear the world on my shoulders for such a chance. "Of course, my Lord, whatever You wish. I will do as You command."

Then the time of your rising has come. You have only to say, 'I accept you, my Father, into my heart' and you shall know My power.

Why waste time? "I accept You, my Father, into my heart."

Now will your jealousy be assuaged. Brace yourself, My son, for this will not feel good.

What?

It hit. Not slowly, or with warning, but like the suddenness of a punch to the face that breaks the jaw with a horrid *snap* that sends a shock of pain and dismay through a body. Every muscle contracted at once, sending my bones groaning and joints crackling. Then the real pain began.

Imagine your nerves slowly being extruded from your flesh, intact and screaming. Now imagine those neural strands gradually dipped into acid, the burning beginning as an irritation that quickly escalates into an inferno that tears reason away. Flensing, grinding, scraping, scouring ... all words so faint to the reality they possessed no merit.

While fire lanced through my tissues, through bones and organs, my mind suffered another, entirely different assault. I fell into the depths of my own consciousness, images of the past flashing accompanying the pain of the present, a counterpoint that only added to the horror of the moment. I wanted to furrow my cheeks until they gushed blood, to vomit until my stomach tore from the effort, but I had no control, only the ability to abide while consumed.

Farther and farther I fell into the depths of myself and blessedly farther from the tearing pain of whatever was being done to my tender flesh. The flashing glimpses of my life began to turn gray, then fade to black, a black that soon became so deep it seemed to suck whatever energy I possessed into its ravenous maw. Colder and colder, not the cold of flesh chilled, but of the soul losing all hope, an absolute zero not only noted by the absence of thermal energy, but also the negation of any spiritual positive.

Colder and colder, until I grew certain that nothing could survive such absence, that I would plummet forever, a frozen soul in the vastness of a metaphysical deep so vast that my mind could not begin to comprehend its scale. It was here, at the end of consciousness and the beginning of forever I felt the stirring of some vast, immeasurable presence. In the void where even atoms ceased to exist, It, did. An immensely powerful something beat against my mind until my awareness curled into a pain-racked ball and whimpered, suffering a cold agony that would have destroyed utterly any frail thing such as flesh. This presence's attention beat down on my sobbing mind, it's regard a blunt buffet of crystallized hate, both for others and of itself. I knew that being wanted everything scrubbed from the universe, to destroy all of creation down to the smallest particle and replace it all with a construct of cold, inhuman perfection that would be both beautiful, stagnant, lustrous yet rotting. I understood in that moment that it was not God who spoke deep into my mind as I knelt by my bed, nor a member of the Heavenly Host, but the mightiest of the fallen, the General of the Rebellion. The first of all angels and the Adversary of the Lord.

Lucifer had come calling, and he called me *son*.

The loss I felt could not be put into words and madness would have claimed me but for the power of the void. I knew then that first of the fallen dwelled in a place of His own creation, a place rendered indescribably cold by His sheer lack of positive emotion, a void propped up by His own icy hate.

I know it is painful, My son, but the reward will be great. You, above all My children, will know immortality. Countless centuries will pass beneath your feet while others wither and die. You will watch Joshua fade into the annals of history. you will create a great house, be the founder of grand dynasty that will rule forever, and your descendants will remake this febrile world into a place of staggering perfection. All will be created in My image.

Then He showed me history as He perceived it. Only later did I realize that the tinted glass of His prejudices colored events to a point where His recollections and reality did not overlap at any juncture. How was I to know what was real? My education included how to take Roman lives, not the factual knowledge of the past.

See now why I decided to leave Paradise because the false god did not like that My idea of how Man should be utilized to make the earth a study of Perfection. Instead he chose to give his most base creation free will, which has been proven an error. The loss of Eden, war, famine, slaughter, slavery and imperfection unending has been the result. Man needs to be ruled absolutely to unlock his true potential, not be given free rein to stumble about blindly destroying the world. This is why I need you, My son. I need you for great works, to be My hands upon the earth to bring about an everlasting paradise for Man. One the with purity of a flawless diamond.

The pain, the emptiness and the visions of the Fall, the War in Heaven, all seen through the unrelenting eyes of the Adversary, unmanned me, twisted my thinking until I became starved not for Joshua, but for Lucifer, for my Father.

Suddenly, with blissful relief, the freezing agony stopped. All the hate, the staggering emptiness of the void and the absolute zero of spiritual negation ended. I found myself floating in a comfortable emptiness, devoid of light, dark or any color in between. It was merely a cottony nothingness that allowed my hurts to bleed away until I floated there in a kind of stupor.

When Lucifer spoke again, His voice brought pleasure, pure and sweet, sending a thrill all through me. *Let me show you the real Joshua.*

Through the nothing came images of the past, my recollections of Joshua filtered through the perceptions of my most terrible Father:

Joshua greets me for the first time as I am introduced to him by my adopted father, Simon. In my memory his smile is loving and open, hiding nothing, but now I saw that his lips form a slight sneer as he grasps my hands and his kisses to my cheeks, where before were humble and honest, now seen as the pecks of a raptor and I felt that my skin should have been torn open.

We, the followers of this new and exciting prophet, are sitting on the floor, legs crossed and drinking wine from small cups. Joshua serves us himself, ladling the aromatic drink from a large amphora. He serves Peter first, then Mark, coming last 'round to me and I saw that instead of the honor previously thought, it was in fact a slight, a subtle insult meant to show the others that I am not truly worthy of his attention.

Eleazar lay dead for four days in the tomb, corruption upon his flesh and Joshua enters. For an hour no one hears a sound from within and without all remains quiet, the only noise is our heavy breathing as we wait. At long last Eleazar emerges and a collective gasp rings throughout the small valley, raising dust. The once-dead man blinks rapidly in the sun, swaying on his bare feet, burial shroud twisted around his body. He says nothing, merely stumbling forward, as if his legs were new to the act of walking, straight into the arms of his family who weep heavily. Joshua staggers out of the tomb, face gray and panting greatly and he peers around, eyes unfocused, fatigue radiating from every pore, every line of his body. We race forward to support our prophet and Luke edges me out and hugs Joshua to his chest and I catch a glimpse of his face before it is obscured by Luke's long hair.

Contempt.

More and more of the memories, all tainted by the filter of my Father's perception and I began to learn the true nature of hatred. It boiled within me, replacing the jealousy. For what reason did I need to feel that green emotion? Was I not a preeminent assassin? Did not the Romans fall like wheat beneath my dagger? I was strong, swift and capable.

With each beat of hatred in my breast came a throb of pleasure, swifter and swifter as my altered memories unspooled like thread from a spindle. Hate/pleasure/hate/pleasure, over and over and over until the hate *became* pleasure greater than an orgasm, until they became one within my thoughts.

It was only then, when the hate formed hard within my mind that I became aware of my body. I lay on the floor in a pool of tears and drool, blinking rapidly, my flesh not mine to control.

"You have kept yourself hale, My son," I said, or precisely, my body said it, I merely observed through the windows of my eyes and portals of my ears. "I will show you Joshua's weakness, how he does not truly understand the people he proclaims to minister. I will show him the depths of their hate." He looked around the shabby little house and I noted with some alarm that the sun was setting. The ordeal, the pain, the infection that was my Father had lasted almost a full day, which surprised me because it seemed like it should have been longer.

Of course, you know the rest. The kiss, the betrayal, the Crucifixion.

The Silver, thirty pieces, thirty *talents* in a grubby little leather pouch. All of it orchestrated by Lucifer as I lay captive in my mind, delighting at Joshua's fall. Every sting of the lash, every hurt, the nails driven into his wrists, all accompanied by blissful hatred stoked by my Father. When the spear of Longinus was thrust into Joshua's side, my Father lifted the pouch containing the *talents* and cut my smallest finger and bled into it, coating silver with His/our blood. I felt His unholy joy at the creation of the artifact and I reveled with Him.

THIS IS THE SEED OF MY story, the beginning. I tell you this because I feel you need context for what is to come, the remainder that will clarify why I have chosen to aid you and your Templars. I pray that you can look beyond any preconceived notions you may have and understand how the events unfolded. I give you this promise: what I have written, what I relate to you, is the truth as best as I understand it. A strange oath, considering the source, but it is the truth nonetheless.

CHAPTER TWO
KNIVES

T HAT BRINGS US BACK TO A dead man emptying at my feet while Simon, my sixth son by a Judean concubine with perfect teeth, watched avidly with glassy eyes. Training day for my Sicarii young, the next generation of Dagger Men to carry my Father's fight forward.

At the time I recently entered my third score of years and my short hair was more gray than black and lack of sunshine had paled my usually olive skin, which was a good thing considering I lived in Rome.

Why Rome? Because that's where the power was. Emperor Claudius, whom I dined with off and on, had recently been poisoned by his wife, Agrippina. Some say that he knew she hid poison in his sautéed mushrooms and took it willingly, happy to die easily instead of leaking his life away around the edge of a dagger. Knowing his harpy of a wife, it would not surprise me at all.

Under Claudius the Empire saw the first expansion since Augustus, including the conquest of Britannia. After enough time elapsed since the Praetorian Guard forced his ascension to the throne, he managed the Senate quite well. A reformer, historian, and a master of strategy, he showed himself to be just the kind of ruler Father wanted, strong enough that his absence would be felt keenly and would pave the way for a more malleable government.

That is where I came in. For decades I played the part of wealthy and influential merchant, Isaac the Younger, a purveyor of wine, olives and, more recently, silk. As well as other items of uncertain provenance and legality, not to mention usury. Riches galore, and with riches came the ears of politicians. By the time I was sixty I had the attention of ten powerful senators who showed themselves very suggestable, as long as gold entered into the equation. This allowed me an introduction to Emperor Claudius, who I found to be agreeable to embrace another Hebrew friend—the first being Herod Agrippa, king of Judea—one who shared his love of dice and *latrunculi*, or Roman chess. One who lost many wagers as well. Soon I became a regular sight at the palace and from there met my ultimate target, young Nero.

History painted him as fat (in reality he was a bit chubby, but you would not call him obese) and stupid, easily led by his shrewish harridan of a mother, but two years after assuming the throne, Nero began severing his ties with his mother, assuming more and more power. He knew what he wanted and how to get it, but was young enough to be somewhat influenced, mainly by his favored advisor Seneca.

I studied the children. Besides Simon, the rest looked on intently, but without the sort of wonderment that came with the spurting of a slave's blood. Wiping the knife on the corpse's breechclout, I said, "All of you are dismissed, except for Simon."

Harsh discipline taught them to leave without grumbling or commotion. In fact, childhood had been whipped out of them as soon as they were potty trained. What remained were well behaved youngsters with no desire to find themselves on the wrong side of the old man.

"How may I be of service, father?" Always polite, Simon stood with hands behind his back and a look of deference on his face. His plain, brown tunic well cared for, showing me that he paid attention to details.

"How do you fare this day, son?"

"I am well, in possession of full health and faculties."

I had my doubts about the latter. "And do you believe in the great god Lucifer, my son?"

"Of course, father."

If eyes are the windows to the soul, then Simon was empty as a broken jug. Nothing stared back as I considered my son. I matched his expressionless stare with one of my own. "I think it is time for you to leave Rome, Simon."

There! A brief spark. Was it fear? Anger? Could he even *feel* such emotions? "Must I go?"

"The Family has use of you in Damascus and Scythopolis as well as Beersheba."

"Judea, Galilee and Syria? So far away." His hands began to clench, and I subtly readied myself for violence.

"How old are you now Simon?"

That took him aback and he narrowed his eyes. "Fourteen, father."

So, he could see, I nonchalantly placed my hand on the hilt of my dagger, as if checking its security. His eyes widened slightly, and he rocked back on his heels. Dominance games. As old as I was, my muscles still had the rigidity and strength of youth.

"Old enough, Simon. I was thirteen when I killed my first Roman. Slipped my dagger between his ribs right into the heart while he was sleeping. So, you are old enough, capable enough, to be of use. I have a particular assignment in mind for you."

This did not sit well, and I knew how he felt. Rome was … well, *Rome*. London, New York City and Moscow all rolled into one, the center of the greatest civilization in the western world. I would not want to leave, either. Rome was where things *happened*.

That taken care of, I sent a slave to the palace to request an audience with Seneca, Nero's chief advisor. I briefly considered sending a missive to Burrus, his other advisor, but we never got on, him being such a fussy, suspicious sort.

My slaves trimmed my beard, keeping the graying mass nice and neat. Beards meant something in every society. In Rome, where most were clean shaven, beards were kept short and clipped like mine whereas in Judea most wore them full. I had long since divorced myself from my homeland and wanted to adopt more Roman styles, blend in a bit more with the men of the Empire. Small things like this have a positive psychological effect on those I dealt with. Who does not like to converse with people that resemble themselves?

As everywhere, how one dressed indicated status. For me, I wore a long silk toga edged in blue, not fancy, but the material, arrived from the barbarians at the end of the recently established Silk Road, showed that I was a rich and powerful man. Red sandals with amber beads on the back indicated my status as a Patrician. Yes, at this time I was a full citizen of Rome, with all the privileges that came with. Believe me, as a foreigner you are treated with a certain amount of contempt and are never truly admitted into the inner circle of Roman society. Thankfully, I had been in Rome long enough that I was now considered part of the furniture.

By the time my slaves had me dressed and perfumed, the messenger returned with Seneca's reply. We were to meet at the lunch hour. I smiled. Very soon.

My home lay near the Porta Sanqualis, the gate in the Servian Wall. In modern terms, I was living downtown. Only large amounts of coin passing into the palms of certain senators afforded me such luxury. Close to the major temples and near enough to the palace for a quick trip. My home, like my clothes, was an expression of my wealth as a trader.

A gift for Seneca under one arm, I arranged for a veiled litter to take me to the palace. I did not care for such conveyances, preferring the strength of my own two legs, but appearances, appearances, appearances.

Diaphanous veils closed, I reclined in the litter borne by four of my largest slaves, big men from Carthage and Gaul, hand-picked for their strength and endurance from the finest gladiatorial schools, or *ludus*. Well treated, given the second finest body slaves (after myself, of course) and food, they were more than happy to spend their days in training and mild servitude than fighting to the death on the sands of the arena. Of course, I was my Father's son, one consumed by ambition and hate, but I knew when to spare the lash and spoil the slave.

There were no wristwatches or cellphones to tell you the time, instead we relied on sundials and water clocks to break time down to manageable levels. The hours, or horae, were as follows: prima, secunda, tertia, quarta, quinta, sexta, septima, octava, nona, decima, undecimal and duodecima. Like most modern western timekeeping, the hours of day and night had the same names. The words *diei* and *noctis* were used to indicate day and night. Of course, since you are a Catholic priest, you know this, but I tend to wax loquacious, so don't mind me. Then again, since you have spent a great deal of time with Cain, my ramblings must seem mercifully brief.

Be that as it may, only my many jaunts to the palace gave me an indication of how long it took to arrive. Less than half an hour, more than fifteen minutes, at a guess. That meant that the Emperor and I were practically neighbors.

When we stopped, the litter lowered to the ground, I descended, allowing one of the slaves to set a small padded bench on the ground that I could emerge in comfort. Before me was the Claudian palace, the home of Nero and Agrippina.

Movies tell you that Rome was grand and sweeping, impressively large and robust. This was somewhat true from where one stood on the granite steps of palace. The reality is Rome was not as big as you would think. Within the Aurelian Walls, Rome was only 5.3 square miles. Consider the Manhattan of today at 33.77 square miles. However, the world was a much bigger place back then, with undiscovered countries just over the horizon waiting for the hard stamp of Roman boots. Barbarians were always at the border, biding their time for the chance to pillage and burn the richest city in the world, so the fact over a million people called Rome their home still amazes me to this day.

It is all a matter of perspective.

I was met by Seneca's personal slave, his majordomo if you will, by the name of Dovinix, a slender Gaul with mousy hair, sharp features and a clean, well-made tunic.

"Merchant Isaac the Younger, a delight to receive you," he said mildly. "My master awaits your pleasure. He has had prepared the noonday meal for you two to enjoy."

I nodded. Lunch, or *prandium*, was my favorite meal because the noon hour was a time of business and negotiations. The food served at the palace was obviously better than anywhere else within the Empire.

The palace, like many buildings, stood square and even, a defensible block of granite and marble faced with smoothly carved columns and surrounded by trees. Gardens were kept within as well for the enjoyment of the Imperial family. I won't bore you with the exotic animals like lively colored parrots and domesticated mongoose used for superior snake and ratting skills. Safe to say that at any moment there lived quite the menagerie within the palace walls.

Led by the slave, I entered the palace and immediately took a right along a narrow corridor that smelled faintly of cedar and across wool rugs covering red-veined marble floors. The windows along the walls had been left open to allow a cool breeze, which swirled the glinting dust in the pale sunlight. After a surprisingly short walk we came to an antechamber walled with tapestries in purple, gold and black depicting the rites of Bacchus, the God of Wine and Intoxication. Not my sort of thing, mind you. My Father had told me of the fallen angels and their fondness for assuming the roles of the false gods people created to explain such phenomena as thunder, lightning, death and such. Why, the Romans even created gods out of their fallen emperors, believing that it elevated worthy rulers after death and they even imagined a god of flatulence. His name was Crepitus and the less said about his worship the better. By the by we came to a small room, quiet and private, an intimate gathering spot for friends.

Near one wall sat Seneca on a sloping dining couch. He rose to his feet with a smile of delight. He was the kind of man people would describe as piggy, with glassy eyes half-hidden by folds of fat and a heavy brow. The face of a simple, obese man, or so he liked others to think because behind the rolls of fat and behind porcine eyes lay a mind as sharp as any I have ever met, worthy of being a tutor to an emperor. He could see through a pile of verbal manure faster than it could be shoveled. His toga, lined in gold, held a few more yards than mine, proof of his greater stature. Not a problem for me, I would rather be seen lesser, yet *be* greater than the other way around.

"My friend Isaac," he crooned, grasping my hands. "So good to see you again. I was just telling Burrus that we should have you here again at the palace." His voice was high and fluting. He led me toward an eating couch of my own. As I sat a bevy of Egyptian slaves arrived in plain white tunics and sandals bearing platters of food. I guessed business would have to wait.

First. "Here is a token of my esteem, for your efforts on behalf of my house." The gift, a small wooden box inlaid with mother-of-pearl, traveled from my hands to his.

"What's this?" He cried happily. "Thank you, my friend." Loving hands ran across the smooth wood.

"For your recent endorsement to include my humble house to participate in trade along the Silk Road. Riches will flood and so I offer but a token of my respect and admiration." I needed no more riches. In fact, thanks to Lucifer's influence, his *patronage* if you will, I had amassed wealth enough to rival the fabled Marcus Licinius Crassus, the military genius responsible for the downfall of Spartacus during the Third Servile War. History had him as the wealthiest man who ever lived. History was wrong. Thousands of slaves, dozens of estates, but he was a native Roman, while I was an immigrant and, thus, normally viewed with suspicion. Rich, but not to be seen as too rich. Keep it humble, keep it under the radar, avoid suspicion and always give presents that are expensive, but not too.

As Seneca opened the box I said, "Saffron because I know you adore it so and purple dye of the most exquisite quality for your clothes, Tyrian purple, in fact. This will put all other purple dyes to shame." Normally the cost of such an item, with all the import tariffs involved would be prohibitive, but my smuggling operation was second to none, although it still cost a fair amount. Taxes were for those without the imagination to avoid them.

"A princely gift indeed, Isaac," Seneca beamed, placing the box carefully on the floor and accepting a plate from a waiting slave. "But food first, discussion second if you don't mind."

"Of course not."

The slaves poured ice water over our hands and rubbed them dry with soft cotton towels as two others brought in a small table for the platters of food. On the largest platter stood an ox made of gold. On its back were two gold baskets, one with black olives, the other green. On the smaller trays there were candied dormice, cold roast ostrich and pigeon, slices of rare beef and skewered thrushes dipped in hot powders and drizzled in honey. Lastly, on a small bronze grill, there were smoking hot sausages smelling of silphium and peppers.

Not everything consisted of meat. There were apples, grapes, pears, dates and cherries along with stewed lentils and peas, and dark, fine-textured bread and plenty of soft butter. I could go on, but the list seems endless and I do not have the time to relate it all here before my plane lands.

We drank wine and water and ate our fill until I thought I would burst.

Lucious Annaeus Seneca gave a loud belch and handed his plate to a dusky slave. Wiping his fingers on a damp cloth, he looked to me. "To the meat of the matter, dear Isaac, now that we are sated."

"Why cannot this be a social visit? An excuse to give presents." A feeble excuse, but niceties must be observed.

A small, cunning smile. "Come now, Isaac the Younger, although at your ripe age that appellation no longer applies, we both well know that you have not become a valuable member of the Empire by not conducting business at every opportunity. Why, I dare say your acumen as a merchant is surpassed only by your ability to read people" He folded his hands on his protruding stomach. "Now if you would, dear Isaac."

Dear Isaac. I had no doubt that Seneca liked me, but not to the degree of true friendship. To invite friendship in politics is to invite weakness and any weakness in that world equated to blood in the water. It was only a matter of time that a passing shark took notice. A shark like me, perhaps. Be that as it may, I felt neither affection nor disdain for the man, only respect for his station and his cleverness.

Before I could begin my pitch for inclusion to the aqueduct restoration project in Capua that would net me a tidy sum for supplying the stone, we were interrupted.

"Just the man I wished to see." One of the tapestries twitched aside to reveal the figure of Emperor Nero, resplendent in his purple *tunic palamata* with gold embroidery depicting foliage along the hem and neck. It strained only slightly against his golden belt. "Isaac the Younger, it gladdens me to see you." He entered with Sextus Afranius Burrus following.

Where Seneca swathed himself in fat enough for two, Nero's other advisor stood short and lean, a perfect musclebound example of a Prefect of the Praetorian Guard. Thinning brown hair and deep eyes decorated a lean face lightly sprinkled with acne scars.

I was on my feet in an instant, back ramrod straight with right arm perpendicular to the ground, palm outward. My "Hail Ceasar!" was followed immediately by Seneca's.

Nero's round face broke into a wide smile, revealing the small gap between his two front teeth. "Enough of that, Isaac," he said. I relaxed, and he took my hands in his. "It is good to see you again. I so wanted to talk to you about something."

"Anything, Caesar." To Burrus. "Hello, Sextus. You're looking fit as ever, I see."

A small, wintery smile came my way. "As are you, Isaac. I swear, there are some of my guardsman who aren't in as good shape as you. I must have your secret." Suspicion laced his voice like salt in soup. If he had his way, I would be crucified at the Porta Latina outside the walls. It was not that he held any real animosity for me, but that he saw in me what I truly was … a predator like himself and successful predators do not tolerate equal company.

"Enough, good Citizens," Nero laughed, who, at the age of seventeen, was not one to stand on ceremony. "I have a question for our friend here, something that has come to my attention. I have need of his expertise." His face fell, and the room chilled. I realized that what was once companionable had suddenly turned dark and menacing. Nero took a step toward me while holding his hand out to Burrus. The advisor placed in the Emperor's hand a wickedly curved and sharp dagger adorned with rubies and emeralds.

"What, good Isaac," purred the Emperor, holding the weapon up until the edge was scant inch from my eyeballs, "do you how about this?"

CHAPTER THREE
DAGGERS

───≈≈≈───

"**U**H …" MY MOUTH WENT DESERT DRY and my tongue felt like a strip of poorly cured rawhide. "A dagger, Caesar?"

A harsh bark of laughter slapped my face. "A fucking dagger he says!" Nero's wide face was now all smiles. "Did you hear that, Sextus?"

"Yes, Caesar."

I managed some spit. "Caesar?"

"Oh, you should see your fucking face, Isaac." Gone was the menace, replaced with warmth and humor. "You thought I was accusing you of something, didn't you?"

My heartbeat slowed in relief. "Yes, Caesar." No other reply would do.

Shrewd eyes narrowed. "Now why would you think that, Isaac?"

"Because politics, Caesar. Anything can happen, it is why I do not indulge, I merely lobby."

"Fucking brilliant, Isaac." Nero patted my shoulder as if I were a favored pet. "No, I needed you to look at the dagger." At my puzzled look he handed the blade over. "I think it's Dacian, but Burrus is certain it's Thracian by the etchings, and an ancient one at that. I know you have some knowledge of artifacts, being a modest collector yourself. What I want you to tell me is who is right? I've got some serious fucking gold that it's Dacian."

Burrus piped in, his thin mouth barely moving to let the words free. "Everyone knows you deal in just about everything, Isaac. Sejanus Livinus tells me that you procured a Trojan cup made of gold. It's the centerpiece of his collection."

That cup earned me an in with Senator Livinus who possessed great influence with city improvements, which led me to hear about the aqueduct project in Capua.

Nero continued to stand, and in his palace, if he is on his feet, no one sits, so I held out my hand for the weapon. Smooth, hard, beautifully weighted despite the crusting of gemstones. I looked closer at the etchings, but it looked as if time had worn them to faint lines marring the bronze. It was a sica, a dagger commonly used by both the Dacians and Thracians as well as Illyrians. A long, curved blade that could almost be called a short sword with the cutting edge on the inside, used for striking around a shield. I examined the blade for a few minutes, flipping it over and over again as each detail gave up its secrets.

"It is not an antique," I murmured. "The blade has been artificially worn, rubbed with pumice if these scratches are any clue." My eyes met Nero's. "So, it is a fake. The gemstones are clever reproductions, but they are just glass. Good glass, actually worth some coin, but glass nonetheless."

"Come on, man!" blurted Nero. "Bad news about it being a fake, but what about the fucking origin?"

Such language. The emperor thought swearing made him sound tough, like a soldier, but it served only to make him seem spoiled and over privileged. Come to think of it …

"Caesar, whoever made this blade, for what reason, although the only thing I can think of is to part others from their coin, pattered it after a Dacian sica. The cylindrical weight at the end of the hilt and how it is affixed to the tang is a dead giveaway."

Good natured laughter filled the room and that round face showed none of the petulance that would decorate it in his later years. "By Jupiter's balls, Isaac, you are a treasure." To Burrus. "You owe me some coin, councilor."

Burrus smirked, a wry twist of his lips. "Yes, Caesar. I can see I was a fool to doubt your eye."

After receiving his wager, Nero chose to join us for some wine and conversation, a stroke of luck for me. There were merchants who would give their right arm to sit in regular conversation with the Emperor, and those of their children, pets and a majority of their slaves as well.

At first the Emperor steered the flow towards gladiatorial combat, a personal favorite of his and possible expansion into northernmost the wilds of Britannia and Germania to stimulate the economy and cement his position in history. The young man desperately wanted to be known as a great ruler, one who brought riches and glory to Rome. The best of intentions, which are the paving stones on the road to Hell, correct? That saying seems particularly apt here.

Eventually, the conversation took a darker turn, one that I waited for a long time to partake with this young man, one that his forebear, Claudius, had dismissed out of hand. "I wonder, Isaac, about this heresy of your countryman," he said, balancing a cup of wine on his tummy while waving a ring-bedecked hand at the ceiling. "The Christians, I believe they call themselves. Rather a nuisance."

A prickle like the heat from the first touch of a woman you have wanted for so long to bed ran across my skin in a delicious wave. I could not have asked for a better topic. It was as if Nero knew the longings of my heart.

"Did you know, great Caesar, that I knew this Joshua they call the messiah?" I asked slowly, letting each word drop like pebbles into a pond.

That raised eyebrows all around and Burrus frowned. As for Seneca, he merely stroked his large lower lip. "The fuck you did?" Nero exploded in a mixture of outrage and amazement. "You never told me that!"

"To be fair, Caesar, we have not many in-depth conversations and I did tell your predecessor over one of our many dinners. Either way, it was quite a long time ago. It seems so dim compared to the last few decades in Rome and I hardly speak my birth tongue anymore. I have become quite Roman in my outlook and thoughts, so much so that I am considered something of an outsider to my former people. It has both hurt and helped my various businesses."

"You never mentioned it to me, and we have had *several* conversations." Burrus frowned even more, while Seneca continued to stare a hole in me. Suspicion piled high on suspicion layered in soft, fluffy pillows of distrust. "Why is that?"

Always the outsider, accepted, but never fully so. It was a role I wore like a comfortable tunic and one that would never go away. No matter how well known around the palace, how beloved by an Emperor, and I truly believed that Claudius loved me in his way, men like Seneca and Burrus would always look at me askance.

"What was your greatest military defeat?" I countered.

Burrus scowled, not used to be put to the question. The expression gave his face the look of a dyspeptic dog. "Why would you need to know that?"

"We have had many a conversation, my friend, and you have never told me of your greatest military defeat. I know you campaigned in Africa, Germania and Caledonia, but never raised those efforts in casual discourse." I held up my hand for silence, not wanting interruption, needing to drive my point home. "For me, the heretic Joshua was a charismatic rabbi who held all he encountered in thrall to the power of his personality and delusion. It is why our leaders allowed Pilate to take him into custody." My next words needed to be chosen carefully and I considered each before releasing them from my lips. "A young man claims to be the son of God and can perform miracles, but only when those outside of his close circle of friends, and no others, are around to observe." A lie, of course. "He encouraged uprising, unrest and fomented chaos within the culture. Of course, he was delusional and had to be disposed of in the most expedient manner possible. Pilate's mistake was to make the execution public, which allowed him to become a martyr. This allowed for the spread of the heresy, which is a poison in the body of the Empire because these so-called Christians will denounce the proper Roman gods attempting to supplant them with their version of divinity."

"Aren't you a Jew?" Nero took a sip of wine, eyeing me more shrewdly than I cared.

"I have lived in Rome so long, Caesar," I replied, "have seen the living heart of Rome, observed its greatness and destiny. How can I not become as a good Roman citizen? I could not return to my homeland if I wanted to. I belong here … in the homeland of my heart."

During my answer Seneca and Burrus began to nod, obviously taken with my rationale. After all, who would not want to be a Roman? As for the Emperor, he pursed his lips. "These Christians, what do you suggest?"

That was simple. Father and I discussed this on more than one occasion. "Get rid of them all, root and branch, before they spread their poison further. No mercy because they will show Rome none."

In the silence that followed I drank my wine and stared, content that the first seeds of destruction for Joshua's followers had been sown.

I PEERED THROUGH THE THIN VEILS AT the crowded streets outside. Clean by today's standards, no loose pieces of paper or aluminum cans, no broken bottles or the rotting remains of tennis shoes. Instead, there was the all-pervasive smell of urine and feces. The streets were canted, sloped toward the center forming a gutter for waste that was thrown there, although there were fines levied against the careless. No one wants to be hit by flying shit. At corners throughout the city there were glazed piss pots used as public urinals. Fullers would collect the urine because when stale, at that point called a 'wash', it was used as bleach for clothes. Couple that with a million, sweaty people and it became a heady mix that sometimes caused the eyes to water.

Still, the city with all its imperfections and perfections inspired me to my work. If man could create such a city out of brick, stone and mortar all without the help of God, then why was Joshua's jealous salvation needed?

Being rich, I had running water for baths and waste disposal and plenty of body slaves to massage my aging libido. Although strong and fit at sixty plus years, the infirmities of age and hard living were writ on my flesh in scars and in my muscles as they attempted to heal after rigorous exercise. All the pops and creaks of joints, the pulsing ache of onset arthritis that radiated outward until knees and fingers felt as if embers had been thrust under the flesh next to bone.

After a romp with my favorite Egyptian slave, Rada, a girl with good breeding hips, uncommon beauty and an enthusiastic disposition, I fell into a deep sleep. The kind of sleep that always proceeded a conversation with my Father.

He carefully set the scene, the bedchamber of the Emperor Claudius complete with gaming board and dice. The bed could have fielded a polo game and the floor was hidden beneath the furs of bear and great cats. Father sat reclining on a couch, a golden cup of wine in His hand and a platinum laurel wreath atop His noble brow. His face remained hidden, not a blankness, but an absence as if my brain could not comprehend what lay between His high forehead and square chin. A blind spot, if you will.

"You have done well, My son," He intoned with funeral gravity, His offal and honey voice as warm as a miser's heart. The power of that voice thrummed through my bones and I thought for the umpteenth time that even a reflection of Him was almost more than I could bear. "I am most proud."

My smile was all teeth. "Thank you, Father. I could tell that Nero lapped up every word like a thirsty dog."

"He will attempt to eradicate the scions of Joshua. Keep encouraging him, My son. Be aware that Gaul will suffer a drought this year, so you must invest heavily in the appropriate foods. This should increase your holding threefold."

With such information was my own empire built. "Thank you, Father." My dream wine tested better than that in the waking world, sweet and smooth and invigorating. "Although I wish I could use the Words, or the Silver." Those thirty talents tucked away quite nicely beneath a loose tile under the bed.

"As I have said, son, your flesh does not contain the capacity for magic, even though t you are My son. No one can add that little fraction of talent to your body, even if you were born anew. I did give you other gifts which will see you in good stead throughout the years."

Ah, yes. Immortality, one of the gifts from Father, although one that had yet to prove its efficacy since I was becoming older and older, grayer and grayer. I sincerely hoped it was not the kind of immortality where I grew older and older, more and more infirm, but could not die. I was too afraid to ask Father. Every time I skirted near the subject His voice grew cold and harsh, rubbing against my skin like a rasp.

"WAKE UP!" thundered Father, the shock of His voice violently shoving me out of my sleep.

The knife descended toward my throat, slashing and I raised an arm in time to save my life at the cost of a lancet of pain. Blood flowed from the deep cut in my forearm and I jackknifed out of bed, my hearth hammering so hard I thought it would burst from my ribs.

Simon lunged at me again with the knife, a strange smile marring his lips. In his hand, a wickedly sharp blade about sixteen inches long, a bit of overkill in my estimation.

"You are quick for an old man," Simon remarked casually, as if we were talking about the price of perfume from Cyprus.

Stupid, talking is for those who have breath to waste and fools and I was neither. My hand dipped under the bed as he lunged over, coming up with my own dagger. There were seventeen secreted around the room, part of my sense of justified paranoia. Sometimes I hate being right all the time.

A Word blasted from my son's lips, Pain. I could not use magic, but thanks to Father I knew the Words. To most, it would sound like noise that they would try to recall but could not. My mind comprehended quite well, which is why I could teach them while remaining unable to employ their uses.

The Word passed over and through me like a ghostly northern wind and left me standing unharmed. Another gift, Words cannot find purchase upon my flesh. No Pain for me, but I planned on plenty for Simon, the disobedient son.

Big, with bulky muscles and a stocky frame, Simon looked every inch a killer, even with his baby face barely showing the first signs of the beard to come. Those were new muscles, not as strong as mine acquired from a lifetime of murder and training. He had speed, I had guile, and, in the balance, I thought the advantage mine.

Moving quick for a big kid, he leapt the bed, but a brutal punch to his cheek split the skin and blood flew as he staggered back to the other side. I did not wait for him to regain his balance, but followed, slashing.

To this day I do not know whether it was age or bloodlust that tangled my feet in the bedding, but I fell on him in a heap. My dagger pierced him as our bodies collided and a hot, wet tearing came from the vicinity of my leg. I felt the warm rush as arterial spray coated Simon from chest to knees and I knew I was dead, only a matter of time before my body received the message.

His grin told me he was aware of my predicament, but my answering smile stole it from his face as he realized my slash took him under his upper arm and the resultant flow matched the one from my leg.

Both of us were doomed.

I grappled with the boy, my left hand an iron band around his right while he employed the same method against my right. We both battered with our knees, striking for advantage. A lucky blow landed against the gush from my thigh and the crippling, deep pain paralyzed my leg. Only pressing Simon against the bedroom wall held me up. Darkness swam in my vision while only a glimmer of that same dimness floated in Simon's. I knew I would die first.

Slowly, straining with every ounce of my fading strength, I pulled his right hand until the fistful of dagger was between our eyes and I saw an expression in my son's face that I never saw before … fear.

Sweat slicked our skin, but my grip was sure, and the tip of the dagger came closer to Simon's eyes until, suddenly, his arm suddenly went slack, and it plunged in deep. There was an initial resistance, then a sudden give as it buried itself to the hilt, through his brain with a gush of fluid, the tip bursting through the skull to stop with a shudder in the wall behind.

Breath heaving, I staggered back, looking at the blood spouting from the hole in my thigh to the beat of my pounding heart. I placed my hands over the flow, but their strength was vapor and my darkness ate at my peripheral vision, working its way toward the pupils until all around went dark and I died.

WARMTH AND A SLOW, MUFFLED *THUMP thump* described my dark universe, a comforting place of rest, of peaceful contemplation of my innermost thoughts.

So nice, not having to worry, floating in wet warmth that permeated my body like the regard of a loving parent and I wished for nothing else but to float there in the great comfort of my dark and thumping domain.

So, this was death. Not so bad. Rather nice, with its pervasive peace and deep heat and even the noise. That thumpety noise, felt comfortable, familiar and appropriate for my new dark universe. Was this Father's doing? His definition of immortality for His son, a pat on the back for a job well done?

Thump thump.

As I drifted in the warmth my life with Joshua, with the Sicarii slaughtering Romans (and did I ever see the irony there) and my ascendency to power after the Crucifixion unspooled across my thoughts. Strangely enough, I still felt the same acidic jealousy as my mind's eye beheld Joshua's face, his calm, serene face.

Thump thump, thump, thump.

Was that a stab of irritation? No, it was an odd, *stretching* sensation along my spine that radiated up toward the base of my skull where it blossomed into a release, not quite pain … more like when one has to urinate so badly, the pain is so intense that when the flow begins the relief is akin to a hot, pleasurable agony. Relief is too kind a word for the feeling.

Thumpety, thump, thumpety, thump.

The darkness throbbed a pulse that I could feel from belly to bones to brain and a live wire of electric pain flashed across my nerves and if I had the breath, I would have screamed. As it was, my lungs contracted in a spastic symphony of aching fire. I lashed out in anger, in panic because my peaceful universe had become a lake of molten agony and I needed to get away.

Desperately I swam through the drumming darkness. The thumping loud, each beat coming so fast that they were a continuous noise that hammered into my mind. My fingers turned into curling claws of agony before they encountered some soft material. I ripped at it, tore with all my strength and a new smell/flavor/feeling washed over my face I clawded away as my universe grew smaller and smaller, compressing me into curl of flesh. I resisted with every fiber of my being.

The wet walls of my peaceful abode lay wrapped tight against my skin and I pushed and pushed and pushed, clawing at the barrier that threatened to crush me into nothing. Suddenly, with sound like the tearing of rotten cheesecloth, the wet, warm barrier gave.

Light, And screams.

BREATH FILLED MY LUNGS AS FLUID left and air rushed in. I had the feeling of razors of ice in the soft tissues in my chest, but it felt wonderful to breathe, although I coughed up thick fluid with every lungful.

More screams, more tearing and the light was so bright my eyes watered, and the pain began anew as my flesh rebelled, aching and stretching and pulling in every direction across bones that creaked and groaned.

My screams joined those all around as I flailed. The light hurt my eyes. A bright white visual overload that paralyzed my brain for a moment and I let loose a yell that seemed to start at my bowels, ripping out through my mouth in a rabbit squeal of pain and shock.

More tearing ... more screams besides my own and buried under the unmistakable metallic *shhhiinng* of a sword clearing a scabbard. Frantically, I moved my pain-wracked arms, swiping this way and that. The air, icy and biting, tore at nose and skin and again what felt like needles pushing up through my bones up out of my flesh and all was pain. It was a raw newness that nearly tore my mind from its moorings.

Carefully, My son.

Father's honeyed voice almost calmed my agony, but it lasted only an instant before the pain returned and I found myself falling, flailing and wailing. My spine met the floor and I lay there for a moment as my muscles spasmed and my joints creaked alarmingly. The painful whiteness that tore at my brain resolved into a dun-colored plastered ceiling. An alien face swam into view and my perception shifted. It was no alien creature, but a man with features twisted in terror.

On my back ... on the ground. My hands came into view, raw and strong and covered with some sort of bloody slime.

"Wha—?" I croaked through a throat that felt tender. The timbre of my voice held a quality I had not heard in years.

The face receded, and rough hands grabbed my shoulder. "Father is that you?" The hands, connected to arms corded with heavy muscle, lifted me from the floor. It took a moment as the world rocked all around for me to find my feet. Surprisingly enough, I gained my balance quickly and spun to face my savior. "You look so young," he added, still shaken.

"Jacob?"

My eldest stared at me with a mixture of fear and awe, fear winning by a few beats. He nodded, mouth agape in shock.

"Why are you in Rome, Jacob?"

He blinked once, twice then a third time before answering. "I am in Capua, father, as are you. You are in my home."

Capua? How? "How?"

Frown lines bracketed his nose. "What is the last thing you remember?"

"Simon attacked me, tried to kill me." The recollection sharpened, and my stomach shrank to a grape. "I killed him, but not before he inflicted a mortal wound."

"Little prick," he swore. "Never knew his place, that one." Suddenly comprehension colored his face. "The Patron's Promise. That's how you're alive."

Yes! The promise of immortality. Only three of my of sons knew the secret. "Obviously, but how am I here?" Something dripped into my eyes, thick as snot and I wiped it away. More of that irritating, blood-streaked slime.

It took a minute, but Jacob finally let go and answered. "My best, most beautiful slave was due to give birth. Turn around, father."

His words chilled me, and I slowly turned. The room I stood in was smaller than most in Jacob's house in Capua, roughly six by eight and decorated with a small, simple bed made of roughhewn planks and straw. It took me a moment to comprehend with my new eyes what I was seeing, but when it did the realization, the enormity, of what just happened turned my bowels to ice.

A fine, looking slave, long hair, dark clear skin and deep brown eyes. Beautiful, I could see why Jacob chose her for breeding. An expression of agonized horror disfigured that pretty face as did the great void under her chin.

From collarbones to pubic bone she opened up like an obscene flower. The ragged edges of the wound curled back from an inside where the organs had been crushed flat, the meat of her body steaming in the cool air. Blood had been sprayed liberally on the bed and wall next to it. A thick, fresh coat that still ran as it slowly coagulated. Jacob's slave ... due to give birth, he said. It was if she birthed a large animal rather than a baby, one that struggled violently to exit her body.

And there it was, the truth. All the pieces from the hollowed- out slave, to the slime and the damage to her body. She had given birth, but it was to nor ordinary animal ... it was me.

This was immortality in the house of my Father.

THE BOOK OF

MICHAEL continued

Chapter Five
Getting Real

———⁓———

"Well, ain't this a kick in the teeth?"

I could only agree as I stared at my own face on the television. It was an old picture, taken about ten years ago, in fact, showing me with my congregation at the Annual Cornhusker Catholics Picnic. Somehow the news made that nice, clean shot of me smiling with my parishioners look grimy and dark, as if I harbored some deep, dark secret. Like what Time magazine did with the infamous OJ Simpson cover photo.

"Once again, this special report from United States: Michael Engle, former Army Ranger and now priest is wanted in connection for multiple homicides at his church in Omaha, Nebraska six months ago. Authorities believe that Engle is fleeing from country to country to avoid arrest. Authorities ask the public to avoid Engle at all casts and to call immediately if he is spotted as he is considered armed and extremely dangerous."

Yeah, a kick in the teeth.

"What does this mean, sir?" asked Milo rubbing his chin.

"It means that Burke is more desperate than I thought." The old playground song flashed through my mind. *Ring around the rosies, pockets full of posies, ashes, ashes we all fall DOWN!* Funny what comes to mind in moments of stress and reflection. Not too long ago it was *Skip to my lou.* Maybe I was regressing. "First mercenaries, now media. He must know that this story won't hold up for more than a couple of months."

"That's all he'll need."

All he'll need. I closed my eyes and sighed. So far, my disguise held as we sat next to the smoker's area in Heathrow, a five-foot wall topped by two feet of plexiglass that was just big enough to house twenty nicotine addicts. Powerful fans sucked errant carcinogenic wisps away from the sensitive nasal passages of the non-smokers. They tended to give the enclosure a wide berth, which was fine by me. Milo and I sat waiting for our plane to refuel and watched the news on an iPad provided for me from our tech *wunderkind*. I receive a new one every couple of weeks. There was enough counter-intrusion software embedded into the 128-gig machine to defy anything the Sicarii could throw at it. I hoped.

As for my disguise, I gained fifty pounds around the middle, a gray moustache and horn-rimmed glasses. Add to that a prominent Cyrano de Bergerac nose and cheek paddings, just the right combination to foil facial recognition software.

The news report began again, the talking head looking grave, almost shocked at the mention of a Catholic priest on a murderous rampage. A slight headache began between my eyes as I exited the news app. "Milo, I need a minute."

That went over like a Grand Wizard for the KKK at a #Blacklivesmatter meeting. Milo's face closed hard, settling into 'I don't wanna' lines. No one took his bodyguarding more seriously.

"Please, Milo. I have to make a call."

There we go. Understanding hit and he stood. "To *him*?"

I nodded.

"I will be nearby." The huge presence of my bodyguard disappeared, not far and not for long, but for the while I found myself in a clear space. Although the busiest airport in the world, Heathrow did have its quite moments and 1 a.m. was one of them.

I tapped an icon on the tablet and the screen swirled with color while I jacked ear buds into the audio port. After a surprisingly short interval a familiar and much beloved face appeared, kind, avuncular, with eyes gleaming with kindness and merriment behind wire rimmed glasses.

"Holy Father," I whispered.

"Michael," replied the Pope in Latin. "My son, it is good to see you again." The happy lines at the corners of those kindly eyes crinkled further. "I have not much time. The spies of the great Adversary been particularly troublesome lately."

One of the greatest shocks I had received during my time with Morgan Heart was not the revelation of the Sicarii, or his destiny as the Anti-Christ (thankfully averted), but the infestation of Vatican by Sicarii agents. Cardinals, bishops, Swiss guards ... all had been penetrated and corrupted by the enemy who had suppressed even the hint of reform within the papal walls. That suppression led to the assassination of at least four popes (perhaps more) and dozens of others who were without stain.

The current crop of Sicarii agents, discovered through careful study and our brilliant cadre of hackers, were left in place and fed just enough credible information to keep their masters happy. A dance of information and disinformation like that when the United States broke the German Enigma code in WWII.

When this Pope had been elected, the Sicarii thought they were helping to elevate a humble, meek man. What they didn't expect was a true lion of God. Humble, yes. Ineffective, no. It had taken a while to penetrate the layers of security, but I had finally managed to meet the man and assess the situation myself. Finding him to be exactly what he appeared, I spent a good hour catching him up on the events of the real war between Good and Evil. He took it surprisingly well.

"Your Holiness," I began. "There's been some news." I took a few minutes to fill him in on Judas Iscariot. Needless to say, he was surprised, but not overly. We had both learned of things that forever changed our perspectives on reality.

"So why the call, my son?" His eyes twinkled. "You do not need my advice on how to wage war against the Adversary and what allies to choose."

How could he say that? He was the goshdarned Pope, for Pete's sake! The man just *sat* there and stared at me through the tablet as if he was in a dentist's reception room reading *People*. "I-I-I..," No words. My head felt thick and my eyes watered slightly. What could I say?

"Listen, my son, for I have not much time. The Lord has chosen a prophet for the first time in uncounted years. You have felt His hand upon your shoulder, His voice in your ear and His armor protects you, so you do not need this old man telling you what to do. Pray to Him if you need guidance. I am here merely to lend an ear and act as your confessor should you wish it." The words were soft, but the tone left no room for argument. Months ago, I learned that although while I was indeed God's envoy in these troubled times, His Holiness had no qualms about pinning my ears back if I spoke foolishness. While pious and humble, that didn't mean he would stuffer my hesitations, or trepidations, to hinder the cause.

"I have an idea, your Holiness."

More sparkling from his kind eyes. "I thought so. Be quick. My new valet has been particularly nosy as of late and will soon return. It does not take long to prepare a nice cup of tea."

Ever since the Family plastered my face all over the news I knew things would have to change, that things were quickly coming to a head. "For the past few months we've been recruiting, and we've been pretty successful. In fact, so successful we managed to expand our bases of operation and personnel. This includes both Cain and the billionaire Arturo Sacci, whom I was very happy to find as devout as I. With Cain's telecom industry and Sacci's transportation infrastructure, we have gone from limping along mortally afraid of the Sicarii to a real fighting force."

"It is because God has decreed this to be the time to gather His forces, and for you to be His general." The humor in his eyes was replaced by determination and absolute conviction.

Although an advisor and confessor, I only met the Holy Father once in person and a dozen times over the Internet. Thanks to Cain, we had all the resources needed in that area, which was a blessing because it seemed as if the Family were becoming quite proficient at encryption analysis and server location. It cost a fortune to stay ahead of them.

"Your Holiness, what do you know of artifacts?"

"Only what you have told me, my son. The Silver, the Grail and one or two others. This is an area of little study for me."

"If you would be so kind, could you search the Archives for a mention of something called Ablewand?"

"Of course, my son. To what purpose does this serve?"

I bit my bottom lip and nodded. His Holiness had more faith in me than I did. "It's time to get aggressive, to escalate this war."

His eyes widened as I related my plan.

Ring around the rosies.

THE BOOK OF

JUDAS continued

Chapter Four
Rouen, France, 1431

———————

"HERE NOW, WHO ARE YOU?" CHALLENGED the guard, lowering a spear. The leaf-shaped blade looked sharp enough to use in a bris. Circumcision by polearm did not sound like a safe method to aid in the continuation of a bloodline.

I spun past the spear head, the shaft sliding along my side, continuing until the knuckles of my left hand made hard contact with the guard's jaw. The second guard barely had time to grunt before my foot found his crotch and he fell with a wheezing gasp. Two hard punches later and both lay unconscious at my feet.

Three seconds from challenge to conquest. Slow. Despite my last rejuvenation ten years ago I was starting to feel the grip of age. I adjusted my brown leather tunic and belt. My hose was rumpled and stained, my shoes badly worn, the clothes of a laborer, perfect for passing unnoticed in the common areas of the castle.

"What is it, you two daft bunglers?" came a voice from beyond a heavy wooden door. "What is all that noise? Quiet this instant or I shall have you beaten!"

Apparently, I had made more noise than I thought. Smiling, I put my hand to latch and sauntered in as if I belonged.

The room that greeted me was spacious enough for a king and outfitted as such. Thick fur rugs dotted the floor and tapestries that could have ransomed a bevy of nobles hung on every wall. Candles and lanterns offered plenty of illumination, aiding the weak midafternoon light streaming through the north window.

All well and good, but what I had come for, who I had come for, squatted over an ornately painted porcelain pot, face suffused with blood and straining, grunting mightily like a hog at a trough. It took him but a moment to detect my presence, although I was not trying to be silent. The man jumped up with a cry, twig and berries swinging comically as he attempted to adjust his smallclothes.

"Please, Pierre, continue your evacuations," I kept my tone neutral as he gabbled at me. Corpulent, Bishop Pierre Couchon of Beauvais was of middle age and fond of drink, which showed in the vessels burst upon his impressive nose. Brown hair thinning rapidly, he looked more a banker or butcher rather than one of my most trusted agents, although trust had become a feeble word to the Sicarii. "I have long since grown used to the smell of shit."

"My lord," said the bishop, smoothing his smallclothes. "I did not expect you."

"Your guards need more training or replacing. They were far too slow and sloppy."

Hazel eyes clouded with chagrin, an emotion I knew was almost alien to his mind. "They were not of your Order, my lord. Simple castle guards provided by the castellan."

I strode thoughtfully across the bedroom, noting the opulence, the large armoire, the bed with its fine sheets and a few strands of long black hair on the pillows. Hair that had no relation to Bishop Cauchon's head, but most likely formerly resided upon the scalp of the chambermaid. No doubt she was lured to the bed by the Bishop's fat purse rather than the sad little twig that swung between his fat thighs.

With the quickness of a lightning strike, my fist found his prodigious gut, doubling him over. A rancid smell told me his smallclothes would need laundering. "You loathsome fool," I snarled. "I give you but one task, to conduct the trial as swiftly and then burn the bitch to ash. Instead I receive reports of attempted rescues by the Armagnacs, failure to obtain a verbal abjuration of her heresy and your fucking *fear* of the Church."

Couchon hawked and spat, coughing all the while until his stomach finally relented its cramping. "I have done all you have asked, my lord," he gasped. Slowly he stood on trembling legs. "She does have agents who aid her. Men and women of some small note, but influential enough to slow the trial considerably." The Bishop staggered to the chamber pot and pulled at his smallclothes, the smell of shit redolent.

I let him complete his movement, preferring to stare as he squirmed uneasily upon the pot. Once I tired of smelling his efforts, I strolled to his desk and toyed with his episcopal ring, which doubled as a seal for official documents. The gold sparkled in the lantern light, the amethyst in the center bordered by an eagle and lion, an ironic emblem considering the cowardice of the man who wore it. Still, cowards were useful and this one more than most.

For five years he answered to my Family, not knowing our true allegiance, his being only to power and money of which we had ample. Only his placement between England and France and his animal cunning betrayed his value to us. Valuable enough that it was I who recruited him and smoothed his rise in the church.

But it was not Couchon and his timidity that brought me to Rouen, but the girl. Near two months ago Pope Martin V, a venal man of great use to the Sicarii, passed into Hell, succeeded by Eugene IV, an equally venal man of violent appetite. Martin possessed enormous desires for the flesh of young women. When I say women, I mean virginal girls who had yet to have their first courses, deflowering them with what he labeled 'the Most Holy Rod of God'. The Sicarii aided in his lusts, providing him ample vessels to slake his desires in exchange for small, yet profitable favors that saw the course of the Family run true and long. It was only toward the end of his excremental life that he became less tractable and had to be put down like a vicious cur, which led to the next manageable pontiff. Fortunately, Eugene loved power more than flesh and the Family provided services to the new pope that saw his flame grow brighter and hotter. Assassination is ever a tool of politics.

The problem with Eugene, however, was his desperate need to kill anything that offended him, and the girl offended his sensibilities more than anything except Saracens. The girl offended him, and, despite the objections of the more pious and honorable cardinals, Eugene wanted her dead in the worst way.

If only he knew the true allegiance of the Family. It amused me to no end that even a flawed believer like Eugene employed the very people that wanted to destroy the Lying God's Christian empire.

Curiosity brought me to Rouen. I could have easily sent one of my hundreds of children and their descendants, but the girl had me interested. Was she that one true thing, a messenger, or a delusional fake? Could she be a general sent by her god? Such a thing to witness, such a thing to see destroyed.

I stared into the full-length mirror next to the bishop's desk, no doubt used when being dressed by his valet. With my coloring and black hair, most would see me as an Ottoman or a Greek, the former suspicious, the latter merely odd. Considering the empire to the east was in an expansionist phase (thanks in part to my Family, whose fortunes always rested in strife and conflict), seeming a Turk would be detrimental to my operation in France, so I made sure to affect a Greek accent and the name Sarpedon. Keeping my eyes on the floor and my manner subservient allowed me access despite my coloring. Who really notices servants?

With that thought I told myself to investigate my own servants in

Eidgenossenschaft, or Swiss Confederation. A chilly but beautiful land positioned perfectly to control trade routes between Germany, Austria and Italy. My Father declared the Cantons (or states) ideal for unification and I had spent one lifetime there already bringing the Confederation about, influencing the various rulers with money and dreams of a Swiss power as a major trade country. The problem was keeping the Cantons unified, their armies from clashing due to old squabbles that dated back centuries.

"Pierre," I muttered, running fingers through my short hair. "Your folly can be corrected. You must hasten things along. Have her sign an abjuration document."

Sputtering from behind as the bishop tried to hide is astonishment and bear down at the same time. "How, my lord? She will not sign. She is illiterate."

"Don't be a fool, Pierre. Illiteracy is not the issue, put her mark on a piece of parchment. All you do is tell her to sign or face immediate execution. Then after a week, you burn her at the stake for heresy, or witchcraft, or dressing like a man. Take your pick. What matters is that it is done."

With a last thunderous fart Pierre completed his evacuation, cleaned himself and removed his soiled smallclothes in the process. I kept my back to the fat man so I would not be bothered by his loathsomeness. I could not stand those who gave themselves so freely to things like gluttony. Make no mistake, I was a fan of all manner of sins, but in moderation. Excess leads to loss of self, which leads to more excess, a vicious circle if there ever was one.

"I shall do as you say, my lord."

"In the morning."

"My lord?"

I turned in time to see his legs disappear beneath his clerical robes. "There is a need to speak to the girl now."

"Why?"

Two steps and the front of his robes were housed in my fists. My face drew close to his. "Because," I hissed. "I wish it. If I so desired I would fuck her raw and give her to the guards." A vein throbbed at my temple and I could feel the heat in my face. "Yours is not to ask why. You are *never* to ask me why. You have one job and one job only, to be *my* creature upon this world, to do my will and never, ever question me. Nod if you understand."

He nodded, jowls flapping. That low cunning of his kept his mouth shut.

"Good boy, Pierre." I held up his ring. "Now where is your sealing wax?"

"Wot's this then?" The guard, a Briton, stared at the letter in his hand. Like most of his kind he came from poorer circumstances and therefore was illiterate. What he did have going for him was size and a simplistic cruelty that shone from his piggy eyes. I liked him immediately.

"This, my good turnkey, is a letter from Bishop Couchon himself allowing his personal inquisitor, myself, access to the prisoner for the purposes of interrogation."

"You don't look like no Frenchman, nor a good Brit. Wot are you then?"

"Greek, my good man. From Athens and like I said, a man in service to the good Bishop Couchon, so I ask you again, please let me see the prisoner." My smile would have warmed the heart of the most forbidding harridan. I worked hard on the smile and it rested upon my face comfortably.

"That be the Bishop's seal alright," mused the guard. His steel cap must have been squeezing his head quite hard because he squinted at the seal for a good moment before finally nodding and returning the letter. "I guess you kin pass." With ill grace he moved his bulk to the side and opened the dark oaken door to the Tour de la Pucelle, the Tower of the Maid, part of Bouvreuil castle where Jeanne d'Arc spent her last days.

I left the French countryside and entered the solitary, three story tower constructed of sturdy, ugly gray stone. What light shone in the main chamber fell fitfully from windows so narrow that even a mouse would have to crab through sideways to pass. Along the far wall a spiral stone staircase wound up to the middle floor where the Maid of Orléans waited for the conclusion of her trial. Another guard, not as big as the first but meaty enough for the job, sat at a rough wooden table, a battered but serviceable sword at his elbow.

He did not question my right to be there, despite my darker complexion and humble tunic. Anyone who made it past the large guard outside deserved to have their time with the girl upstairs.

Not bothering with pleasantries, I climbed the stairs and knocked on door at the top.

"Enter."

Most would think Jeanne a petite woman, a waif of the Lying God who could calm savage beasts with a glance from crystalline blue eyes. The person that greeted me was a big girl, a farmer's daughter with work-roughened hands and broad shoulders that told of great strength. Wide and strong, with high cheekbones and skin lightly scarred by acne, she was no great beauty, but those eyes were striking. Such a deep and startling shade of blue, they captured the viewer in an instant, penetrating, probing and vastly intelligent. Backed by the utter conviction of her religion, I could see why men laid down their lives for her.

A plain white shift covered her from neck to ankle, a little stained, a little threadbare, yet she wore it like the finest robes of state. I reminded myself that this was a formidable opponent and not to judge her by gender.

"The fallen Israelite," she said softly, startling eyes placid.

A cold chill hit my bones. "Excuse me, *mademoiselle*?"

"You are the scion of the Adversary, are you not?" She quickly crossed herself. "Here to slake his curiosity, no doubt."

No doubt at all. She hit the nail with such precision that my lips grew numb as I struggled to answer. Finally, I settled on a little, known tactic called 'the truth'.

"You are correct, and astonishingly perceptive." I tried for a smile, but it died before being born. For a man who is reborn from his own descendants, ripping through the flesh of the host mother, growing into manhood before drawing a breath, I found myself floundering in the face of this remarkable young woman.

I could have sent another in my place, but if Jeanne d'Arc was truly the Lying God's chosen messenger, then the duty should fall to me, the messenger of the Fallen, the Founder of my Family. It seemed only fitting, for only someone of my vast experience could withstand the hypocrisy of the Christ uttered from the mouth of his hand-picked lackey. Besides, it looked to be a bit of fun, something of a rarity of late.

For over a thousand years I died and rose again in a welter of blood and tissue, each new life a horrifying death for the women my family chose as brood mares. Nor more wives because who would wish to become close, have deep-rooted feelings for someone who could die messily should I need rebirth? We had learned to separate our feelings, taking women only to bed and breed, never to make part of the Family and the females born to us were of use as honey traps, their charms in aid of assassination and the collection of intelligence. Every so often they were used to cement relationships with various heads of state, to augment the power of the Sicarii and to plant our seed in as many royal lines as possible. This led to influence, this led to control and control was part and parcel of Father's plan.

Jeanne d'Arc had been a thorn in the Family's side for the past couple of years, her victories interfering with Britain's scorched earth policies (a policy provided to Henry V by a many-times great grandson of mine named Bartholomew whose talent for anonymity and intrigue was second to none). England wanted to rule all, and the Sicarii would ride to greater glory upon the house of Lancaster's shoulders. Father advised me to be wary of the girl, saying that the minions of the Lying God were clever with their falsehoods.

With a sigh, Jeanne wandered toward the far end of the circular room some forty paces away. She had the run of the middle section of the tower, large enough for a couple of families, but sparsely furnished with only a small table, a three-legged stool and a cot for comfort. Light came from three narrow windows set at six feet. The stone of the interior was the same as the exterior, crude, ugly and rough, offering no ease to the eye or soul. This was a room built to punish the occupant with despair, leaching hope and light and joy from a body as surely as a cut to an artery leeches blood.

"The Lord sent an angel to tell me of your arrival, Sir Enemy," she said absently. "His arrival was accompanied by the soft sound of golden bells, like all angels." A roughened finger pointed toward the ceiling. "He floated there, clothed in samite, golden of skin and informed me of you."

I could not help myself, fascination had set in. "What did he say?" My voice barely stirred the air. This was no madwoman, but a true messenger. I could see it, taste it upon the tip of my tongue. The room held an electric air that ran like insects across my skin.

"That you are lost, lied to by the Adversary. That there is within you a seed of goodness. Great goodness should you allow it to flourish."

Breath returned to my lungs in a rush and I shook myself like a dog. Her voice, made hoarse by shouting battlefield commands, nevertheless held a seduction that nearly had me sucked into her religious mania. "It is you who have been lied to, *mademoiselle*. Your faith has blinded you to the world all around. There are mysteries you have not dreamt of in your little corner of France, mysteries that would leave your mind in a perpetual state of amazement."

Without turning she said, "You are speaking of the magic of Words and the existence of elemental intelligences that oversee the natural orders of the world, are you not?"

If she had sprouted bat wings and a tail I could not have been more surprised. She turned and fixed her blue eyes upon my astonishment.

"The Lord has been kind and granted me visions and gifts, Sir Enemy." With that she muttered a Word.

It slid into my ear and out the other without disturbing the gray matter in-between, leaving no trace of its passage. So, it is with Words, if one is not a magus, then they are immediately forgotten upon utterance. All I knew is that Jeanne d'Arc spoke a Word, but its meaning was void and that frightened me more than a dagger to the liver. One of my gifts from Father was the knowledge of Words, yet the meaning of this one escaped my grasp. A Word unknown to the magi, to Father.

Of course. It made perfect sense ... how a young girl could go from farmer's daughter to general so quickly and be so effective in combat. Such miracles in front of the men would explain their devotion and willingness to follow her into war's red embrace. For a moment I was so stunned I could not move, could not breathe.

Another Word shattered the air and I felt a tingle along my skin which slid away, and I came back to the moment. "Words have no effect upon me," I snarled, balling my fists until my knuckles cracked. "I have long been immune to such."

For the first time she was rendered speechless. I reckoned that the angel of the Lying God conveniently forgot to inform her of the immunity to Word magic granted me by my terrible Father's temporary possession of my body all those many long years ago. Regret at the inability to use Word magic fled at her demonstration.

"Merely a Word of Knowing," she said finally, hand to mouth and eyes bright. "So, I could know if you attempted to guile me with falsehoods."

A Word heretofore unknown by mortal man? This begged the question of how many Words existed in Heaven and Hell? As many as the angels in the Eternal City or demons in the Damned Tunnels? Was there more to Word magic than was possessed in my philosophy? Was this Word of Knowing the tip of the iceberg, so to speak? I took a moment to ponder this information.

Much like the Word of Truth, which forces the subject of the spell to speak truthfully when put to question. Yet this Word of Knowing, by her admission, seemed more passive, merely sensing when someone lied or did not. Her attempt to use a Word on me offended.

"My lies? My lies?" Anger wormed its way through my heart and brought heat to my cheeks. "How dare you? Do you know who I am? My history? I think not, *mademoiselle!* I am the one true constant in the world, the man who has seen it all, from the elementals that spin the sun in the heavens to the basest, darkest sins of mankind. Without me, you have no Christ to worship, no cross to carry about your neck on a fine gold chain!" My breath became labored and it took all within me not to lash out. "Without me, the sacrifice of the so-called Son of God would never have happened, and you would be worshipping some Roman deity and dropping whelps for some smelly farmer's son. *I* am the reason you became a messenger, so I want a little *fucking* respect!"

Jeanne grimaced. "No offense was intended, I assure you, only the truth."

My breath was ragged, and it took a few moments for me to get it under control. My teeth felt dry and veins stood out on my neck. I had not felt this kind of anger in centuries. For a moment I reveled because this was life, this fury told me I lived, I breathed, and I still retained the purpose that set me on my path. Centuries had a way of dulling the edge of resolve.

Those crystal blue eyes were fixed at my side and it took a moment for me to realize that she stared at my hands still bunched in furious fists so hard the knuckles shone white. Slowly I unclenched and felt pins and needles along my fingers.

"Please excuse me," I began. "My behavior was quite rude." Apologizing hurt, I was out of practice, but I needed … no, *wanted* information from the Maid. Something, anything to aid in the advancement of the British cause during this war. Family interests lay with the British and King Henry's victories gave the Sicarii greater reach, greater influence. You could not have too much power.

"You want something."

The words sliced through me and I could feel her regard on my skin. Her power near humbled me it was so great. "Yes. Yes, I do."

"Make your offer, Sir Enemy, then leave me be. I must prepare for my death."

"Perhaps that can be prevented."

"I will not abjure the Lord or His word." Hard finality weighed her words.

A pause. "Then tell me of your army's disposition, supply lines, the names of your commanders and further plans for confrontation. Give me this and I swear by my Father that you will live. Tell me what I wish, and you will be free." The offer stunned me because I had no clue I would make it until the words left my mouth, but I meant them.

Father was going to be very cross with me. He wanted her dead, the sooner the better, but I needed the intelligence and perhaps could earn a measure of forgiveness for disobedience if the House of Plantagenet were to finally wrest France from the House of Valois. This kind of risk, traveling to Rouen, bearding Couchon in his lair and confronting the Maid had me tingling with excitement. It had been years, decades, since I took such risks and the energy was almost sexual in nature.

Jeanne's reply, however, brought me crashing down to reality. "No. No, Sir Enemy, I cannot betray my countrymen thus. Not even if doing so would cost me my life. My immortal soul is more valuable than mortal flesh."

For some reason my eyeballs felt far too large for their sockets. "Do you understand the consequences of refusal, *mademoiselle*?" I asked, moving closer until we were nose-to-nose. To her credit she did not flinch or draw back. Instead, she placed her hands behind her back and fixed me with her blue gaze. "You will be burned for witchcraft. Except for crucifixion, I cannot think of a single death that comes close for sheer horror and pain. Only I can save you from such a death, so I urge you to reconsider. I know how your god works, that if you give me this information you can ask his forgiveness and it will be given. Your soul is safe with his forgiveness."

She shook her head before I finished. I knew what her answer would be. "I am sorry, Sir Enemy, but what is that forgiveness if I cannot forgive myself? If I do this I will be unworthy of His forgiveness and cannot ask for it."

I turned away, cursing. The Lying God's hooks were in deep and she would never betray the information needed. No matter, the House of Plantagenet would prevail. France would be Henry's soon enough. Not even the Knights Templar, officially disbanded a couple of decades previously, lurking about like stray curs in the shadows nipping at Sicarii heels, could stop our righteous ascension and the furtherance of Father's holy plan.

"Goodbye, Jeanne d'Arc." I said over my shoulder reaching for the door. "You have made a poor decision."

My shoulders hit the rough stone wall and my breath left in a rush, my guts cramping around a tight, hot ball of pain. I was tasting the floor and my arms were wrenched backward and up, a hard knee between my shoulder blades. I had not heard her move, no telltale swishing of air as she attacked, only the startling pain of the punch to my gut and the floor to my lips.

"Sir Enemy," she breathed into my ear. "Make no sound and I will not destroy your shoulders."

Intolerable! Subdued like the rankest amateur! Humiliation and shame warred with the anger that flowed hot within my veins. "Get off me," I grated, making sure my voice did not reach above a whisper.

"I certainly will, Sir Enemy, but first you will listen to me and do so with your complete attention. Do you comply?"

What choice did I have? "Yes." The word hurt as it exited.

The pressure on my shoulders eased and the knee between them disappeared. "Good. I do not care if you rise or lay there, simply listen."

Regaining my feet, I rolled my shoulders to loosen up. Jeanne stood under the far window, the light haloing her dark hear, cut close to the scalp and to the skin in the back in warrior fashion to better seat a helm. The manly cut made her look more a woman, not less, a fact I found most curious.

"You call the Lord the Lying God, one of the most profound untruths in Creation. Let me tell you why."

I gave her a gimlet stare, crossing my arms. "Do enlighten me."

"The Lord has given unto me knowledge that will show you, the Lost Disciple, proof of His good will and love for even the most wayward of His children. You are aware, of course, of the writings of John of Patmos?"

"You are talking about Revelations, that load of manure foretelling the end of the world."

She nodded.

"Of course. It's laughable. A fairy tale created by a delusional man on a lonely island in the middle of nowhere."

"It is what is to come." She spoke the words with such peaceful authority that I believed her. I did not wish to, but I did. Her certainty was contagious. As I stared, trying to find words, she made no motion. Motes swirled in the beams from the windows, insects crawled upon the walls, but we two stood motionless as if the world had no impact upon our bodies.

She continued. "You will be given a directive by the Adversary, the one you call your Father, to begin a quest for the one he will call the Redeemer. This man will be of your lineage and will have the use of all twelve Words of magic known to mortal men, practice Alchemy and be able to use all thirty of the Terrible Words contained in the Silver, the betrayal coins. Your payment from the Romans."

My knees locked so I would not fall. How could she know about the Silver, the *talents* I received for betraying Joshua? How could she know any of this? Head spinning, I turned away before my face divulged my emotions, which was a stew of many ingredients. Sudden nausea gripped me, and I bit my lip to keep from crying out. Father mentioned the prophesy of Revelations, calling it a convenient fiction, a dream conjured by a mad god. Such things were beneath Him and He would have no part in Heaven's plans for the future.

"How can you know this?" I demanded.

"The Adversary is nothing if not predictable. He has always wanted perfection, a world without defect, but such a world cannot exist because of man's imperfections. To make Mankind perfect, one must erase free will so there would be no strife, no greed, no sin." She took a deep breath. "What the Adversary does not understand is that removing free will does not induce perfection, but rather creates another flaw in Mankind that would ultimately destroy the perfection he seeks and to kill Mankind utterly would deprive him of the worship and reverence he so desires. In short, Sir Enemy, your father is betrayed by the lust for perfection he seeks and refuses to see the truth because he thinks himself perfect. Only the Lord God is perfect, not his children."

"Then why seek perfection?" I asked quickly. "If we can never be perfect?"

"Who says we cannot be perfect, Sir Enemy? Perfection comes at a cost, which for most is the death of the mortal body. It is not the goal of perfection which is important, but its pursuit and the trials one must overcome that purifies the soul. Like metal in a crucible, the impurities will float to the top, ready to be skimmed off."

I blinked. An expert in metallurgy now? The Maid had more skills than I could account for. My head whirled. So much information and her description of my Father, in the dark places of my heart where truths are laid bare for the inward seeing eye to behold, was surprisingly accurate.

Father's pride was the stuff of legend, but like all good legends, it was based on solid fact. He could tolerate disobedience as long it furthered His cause, which was to throw down the Throne and remake Heaven to His liking, and thus remake the world. His hatred of the Lying God had no limit, no end point to say 'here and no farther' and the source of that hatred had grown from the humblest of seeds.

Us.

When the Lying God created Heaven and Earth, all was perfect, a thriving world filled with all manner of cunning and beautiful beasts for all higher beings to enjoy. The introduction of Man angered Father, but it was something He could live with because there lay within Man's simple flesh a spark of greatness that could be nurtured, coaxed into life. Father began to see the glory of Man toiling endlessly to reshape the world in honor of the Angels. Then the Lying God performed the one act that tore Heaven asunder.

He gave man a soul. With the gift of a soul, the Lying God gave Man a measure of his grace, thus elevating Man to be the equal of his first-born children, the angels. The gift of souls tore Heaven apart as angel fought angel and the streets of the Eternal City ran with divine blood.

Not an easy thing to put behind you and Father never had. Because of His great and terrible pride, He would never bend a knee to His creator and ask forgiveness. Instead, I knew He hatched myriad plans from His seat in Hell, plotting to the moans of the damned. His patience was such that if it took millennia, He would gain His vengeance, but at what cost? What form would that vengeance take? These thoughts kept me up late at night more than once. If I could not trust Father, then what was the point of ... well ... *everything*?

The centuries since my first death had been spent expanding the Family empire, becoming rich and powerful beyond my childhood imagination and there was little time for reflection because there was so much to *do*. But immortality wears thin, constant rebirth into the bodies of one's descendants invokes philosophical thoughts best not shared with my Father, the Family Patron. I feared that if I gave those thoughts voice, Father would become cross, and render me to my component humors.

My next words startled me. "I am necessary, mademoiselle. What is light without dark? Day without night. Without me, your god would have no meaning." Why was I trying to justify myself? Some small part of me was screaming.

"It is true that many things are defined by their opposites, Sir Enemy. I am the Messenger of the Lord and you are the Messenger of the Adversary, both of us at the opposite ends of the board, but there is still within you that which is kind and good. It is buried under the lies of the Adversary, but it still exists."

Throat clogged, I merely shook my head in negation, vision wavering. Then I felt two strong, calloused hands descend upon my shoulders. "I know I must die, Sir Enemy, and that is your doing, but know that I forgive you."

Lips softer than sighs brushed my cheek. I still feel them.

CHAPTER FIVE
HUNGARY, 1610

———— ～～ ————

"YOU CANNOT GO, FATHER," SAID MY son. As of last count I had fathered over four hundred, but Michael (trust me, as I convey this I see the irony), for some reason, proved to be a favorite because of his keen mind and absolute loyalty. Short, broad, with hugely muscular arms and a face carved from wood, he was my choice to lead the Family whilst I traveled.

The road, more a muddy trail winding through the Hungarian countryside, did not register upon my consciousness as I recalled the conversation a fortnight earlier.

"I can, and I will, Michael." My voice was diamond and the grudging look of acquiescence that passed over his face said more than words ever could. Good boy. Always listened to his father, unlike dozens of his brothers and sisters over the centuries.

He still gave it one last try, though. "Take William with you, at least. No one is better with a sword, which could come in handy where you are going."

I strode across the big room I used as an office and opened the double doors to the balcony. Far below and about a mile away lay a lake so crystalline pure that I could see the bottom from my vantage point atop the western tower.

As castles went, it was a modest affair considering the Family's vast wealth, but by Swiss standards it bordered on ostentatious. The Swiss were a strange people combining the unusual dichotomy of humility and pride, but for them it somehow worked. A tiny yet fierce country ripe with wealth and good taste, it was the quiet giant that lulled others into believing it was not worth conquering. Years upon years of political maneuvering and bribery saw to it that it was left alone to prosper, a perfect home for my Family.

"William is a good choice," I replied. "But I will travel alone."

Michael sputtered, but kept his peace. Good boy. I left to prepare my kit for travel.

Sadness dripped from my pores like sweat, but I kept the Family from seeing it lest they think me weak. Lately my spies reported grumblings from the head of the Family concerns in other countries regarding my complacency. They desired to foment unrest, warring with the prosperity brought about by peace. All I could say that the time was not yet right to dip the world into chaos, but kids will be kids and rebellion is often the byproduct of youth.

As for the sadness, that was brought about by Father.

I plucked at the white shirt peeking out from beneath my tan tunic and half-cape. Summers in Switzerland tended to have enough bite to bring apples to the cheeks. Although the air nipped, what chilled me was the dream two days ago, another Sending from Father. This time He dressed as a king upon a throne of ivory feathers that clacked with each tiny movement. I stood as a supplicant staring up at a visage too bright to comprehend.

"You have pleased Me, My son," He rumbled in a voice like the breaking of rocks. "My Family has grown strong. Now it is time to begin the second phase of My plan."

I jumped. Second phase? I did not know there was more than one. "My Father?"

"You have heard of the prophesy of Patmos written by John?"

Chills puckered my skin and I felt the blazing mark of Jeanne d'Arc's kiss upon my cheek, still fresh after two centuries. "Yes, Father, you informed me of it a few centuries ago."

Claiming that since the prophesy was written, the Lying God would expect his most rebellious Son not to proceed with the creation of the Redeemer, the one who would fight the foul Nazarene at some distant future. Father stated that He would not be manipulated in this manner and would proceed to do exactly what lay on paper. My mind fled back to the Maid and her assurances.

"And you, My son, will write down the new magics I have conceived for the Family's use, magics so potent as to render even the Words sterile."

"What magics, Father?" I asked in that dream while tossing and turning in my bed, startling my newest concubine, Helga.

"Blood Magic, My son." He told me the source of the magic. My stomach turned at the thought of sacrificing innocents to create runes of power of tremendous efficacy and just when I thought it couldn't become worse, that my soul could not possibly endure more staining, He told me of the enhanced breeding plan. For centuries under His guidance I took meticulous care for choosing breeding stock (women, of course) with the physical and mental attributes necessary to produce the perfect assassins. Intelligence, strength, speed and endurance were the traits most often looked for, while defects were not tolerated. Those who did not fit the rigid physical requirements found themselves on a ship to wherever the most profit could be found for slaves. Now, however, Father laid out a more incestuous design that not only placed a premium on optimum physical characteristics, but magical ones as well. He wanted a twelve Word magus with access to all the Terrible Words ensconced within the Silver, not just one or two. This perfect Family member, the Redeemer, would be immune to the debilitating effects of the Silver and that would unlock near unlimited power. To obtain such a thing, Father wanted His scions to implement those assassination skills taught at an early age upon their siblings to prove themselves worthy of consideration, proof of superiority through the assassination of their kin. Slavery was bad enough, but I followed Father's directives in that regard because, with slavery came life and with life came some joy, some hope.

Apparently joy and hope were not high upon Father's list of priorities. With the news of Blood Magic and the new direction for raising Sicarii young came another task, a person to be brought into the hard arms of the Family as prime breeding material.

I re-entered my office and saw Michael with his chin resting on his large fists. He looked perfect behind my desk and that brought me to a decision. I rubbed my cheek where the kiss still burned softly.

"Son," I said. "Since these missions do carry a small amount of danger, I am appointing you my heir. Fetch me a quill, paper and sealing wax." I toyed with the signet ring on my right index finger. Yes, time to put such things on paper to cement their meaning.

That garnered me a look. "You cannot die! How can I be an heir?"

"Just in case. The world is an uncertain place." I quickly detailed where I kept the Family History, which is now called the Codex. "It will be up to you to continue our mission as laid out by the Patron should I not return." In that history was laid out the details of Father's most recent directive, the plan and the workings of Blood Magic. I suppressed a shudder, realizing I trod a perilous road. My immortality usually garnered me some measure of safety, but Informing Michael of the possibility that the enemy might find a foil to it could lead to misbehavior by my descendants.

"And how can that be?"

"The agents of the Lying God are numerous and powerful. Even I cannot endure forever. Should I not return you will learn this lesson to your dismay."

RAIN BEGAN AGAIN, DRIBBLING DOWN MY waxed greatcoat and pouring off the brim of my broad hat. The horse's hooves made sordid squelching noises in the mud and I looked up to see the Little Carpathian Mountains rise before me, a castle, drear and dark, at the peak of one of the foothills. In the flatland below lay a small village as dreary as the looming castle, half flooded with runoff. I gave the reins a flick and the tired old mare snorted but picked up the pace.

The horse and I plodded into the small village without fanfare because there was no one to notice. The rain was keeping everyone indoors, not that it did much good considering the state of most of the thatched roofs. If this place ever saw any prosperity it had long since departed along with most of the paint and pride, but it still boasted an inn and it was there I set my sights.

Inside the common room smelled of rot and the thick odor of unwashed bodies, of which there were quite a few, men who ranged from grossly fat to gaunt, all with the same near hopeless/helpless stare of those long abused. A fat barman gave me a sour look just before I removed my hat and placed it on the bar. I recognized hate when I saw it.

"We don't serve Turks here. Begone, heathen." One meaty fist grabbed a stout oak truncheon from beneath the bar. From behind came a soft rustling.

With every rebirth my features remained the same as my original entrance into this world, so it was no surprise to be considered an Ottoman.

I flung my coat the floor, revealing the sword at my side and the brace of pistols at my hips, and reached over the bar grabbing the barman's throat with one hand and the truncheon with the other. "As a son of Greece," I said. "Being called a Turk is a deadly insult." My eyes became hard and pitiless. "One for which you will apologize or die." I raised my voice. "If you two don't sit down *right now*, I will give you each an extra mouth to breathe through." The sound of a pair of behinds hitting benches reassured me.

"My apologies," gabbled the barman when I gave him air enough to speak. "I should have asked your provenance. Begging your pardon and all." He sagged, dropping the truncheon when I let him go.

"There," I beamed. "Now we are friends." My coat was back on and my weapons hidden. A silver coin clattered to the bar. "Food, ale and a room. Preferably without fleas."

That silver disappeared as if it was made of smoke. The barman gave me a gap-toothed grin through the rotted remains of his teeth. All sins forgiven. There was a lesson in there somewhere, I thought. "Right away, Sir Greek." A large leather jack of ale appeared in front of my elbow.

"My name is Mavros Polodides," I declared loudly facing the men of the village. "Mercenary and gentleman and I am here to join the service of György Thurzó, who I believe is standing in for the late, great warrior Ferenc Nádasdy, peace be upon his soul. I hear he is need of good men and I am seeking an honest master."

All eyes suddenly avoided mine and an ominous quiet descended.

"What?" By my Father the beer was awful. It tasted of road sludge and failure. I resisted the urge to spit it out and manfully endured another sip.

One man, possibly the bravest of the bunch, stood. He was one of the rail-thin ones with sunken, sallow cheeks indicating an absence of teeth. With a deferential dip of the head he said, "Begging your pardon, Sir Mercenary, but György Thurzó is here to arrest our Countess Elisabeta Bathory on the crimes of murder most foul."

Of course. The woman Father sent me to bring into the Sicarii fold.

"Murder?" I mused, pulling at my lower lip in false consternation. "Murder is sport for the nobility. Why, I can hardly count all the poisonings and backstabbings there are so many. What makes the Countess special."

That was the limit of the man's courage. He sat down and placed his face into his leathern jack of ale. From behind the barman cleared his throat.

"Yes?"

"You see," he began with much hemming and hawing. "Young women all around these parts have been going into the castle. The Countess hires them, you see. Hundreds over the years to be chambermaids and ladies' maids and scullery maids and the like, you see. All going in, but none ever come out. Their menfolk, husbands, intendeds, mothers and such, never see them again … all gone as if they never existed." His eyes grew wet. "My own daughter got herself a job nigh ten years back and I ain't never seen her again. She never came out of the castle. Don't you understand?" Tears began to grease his fat cheeks. "I think the Countess *eats* them!"

An awful silence beat at my ears and the men continued to avoid my gaze.

"So György Thurzó will bring her to justice, then." I gave them a huge smile. "That is good. Your village and all those around will be free. This is good news, yes?"

The greasy-faced barman replied, "It would be, but the Countess has hired her own mercenaries and they, along with those loyal to her, have locked up the castle tight. György Thurzó will have to invest in a siege to pry her out. She has enough men that not even the King can reach her. The castle was designed to be impregnable. Justice will not be done."

Well, that was a sticky situation and one that called for a clever assassin. Good thing I happened to know of one wearing my shoes.

"You men should not worry," I said with a smile. "With Mavros at György Thurzó's side I am sure that the Countess will meet her fate." I drained the jack despite the brews awful taste.

No one joined me. This was one downtrodden lot who could would not recognize hope if it slapped them in the face. I glowered at them. "Come now, men, how many soldiers can she possibly have? They will run out of food eventually."

Mumbles and grumbles. Finally, one man in the back with the wide shoulders of a blacksmith said, "The Countess has at least two hundred veterans of the war with the Ottomans in her castle, not to mention foodstuffs galore. The castle is fed by a spring as well. They could wait in there until judgement day."

Interesting and even more interesting. It seemed as if the Countess was holed up like a rat within a wall. Once again, there was Sicarii in my shoes who had vast experience at the art of rat-catching. That is, if one substituted the word Roman for rat.

Castle Csejte, on its high hill backdropped by the Little Carpathians, boasted a single tower with sturdy walls forming a rough triangle. Smaller buildings huddled close to the tower, possibly storage or housing for the castellan and other well-placed Bathory servants. Not a large castle and grounds but situated so that it had a clear view of the only road that wound up the hill. Not a tree or shrub could be seen, no place for cover. From the center of town, I could see the vague humps of helmets sticking up from the walls. Sentries armed with crossbows, no doubt, and possibly rifles, although it would be hard to keep powder dry in the damnably wet weather. Just as the cloud hidden sun kissed the horizon, it began to snow, and I hoped it would grow heavier and heavier, hindering the sentries on the wall.

"See," said the barman as I re-entered the inn. Most of the men still sat mulling into their jacks of ale, although a few offered slight smiles. I had spent the better part of a silver buying rounds for all present and they were happy enough to see how far my generosity extended. It also set more tongues wagging and I learned that over the years the Countess preyed without remorse or pity, virtually laying waste to the female population for at least three days ride all around. The only women that remained were those who were too old or too canny to venture toward the castle.

"If you want to see György Thurzó, Sir Mercenary," said the blacksmith around his jack. "Then you'll find his camp a mile west of here. Buy me another two rounds and I'll take you myself." This brought a chorus of protests from those who had not thought of that, but they shut up as the blacksmith glared. "He hired me to replace some shoes for his horses what threw their old ones."

The last thing I needed was to see the Palatine of Hungary sent by King Matthias II. I had my information and I had my destination. What I needed was the cover of night and a decent meal. Looking around the inn I ventured that one out of two would have to do.

CHAPTER SIX
THE CASTLE

———⌇———

THE HUMAN EYE RESPONDS TO MOTION. When we hunt, we look for movement, a breaking of the environmental pattern. That is not to say that we cannot see what is motionless, it just tends to be a bit harder, especially at night.

A half-mile uphill would normally seem a lazy stroll, perhaps a slight burning in the thighs, but nothing strenuous unless one wanted to make a run of it.

I had scared the barman (who was also the innkeeper) white with my sword and pistols that I felt comfortable enough leaving most of my possessions in my little room with only the fleas to keep them company. That did not prevent me from wedging the door shut and exiting the window. No need to advertise my absence.

The snow fell harder, thicker, masking my presence somewhat from the castle guards, but I kept my movements even, steady, avoiding the road entirely for the straight route over dead grass and around tree stumps.

Pretty soon the snow became thick enough that I abandoned my slow, steady pace for a brisk trot, the chill air breezing through my thin clothes. Loose black trousers, shirt and soft, kidskin boots. A long black scarf was wound round my head and across my face so only my eyes showed, the image of a man up to no good.

In the days before firearms I would have worn armor, but now traveled without. A brace of pistols lay strapped under my shirt along with my powder horn to keep dry. Nothing more embarrassing than to have a man at your mercy and your hand-cannon misfires. For such an occasion I also carried a few throwing knifes, a garrote, a short sword strapped to my thigh and a lead filled kosh when I wanted to subdue, but not kill. There were a few more small items secreted about my person, not so much to slow me down, but enough to make swimming problematic.

Weapons were all good to have, but the human body, along with the disciplined mind directing it, is far deadlier than any gun, sword or knife.

A little over a century ago Father instructed me to send a brace of my best sons (or grandsons, great-grandsons, etc.) to the lands of the far east, the place of the Mongols and Chinese, so send them I did, although curiosity almost compelled me to go. They would be guided by dreams and portents to the desired place and the extent of their mission. Nearly a year later they returned, hardened and lean to the point of gauntness, with a man in tow.

White haired despite having less than two score years under his belt, the man from China called himself Grandfather Lok and spoke fluent Romansh, having learned from his two Sicarii companions during the long trek home. Reed thin, he radiated vibrancy and power, yet remained deferential and mild mannered. It took me less than a minute to realize that he was the possibly the most dangerous man I had ever met and the reason why Father brought him to us.

Unarmed combat. We Sicarii could kill with virtually any weapon, in fact I had once disemboweled a Roman *legatus* with wooden spoon, but the art of fighting unarmed was left to wrestling around on the floor until one opponent managed to break the neck of the other. Grandfather Lok's job was to teach the Family the way of unarmed combat.

For the better part of a year I studied under Grandfather Lok's disapproving eye until he decreed that I was little better than execrable at *Quan Fa,* the name giving to this martial art. During that time, I learned his tongue, as Father mandated, and the reason why Grandfather Lok so willingly departed his native China for what he termed as the 'barbarian west'.

A former monk, Grandfather Lok had an obsession, perhaps compulsion, for tall women. They … disturbed him and any that topped his own middling height had him itching so fiercely with lust and … other dark desires that he became quite unmanageable to the point of mania. This made him quite amenable to the thought of departing his native land. A dream featuring the ruler of the Ten Hells, Dìzàng, urged him to trust the two round-eyed barbarians that would soon come his way.

Father, it seemed, was not without a sense of humor. Manipulation as well … I believed that Grandfather Lok might not have felt the itch of his dark desires so intently had not Father stoked their flames somewhat.

Grandfather Lok was long dead, but his legacy remained deep in the muscles and bones of the Sicarii. Killers whose bodies were weapons enough.

Thicker and thicker, the snow almost totally obscured the castle. I picked up the pace, legs pumping, breathing in through my mouth, out through my nose, eyes never straying from my purpose. Within a few minutes I came upon the outer wall so suddenly I skidded to a stop a scant few inches from breaking my nose against rough stone.

So up I went.

Like most backwater castles, the defensive wall had plenty of nooks and crannies for an enterprising rock climber to ascend. No limestone sheeting to prevent what I dared, no chinking or smoothing, the inhabitants obviously felt secure upon their hill, safe with an easy killing field eyed by archers and sharpshooters. It spoke not only to a certain amount of frugality, but to arrogance as well. People living on top of their hills rely far too heavily upon nature's defenses rather than their own.

Foot by foot I climbed, well hidden by snowfall yet not wanting to risk any sound that might alert a passing guard. At this point, some twenty feet above stony soil, I was easy pickings for a man with a good eye and steady hands.

At the top I pulled myself over, keeping low and slow, hiding in any available shadow. To my right, the tower with its narrow windows streamed light onto the falling snow. To the left some sixty feet away, stood a guardhouse built along one of the points of the triangle above a steep drop off. Down below in the giant courtyard were dozens upon dozens of tents, many lit from within with small fires along the walkways between. Mercenaries and levies, no doubt, summoned by the Countess to withstand a siege. She had enough men to give the Hungarian king pause.

Footsteps. Careless, loud and unhurried. I made myself one with the darkness and waited. A minute later a guardsman in rusting chain and heavy boots came crunching my way through the snow atop the wall, a small lantern in hand. Before the light could reveal my location, I struck, taking him to the ground, one hand clamped to his mouth, the other around the knife he felt at his throat.

"Quiet, or you are dead," I hissed into his eyes. "Nod if you understand."

He understood.

"Good. Where is the countess?" I removed my hand.

Fear scrunched his face until he looked somewhat less than human. "T-top of the tower."

I smiled. "Thank you." And thrust with the dagger up under his jaw, through his soft palate and into his brain. He died quickly, cleanly. I had no ill will toward the guard, after all he was just a hired hand, but I could not let him live and taking prisoners was out of the question.

"Sorry, my good fellow," I muttered, rolling his body off the wall and onto the hill below.

To the right then. There I encountered one more guard, but quickly dispatched him as well without even a *clink* of chain to give me away. He joined his fellow at the bottom of the wall.

From my vantage point, I studied the courtyard. Not well lit, merely a few torches sputtering amidst the snowfall. Plenty of shadows in which to hide.

The tower was accessed through a single door at courtyard level. A length of thin rope wrapped around my waist allowed me to descend easily and without mishap. There were no guards, the men were tucked quietly away inside their tents and the guardhouse. Who would be foolish enough to assail the castle at night?

Not for the last time I felt the familiar burning of Jeanne's kiss on my cheek and for a moment it nearly robbed me of much needed concentration for my sneakery. I crouched at the base of the tower and placed a hand to the burning spot, calming my nerves.

Security being as lax as it was, I strolled right on into the tower without raising a hue and cry. Inside the roughly triangular tower there were four men in somewhat rusty chain hauberks squatting around the hearth in on corner, warming their hands against the chill that permeated the air. A fifth was drinking from a leather jack, his buttocks firmly planted at the rough-hewn table that dominated the center of the room. He looked up in surprise, his iron cap at his elbow, joining the chain mail that puddled there.

"Here!" he belched through a black mustache that obviously doubled as a repository for leftover food. "Whatcher doing here, and in that getup? What areya supposed to be?"

I stretched as I walked calmly forward as if I belonged. "Oh, what a foul cold night it is. Snowing like a right bastard." My Hungarian was flawless, one of the benefits of immortality.

The other four men did not bother to look, too intent on warming their hands.

"That it is, brother," the fifth soldier settled back down on his stool, blithely unconcerned about a strange man wrapped head-to-toe in black clothes barging in during the middle of the night. We were all fellow soldiers here, were we not? "Take off that getup and join the fire. Are you one of the mercenaries?"

"Yah." I made as if to remove my headwrap.

"Ah. Where you from? Seen much action?"

A few steps forward, hands around my neck to secreted sheaths, filling fingers with weapons. If the soldier had been sober, this might be a different tale, but long hours, boredom and drink robbed him of necessary paranoia. Casually, I stabbed him through the eye before he could take in the color of the skin around my eyes and let his suddenly limp form slump against the table.

No more time.

Whirling like the dervish of legend, the two long needles, both nine inches, tapering to fine points, buried themselves into throats. Spinning, I tore one out in a spray of blood and rammed it through the temple of the fourth guard where it lodged in his skull. Letting go, I grabbed the fifth guard by the chin and the back of his head and twisted violently. His neck snapped so loud that I near mistook it for a gunshot. His eyes rolled until only the whites showed. He fell at my feet and I stood there, calmly assessing the situation. It took all of three seconds to kill the five guards. I silently thanked Father for their indolence and proceeded to wedge the door shut against any who might have heard the snapping of bones. For a moment I stood there, panting not with effort but with the anticipation of more violence. Contrary to popular belief, I do not revel in death, although I deal it well.

Five dead below and an unknown number above. Lax security for a countess who so heavily transgressed against her people.

Simple stairs with no bannister led up to a door. No shouts, so the death of the five soldiers had been quiet enough.

The door was unlocked, and I walked through with the same nonchalance I exhibited entering the tower and was greeted similarly by a scarred soldier standing at the foot of the next set of stairs.

For the briefest moment I was distracted by the scars. Only the skin of his face was visible, the rest hidden behind a well maintained chain hauberk and coif shining with oil, but what showed was enough. Skin like melted wax, pink and raw-looking, slid over his face, pulling at his eyes, making a stub of his nose. Of his lips ... well, there were none, only a hole backed by blackened teeth. Pitiless blue eyes bored into mine and we held that moment for what seemed an eternity.

Flashing steel caught out of the corner of my eye and it was only centuries of finely honed reflexes that saved me from decapitation as I ducked. Razor-sharp death swept overhead, and I thrust out with one arm, the knife I had palmed flying through the air hard enough to imbed up to the hilt into the eye of my assailant. He died without a scream, streaming blood and fluid from the ruined socket

Oddly, the scarred man did not make a sound, merely drawing a wicked looking hand axe with a small straight spike on the end and a curved spike opposite the blade for hooking through chain. He spun the weapon his hand as if it weighed nothing, his fingers nimble and then he grinned.

There are things in this world that can, in the words of today's youth, make you lose your shit. The touch of one's first love, a first kill, finally confronting mortality, to name a few. That smile left them in the dust. It caused my scrotum to tighten and my guts to squirm. It was the smile of a man comfortable, more than comfortable, of killing thousands of people regardless of age, race or gender. I would not have been surprised if that axe seen the throats and skulls of entire villages.

I nodded. Here stood a dangerous man, a man worthy of respect if only for the skill he displayed. I drew a brace of fighting knives and he nodded in return.

No words, just action. We flashed toward each other, blurring and twirling. The axe missed my nose by a fraction and I thought the soldier overbalanced in his heavy hauberk, but the wicked spike on the back end came around and tore a gash through my right arm in a gush of white-hot pain.

First blood.

Cursing would be a waste of breath. I flashed the knife in my right hand toward his throat while striking out with my left foot. The scarred man danced back, avoiding both attacks with ease. I pressed, dancing in with knives spinning, trying for a vulnerable spot but my opponent put his hauberk to good use, placing chainmail where needed to repel edges while the axe appeared as if by magic to deflect needle tips.

Again, we joined to the sound of clashing metal. I deflected a swipe that rang like a bell and numbed my left hand. The dagger went flying along with a small section of skin. I took a few steps back, but the scarred man followed, sure of his advantage, but I still had more weapons. The sword at my thigh cleared the sheath and swept outward, drawing a line of red across scar tissue along a cheek, causing him to retreat, keeping those cold eyes on me.

Damn, he was good.

I pressed what I thought was my advantage, swinging and stabbing, trying to turn his insides into his outsides. Every attack by my short sword met hand axe, every knife thrust by chain armor. Spinning, the sword arced toward exposed flesh and the axe was there, but so was my foot, which hammered hard into my opponent's thigh. For a moment he wobbled, and I had him, he was mine. The sword licked out, a jab ready to tear through chain, victory fueling the thrust.

Pain, a cold stab in my gut as the tip of the sword slid into his and we both staggered back bleeding. We both took a moment to assess. The straight spike of his axe had punctured my gut while my sword pierced his. Both of us wounded, not badly, but bad enough.

"Damn," I grunted. "You are good."

He nodded and grunted in return.

"Cannot talk?"

A nod.

Mute, then. The issue of him raising a hue and cry seemed solved. My gut hurt. The blood was not spurting, but there was plenty of it. I noticed his tabard consisted of a plain gray piece of cloth, not colored or the heraldric green dragon curled upon a field of red which was the Bathory coat of arms. A mercenary then ... hopefully. "How about I pay you to come work for me and we can put this unfortunate event behind us? I have no desire to be killed and no desire to kill you."

He cocked his head to the side, eyes narrowing. With his non-weapon hand, he rubbed his thumb and forefinger together and I felt a surge of hope. Money, he was asking how much the pay would be. While my wound was not fatal (only an inch of spike at penetrated, but it hurt something terrible) I had been around for a good long while and really did not want to tumble with this man again. My gut shuddered in pain and another dribble of blood soaked into my clothes. Another reason to wear black ... it hides blood beautifully.

"You work for my Family and you will want for nothing." I paused to let that sink in, then finished, "Ever."

Slowly, almost glacially, the hand axe lowered until it was held loosely at his side and I carefully sheathed my knife and sword. Raising a finger, he bade me to stay and I stayed, curious as to what he was about. This gave me enough time to see that this room differed from the one below as that one differed from the courtyard. Rough stone walls were hidden behind tapestries depicting hunting scenes and a large bed lay under one of them. Furs of all color lay scattered about, at least a dozen different animals hiding the cold floor. Instead of the hearth, there were a pair of braziers providing a pleasant warmth, although the air was close with smoke.

It was opulent, but not overly so. I stopped my examination when the scarred warrior returned from a small writing desk with a fragment of parchment and quill and ink in hand.

'I can want a lot. How much gold and what must I do?'

Ah, a literate brute. Better and better. "I have more money than you can dream of, my good man. As for the doing, I think we can find something for you. Perhaps as the bodyguard for my Family against a particular thorn in my side."

'Which is?' he scribbled with the quill on another scrap of parchment.

How much to divulge? The answer could set us to fighting again, if he was a follower if the Lying God. I stroked my lower lip thoughtfully and decided to take a chance. After all, it seemed a safe bet considering the woman he defended. "The Knights Templar." Most thought them disbanded by Pope Clement in 1308, but I knew the truth. They still fought their battles against the Sicarii and were harder to kill than cockroaches.

He grinned, a twisting of scar tissue. I raised an eyebrow and he pointed to his mouth, opening wide and showing me the stub of his tongue.

I considered the nub of flesh. "The Templars did that?" If so, Father provided me with a most puissant ally, one who would have no problem tweaking the Knight's collective noses.

A nod.

"Why?"

Scribble, scribble. 'I practiced magic. Could cause pain with a word.'

The world tilted under my feet as I absorbed that statement. A magus, a user of the Word of Pain. Of all the punishments to inflict upon a magus, the removal of the tongue was the worst. Most would kill themselves after such mortification. The fact that he lived and thrived told me much about his fortitude and determination.

"If you join me, not only will I pay you an obscene amount of money, but you will have ample opportunity to kill as many Templars as you can stomach."

That got him. *Scribble, scribble.* 'What do you want me to do?'

"Let me pass. I need to see the Countess and you will make that happen. When I am done, you and I will exit this castle and head to Switzerland where I live. There you will be made part of my Family," I paused. "What is your name? It seems rather rude not to inquire."

Scribble, scribble. 'Bolivar.'

"Bolivar, then. You stay here. I'll be back."

Most would wonder why I would so willingly trust a treacherous lout like Bolivar. The truth is I did not, not one whit. However, I have developed over the long years an ability to read the faces and eyes of those I dealt with, even one as scarred as Bolivar. I knew that while his loyalty was as thin as tissue, I could count on his greed. It was in his best interest to aid me, pure and simple. I could always rely on such motivations and knew how to manipulate such things.

He pointed toward the ceiling three or four times making wild googly eyes. I shook my head and he scribbled some more. 'Dangerous.'

Of course. I nodded and headed toward the stairs, holding my stomach. Before I made it up two steps another scrap of paper was thrust in my face.

'Good Luck.'

Chapter Seven
Countess Me Out

⸺⟨∾⟩⸺

T HE NEXT LEVEL UP TURNED OUT to be dark as a miser's heart. The chill
in this room prickled my skin and I took a few moments for my eyes
to adjust. When they did I noticed a faint line of light forming a rectangle
far above. A door, I supposed. Keeping my movements careful so as not to
stumble in the dark, I started to climb the next set of stairs.

"I have been waiting for you." The voice came from nowhere, everywhere.
Female, sultry, filled with the promise of sexual intimacy and more, throaty
and low.

Not answering would have been rude. "Who are you?" I asked the air as
I ascended.

"You know who."

Of course, I did. "The Countess Bathory."

"Yes."

"Come up. I won't bite."

I was not sure of that, but I still climbed those stairs. Call me what you
will, but I possess bravery and my own sense of honor. I gave my word to
my children that I would go to Hungary to seek the Countess Bathory for
the Patron, my Father, and there was nothing that could dissuade me from
the task.

"Come, you are welcome here."

Somehow that was scarier than any threat and I felt a shiver from balls
to the base of my neck.

At the top I opened the door, the latch moving soundlessly. As the oak
moved, a pungent wave hit my nose, a familiar coppery smell I knew better
than the face of my first born. Blood. A *lot* of blood.

The room was dimly lit, bare blue flames dancing on the thin stubs of wicks, the lanterns set in niches at shoulder height. Tapestries hung from the ceiling, dividing the room and adding menacing shadows. So much blood smell caused my stomach to churn and for a moment I became dizzy, but I mustered myself and stepped further into the room.

There is a sense, a *feeling*, when magic is performed. Elemental, Botanical, Word, all the different practices and, although I cannot perform it, I can feel when it is utilized. That same feeling skittered across my skin like a multitude of ants and the hair at the nape of my neck stood on end. I did not know what uncanny forces swirled around me, I only knew someone practiced.

"Come further, Oh Great One," came the alluring voice from beyond the tapestries.

Two more steps and my skin itched abominably.

Another two and I was at a tapestry displaying a bacchanal, the women voluptuous, the men far exaggerated. I lifted my hand to move the scene aside when suddenly I understood the reason for ants-across-the-skin feeling.

The room was larger on the inside than the towers dimensions could account for.

This was magic on a scale I had never heard of before and it left me breathless. As my eyes adjusted to the dim light, I saw that the walls were covered in runes, strange glyphs a foot in diameter, hundreds of them. Black lettering that almost obscured the dull gray of the stone beneath.

"Hurry, please, my bath will cool far too soon."

Her bath? I wanted to scrub my skin until it bled just to negate the skittering feeling of magic and she complained about her bath? However, it seemed she expected me, so I doubted the dangers deeper in were physical in nature. I turned back to the tapestry and moved it aside. Jeanne's kiss raised fire on my cheek.

What hit my eyes nearly tore my jaded perception of life to shreds.

Sixteen women, girls actually, most just beginning to see the downy fuzz between their thighs, hung by their ankles from the ceiling far above (here in the center of the room, the ceiling seemed to soar to a height impossible to account for from the outside), newly made mouths on their throats still dripping red. Directly beneath these girls lay a large tub sunk directly into the floor, a repository for the blood they had spilled.

Standing under the dripping, arms caressing the red into the skin all over her body, stood a woman clothed only the falling fluid.

Immediately I felt a sense of arousal, despite the grisly scenery. Elizabeth Bathory, from her long, dark hair to her toes, radiated lush sexuality. From firm, ripe breasts to the blood-covered patch between her legs, her body begged to be kissed, fondled, stroked and licked. My eyes could not stop feasting upon the glory of this slender, yet voluptuous woman who showed no evidence of either middle age or the birth of two children. In fact, if someone were to ask, I would have pegged her age to be no more than twenty, if that.

The part of my body least given to thought urged me to take her right there and then despite the thick, almost visible smell of blood. Take her, ravish her, possess every beautiful inch of her and by the look in her liquid brown eyes she wanted that as well. Rubbing red onto her nipples she beckoned, smiling through blood and the pain and despair that hung in the air like a cloud and I dropped the knife from my hand with a harsh clatter, ready to lose myself in her arms. There was the pulse thunder in my ears and heat, sweet heat, in my loins that near drove away all thought, all reason because something primal rose up, rearing its ruddy head behind my eyes, ready to take all control and use my body for baser purposes.

It was the kiss that saved me.

As my booted foot made ready to step into gallons of blood, the kiss burned my cheek with such a frightening intensity that I thought I heard flesh sizzle and the grinding pain of it shook me out of my torpor. Just in time to catch a glint of metal between the Countess' fingers.

A razor, sharp and slick, no doubt the one she used to slice the throats above. I shook my head and took a step backward, then another until my back touched a tapestry.

Elizabeth's face formed a moue. "Aw, lover, why do you flee? Am I not desirable?"

I was proud that my voice did not emerge as a squeak. "You are, but that blade is not."

A flash of annoyance, gone as quickly as it formed. "Pay no attention. I merely judge your merit."

"Meritorious enough, Countess." I made connections I should have ten minutes ago. "You told Bolivar to let me pass."

"Yes, should you show adequate respect. It is obvious you did." She pinched her nipples and moaned.

I bit my lower lip until it bled, the sharpness of my teeth keeping my mind on task. "You said you were waiting for me, that I was welcome."

"I was, and you are."

Pointing toward the razor I said, "Strange way to show welcome." A gesture to the bodies hung above. "Unless this is how you welcome people."

Laughter like sex given sound caressed my ears. "Bathing in the blood of the virtuous and young keeps me youthful. Your Father informed me of your arrival, said I should test your mettle since it has been several centuries since you last used your Sicarii skills."

Anger heated my cheeks, but I kept the emotion at Father's betrayal at bay. "I was told to bring you to the Family home, to make you ours." I rubbed my burning cheek. "Why?"

"Because of my magic."

"Your magic."

"Blood Magic."

Puzzle pieces clicked together in my mind and I let out a great breath. Of course. Father said Blood Magic would be the next component in the Family arsenal, but he refrained from the mechanics. Countess Elizabeth Bathroy must have stumbled onto the secret and now Father wanted it brought into the Family. I glanced at the runes and realized they were drawn in blood, blackened with time, clotted with foul power. Hundreds of runes ... thousands. So much blood, so much magic. Magic enough to render the inside of the room larger than the outside. The power staggered me, and I felt a momentary sickness, as if some limit to my endurance had been reached, or a line not seen crossed.

"How?" was all I could ask.

Elizabeth smiled prettily, wicked and charming. "Years of practice. The inspiration came from a scroll brought back from the Ottoman Empire by my late husband Farenc. This scroll, painstakingly translated over the course of several years, yielded the first bitter seeds of Blood Magic." Her sultry voice became dreamy. "I knew I had found the secret of everlasting life and the start of an entire discipline of magic long since forgotten. Armed with this knowledge, I began to experiment.

"At first my efforts were in vain." Bathory began to slowly pace in a circle, sluggish ripples following her footsteps. Every now and then she would dip her cupped hands into the blood and rub it on her skin in sick and sensual display. "But soon I discovered that it was the blood of virgins and the young that offered real results. My first shower of blood took years from my face, sagging lines disappeared from my body and my breasts, droopy from childbirth, became full again." She fondled the objects of discussion.

"Many had to die for me to winkle out further secrets. Those first few runes in the scroll were the templates for others to come, the ones that created this room, the ones that allowed me to cast spells on my soldiers, on my husband. Thus ensorcelled, I kept secret my efforts for many years though I depleted my lands of the young and virtuous."

"Your spells were not enough, I see." My mouth tasted of dust and ash and my cheek blazed.

For the first time her perfect face formed a frown. "No. It was not. I prayed to your Father to send me aid and He came to me in a dream and told me that if I gave His descendants the secret of Blood Magic, He would gather me into the bosom of His Family, the Sicarii, His righteous hand in this world."

Madness gleamed in her eyes and I suppressed a shudder. Insanity like that would be harmful rather than beneficial and I had no doubt that she would become worse as time wore on, not to mention the demand for sacrifices to keep her young. Such things could tear apart my currently stable Family.

"You have this secret?" I asked.

Elizabeth pointed, and I saw an ornate writing desk against the far wall beneath a particularly large rune that reminded me of Golgotha in its broad shape. On the desk lay a small book, barely the length of my hand and almost as wide and maybe a half-inch thick. Inside were painstaking drawings of the various runes I saw splattered on the wall along with their effects written in a small, tidy hand. Toward the end of the book were descriptions of the kinds of blood needed to power the spells. Like my Father had told me and as the Countess noted in her precise handwriting, the blood of infants proved the most efficacious.

"Take me," the Countess crooned, rubbing her skin. "Take me to your home. Fulfill the promise of Lucifer. Make me Sicarii."

I touched my cheek. It felt hot.

"Take me."

Would I? Could I?

"Come, first son of Lucifer. I bind you to your Father's dark promise."

My Father's promise. I felt sick. His promise, not mine, but I was at least honor bound to do *something*. Heart heavy, I tucked the book in my shirt and faced the wall of runes, their crusted black lines holding no answers to the anguish in my heart.

"But know that I forgive you."

Why did Jeanne d'Arc's words still haunt me near two centuries later? I had lived several lifetimes since then and in each body, I felt her kiss upon my cheek. Why did I feel such remorse and why was I doubting my Father?

The book was a large weight in my shirt and I realized that answered my question. For centuries I carried out Father's whims, killing those that I believed needed killing to further the Family cause, but what could justify the death of infants? Sleep sand gritted under my fingertips as I rubbed my eyes. So tired, a malaise not of magic but of the spirit.

"Jeanne," I whispered, surprising myself. "Give me a sign. Tell me what ails my soul?"

I expected no response. How could I have? The Maid's ashes lay scattered across the French countryside along with heat blasted bits of bone. She resided beyond the veil of life and was never coming back, no matter how hard I wished.

When the words did come, it near unmanned me. *"But know that I forgive you."*

I jumped, startled. They sounded as if whispered in my ear. "Did you hear that?" I demanded of the nude countess.

"Hear what?"

Her stare still brightened the room with her insanity and I turned away. "Nothing."

"Jeanne," I whispered again, afraid. "Is it you?"

"Who are you talking to?" the Countess asked. "Do you pray to your Father?"

Pray to him? What a thought. It never occurred to pray to Father simply because of the familiarity we shared through dreams. He appeared superior in every way, He showed me a modicum of respect and, if not affection at least a kinder sort of regard than paid to others.

"I do not raise my voice in prayer, Countess. It has been uncounted years since I last gave voice to one."

"Then who do you talk to?"

But know that I forgive you" My cheek blazed as the words hung hard in my mind and I stumbled, catching myself at the last moment. When I rose, my hand caressed my cheek and I knew what I wanted to do. What I felt I must do.

Suddenly feeling lighter, my shoulders free of the weight of my conscience, I straightened and faced the Countess, feeling so much better than I had in a long, long time. "Goodbye, Elizabeth Bathory," I said gravely, gazing into her madness rattled eyes. "I hope you find some mercy in this life because I do not think there is any waiting in the next."

For the first time since I arrived she looked startled, and a little afraid. "What? What do you mean? You must take me to your home! It was promised!"

I put my back to the madwoman and exited the room. "His promise, my lady, not mine." The door shut on her shrieks of anger and dismay.

When I reached Bolivar, it was to find him sans hauberk and I saw that his finely muscled torso was almost as scarred as his face, flesh like melted wax covering his hard muscles. A large bandage had been wrapped around his midsection, a tiny blot of blood marring the gray cloth above his navel. He raised an eyebrow as I closed the door on a dim cry from above and was rewarded with its absence. Apparently, the magic in that room prevented her screams from piercing far through stone.

"The Countess will not be joining us," I remarked drily. "Pack what is needed, we will be leaving shortly. Are there any bandages left?" Seeing his midsection reminded me that mine needed tending. A wad of soft cloth flew my way and I caught it absently. "Does it bother you that she will not accompany us?"

An emphatic shake of the head. Elizabeth's madness held no fascination for him. Good, this would make things much easier.

When I was done with my ministrations and had once again donned my clothes, I pulled my sword. Bolivar drew his wicked hand axe. "We kill as many as possible, then open the gate and make our way to the village. I have a horse at the inn. Do you have one here?"

A nod.

"Good. This will not be easy."

He shrugged.

I nodded. "Let's go home.

CHAPTER EIGHT
CONSEQUENCES

———

"**Y**OU HAVE DISOBEYED ME." Father's dream voice hammered into my skull, shooting pain to the base of my neck.

Bolivar and I had returned home to no fanfare. The Sicarii did not believe in it, however he was greeted with deference and respect and given a room in our castle fit for one of royal blood. His scars drew no special attention, we all had marks of strife upon our bodies and I immediately put him to work teaching our young how to wield those weapons with which he was most proficient. It turned out to be quite a few, up to and including a bladed whip.

The small book of runes I destroyed after transferring its contents to the Family history and noting my interaction with the Countess. I made no mention of breaking Father's vow, only keeping to the bare bones of the tale.

As for Castle Csejte and its inhabitants, we killed very few, only enough to sow confusion, then we stampeded the horses through the front gate, after opening it for György Thurzó and his men. It seemed I was not the only one who considered a night time raid under cover of a snowstorm, merely the first to do so. Within an hour the castle was his and I, along with Bolivar, were catching what sleep we could in that smelly village inn.

"Pay attention!" The roar shook the dream world and almost split my skull apart. Gone was Father the beautiful, yet mysterious, figure. What remained was a dark presence that could not be defined, but the overwhelming sense of menace and anger proved definition enough.

In that dream place I stood, the only occupant of a sere plain of dried, cracked mud and sterile wind. No features dotted the horizon, only a sense of overwhelming sameness and desiccation, as if the entire world consisted of flat, fractured earth. It came to me that I stood there naked, but I paid no mind to my lack of clothing because the presence that filled the sky, that dark shape that had no definition, took all of my attention.

"I am Father. And I am aware I have disobeyed You."

Father's honeyed shit voice flowed down to me, insubstantial yet thick and gelid. "Why do you disobey Me, My son? You have been an exemplary offspring, yet you break a promise I made to the Countess Bathory and My word is never to be broken."

"Her madness would have destroyed the Sicarii, or at least brought unwanted scrutiny. Better she meets a hangman than harm the Family."

"THAT IS NOT FOR YOU TO DECIDE!"

How can a dream reflect so much pain? Barbed hooks shredded my skin from the inside out, tearing and splintering bone, popping my eyes like cherries beneath a boot. My blood boiled, steaming into the air and a fist made of molten iron squeezed my brain, vaporizing tissue while my organs were plucked by parasites with needle teeth. A razor slowly slid through my penis and testicles, carving them in to tiny chunks and my tongue stretched out of my mouth, longer and longer until it tore at the base and I began to drown on scalding blood. No breath remained in my lungs for I had no lungs to draw in air, they were flapping out of the hole in my back where my ribs used to be, a gross parody of the Viking Blood Eagle.

The enormity of my suffering had no boundaries, it went on and on as what I thought was destroyed was destroyed again and sometime later, possibly during the moment when my ribs were yanked apart by sandpaper hands, I found the ability to scream for mercy.

Much to my surprise there came a relief so immense I almost slipped into deeper unconsciousness, I found myself whole and trembling on that cracked plain, curled into a fetal position, covered with sweat and vomit.

"You do well to remember Who you are fucking with, boy." If Father had once regarded me as favorite, a son He was proud of, it lay far from His voice. Instead, contempt and hate dripped like foul acid from every syllable. "You do not gainsay My word."

"Jeanne, help me." The words coughed out of a raw throat.

"What?" For the first time I heard surprise in his voice and it made me … hopeful.

"Jeanne," I croaked. "Help me."

"You cry out to that whore? You *dare*?" The air above congealed, the dark sky of my dream becoming something pregnant with loathing and despair. I knew that any second now the suffering I felt earlier was but the slightest prelude of the attentions He was ready to inflict upon me.

"Jeanne …."

My cheek *blazed*.

Father screamed, agony and hatred combined to split the sky, to sunder the world beneath my curled body.

I woke.

Out of bed, clothes hastily thrown on. No thought, just action. My burning cheek reduced to a pleasant tingle. Had to run, had to hide. For some reason I knew my connection to Father had been severed, but by what agency I could only speculate. My bet was on Jeanne's blessing, those lips upon my tingling cheek and her profound forgiveness of my trespass against her.

There, a bundle of clothes, a few weapons and a pistol at my belt. Ready to go.

"Going somewhere, father?"

Michael in the doorway, blade in hand, curved and terribly sharp, the edges silvery, gleaming. A type of one-handed sword called a kilij, made famous by Vlad Tepes and capable of both draw and impact cutting. A person with the requisite skill could slice a man in half with such a weapon.

Michael had plenty of skill and the muscle to put it to good use.

I faced my son, hand on my pistol, ready to draw and fire in an instant and by the widening of his eyes he knew I had him cold.

My hand fell away. "No, son," I said mournfully. "I cannot kill you."

More people came into view behind him. Family members all and all armed. A muzzle pointed my way. Michael raised a hand and it withdrew. "The Patron has given orders. I am the new head of the Family now."

I nodded. "You will be a fine leader, son."

"You know what I must do?"

Another nod, no words.

He lifted the kilij. "I have no choice."

My smile held more bitterness than sadness. "I hope before you die, Michael, that you come to realize that there is always a choice."

Death came with a flashing, silver edge.

BIRTH BEGAN LIKE IT ALWAYS DID, starting with pain and a horrible constriction as if I was suffocating under the world's largest, extremely wet pillow. I pushed back, knowing that any moment there would be the same tearing, ripping sound accompanied by gouts of blood. My tissues would start to burn with the need to grow and, phoenix like, I would emerge from the corpse of a woman who died a horrible death.

Instead the constriction continued, and I felt myself *pushed*, squeezed through a short tunnel of flesh until my face, slimy and gross, suddenly met air so frigid I cried out in sudden pain, which brought out a coughing, hack that brought that cold air to my lungs.

Light, overwhelming, searing redly through my closed lids and it provoked more gurgling cries. My tongue felt heavy, useless, a thick pad of flesh barely under control and my limbs weak, flailing against the cold air. Hard hands gripped my back and I felt myself lifted.

The experience of over a hundred rebirths told me something was amiss, so I pulled myself together, weathering the shock and the pain of the light and forced my eyes open. All I could see was a blur, a head-shaped mass that failed to resolve no matter how I blinked. My head began to pound as the light speared my skull. I felt soft cloth wrap my body and I relaxed as the chill air loosened its grip.

It took a few moments, but the blur cleared somewhat, and I could see Michael staring down at me, a frown on his face. "Hello, father."

I gurgled, unable to control my mouth. The rebirth hunger was ravaging my stomach, but I could not ask for food, my betraying lips refused to work.

"Speaking seems beyond you, so let me inform you of the situation." He took a deep breath. "As I said, I am now head of the Family. Our Patron refuses to speak to you and will communicate only with me. With that being said, you are hereby condemned to be a prisoner forevermore, to grow old in captivity, to die in captivity and to be reborn in captivity. There is no appeal for this for this is His word and it is resolute. Know that you will be forevermore born in a female body, given birth by one of our breeders and, as such, will serve as a breeder yourself until you can no longer bear children." A pause. "Speaking of which, no more will you grow into adulthood upon your rebirth. From now until time erases the sun from the sky, the normal cycle of aging will apply." He neared, and I could see well enough now the strain upon his face. He was always such a dutiful boy and despite the cruelty of the Family business, he maintained a lighter heart than most. "The Patron promised you immortality, father, and will never break His word. It is just now that your immortality will be on His terms."

A dry laugh devoid of humor shook Michael's body. "I guess it always has been."

I cried. What more could I do?

CENTURIES PASSED WHILE THE FAMILY KEPT me in isolated comfort, a breeding machine. Every businesslike coupling a rape, every birth a lesson in the pain of conception and aborted motherhood. I never saw my children, they were taken from me the moment they took their first breath, leaving me with sore nethers and aching breasts full of milk. The first few times nearly broke me, but after the first two lifetimes, I became numb to the ordeal.

I will not bore you with the sordid details of how I learned to cope being born a female, growing up, dealing with the annoying complexities of menstruation and losing my virginity as soon as possible. Safe to say the

Family wanted safe and healthy births and that is the only reason Father did not have me gang raped every lifetime or tortured to death with hot pincers. Our Family Patron is, unbeknownst to most, a frugal being. Still, childbirth is hard on the body and as soon as I grew too old to breed, I was put to death, usually quickly so as to re-incarnate and start to process all over again.

Many a night as I lay in my bed aching for sleep I wondered why Father did not just have me grow to full maturity upon my birth, as I did when rebirthing as a male. Perhaps he enjoyed my constant consternation at having to grow as a child with an adult's mind. His ways, while not that mysterious, are never without a purpose.

Each incestuous breeding brought forth issue, a daughter or son, some deformed because of inbreeding, some beautiful and powerful, examples of the ultimate being Father needed to permanently house a fraction of his consciousness. His fingerhold into our world.

Let us move this story forward a few centuries, to 1976, my last rebirth. The end of the Age of Rebellion and the beginning of what the Americans called the Me Generation. Like every rebirth, I was tended to with cold, yet meticulous efficiency. My plight was not common knowledge in Family history (what became known as the Codex) but existed as oral tradition between one Family leader and the next.

In 1990 I had my first period, a year or so later than I was used to, but not unusual. This iteration's breasts were smaller, the hips slimmer, my hair not prone to length, becoming frayed and thin beyond my shoulders, so I kept it short. A buzz cut.

Since my periods could not be hidden from the Family, I was visited by Julian the next day, the first day of copulation to produce superior offspring.

Slender despite the beginning of middle age, back straight, hair slicked back from his high forehead, he seemed the epitome of sophistication and breeding. Only when he opened his mouth did his ugliness show.

I was sitting at a small makeup table, staring into a mirror with a sort of emotional detachment usually found in etymologists as they pin insects to corkboard when Julian arrived. I pretended to examine my face as his expensive Italian loafers swished through gold shag. Good looking in a severe way, I thought, not beautiful by Family standards, but the kind of looks people label handsome or striking. My muscles were hard from daily exercise, although I long since gave up hope of escape. From the first the Family had four of their best guarding me at all time, leaving nothing to chance. It was both a symbol of their respect for my abilities and a gigantic pain in the ass.

"Are you ready for the breeding, Judas?"

Julian took great care to call me by my … more commonly known name. I think it amused him greatly, tweaked his sense of power that he held the illustrious Founder under his thumb. As a young man, the most promising and ruthless Sicarius of his generation, he had fathered two of my children, the last one having killed me at the ripe age of forty-six. I held no anger for the child, he was blameless. It was Julian for whom I saved my rage.

"Get your rape over with," I said tonelessly, my heart a stone in my chest. "You are boring me." I would take it, like I had for hundreds of years. Once I killed myself, hung with my own bed curtains. For the next two lifetimes I lay tied to the bed, let up only for toilet breaks so I would not develop bed sores. A hard lesson learned.

Fingers toughened by years of martial arts training caressed my shoulder. "In your previous life you have given me two fine sons, and both show more promise than even I at their age. Perhaps the greatest promise of all. I think it is time for you to bear me another son, a son who can sit at the head of all tables and clench this world in his fist."

"I do not care."

"You should. They are fine boys and your contribution to the Patron's plans has been invaluable. Of all our breeders, only your children have the most promise."

Enough. I stood and put my hands on my hips. "Get it done or get out. I am tired of this."

Julian smiled, an ugly expression on his normally handsome face. "Tomorrow morning. I have a meeting with the Prime Minister of Great Britain and I really should not be late. I thought to give you fair warning of my arrival." This was said with his usual sadistic charm. He wanted me to squirm and fret and try not to panic at the thought of my impending rape. As a younger man he showed no gentleness and did not care if he caused me pain and I knew this next time would be spurred by a desire to humiliate me further. He wanted my fear to tear me down, to make me less of a person, to cry and beg and weep at his ministrations.

Fuck him.

Anger clothed me like a warm blanket and I turned from him without a word. He knew I would not attack him, just as I knew there were cameras on us at that second, recording every instance in case the four Dagger Men needed to intervene. They would not kill me, but there was no restriction upon pain and in the last few centuries the Sicarii had become masters of the subject.

Gone were the freedom fighters trying to overthrow Roman rule. Meet the new boss, same as the old boss.

One of the tortures provided was lack of entertainment. No television, newspapers, books or radio and there were only so many hours in the day I could dedicate to martial arts. I had nothing to else besides staying fit to pass the time save my memories. Memories and the construction of a what-if worlds … what if I had not betrayed my friend, what if I had freed Jeanne.

What if.

Thump …

My imaginary world with my imaginary wife and children vanished like a popped soap bubble, the sudden noise a harsh reality against fantasy. I sat up and waited. I knew that sound, had heard it often enough in my Sicarii days … the sound a body makes when it hits the floor.

I waited.

The door opened.

There was no weapon for me to draw, but I still had my martial arts training and was ready to deliver a flying kick that could snap the neck of a bull. Just as my thighs were ready to propel my forward at vicious speed, the figure in the door had me in the sight of what I could only assume was a pistol of some sort. Unlike a normal black powder weapon of wood and steel, this seemed to be small, shiny metal box with a long handle. The hole in one end dribbled fine smoke and I suddenly knew that any violent movement on my part would be met with death.

"Who are you?" asked the wielder of the deadly box in German.

I stared at the man dressed in tight-fitting black clothes. He had longish hair parted in the middle that fell in waves to his shoulder. A short beard decorated the wide, homely face of a peasant. "Who are *you*?" I replied slowly in the same tongue.

"Quick fucking around," came another voice whipcracking through the door.

"I found a girl," said the man with the unusual gun. "Young."

The owner of the voice appeared behind the man. He had a puckered scar on his left cheek. "Is this the one?"

Could this be help? Saviors? No time like the present to find out. "Can you help me?" I asked. "I am a prisoner here."

Scar Face narrowed his eyes. "What kind of prisoner?"

"A breeder."

That took him aback. He conferred with the first man for a moment, then, "Come with us if you want out of here, girl."

He did not have to ask twice. I was in the hallway in a flash, barely noticing the bodies of my four guards and the blood that streaked the walls. Six more men and a hard-faced woman, all dressed in the same black, tight-fitting clothes, stood there, tense and ready to deal death. Each carried those metal boxes I assumed were guns of some sort.

"Who's she?" asked another man, lean and tall.

"Prisoner," said the scar faced man. "I think she's the one."

No argument. Without another word I was whisked away with brisk efficiency.

HOW CAN I EXPLAIN THE OVERLOAD of information that comes with a paradigm shift of perception? For hundreds of years I was kept prisoner, never given access to technology of any sort, the only markings of the passage of time the different styles of clothing provided and shown by the various heads of my Family.

Think of a person whose last known technological development was the flintlock pistol. Then add four hundred years in an eyeblink. Strange boxes with wheels that made the damndest noises that gave off odors like burning peat. Buildings so tall I had to crane my head all the way back to capture the height. Boxes that played music, some of it so discordant that it made my ears ring and my eyes water. I was later told it was an orchestra called Led Zeppelin.

I was taken to a warehouse in Munich (after a white-knuckled plane ride that had my stomach rebelling and sweat pouring from my skin in rivers. I think that the flight attendant thought I suffered from the plague) where I would be, in the terms of my saviors, 'be debriefed'. Even though a prisoner of the Sicarii, these people handled me with grave caution and respect, perhaps fearing that I was some sort of spy or Dagger Man agent. There I met a man named, ironically enough, Roman.

Ignorant of modern times, only able to communicate efficiently because I lived through the changes of languages of my captors, I kept my story short and simple. I was Constance, a minor member of the Family whose sole purpose was to produce viable offspring. Period, end of story.

Roman, medium tall with wide shoulders and skin parchment white, looked at me impassively from across the table at which we sat. He wore a suit I knew from Julian was called a three-piece, but no tie. Julian's seemed nicer, fitted better. The one on Roman hung poorly and was the color of old feces.

We sat in a warehouse that lay open and echo-y all around, damp, dank, dusty, musty and dark. Long abandoned, full of rats. I kept my attention on the lights. Lightbulbs fascinated me, even though staring at them hurt my eyes. No smoke, no flickers, just a strong outpouring of illumination that robbed the area of shadows. I desperately wanted to touch one.

"Stop that!"

I came back to myself. "What?"

"Haven't you ever seen a lightbulb before?"

It had a name. "Lightbulb," I said in wonder. "No. Never before."

This seemed to puzzle Roman mightily until Kurt, the first of my rescuers, said, "Her room was lit with oil lamps. No toilet, either. Just a chamber pot.

You should have seen her on the plane. I had to slip her a sedative, so she would remain calm."

They continued to talk, so much jabbering because I was not paying attention. Then more jabbering, heated, intense. I almost paid attention, but the lights were so beautiful. I could see a glowing thread looping within the glass sphere above me, yellow white like the sun and it brought a smile to my face. Would that lightbulb burn my fingers if I touched it? I considered this marvel as it shone from its metal hood while the two men decided my fate. It did not matter, I knew they would not hurt me and that I was free.

Free.

Has there ever been a more perfect word? Taste captivity, have your existence confined to a room, even a plush one like my former cell, and abandon hope that there is an outside world for you to experience. Freedom becomes a cruel jest, but when experienced, a drug more potent than love, or hate, or hope.

Freedom.

"Young lady, please come back to us." This was a new voice, old and quavery. A woman's voice.

Out of the darkness of the warehouse and into the light of the bare bulb overhead walked an old woman. Ancient, really, with translucent skin like crepe paper heavy on her face and hair white as snow. A black dress covered her from neck to ankles and though she looked as if she would blow away in a stiff breeze, her steps were sure and firm, her blue eyes blazing with will and intelligence.

"Ada," said Roman. "You shouldn't be here."

"Pish," came the reply. "I am the leader of the Templars, I go where I wish."

The Templars!

Ada's wrinkly face smoothed with delight. "Ah, she knows *that* name!"

Betrayed by my own face, I closed it down and stared at the table. The Templars, the enemy of my Family. For a moment I felt a stab of fear so powerful I nearly wet my dress. My intellect took over from my immediate fight-or-flight response and I began to process the information. The Templars had rescued me, had expected me ... therefore they must be an ally rather than an enemy. Why should I fear? Was not my Family now my enemy?

I looked up.

Ada shooed Roman from his chair and sat. "This one is smart, she knows what's what and has already figured out a way to use us. I can tell." No accusation, just bald facts. She continued to pierce me with her blue stare as she talked. "She could be valuable, or she could be useless to our cause. I have not decided which."

"She has a name," I said.

The old woman nodded.

"Constance," I supplied.

"Of course."

"I am not your enemy."

"Of course."

"Neither am I a friend."

"I know."

"Now what?"

"That is up to you, young lady."

Color me surprised. "Me?"

"Do you know how we came to rescue you?"

I was keen to find out and said so.

Ada leaned forward and assumed a conspiratorial air. "I had a dream."

Of course. I let my face convey my skepticism.

Brittle, old lady laughter. "Joan of Arc came to me in a dream and showed me a chateau in Switzerland. She said hope was imprisoned and must be set free. Very powerful things, you know, dreams."

Jeanne! My heart beat in my chest and sweat bloomed on my upper lip. My fingers caressed my suddenly burning cheek. Ada blurred in my sight.

"You know what I am talking about, don't you?" She sounded satisfied.

I only knew part of this riddle, but I nodded anyway. Jeanne!

"We Templars have freed you. God has delivered you unto us and now I must decide what to do with you. This is an important decision, young lady, because visions of saints don't come our way often, so when they do we pay particular attention. Do you understand."

Not daring to speak, I nodded.

"What do you think we should do?

It took a while for the lump in my throat to dissolve. "I would like to go," I husked. "Some place remote, where this big world will not hurt so much."

"I imagine, as sheltered as you have been, that it is a strange place." Ada smiled. "There is a country I think that would suit you well."

"Ada, I don't think this is wise." Roman stepped forward, arms crossed. "We can use her. Even sheltered, she's a mine of information."

"Hush, Roman."

Roman hushed. That was Ada's power, total command. Roman may not have liked the command, but he obeyed.

"Tell me girl, have you ever heard of Kathmandu?"

CHAPTER NINE
NEPAL

———————

BEFORE THEY LET ME LEAVE GERMANY, the Templars did what they could to catch me up on world history for the past few hundred years. So much changed. So much stayed the same.

More efficient ways of killing people came as no surprise, the average pistol being able to shoot seven people in a matter of seconds was certainly an improvement over one every minute and the business of a quick reload had my head spinning. The pistol had become a weapon so simple that a toddler could easily use it. This saddened me somewhat.

My introduction to small arms came as some surprise to my instructors. By the end of the first half hour I was grouping bullets center mass on a paper target from one hundred feet away. Considering my efficiency with black-powder weapons, learning modern arms was child's play.

Proving myself with hand-to-hand was no surprise. Every member of the Deschamps family was schooled in martial arts, including the breeders. Convincing the Templars of this was easy once I felled a brace of them at one time, much to Ada's amusement.

If you are wondering why the Templars would consider letting a fourteen-old-girl fend for herself, do not. I had a chaperone, of sorts. Kurt, the first man I saw outside of the Family in four hundred years was there to accompany me, to be my guardian until I came of age and tackle the world alone. Four more years.

He was less than thrilled at the prospect, but like a good, obedient Templar he took the assignment with only a modicum of cursing and chest beating. I hid my laughter. Some non-Family companionship was just what the doctor ordered. Too long locked away, so long that I believed by the normal definition I was not sane. Not by a long shot.

I watched the mountains pass far below me as I wondered about how I would fit into this unusual world I now inhabited. The mental exercise kept me from pondering how an enormous metal contraption could fly through the air without crashing.

"Let go of the arms," Kurt commented drily.

My head whipped from the window. "What?"

"Your knuckles are white on your seat arms. No reason to advertise your terror."

A drop of sweat hit my eye and I blinked rapidly. With a great deal of effort, I uncurled my fingers and I studied my nails. Painted. Strange that women were expected to paint their fingernails. It looked good, though. Deep burgundy, the color of old blood. I tilted my head toward my chaperone. "How does this thing stay in the air."

He pointed out the window. "See those big egg-shaped cylinders under the wings."

I nodded.

"Engines. They provide thrust."

"But we are not crashing." Surely that was not a hint of fear in my voice. No, it must have been fatigue.

"Put enough energy behind it and a brick can fly. The wings keep us gliding. When we land, wheels will cushion the blow and allow us to coast to a stop."

Images of the giant plane on a wagons wheels caused a nervous chuckle. Kurt smiled and went back to reading.

That is another thing. Reading! Most of the people on the planet achieved a level of literacy not seen in the old world. Why, you could buy a book just about anywhere! Even an airport! Who would have thought it?

We landed at Tribhuvan International airport within a matter of hours, the descent and landing not a worry anymore because staring out the window as we flew eventually desensitized me to my peril.

I wore tight, blue trousers made from a cotton called denim. Very tough and much better than hose. Over that was a long-sleeved shirt depicting a drawing of a big-nosed creature, somewhat like an ugly dog, covered in orange fur with the words 'Ha! I kill me!'. I was told the 'alien' being depicted was from a comedic entertainment show created in America and was very popular over there. I concluded that America must be a very unusual place.

You, of course, know what an airport looks like. Blocks of poured concrete, vast echoing chambers filled with the infinite variety of humanity, the air filled with their chatter along with various voices throbbing through the air like the pronouncements of lazy gods. Not a sensory overload for those born into the time but imagine distilling the essence of all that seeming chaos down to a thick sludge of input and multiply it by one hundred. That is how I felt, that was the bedlam that threatened to tip what sanity I had left to the breaking point. I became most grateful when I felt Kurt's calloused hand gently take mine. In that second, he became my anchor to reality, my magnetic north.

"Hello, sir, do you have the time?"

Latin. Someone asked a question in *Latin*.

We stopped suddenly and looked at the speaker. A little brown man with a wide smile dressed in dun trousers and a short-sleeved shirt with opalescent buttons down the front. His forearms were huge, corded with muscle.

"There never seems to be enough time," replied Kurt in the same tongue.

"God gives what is needed."

My chaperone smiled and extended a hand. "Daniel?"

The other man took it and shook hard. "Yes. Kurt?"

"Yes."

They smiled at each other as if they were old friends and I concluded that the greeting consisted of a sign/countersign to verify identity. It is what I would have done.

Daniel pierced me with his dark eyes, the smile never fleeing from his lips. "This is her, then?"

I extended a hand. "Yes, I am she. Good to meet you Daniel." His grip was firm, and I had the impression that he could have reduced the bones of my hand to powder if he so desired.

"Good. Come with me."

"Where are we going?"

Daniel winked. "I'm told that you are not used to the wide world. My cousin lives in a village far from here and has agreed to take you in until you can fully acclimate to the global norm."

Global norm. Nice. "Who are you, Daniel?" I asked, not budging. Kurt had withheld information during the flight and I was starting to feel particularly mulish. I needed answers.

He was more than happy to provide, it seemed. "A former Templar."

"Former?"

A shrug. "Perhaps not former, but family obligations mean that I don't travel out and about battling the Sicarii."

Kurt clapped the small man on the back, a blow that would have staggered a normal man, but Daniel barely moved an inch. "Here standing before us is a real, live Gurkha."

"Say what now?"

"A soldier from the Gorkha region of Nepal," said Daniel offhandedly.

"We gained some notoriety."

"Don't let him fool you, girl, he and his are the best of the best. The most coveted warrior in all the world. I'd rather fight Israeli Commandos than the Gurkhas."

Time came to a stop, the world all around clipping into wedges of frozen activity as my mind went to a deep, dark place. The pair began to look worried as I stood there. Kurt raised a hand to steady me when I said, "Israeli Commandos? Israel is a thing?" Why had the Templars not informed me during my impromptu History lessons?

"By the Lord, girl, you didn't know?"

How could I express my shock at there being an Israel. In my time (my original birth time, that is) it was merely a Roman vassal state, having been laid waste by the Egyptian pharaoh Merneptah centuries before my birth and fought over like a bone amongst curs for several more. During the Bathory incident it found itself part of the Ottoman Empire, a land of lost identity, a place for a lost people.

Israel. A siren song, a place out of legend, a dream. Reality. Finding my voice again was difficult and my mind tried to wander to places of unknown wonder, but my current situation needed me to be mentally focused, so I forced my thoughts into some form of cohesion. "This place where we are going, how far away is it?" Time enough to mull this revelation later

Once again Daniel's smile split his face. "A few hours from here. We'll take a Jeep most of the way, then walk the rest. You up to a walk, young lady?"

"If it gets me farther from the Sicarii, I will walk to Africa."

SUMMER IN THE NEPALESE MOUNTAINS COULD be called winter almost anywhere else. Except Switzerland. I found it amusing that I escaped from a place that was similar to the one in which I now hid. It seemed that my current incarnation was beset by irony.

Color assaulted my eyes as my thighs burned and my lungs heaved. I had forgotten the infinite variety of hues that came with wildflowers and was entranced. The simple joy at staring at flowers occupied my attention. My body moved of its own accord, following Daniel while Kurt plodded along behind. The two men seemed content to travel in silence, perhaps enjoying the sight of a young girl craning her head around to take in the sight of mountain vales and rocky summits.

So much to see. "It's beautiful."

"Yes," Daniel replied, pointing ahead. "There's the village."

I followed his finger and saw a cluster of buildings a couple hundred yards ahead, slathered in shades of saffron and orange.

"We'll be safe—" Daniel began just before of the front of his skull abruptly came apart.

Sharp *pops* sounded through the air and my mind went into the warrior's place, a state where all was reduced to relevant and irrelevant data.

"Shooter," barked Kurt from behind. "Run."

Good idea, but not the direction he wanted. Instead, I ran toward the village, tired legs suddenly invigorated. From behind came a few choice swear words, some I had not heard before. It seemed the Templars liked their cursing just fine.

Flashes of light and the ground beside me became peppered with sudden holes followed soon after by the sharp report of gunfire. My pistol, supplied by poor Daniel, found its way into my hand. A tug on my jacket, a hot run of pain along my arm and my calculating mind realized it was a graze, nothing serious, but I did juke side to side a bit to present a more difficult target.

Closer now. I could see the shooter, a man on one of the flat-topped buildings, the eaves covered in saffron bunting. His hands worked over the rifle, sliding the bolt back, ejecting a cartridge. Had it been fully automatic, I would be dead, but he was quick enough to betray considerable time at practice.

Fifty yards. Too long. A slip to the left and a bullet whizzed through the spot my head had been.

Thirty yards, close enough. The pistol in my hand, the 9mm came up and I fired at a dead run. The round took the man under the left eye and dropped him hard, along with his rifle.

At the building, the furthest outlier, the first seen from the little mountain path we walked. Twenty feet above my head on the roof lay a rifle and the corpse, too far to climb quickly. I had one clip in and one in the front pocket of my heavy jacket.

Killing Daniel served no purpose, unless the people of this village were trying to hide a crime, but that made no sense if his cousin lived here. I needed more data.

Kurt was bellowing like a bull and I cursed. The fool would get himself killed. That thought came true as he suddenly stopped and raised his pistol, firing three shots in rapid succession before his chest erupted in crimson flowers. He fell on his back.

Reaction now, no thinking. The shots came from the main street, such as it was. I peered around a corner to see a small man in ragged trousers, sandals and short sleeves run toward the fallen Kurt. I put two rounds into his chest and left him to bleed out, but not before confiscating his rifle.

My small arms training was confined to pistols and revolvers, not to rifles. It did not look difficult to use, but I had no time to learn. Voices screamed from farther in the village, just out of sight and to the left.

I made acquaintance with the nearest home, not surprised to encounter emptiness. It was a largish single story, but simply furnished and easily searched. A quick study of the main room showed a trap door to the roof and I took it. From there I ran to its neighbor and jumped, catching the lip of the taller building's roof, pulling myself up.

Now I had a view of almost the entire village. Boomerang-shaped, it threaded along the side of the mountain, curving to my left, a line of buildings along a main road constructed of cobble. Most of the houses were roofed in thatch, although the taller ones like the one I stood upon had large, wooden shingles grayed by weather.

In the center of the village milled the inhabitants, clustered together in fear. Standing around were at least a half-dozen rough looking types holding rifles (I discovered later that these were called Lee Enfields, a British Army standard from 1895-1957).

One of the rough types possessed keen vision because the next thing I knew there was shouting. An indecent number of rifle barrels pointed my way. I threw myself flat and scrambled down to the one story and back through the trap door, landing awkwardly. A bolt of fire ran from my left foot to the base of my brain, but I could stand, albeit gingerly.

Gunfire and the front door became toothpicks and I threw myself flat again to avoid eating lead and fired three shots. A scream answered the third.

Before I could fully stand two men charged through the doorway and I fired three times at the nearest. He screamed and fell, sliding to stop a couple of feet away while the second took aim with his rifle. I screamed, launching myself toward him, my ankle a white-hot mess. I did not feel it because there was dying to be done, him or me. A shot, a flat bark and the whine of a bullet missing me by inches. From my charge I spun low, sweeping out and clipping his ankles with the heel of my hiking boot. He fell, hands grasping for my throat. I grabbed his little fingers in my fists and thrust my hands to the side. Both digits *popped*, and he screamed, but not for long. My elbow found his throat and his larynx gave with a *crunch*. I left him to flop his life out on the floor as more bullets pummeled the house.

Blood flowed from my left leg, a wound I had not noticed but there was no pain, only the determination to live. More bullets, glass shattered, plaster fell from the ceiling.

Someone shouted, a language like gargling with thick oil.

One clip left and two rifles I was not sure I could employ with any efficacy. Not good odds. I needed to get close.

"Do you speak German?" I yelled, trying for frightened.

More gargly language. Then, oddly, French. "You come out, you live. Promise."

Sure. Still, I was outnumbered, the odds grim. "Yes, I will come out. Do not shoot."

"Throw guns!"

Damn, a smart villain. I complied, saying goodbye to the pistol followed by the rifles.

"Out! Hands in sky."

Right. In sky. I stood, no longer a cool killer, but a young woman filled with anger. My heavy jacket hit the floor and with efficient jerks I tore my long-sleeved t-shirt to shreds, defacing the cartoonish alien. "I am coming out."

Light stabbed my eyes, blinding me for a moment and rough hands grabbed me, groping and insulting. Brisk shoving had me in the middle of the tiny village, a square no bigger than my bedroom/prison in Switzerland.

A quick count. Six men carrying rifles, one with a pistol, which was pointed at my face. The pointer (the leader of this bunch, I assumed) was my height with a snarly face and ragged clothes. I judged him to be in his mid-forties. Most of the other men, as raggedy as their leader, focused their attention on the inhabitants of the village, who were forced against the buildings at gunpoint.

"What, bitch, did you do to my men?" he screamed in truly terrible French.

"Dead."

Growls all around. I tried not to cringe because dying would mean falling back into the Family's clutches, a fate I thought to be worse than death. Raggedy man's face worked for a second before he noticed the state of my clothes.

Remember, I was only fourteen in this incarnation, but already woman enough with curves in all the right places and rather attractive, if I do say so myself. I could see the cold calculation in his piggy brown eyes. A rough hand squeezed my breast. "We use you good, bitch. You be ours for a long time."

His first mistake was not killing me immediately. The second was coming into range. I enveloped his gun hand in mine, lifted it high overhead and brought the arm down hard on my shoulder. His elbow bent the wrong way with a wet *snap*.

The pistol in one hand, I reached down with the other and grabbed handful of crotch through a thin layer of gabardine and squeezed. His mouth opened, but no sound emerged.

I fired, taking the nearest raggedy man in the throat. The second shot took another in the chest and by the boneless way he fell, I did not have to worry about him rising to take vengeance. Time elapsed: two seconds.

The other men began to turn, rifles rising. I spun, shooting. One bullet entered under an armpit and the man howled like a rabbit in agony. Another man died with a bullet through the eye, blood and brains spewing out the hole in the back of his head.

Click.

Empty.

Oh, shit. Two more shooters. I threw the gun at one and was pleased to see it hit his wide forehead. The man dropped, clutching his face. A bullet passed between my legs. I ran before the last man could take aim, my ankle burning with pain. I jumped at the man and I must have looked the epitome of the spirit of vengeance because he screamed, dropped is rifle and ran, sandaled feet flying.

I ran after him, angry now, blood pumping, the pain in my ankle of no more thought than a splinter. I had given birth to at least a couple hundred children, how could a sprain even begin to compare?

The man looked back as he ran, his face a rictus of fear. That was candy to me. My blood was up and the chase on and at last there was something to focus several lifetimes of anger on.

My tackle took him low, his face planting hard on cobble, teeth shattering. I climbed him like a spider monkey and grabbed two fistfuls of greasy black hair and began to pound his face into the street.

Wham. That is for you, Julian, for your sickening smugness.

Wham. That for Elizabeth Bathory, the vilest woman ever to walk the earth.

Wham. For me. For being such a dumb shit all those years ago. For betraying my friend out of jealousy. For being weak.

For being wrong.

Wham. The last one for Father, the real liar. Fuck you.

I could not see. Could not do anything except hug myself and cry. Centuries of bitterness and loneliness and sorrow erupted, smearing the world.

Soft hands touched my hair, my arms, lifting me gently to my feet. I blinked away tears to see myself surrounded by women. Young, old, short, fat and thin. All types. The entire female population of the village. They were staring at me with a mixture of reverence and compassion. One of them, dressed in a loose-fitting deep burgundy shirt touched my cheek. "You saved us," she said in French. She was missing a front tooth and her hair was threaded with gray. "Thank you."

I nodded, not trusting my voice.

Later, I found that Daniel's cousin, a former Gurkha himself, had been the first to die, shot from behind by the raggedy men. Bandits. A group of men new to the area, they had the ability to simply disappear into the mountains, thus evading what law enforcement happened to be nearby. They had never wandered this far to the east of Kathmandu and their attack on the village had been a complete surprise.

The woman, Jiviya, was the widow of Gajendra, Daniel's cousin. She had learned French from her husband, who, in his youth, was well traveled. "Now we have no one trained to defend us," she lamented while bandaging my wounds. Her short fingers were as calloused as any man's.

My heart went out to these people. Their lives were simple, yet rich and full while mine had been … complex and empty. The full force of that knowledge made my stomach churn with acid.

Kurt's corpse lay near my feet. I hardly knew him save that he seemed a decent sort. Daniel as well. They needed a proper burial.

I looked around as Jiviya finished her ministrations. A young girl, perhaps seven, came forward out of the crowd of women to hand me cup of water. It tasted better than anything.

"You need a protector," I said between gulps. "I need a place to stay."

Something like hope blossomed on Jiviya's face.

THE BOOK OF

MICHAEL continued

Chapter Six
Get to it

THE WOMAN WHO HAD BEEN ... check that, who *was* Judas Iscariot set her tea down and calmly regarded me over the steaming mug.

"That is pretty much the whole of it, Father Engle," she stated. "There is much more, but it is not germane to the struggle."

I was still wrapping my head around the whole Joan of Arc thing and Elizabeth Bathory. It's not every day to talk to someone who seen so much history. Except for Cain, of course. You'd figure I'd be used to it. Outside the lights of Bruges winked off the canals.

Located in province of West Flanders in the Flemish Region of Belgium, Bruges is a mix of a fairytale medieval western European city and Venice. Canal based, the city couldn't be more picturesque if it tried. Considering that Belgium is often overlooked because of France to the south, it seemed a good spot to hole up while I waited for my compadres to make contact.

It didn't take long for Maggie and Cain to show with Judas in tow. The woman, still had trouble with that, looked lithe as a panther and about as dangerous, proved deferential and polite, if a bit distant. Soon after she continued the story that she began with the email, one of evil, hope, despair, regret and madness. It brought to mind her own questions about sanity, so I treated her with kid gloves.

For the first time since I took power, the majority of the Templars (not a large number, mind you) were in one location, waiting for me to come up with some divinely inspired plan that would crush the Sicarii but good. I was humbled by their faith, not to mention worried to the bone.

"Thank you for your story," I said quietly.

Judas speared me with her deep brown eyes. "You do not look the part."

"Excuse me?"

"Of a priest. You do not look like a priest."

"I imagine your interactions with the clergy were somewhat limited."

She shrugged. "I placed a few in the Vatican. There was a couple of popes as well."

"Alfons and Rodrigo Borgia."

A small slant of a smile. "You know your papal history."

"Rather practical in my line of work. What do I look like, then?"

"A young warrior, a Norman brute. Put you in armor and you would look every bit a Knight Templar."

Nice. Trying not to feel too proud, I said, "Not so young anymore, I'm afraid. I hit 46 soon."

Her eyes widened. "You are blessed indeed because I would have placed you at no more than thirty. God has plans for you."

"Don't you mean the Lying God?" At her wince I continued, "That was rude. Forgive me, that was petty."

"But deserved," she replied quietly. "I understand your trepidation at my presence. You have every right to kick me out into the cold, but I am here to help."

And I could use all the help I could get. "How did Cain know where to find you?"

"It is a long story."

I stretched my arms above my head and my shoulders popped. "Too tired for more stories. I have to think of something to counter the Sicarii soon."

"You are the prophet of God. No doubt you will be inspired."

I stood. Meeting adjourned.

OF COURSE, MORNING STARTS AT MIDNIGHT and that's when the voices outside my door woke me out of an exhausted slumber. No dreams, only the blessed oblivion that comes with overwhelming fatigue.

"Wake him."

"Shhh ..."

"Milo, it's important"

"You always say that, Giovanni."

"Because it's always true."

"Shhh!"

Well, heck. No sleep for the weary. "Enough! Come in already." The door opened. The hallway light rammed into my eyes. I turned on the bedside lamp. "What is it?" Coffee. Lots and lots. I asked Milo for a cup (didn't he ever sleep?) and motioned Giovanni to get on with it.

Skinny to the point of skeletal, Giovanni looked like an Italian stereotype:

pencil thin mustache, olive skin, slender with slicked back black hair. He wore three-piece suits like normal people wear underwear … all the time. Expensive ones, too. Linen and silk so they shone in the dim light. This one was a light gray with salmon pin stripes. He held a custom-built laptop that almost looked too heavy for him to lift.

I waved at his computer. "Gio, do you sleep in that thing?"

He just couldn't get with the small talk. Where was that coffee? My brain was functioning like a knock-off iPhone. "Sir, I did what you asked, and I think I have something!' He was so excited I thought he would vibrate out of that suit.

"Gio, Gio … slow down. Take it step by step." Milo chose that moment to enter with the coffee and it tasted so good I almost blasphemed. Instead, I settled for an *aahh* of contentment and propped myself up to a more decorous seated position in bed.

The laptop plopped down on my … well, lap. Lots of code and a moving graph in one corner. "Look at that, sir."

"I don't speak computer, son. Just tell me."

His face fell. "Sorry. Well, I did as you asked and then kept up the snoop, not looking for Burke, but his number two man, Fergus. That's when I got a hit."

"Of?"

"Oh, I managed to hack his secretary's workstation, discreetly of course, I left no trace, and found out that there was a flight plan filed under one of his known aliases."

"An alias, huh?"

"Yes, as he does when he wants to travel incognito. That was brilliant, sir, having us search for flight plans like that."

Not so brilliant. It was an idea I had a few months ago and it carried a certain … risk. I had a strong suspicion I could only use this tactic once. "And what do we know?"

"He is taking a private jet, one not registered to the Deschamps family, to Dulles International. It was booked for two."

"His personal assistant?" Surveillance of Burke's second-in-command revealed that he traveled with a brawny woman named Margaritte who acted as his assistant and bodyguard. Although he was capable of guarding his own body. From what Jude told me, he was a magus in his own right and a trained Sicarius, but it never hurt to have an extra pair of hands filled with guns in a tight situation.

"Yes, we believe so."

"And?"

For the first time since I sent him on his task, Gio's tired face split in a wide grin. "If we can get close enough without being spotted, it will work."

"You're sure?"

"Yes, sir."

At that moment Judas entered wearing a tank top t-shirt and boxer shorts. They had little yellow duckies on them. "Sure, about what?" She crossed her arms and leaned against the door frame.

It was getting to be like a Templar convention in here. "How much did you hear?"

She shrugged. "All of it. Voices carry in these old houses."

Of course. I raised my voice. "Cain, Maggie, get in here."

There they were. Judas' eyes widened slightly in surprise. Cain merely smiled while Maggie strode in, big as all get out, and took a seat on one of the two comfy chairs. I really wasn't dressed for a meeting and my hair stuck out every which way.

"You two are starting to be predictable."

The amazon shrugged, unabashed the had been caught out. "Like she said, sound carries in this old house. I could hear Gio over the television."

Cain piped up. "Although I find Belgium delightful, quaint and beautiful, the content of entertainment provided *sans* lucre suffers in comparison to even the drivel that the American's slop out with great regularity. It is as if the joy of quality programming is lacking in the fundamental nature of the Belgian people. As a leader in the communications industry and a provider of quality, non-reality-based television, I find myself rather insulted by the fare offered at this late hour. I mean, who really watches *Miami Vice* anymore?"

Judas cocked her head to the side. "Miami what?"

"Oh, dear Lord in Heaven, stop!" I rubbed my eyes with one and while taking a sip of coffee with the other. "Okay, quick recap, no Q&A. I thought it would be a good idea to check on flights booked under known Deschamps aliases. They do this to conduct covert business. Fergus, Burke's number two, has booked a private plane out of Heathrow and we are going to intercept him."

The question I knew was coming came from Maggie. "How are we going to intercept the second most powerful member of the most dangerous organization in the world in the busiest airport in the world."

"Gio."

At my prodding, he said, "Not intercept him, per se, but merely get close enough that I can remotely scan his electronic devices for data we need."

"Say what now?"

"The problem with finding Burke," I said, smoothly, cutting off Gio's no doubt technical explanation. "Is that we don't know any of his aliases. He hasn't been back that long and has not established any sort of pattern or routine we can discern. Heck, he hasn't even been to the Family estate in Switzerland, so

I figured we would chase the next best target in hopes of locating him."

"Fergus," said Cain.

"Fergus." Another sip of coffee. "No offense, Cain, but while your people are great at breaking encryption and general hacking, we Templars have the best, recruited the best." Hackers were among the first I recruited. This war, this bloodbath between good and evil would be fought digitally as well as physically. The new battleground where data was blood and money bone. "Gio has a device that can remotely scan any electronic storage medium."

Cain stroked his short beard. "This device is known to me. One of the multitude of shell companies (belonging to myself, of course) that conceived, developed and first implemented that particular bit of technology, an endeavor that, if I am not mistaken (and I seldom am, mind you), exceeded fourteen million dollars in total expenditures. Said device belongs to me. To be more precise, the United States government with all its powers, the NSA with its multitude of technologies implemented solely for spying on any and all, have not caught wind of that fair bit of advanced machinery. My question to you, then, is *how the fuck did you get it*?"

If I didn't know better, I would've said Cain sounded peeved, perhaps irritated to the point of putting together a plethora of terse and succinct sentences. I caught a glimmer in his eye. He was amused but trying not to show it. "I did say we had the best hackers. You should've had the specs on a stand-alone air-gapped computer."

"They *were* on a stand-alone air-gapped computer!" he almost shouted. The veins in his neck stood out in stark relief.

"Oh, well your facility in Mobile, Alabama should have better security."

"Why didn't you ask for the technology instead of stooping to acquire it by means less than legal?"

"Where's the fun in that?"

Cain's sudden laughter filled the room and I winced at the volume. After he depleted his share of mirth, Maggie said drily, "You said 'we.'"

"What?"

"Mike, you said we. That's the first time you used that word in association with the Templars."

Well, what do you know? I sure did. I reckoned I finally conceded that I stood at the head of the Templar organization. It hurt to think about.

"There is one complication here, however, my young Templar leader," said Cain, moving to the foot of the bed to give me penetrating stare. "If it is indeed the same device, then one would have to be within ten feet of the computer one wishes to scan. Considering the level of paranoia possessed by every member of the Sicarii, entering into such proximity to use the device would be met with a swift, and in most cases, fatal response seen only in a movie starring an aging, yet still musclebound, Austrian action hero."

"Gio?"

"Yes sir." My best techie sounded mournful, his normal bantam cockiness absent. "So, I think I should be the one to do it. You know, get close."

Grumble, grumble, mumble, mumble.

"No, Gio. You're too important and I won't risk you."

"But—"

"But me no buts, Gio." Did I just say that? I was starting to sound like an officer. I wanted to weep. Another sip. The coffee was starting to get cold. "I'll do it."

That got some attention, none of it good. I calmly weathered the storm of denial, finished my coffee and handed the cup to Milo with a mouthed thank you.

"Shut up!" In my best drill sergeant voice, the words cracked through the air like a rifle report. They shut up, even Cain, which was a minor miracle. "If anyone has something constructive to add, perhaps an *alternate* plan, that would be wonderful., Simply hollering in my direction gives me the itchies." I crossed my arms in the best example of stubborn body language I could muster while sitting in bed wearing nothing, except boxers and a t-shirt.

"What we need, sir Michael," said Judas calmly from her place in the doorway. "Is for someone the Sicarii *does not* know to do the deed. I understand there is something new called *facial recognition* employed by the Family that will spot you if you attempt to enter the airport."

I waved a hand. "Easily bypassed with good makeup. Facial prosthetics are only getting better."

Suddenly, the bed was ringed with bodies, arms crossed, and grave looks bordering on angry. "What?"

Cain spoke for the lot. "No."

"No?" Then. "Send someone else."

Maggie. "Me."

Judas. "Me."

"Me. Me. Me …"

Oh boy.

One of the most difficult aspects of leadership is knowing when your position is untenable. I reached that point and, brother, it hurt a ton. I waved my hands in surrender. "Okay, okay. Fair enough. Call me done, but I will be there in some capacity and …"

Lightbulb-over-the-head time. I grinned. "Oh, guys, did I ever get an idea …"

They did not look reassured.

Chapter Seven
You Call This a Plan?

———————

"**I** HAVE YOU, MAGGIE."

"Good. How's the feed?"

Pretty good. In color, great resolution considering the camera was in a button at the top of her tight-fitting black blouse. "You're fine. I can see everything fine."

"Just as long as you can get to me."

"I can, and I will if need be. No worries." I looked to the other screen. The van I sat in had that subtle fried chicken smell of old sweat. "Have you, too, Henry."

Henry Novacek was one of the new guys, sort of the poster boy for Marine recruiters everywhere: straight up and down, flattop haircut, strong jawline. Young. Too dang young for my taste, but our man (or more precisely, woman) in New York provided a dossier that included three tours in Iraq, a long history as a devout Catholic and a moral compass as steady as it gets.

"Thanks, boss," he replied keeping his eyes on the hotel front while pretending to read a newspaper. "Just tell me what to do and it'll get done."

"Just like we planned, kid. Just like we planned."

Not that plans ever survived first contact with the enemy. That's a truism that goes back to when the first caveman chucked a rock at his neighbor.

Ring around the rosie ... I shook my head, hating that nursery rhyme. It would not leave.

Maggie said, "I've got eyes on the target."

The screen showed the entrance to the Bulgari Hotel, London. A black stretch limo at the curb idling away while the doorman held the door for a well-dressed man with ginger hair. My mind filled in details in the blink of an eye: fit, slim-hipped, deep labial lines around his mouth. He looked like he sucked a hundred lemons a day.

Fergus. Matched the pic in the file on my tablet. Three other, heavies ... bodyguards, escorted him toward the car followed by a woman stout enough to qualify as a fullback for the 49ers. His assistant-cum-bodyguard ... whatshername.

"You know what to do, Maggie," I said into the microphone. From behind me, scrunched up on his tiny seat, Gio prayed.

Finding Fergus wasn't the hard part. Not at all. Our intel told us that he had a peculiar love for the Bulgari Hotel on Knightsbridge across from Hyde Park. It only took a short amount of time to locate him. We set up surveillance after he checked in. The next morning had me and Gio in a plumber's van down the street and our two operatives planted in the daily commute crowd ready to make contact.

It hurt, not being in the middle of the action, to send others into harm's way, but I had to trust that Maggie, a powerful magus in her own right, knew what she was doing. Henry, however, despite being a veteran, seemed like such a kid, wet behind the ears and raring to go get himself a handful of glory. That usually translates into getting dead quick.

Maggie's voice rang in my ears. I turned the volume down on the headset. "Yo, Fergus, my man!"

Burke's second stopped as if he'd hit a wall, head whipping toward Maggie who was bearing down on him like ship under full sail. His four minions reached inside their jackets. "Not here," I heard him hiss. Their hands emerged *sans* hardware.

"Well, well," drawled Fergus, hastily plastering a pleasant smile on his face. It looked like something he saw a person do once and imitated it poorly. "To what do I owe this fine meetin' and all?" If his Scottish burr were any thicker it would've landed on the sidewalk with a *splat*.

Maggie looked around at the morning crowd. "Good to see you're playing nice. Wouldn't do to see you accosting a woman in the middle of London."

"Henry," I said. "Get it going."

Gio added, "You only need fifty seconds. Don't make it obvious."

"Got it." The young man mimed talking on a phablet, one of those smartphones so big they doubled as computer tablets. He managed to mumble, just audibly enough, a bunch of 'uh-huhs' to be convincing along with a smattering of 'yes dear' and 'you know I will, darling' for show.

Come on, kid, I urged. Keep it natural.

The four heavies had their eyes on Maggie, leaving Henry to work his magic. I knew that the phablet was the scanning device, functioning not at all like a phone. From Maggie's camera I saw him remove the device from his ear and press a button.

Game on.

Fifty seconds.

"If you use your sight, Fegus," said Maggie loud enough to keep his attention on her. "There are quite a few sprites and larger air elementals close by. Don't get nervy."

"My guess is yer havin' a few of yer bonnie Templar bitches close by for support. A sniper or two if I'm not mistaken."

Forty-five seconds.

Lord, but he was laying it on thick. I felt a prickle at the back of my neck. Games within games. Nothing simple when dealing with the Sicarii.

"You're not mistaken. For a change."

He spread his hands. "Then why are ya here? To take me out, I reckon."

Forty.

"Why can't enemies talk, Fergus? Perhaps I came to make you an offer you would be foolish to refuse." A goodly pause. "Join us."

For a moment the dapper Scotsman looked nonplussed, then he gave a short bark of laughter and within seconds he and his minions were busting a gut, tears running down their faces.

Uh-oh,

As if reading my mind, Gio said, "Not quite the reaction I expected."

"You can say that again."

"Not quite the—"

"Gio," I warned.

"Sorry. Couldn't help myself."

Thirty.

Sweat dripped into my eye and I blinked furiously. I wanted to leap out of the van, to yell for the backup to shoot, to kill Fergus and his men before everything became pear-shaped. "Gio, how does it look?"

The hacker stared at his screen. An indicator was tick-tick-ticking its way to one-hundred percent. "Just a little more time, Henry," he said, wiping his brow.

I thumbed the open coms button. "Everyone ready?"

Twenty.

"Bravo one, ready." From Milo's voice you'd think he was talking about the weather.

"Bravo two, check." That was Alanna Dicicco. Tough as nails, pretty as a peach.

"Bravo three, ready." Orson Chambersmythe. Impeccably British and could shoot the eyes out of a hummingbird at five hundred yards. My backup in case things went from bad to carnage.

Ten.

Fergus planted his hands on his hips. "Let me offer ya somethin' ya should consider right well, lass." The smile that now blossomed on his face was light years away from pleasant. "How about ya come with me and ya won't die."

It was Maggie's turn to laugh.

Five.

"Ya don't think yer here by accident, do ya? Ya think we didn't see yer cyber boys sniffin' away around our wee little systems? Did ya consider that we letcha find me in order to draw ya out?"

Oh, shit.

Zero.

Then things went pear-shaped.

The sidewalk around the group and the street around the limo flowed upward like liquid cement defying gravity, coming to a stop twenty feet in the air and drawing a plethora of oaths from the passerby. There came the sound of a horn and a large crash as a blue Vauxhall Corasa hit the barrier and crumpled like an aluminum can in the fist of a giant.

By the Lord! "Everyone!" I shouted. "Go, go, go!"

A crash filled the headset as in front of my incredulous eyes mayhem erupted.

In Milo's small room, the door exploded inward, three men in blue jeans and heavy jackets leapt in like spiders, hands filled with death. Silenced weapons spat bullets that streaked toward the large man.

In Alanna's room a heavy boot destroyed the lock on the door and a large man, larger than even Milo, sauntered in holding a .44 revolver that looked tiny his such a big hand. A scarred face smiled as he pulled the trigger.

In Orson's room two women tore through the heavy door as if it were tissue paper. They also leapt in and began shooting before the Englishman could react.

All three of my people wore minicams attached to front buttons of their shirts, all of those sending me a clear picture of imminent death.

I thought it had been clever putting all three in empty offices (in Milo's case, a not-so-empty office, but the newly filled Templar coffers bought us a certain amount of privacy) facing the hotel. Turns out I had been outmaneuvered.

Almost.

Bullets streaked toward Milo, his death assured ... that is until they reached some barrier, some strange force that caused them to suddenly stop, smoking, in midair some few inches in front of his face.

That was my ace-in-the-hole ... sprites, minor air elementals. A couple of years before I met Morgan, he wrote of his adventures against his Family, the time he obtained the *Codex Infernales*, or the Judas Codex. He told of a magic called a Denial, a sort of imposed field where certain elementals cannot enter. The Sicarii had used a Denial to guard the Codex, forbidding air elementals from entering a place called SwolTech. Air has a real problem with being told *not* to go somewhere. Seemed like that element's temperament mirrored that of a seventeen-year-old boy in the full flurry of testosterone-fueled rebellion. And it held a grudge like you wouldn't believe and was more than willing to help when Cain gave the call.

The sprites, invisible to the cameras, managed to keep bullets from turning Milo into a flesh colander every time the Sicarii pulled the trigger. Without a sound, Milo charged the group, discharging his own pistol at the first man, who danced a death jig before falling. Before he hit the floor, his compatriots had already drawn wickedly sharp knives and set to attacking my bodyguard.

Alanna sidestepped an axe kick that would have pounded her into the floor like a tent peg and punched, hitting the giant's calf with a well-placed knuckle. The big man grunted, a sound like the cough of a jaguar, and went for a spinning backfist. She wasn't there to receive it. Instead she was airborne, whirling, wrapping legs like pythons around the man's neck, grabbing one large hand and savagely biting the thumb while squeezing her thighs together, her weight dragging him to the floor.

As for Orson, the bullets were of no use to his enemies, but before he could draw his own weapon, a boot connected with his throat, *crunching* his larynx and he choked to death with a high-pitched wheeze. I felt my temples throb as the sounds of his agonizing demise hammered into my brain.

"Cain," I said. "Orson ..."

"Say no more," he replied over the headset. "I will attend the lad's killers."

That was my real back up plan. The world's oldest man and strongest magus held in reserve in case of emergency. During the planning session I almost included Judas, but still couldn't bring myself to fully trust her. Call it a failing of mine, or a judgement call.

What about Maggie? The monitors installed in the van gave me a close up view of the action, but Maggie's was a bit dim. There was enough light to catch some of the action.

One of her boots took a minder in the knee, striking with rattlesnake quickness and the leg bent the wrong way, the sickening wet sound of breaking bones filling the speakers. A hand the size of a dinner plate slammed into her jaw, standing her upright while another doubled her over. There were just too many and the monitor became a jumble of confusing images as my stomach tried to curl in on itself.

"Father," Gio cried, clutching his elbows. "We have to do *something*!"

"Just keep an eye on the limo," I snarled, reminding myself it was me I was angry with, not him. Things were spinning in directions unknown. The old saying, 'plans do not survive the first contact with the enemy' couldn't have been any truer than right now. I hoped, dearly hoped, the remnants were still viable.

As the two women who killed Orson turned to leave, Cain was upon them. No guns, no knives, just flashing fists and feet. The first woman took an overhead right that flipped her on her head. The snap of a neck echoed around the room. The second woman took some time to kill. She was skilled, her ability at Krav Maga and Aikido fluent in every liquid motion. Had it not been Cain, she would have wiped the floor with him, but it *was* Cain, the man who had fifty-thousand years of martial practice.

She never laid a knuckle on him.

"Done." That was all he said, a single word uttered in such a dead, hard syllable that it rang in my ears long after it was spoken.

"To the limo," I replied. He disappeared out of camera range. I cut the feed.

Back to Alanna. Both were back on their feet. I saw the big man's hand bleeding profusely, a jagged, red emptiness where the thumb used to be. She stood with hands cocked, raised and ready for action while the big man stood on shaking legs. His wide face and blunt features reminded me of a statue, but statues didn't bleed and grimace in pain.

A high, spinning kick that should have connected, but the man suddenly sidestepped, unusually graceful for such a big guy. His flat slap to her head flung blood from his hand to decorate the wall. Alanna fell to the floor. She did not get up.

I felt my stomach roll. "Cain … reroute to Alanna."

"Almost there," he replied.

Next screen. One assailant down, head twisted round at a one-hundred eighty-degrees from the front. It takes considerable strength to break an unwilling neck, but Milo had plenty to spare. It looked like he used it well.

A knife suddenly appeared, and he blocked the thrust that would have opened him from crotch to sternum like a trout. His fist knocked the assailant's knife away. A hard jab took him in the jaw, but his head hardly moved. He speared the attacker's eyes with stiffened fingers, burying two digits up to the palm with a wet squelch. There was a scream, long and agonized, a wail of dismay and pain that raised the hair on the back of my arms. The man fell, clutching his face.

One left. This man, this Sicarius, moved with fluid grace. Tall, lithe, dusky skinned and black haired. He looked a lot like Burke, enough to be a cousin.

Or brother.

This man smiled, a wicked thing full of anticipatory malice, and spoke a Word.

Oh ... well, that was unexpected. I bit my lip as the sound crawled through my ears and out again. A magus. Good thing we prepared.

I could almost feel the paste smeared on Milo's chest heat up as the Word washed over him, absorbed into the counter spell unguent prepared by Cain.

As for Milo, he attacked so fast the Dagger Man's smile didn't have time to fade before a meaty fist spread teeth across the room. "That's impossible!" screamed the man from the floor, eyes unfocused. Holes like accusations marked the places where his teeth had been. "Impossible!" My bodyguard's foot put paid to the rest of his life.

In Alanna's room, the size twelve boot descending toward her head suddenly stopped, then disappeared so quickly it was as if someone deftly edited the scene. There was a couple of hard thuds and a cracking sound and the next thing I saw was Cain, wiping his hands on his trousers before offering one to Alanna. Blood crusted his fingernails.

Dark, blurry shapes dominated Maggie's screen, still a jumble of half-seen images and grunts. The elemental wall, cement gray streaked with black asphalt, was now surrounded by amazed gawkers. I wanted to bolt out of the van and run to her help, but that would be suicide. Not part of my belief system.

"Father look!" Gio pointed.

The elemental wall of concrete started to melt, flowing, reforming, stretching like taffy, resuming the form of street and sidewalk. It happened quickly, and it left the limo exposed once again. Without hesitation it raced off, wheels smoking, the crowd screaming scrambled out of its way.

"Everyone," I hollered. "Our quarry is leaving." I turned to our driver, a hard-faced woman named Lenore. "After that limo. Don't lose it."

The chase was on.

CHAPTER EIGHT
HUNT AND HUNTED

＊＊＊

F EW THINGS SUCK IN THIS WORLD like tailing a car through metropolitan London at the height of rush hour. Being chased by a helicopter gunship through Paris while being a passenger on a motorcycle topped the list by a hair, but London came a close second.

There was no blazing through the streets at eighty miles per, no screaming pedestrians or yelping dogs we almost squashed into paste. Not in London, not with streets full of Fords and Smart Cars, double decker buses and motorcycles, pedestrians and cyclists. It was New York on steroids, Paris pumped full of performance enhancing drugs, mean, fat and sassy.

Slowest car chase ever.

That didn't stop my heart from lodging firmly in my throat the whole way, though.

"Do stop struggling, my dear Maggie." Fergus smiled wide, every freckle captured by the high-res camera. The interior of the limo was well lit, and it was roomy enough to accommodate the five people rather easily. "You will only get hurt." The Scottish burr remained, but now it was softer, almost undetectable, replaced by smooth vowels. "When we set this trap, I thought we would catch a Templar or two, but we absconded with the woman who helped Olivier kill Julian." Wide, wide, wide, was that smile, teeth gleaming. The grin of a predator. "The boss will be *so* pleased."

We were on something called Cromwell Rd, I think. I wasn't paying that much attention to the outside world. My focus was on the limo. "Maggie, we're right behind you," I said into the microphone. "Don't worry, we got your six."

No reply. Not that I expected one. She had to keep her cool and not be seen reacting to voices that weren't in the limo.

One of the minders, a broad-shouldered brute with blond hair, leaned over and whispered to Fergus, "Our people have not checked in."

A look of annoyance crossed the Scot's face. "Then consider them dead unless they show up later. I have a feeling Maggie's backup included Cain, the man she's been seen bouncing around the world with."

The minder nodded, paling. Cain had that effect on the Sicarii.

"Check her for bugs."

"Gio!" I barked. "Turn off her tracking devices, all but one."

She had three. Boot, lapel and button. All could be remotely activated and deactivated.

"The one in her lapel and button are off. I left the one in her boot on. Hopefully that will satisfy them."

"Good job." To the driver, "Lenore, where are we?"

"Slowly heading southeast, Father." She was hunched forward, gripping the steering wheel tight, knuckles white. "Got four cars between us, but someone's gonna spot this van if we keep on their tail like we have been. We're not exactly subtle here."

"No worries."

On the monitor, events unfolded. "Found one." A boot went flying out the limo, eliciting several honks.

"Kill the camera and audio." The monitor winked to black. We waited a tense minute or two.

"Want me to turn the camera back on?" Gio asked, sweating bullets.

I bit my lip. "Not yet."

It was a credit to Gio's faith in me that he didn't object. He nodded once, long jaw clenched and went back to his tablet computer.

"Lenore, back off a couple more car lengths, but keep them in sight."

"What the Ferris Bueller are you talking about?" She sounded pissed.

Gio looked at me and mouthed *Ferris Bueller?* I shrugged. Lenore's face was dripping with sweat and I reckoned she felt more than a little stressed. "Trust me, Lenore. I got this. Gio, when we pull back two car lengths, turn the camera back on."

Lenore managed to slow enough to let a couple of subcompacts get in front and when I gave him the nod, Gio turned on the camera. Audio crackled in the headset.

Three minders dressed in black business suits faced the screen, one rubbed his knee and flexed it gently. Fergus knew the Word of Healing and had repaired his bodyguard's damaged joint.

"Now about those pesky little sprites of yours," Fergus said, drawing a crude dagger from the inside of his jacket. "Crack the windows a tad," he ordered one of the minders.

I went cold because I recognized the weapon he held in his hand. I carried the twin. Silver runes adorned the black leather sheath. He drew the dagger. A misericord. Like Ablewand. A sudden wind swirled inside the limo, dragging bits of paper as it fled the car.

"This is Denial." Fergus waved the artifact around. "Like the spell of the same name, it forbids elementals, banishes them, but only in a ten-foot radius. You have no help now, Maggie dear. Don't try any Words, I will counter them."

A tug at my elbow. "I have the files from Henry. One already decrypted … it has Fergus' itinerary for the next two days. The other is only a few kilobytes but is heavily encrypted. It will take me a bit longer on that one, a matter of checking known Sicarii decryption keys." Gio bit his lip as he stared at his laptop.

I nodded and returned my eyes to the monitor. The van swayed a bit and from the front came soft swearing. Lenore sounded more pissed than usual. A former Mossad agent, part of the Kidon unit of the Caesarea department, she came to the Templars via the Holy Father's connection in Israel. Funny how ultimate evil brings those of differing faiths together.

"Where are we going?" asked Maggie.

Fergus seemed not to hear as he sheathed the dagger and hid it inside his jacket. "Do you mind telling me what you know, dear Maggie? All the little secrets you are privy to? I promise to make your death quick and clean. Otherwise, if you make me work for the information, things are going to get sticky. Not that the boys will mind."

Maggie's next words were unprintable. Inventive, but unprintable.

Fergus was not impressed. "Such a mouth. Before you die the boys and I are going to fuck-start it. Break it in for what it was intended."

"Easy," I breathed into the microphone. "He's trying to rattle you." As for me, I felt plenty angry for her sake and wanted to reach out through the camera and yank Fergus' spleen out through his nose. She was made of sterner stuff and stayed quiet. I knew she wanted them dead in the worst way.

"Got it!" Gio crowed, startling me out of my skin. Lenore did some more swearing and the van juked to the right for a second, nearly sending me sprawling. "Sorry," he mumbled after I tossed him a stern glare learned from the best Drill Instructors the United States Army had to offer. "I decrypted the file. It was sent using one of the older keys, one we only recently uncovered when we hacked United Arms a couple of months ago."

United Arms. I rubbed my cheeks. An American arms manufacturer, part of the Deschamps conglomerate and a leader in the creation of weapons of mass destruction. We learned through our sources in Washington (yes, there *are* honest and good politicians. I was as surprised as anyone) that they would win a DOD contract if the testing of a new weapon were to be successful. We infiltrated their major facility in Arkansas and accessed their computer system and altered the schematics for a new weapon prototype of the M61 Vulcan cannon capable of firing 10,000 flechettes a minute, turning *anything* into Swiss cheese in a matter of seconds) just a hair, just a fraction of a centimeter.

We reached out to our man in Washington, who suggested that the test would be best demonstrated by a unit fresh off the assembly line. During the demonstration the only thing turned into confetti was the weapon itself. Embarrassing to be sure, but what hurt more was the loss of the contract, which would have aided them in the hostile takeover of their biggest competition, the Allied Arms company.

"An older key?"

"At least three years old according to code date. It looks to be several kilobytes of text."

Why would Fergus have a file encrypted with such an old code? I mulled that for a second, then said, "Read a little bit, find out what's what."

Meanwhile Fergus peppered Maggie with questions, not really expecting her to answer (and she didn't) but to see what kind of reaction he could provoke. Most were about yours truly, where I hung my hat, my command style, resources etc., etc. From the anger crinkling the corners of his eyes, her face must have been carved in granite.

"You're doing great, kiddo," I purred into the mic. "Let him talk, I'll tell you when to get physical."

Before I could say more the back of the van opened letting in an indecent amount of sun and a smiling Cain, scaring me out of five years of life. I looked out the front and saw we were zipping along about thirty mph and he hadn't even broken a sweat or seemed winded. The back door slammed shut hard enough for the monitors to rattle, causing Lenore to spit out some blue words. Gio squeaked then went back to reading.

"Not late, am I?"

"Planning on giving me a freaking heart attack?"

"A fine specimen such as yourself is hardly at risk for a myocardial infarction, no matter your advanced age."

"So, says the ancient son of Adam."

"Touché." Cain dazzled me with a smile. "What is currently in play with the lovely a nd talented apprentice of mine? Is she in dire circumstances and in need of rescue?"

"In the limo with Fergus and four of his minders."

He *hrumphed*. "It seems rather unfair odds if you ask my opinion. The young Sicarius should have employed more personnel."

"They are trained Dagger Men, Cain."

"And she has survived half a decade as the Valhalla Club's champion."

True. Run by fallen angels who took on the aspects of the Norse Gods, the Valhalla Club was a fight club, but instead of fists and feet they used axes and armor. From what I understand most of the warriors retired missing digits at the least, losing their lives at the most. Blood ran in rivers through the graywater pipes beneath the club.

"Holy ... crap, Father," Gio breathed. "This is it. The Holy Grail." His face shone as if with an inner light. "Everything we need to know about Burke."

I felt my eyes go wide. "Everything."

"Everything."

The mic was uncomfortably close and a drop of sweat rolled down my temple. I desperately didn't want to say the words that would set loose the hounds, didn't want to be the cause of bloodshed.

I knew my duty.

Of course, Cain read my mind. A habit that annoys, for sure. "Whether you choose to believe my words, young man, I offer nothing but the naked truth. Not as I perceive it to be, but as it lays for all the world to glimpse." Cain chuckled, a hard-edged sound that implied no mirth. "Although raised from infancy to regard their Patron as the pinnacle of the Divine, they do not, and have never, resided in a vacuum. Those men in yon limousine would no more take pause at committing the vilest atrocities than you would admonishing the venal for a multitude of sins because the Lord that we worship, the one that gave mankind a measure of His grace and that spark of divinity called a soul, also bestowed the greatest, most cherished gift of all."

"Free will," I murmured.

"Quite. Those men chose their measure in life, chose their destiny with eyes wide open even though somewhat shaded by their Sicarii brethren. The truth has always been manifest for all to see ... in a sunrise, the cries of birds and the soft wail of infants. To call violence upon those who breathe blatant hate from their nostrils, whose existence has been dedicated to the overthrow of all that we call good in this world is not a sin.

"It is *justice*."

What could I say? I gave a nod and opened my mouth. Nothing came out.

A large hand settled lightly upon my shoulder. "She is not only my apprentice in the ways of the magi, but also a student of combat. Maggie will win out."

The words finally passed my lips, bitter as gall. "Kill them." No euphemisms, no clever play on words. Just a sentence of death.

One bare foot and one boot lashed out, a hard heel connected with a meaty crunch on a chin. The bare foot hit without a crunch, but the effect was the same. Heads snapped back, necks breaking. At the same time, her right hand flashed, the edge smacking against Fergus's throat. He began to choke and gag, spittle flying from his lips. No Words from that man for a while, I guessed.

Two minders to go.

A gun came into camera view and a feminine hand grasped the barrel. Flame sparked out the barrel in a flat *crack* and a bullet hit the third minder sitting across from Fergus between the eyes.

Maggie twisted her wrist and with the other hand jammed the barrel of the weapon in the last minder's mouth, the sturdy woman, shattering teeth. Flesh rendered the next bark of the gun quiet and blood streamed from ears, nostrils and eyes. The woman folded up on herself and slumped.

"I'll take that," said Maggie, reaching into Fergus' jacket and pulling out Denial. Nodding once, she calmly stabbed him through the eye and he stopped his gurgling, thrashing only once before dying, face red and bloated with blood.

The windows were bulletproof, but the mirrored glass partition between driver and passengers was not. It gave with a crunch and Maggie held the barrel to driver's neck.

"Do what I say, and you get to live," she said.

He did exactly as instructed.

THE BOOK OF

BURKE

Chapter One
Back

———〜〜〜———

Fergus:

By now you know that I have returned. Because only a few executive members of our organization are allowed access to Project Century, I have chosen you to be the recipient of this knowledge. We have housekeeping to perform and when the dust has settled, to use an Italian term, you will sit at my side as my consigliere.

Blaine was a competent business man but proved to be a fool when running the Family's true concerns, and such fools cannot be tolerated. It is time to return to our roots, take an aggressive stance and prepare the world for Century and the ascendancy of the Patron. Because you will sit at my right hand, I have prepared this document, so you may understand Century and ready yourself to participate in the project. With the now operational project at our disposal, the Templars will tremble and we can finally, once and for all, dispose of Cain and the priest.

For the Glory of the Patron
Burke

Sticky light gummed up my eyeballs and made my head hurt. I tried to blink but purple colored my world. A shock hit my body, jazzy tremors that had me shaking like a palsy victim.

"Sorry, sir. I am removing the electrodes as we speak. Please hold still."

I knew that voice, but the memory of it wouldn't surface through the sludge of my mind. I tried to form words, but a gluey something held my mouth shut and the sticky light seared my eyes. Anger ignited within. I was never a patient man and my inability to move and the pain that poked my brain put me off my feed.

"Glrg." Was that the best I could do? The anger morphed to a simmering rage. Julian always said that was my greatest flaw, my blood running too hot for my own good. It led me to rash action and foolish underestimation of my enemies. It hurt to say that he was right. It takes a certain amount of courage for honest self-reflection and courage was something I never lacked.

Back in the day, when I was young, barely out of small pants, I told Julian and the rest of the Family I had eleven Words, that I was a magus to fear and the Olivier was nothing. I felt so clever hiding the fact that I had all twelve Words, that I was the most powerful Magus ever. The Chosen One.

The Redeemer.

Damn Olivier for having twelve Words. Not only twelve Words, but an even a greater facility for the Silver than I. Twenty-two of the Terrible Words stored in the Silver were mine to command, but Olivier could use all thirty and that meant only one thing. He was stronger than me, stronger than Julian. Stronger than anyone.

That stung. Worse than I could even say. and it kept the anger smoldering in me for years after he disappeared. It was a cancer that ate at me, gnawing at my pride. I knew that even though he could technically out-magic me, I was smarter, I had the iron to do what was needed, to *be* what was needed.

We captured him, tortured him to gain information on the location of the Silver, but once again he beat us. He beat *me*. That caused the anger to become a true infection, pustulent and vile, a tearing at my soul and consuming my nights, driving my research. I had to find Olivier. Had to retrieve the Silver.

Had to kill him.

I never found him, though. That rankled.

Tolonen. That was the name. I went for it. The name came out somewhat ungarbled.

"That's right, sir. I am Dr. Tolonen."

Good. Thought so. Tolonen. Met him a couple of times with relation to the Century Project a few years ago.

Why Tolonen? He should be in Finland overseeing … oh … *shit*. A chill blasted through the purple gumminess, through the light that hurt worse than a migraine. "Dead. I died."

"Yes, sir. Please calm down. Let me remove the electrodes and clean you off."

"Elec—trodes?"

"What do you remember?"

What was that taste? The purple gumminess had a … sweet flavor. Bitter as well. "M-most everything." I gave it another thought. Voids in my mind, light in my brain. "Turn off the light."

"It is very dim in here already, sir. Any dimmer and I won't be able to see well enough to minister to you. Your eyes and your brain will adjust soon. Now, you said you remember 'most everything'. Can you explain."

A cool something wiped my mouth, removing the sweet/bitter taste. Tolonen began to gently wipe my eyelids. "I-I remember my early life, some portions of the last decade, but there are ... voids, holes I can't account for. Is that normal?"

"Perfectly normal. Tell me, do know where you are located?"

"Finland," I replied, mouth coming along nicely. "Project Century labs."

The cool something wiped away the purple and I was able to see somewhat. The shape that loomed over me must have been Tolonen, but all I saw was a big blur. "Good. Tell me what you know. and I will fill in while I take care of you."

For some reason Century was clear as bell in my memory and the words came out as lips and tongue became more operational. "Seventy years ago. Project Century was conceived. Cloning with accelerated growth so our ranks could be replenished quickly. The idea was sound, but when the first fast-grown clone was successfully produced in the eighties, it died within five hours of being decanted from the pod." I licked my lips, tasting the remnants of sweet and bitter. "Despite proof of concept, the bodies didn't last long without a soul, so Julian came up with the idea that if the Patron were to release a soul from Hell into the new host bodies, then they might have a chance at life again, be who they were."

"Very good, sir. Spot on. Please continue."

"Problem was the memories. Souls do not equate to memory. The newly revived lived but had the minds of children and had to be reeducated. This was the nineties. A new approach had to be found and it was. Mind mapping."

Something blocked Tolonen's blurry body and a hand pulled me upright, or almost so, and the lip of a cup hit my mouth. I drank greedily. Not water. Something salty and sweet and faintly vile. I figured it must contain some of the elements my body needed. My new body.

"Thank you," I said when the cup was empty. Tolonen was coming into focus. Tall, almost gaunt, with dark brown hair and puppy dog eyes. "Mind mapping. Recording the brain, downloading memories, experiences ... all the data. Mandated by Julian to be done once a year by every Family member, although most didn't know what the procedure intended. I was one of the lucky few in the know.

"For five years my mind has been mapped, ready for me to be reborn in the eventuality of my death." I laughed, hacking up phlegm. It hurt. "Which is what happened. I must have died." Damn. With clearing eyes, I looked around. My new body rested in a tub of purple goo, electrodes attached to every major muscle group, the wires disappearing into the translucent slime. I recalled that when the bodies were quick-grown, electrical stimulation was needed so the muscles would develop properly. "How many others have been decanted?"

Those puppy dog eyes looked away. "You are the first, sir." He licked his lips. "Well, technically not true. The first to survive decanting. It took some trial-and-error to perfect the process. I can assure you that we can start decanting more and more of our members, bringing back those who have donated cells to the project."

The first! I would have been elated but my stomach took that time to let out an enormous rumble and I realized I was *famished*. My joy at being alive (again) would have to wait. There were only two things that mattered. "What happened to me? I need food. Yesterday."

"I have a dossier prepared with all the information you require. When I am done removing the electrodes, I will assist you in cleaning up and providing a meal."

A dossier on my death. The anger reborn in my gut told me I wouldn't like what I found.

IT TAKES A BIG MAN, FERGUS, to admit when he's wrong and I was so very wrong when I discovered Olivier's hideout in Nebraska and tried to take him on by myself. My arrogance led to my destruction. I can be a big enough man to admit I was a fool. Death provides a certain unique perspective on life. The anger I now feel coursing in my veins is a dull thing compared to the fury that dwelt there before. In the time since my resurrection I have been given to more philosophical thoughts, which I believe have helped me cope as the new head of the Family.

After my decanting, I spent three weeks in physical therapy, catching up on the two years since I died and the bloody cock-up that was Blaine. I never liked that boy. Too American, brash and impulsive despite being a fine businessman. His breaking of the Accords with Cain was a most egregious and foolhardy act. He should have sent an entire SS team to take out the priest, not the Giggler. Michael Engle is far too powerful to leave to the talents of a single individual. Now that Engle has been introduced to the Templars and Cain has entered the fray, we are in greater peril than ever before. We don't have the Silver and only a few artifacts to aid our cause, so the successful completion of the Century Project is the Patron's answer to our prayers. Now we can resurrect the finest Sicarii who have ever lived. Seventy years of stored cells, incredibly valuable DNA that can tip the balance permanently in our favor.

You have spoken to the Patron, but you don't know the full details of what's to come. Allow me to illuminate.

A BUILDING BURNED IN NEW YORK CITY, one of its many high rises. What made this one special was that it belonged to the Family. It belonged to Blaine and he was inside that heap of burning rubble, his remains becoming bar-b-que.

Some media anchor babbled on about the story we planted, about some sort of terrorist act aimed at an imperialist global conglomerate, a hate response of religious extremism that had every news organization scrambling for experts on the subject. No one bothered to doubt the story, not in a time of fear, fear fostered by the Family. Conflict is good for business.

I flicked the television off and took a drink of some single-malt scotch. Electric stimulation of forming musculature kept me from being as weak as a kitten, but I still was not up to snuff, not as strong as I used to be. My hand shook slightly, the amber liquid sloshing a bit. A drop hit my wrist and I licked it up. No need to waste good liquor.

My bodyguard, Hans, stood at the door, as immobile as the furniture, blue eyes flat and unblinking. Thick beard, thick shoulders, thick wrists ... thick everything. Quite possibly the strongest human being in the world stuffed into a ten-thousand-dollar suit. Unlike most serial killers, he had impeccable control over his dark urges and since I had need of good help, we struck a rather simple deal ... I gave him wheelchair bound women to abuse and destroy and he gave me his absolute loyalty.

My gaze flicked to his massive form, the tattoos on the backs of his hands, around that thick neck and behind his ears. Rust red coloring still inflamed from their recent application.

"Hans, give me a moment."

He disappeared through the door, silent for one so big.

Three weeks of physical therapy and two hours with the Board to cement my leadership. Not that it was necessary ... when the Patron said jump, we didn't land until he told us to. Blaine's descent was as swift as his rise because the Patron deemed it so and because he failed his talent, let his cockiness destroy reasoned thought.

I was him a couple of years ago. Now ... now I was made of sterner stuff. Wiser, perhaps, possessing a cooler head.

The area in front of my desk was large enough to park an Escalade, the carpet a soft beige expanse suited to what came next. From a brass urn I poured the ashes of a child molester in broad arcs, carefully creating cabbalistic symbols. Then came the black fluid called Unholy Water sprinkled at the cardinal points, each drop precisely placed.

Most people whose eyes were not veiled, wide open to the real world of Words and elementals had not heard of this next thing, this different sort of magic. Only a handful of magi throughout the centuries had known of its existence, knew its name. Not Botanical Magic, not Elemental Magic, it was Angelic Magic. Also called Enochian Magic after the Language of the Angels.

As the last drops landed, I began to chant in Enochian. The words are not for your ears, Fergus, unless you assume the throne. Safe to say, it sounds like an unlikely marriage of Finnish and Hawaiian with a few dollops of the Language of Air thrown in for good measure. The words constituted the opening of a path, a clarity of perception and a loosening of the bonds between spirit and flesh.

With the brass bowl of Unholy Water now resting on my desk, I sat in the middle of the curves and arcs, the heaps and dots of ash and Unholy Fluid smoking on the carpet, sitting crisscross applesauce with my hands on my knees. I was careful not to touch the ash or the water., The results of such a mistake would be more than a little drastic. Most likely I would melt into a putrescent puddle of amber fluid.

I kept chanting, repeating the words over and over again, waiting for the results of the spell. After a while, I began to notice a curious graying at the edges of my vision, as if the world was slowing being edited from my reality. The grayness ate its way toward the center of my sight and I had to stifle a stab of fear, forcing myself to continue.

All gray. Still chanting, sweat slicking my skin as the words passing my lips became muffled. I closed my eyes. I would not show fear, would not give in like an animal in a trap. If this went sideways, I would die with my dignity intact, not like a little bitch.

"You can open your eyes now."

I knew that voice. Shitfire, did I ever. It was *Him*. The God of the Family. Lucifer. Slowly I cracked my eyelids and let out a slight bark of amazement.

A room. An office, with a nice, thick Persian rug cushioning my ass and a walnut desk dominating my field of vision. I slowly rose to my feet, smoothing the lines of my Desmond Merrion suit. No sign of the speaker.

The wall behind the desk consisted of oak shelves filled with books. A quick squint revealed it to be an impressive collection of legal texts, the kind one would find in our London and New York based law firms. The chair, black leather and overstuffed, was empty. Once again, no sign of the speaker.

A wet bar ran along the wall to the right and my mouth watered at the impressive array of alcohol displayed there.

"Go ahead, fix yourself a drink. I will take vodka, slightly chilled."

I jumped and looked around. No one. Merely me and the office. I absently noted that the Persian rug was devoid of ash and Unholy water. My spell had worked.

Two fingers of Pappy Van Winkle 23yr old reserve for me. My fingers shook slightly, the only evidence of my uncertainty. I added three cubes of ice to a stainless-steel shaker and poured in a couple shots of vodka, tightened the lid and shook slightly, popping the pour cap off and draining the now cold fluid into a crystal tumbler. My mouth went dry as I noticed that the office had no door. no exit.

"Thank you, My boy." A hand came into view and took the tumbler. I turned.

If you're looking for a detailed description of what He looks like, then you're going to be disappointed. His ... aspect was beyond my mortal comprehension; it didn't really register upon my visual cortex. All that is left to me are impressions: a strong chin, a high brow, hair so finely golden as to be gossamer threads of light. These details floated around in my mind without coalescing to a stable, comprehensible whole. I did have an immediate sense that this was a being of such intense beauty that to glimpse more than what He allowed would turn my brain into ash in an instant.

"Hello, Burke. Good to see you again."

I sipped my bourbon. Smooth, buttery, with a large body, some sherry notes along with dried fruit and creamy vanilla. The Americans could sure create a fine brew. "Again, sir."

"Of course. You were dead once." Lucifer took His seat behind the desk and I had to avert my eyes to avoid a headache. His voice sounded as it always had, rich and avuncular, sweet with an undertone of offal. "That is, before I let your soul flee from this realm."

"I am in Hell, sir?"

"Yes."

Oh.

"You look uncomfortable," he continued, the tumbler disappearing into the blank spot of his face. "Have a seat."

And there it was, a chair. Simple, wooden and not in the least comfortable. "Thank you, sir." I took a deep breath, ready to tread onto unfamiliar territory. "Hell looks like an office?"

His laugh made my stomach perform a slow roll. "This is what I created to accommodate you, Burke. Had I translated you Hell without this ... anteroom, your body would be rendered to its component atoms in an instant."

"Thank you then, sir. The spell you emailed me worked perfectly, of which I am profoundly grateful."

"Of course, it worked. It is the same spell I handed to every Family head since ... the Founder disappointed Me."

I nodded. While the original *Codex Infernales* remained lost, Julian had the foresight and a certain contempt for tradition to have it digitally stored. In the past few weeks I had caught up on the Family history, as well as the intricacies of Blood Magic. Some information had been lost, however, remaining with the original work. Why, I don't know.

"Strange," I murmured into my drink. "An office. Very modern."

A well-manicured hand waved at the wall to my left and it disappeared. What replaced it was as hard to define as the Patron's features. Blackness, a dark like the crushing heart of a singularity, it sucked at my soul through my eyes and I felt that if I kept staring, the pressure of it would pull me in and I would be lost. No, worse than lost. That word does not encapsulate the true meaning of what would happen on the other side of that blackness. I suddenly knew that it would be more horrible than I could describe, an aching coldness, an absolute zero where all laws of thermodynamics cease to have relevancy.

"Hell is not brimstone and fire, red hot hooks tearing at flesh. No, My young one, not by a long shot. Hell is the total absence of everything, anything that could impact upon the senses. There is no light, no dark, no up, no down, only an eternity of utter emptiness where souls suffer not the pain of physical agony, but the sweet anguish of nothing." Lucifer took another drink of His vodka. "They say that staying too long in a sensory deprivation chamber drives people mad. They begin to hallucinate before their marbles become lost. My guests, being souls without flesh, are subject to pure, crystalline sanity. They do not have the comfort of madness. No shelter of a mind lost. Only abject clarity that has no end. A perfect sameness that has no end or beginning. It just is."

I couldn't help myself. When life offers you the opportunity to meet the Patron, you sometimes take a risk and ask some questions that may seem indelicate. "This pleases you?"

Silence. It stretched like taffy and I began to sweat ... until He began to chuckle. "I am pleased by what I have wrought here. It is perfection, as is the suffering of those I find ... less than worthy of My attention. For Me, it is candy." His regard focused on me and I felt a pressure upon my mind, a mild presence that raised my blood pressure, bringing a flush to my cheeks. "My descendants, such as yourself, have no worry of such a fate, My mercy is infinite. As long as you do not fuck up." A slight pause. "Like you did when you decided to take on Olivier alone."

That warm flush of blood became a cold sweat in less than a second. "I'm sorry, sir. I was rash and such a mistake will not happen again. At least you have his soul now to toy with however you wish."

The Patron sat there, silent, His regard a steady, almost smothering cloak upon my senses. It suddenly came to me then that Olivier's soul *wasn't* with the Patron, that it somehow escaped his grasp. It also came to me that if I voiced such an opinion aloud you wouldn't be reading these words. Instead, you would be answering to a new Family leader. The ground on which I found myself seemed more fragile than rotten ice.

"Uhem … ah, well, sir," I said, trying to get the conversation back to a more convivial territory. "You called me here and I came. What can I do for you, sir?"

He drummed His fingers on the desk top, the sound slightly muffled by the blotter. He sat there, drumming and staring until I couldn't look at Him anymore and I cast my eyes to the wall. The blackness was gone, replaced by painting of a wolf howling upon a hilltop beneath a pregnant moon. It was crude and unsophisticated, the artist having little understanding of proportion and composition. I wondered why the first angel would have such a poor example of art in His office.

"Pay attention, boy. The time has come."

I didn't bother to ask what time … it was *the* time. The time of the Redeemer. I felt a rush of delicious terror. All I could do was nod.

The Patron seemed pleased. "Good. Now, go and prepare for the Rite of Ascension to be performed this year at the appointed hour at the sacred site. I trust you will not fail Me?"

"No, sir."

"Fine. You have pleased Me, and I have given you this second chance. You may not be the perfect vessel for My might, but you are the best seen since I began this endeavor. You have the rituals and the diet needed to cleanse your body. Rejoice, for My hour is at hand and the world shall tremble at My magnificence."

The office disappeared, only to be replaced by my own. I sat sweating in a pile of ash, overjoyed and terrified. I am the Redeemer, the living conduit for the Patron in this world.

Our time is nigh, Fergus. We shall sit at the table and dine upon the fruits of this world and shape it to our desire.

THE LAST BOOK

THE LAST BOOK

CHAPTER ONE
MICHAEL

———~~~———

ARTH GIVES WAY TO THE ONSLAUGHT, unable to withstand the flow. Elementals, slow and ponderous, refuse to stop the deluge. Saltwater and fresh, bitterly cold and relentless as gravity, seep through the spaces between rock and where there was no space, small water elementals carve them, chewing through stone as if it is soft cheese.

The waters from the gulf eat their way north while the multitudinous lakes in the area lend their mass to the effort. A local fisherman, boat caught in a swirling eddy, cries with alarm as the lake, small but well stocked with fish, drains three feet in a matter of minutes.

And still water rushes, more and more lakes lose valuable inches and feet, draining deep into the earth and rushing toward a central point, tearing at the earth with liquid fingers.

In southeast Finland, in what was once the South Karelia region, there is a municipality on the shore of the lake Saimaa about nineteen miles from the Russian border. The placid waters, clear and cold, now roil as if the depths boil at unimaginable temperatures. The inhabitants closest to shore, turn on their lights and peer worriedly at the agitated surface. A man exits his small home, dressed against the frigid Finnish autumn, electric torch in hand, casting illumination at the waves that slap at a wooden dock. His small fishing boat bobs as if in the grip a violent storm, though there is no wind of any consequence.

Water touches his rubber boots. "Vittu," he mutters fearfully.

The water recedes from his toes, the level dropping a foot in less than ten seconds and the man looks out at the lake, eyes aided by the torch. Far out he notices a hump in the troubled water, a rising curve of darkness as if a fist had punched the lake from beneath, deforming the surface.

Twin columns erupt, watery arms fifty feet long bearing four fingers follow shortly by a globular head, an almost perfect sphere twenty feet across, marred by a slash of a mouth and swirling vortices where the eyes should be. The surface of the head ripples slightly in time with waves below. The head rises, borne aloft by a column of water that is the body. At full height, the elemental tops seventy feet, from crown to where waist joins seamlessly with the rioting waves.

The man stares. The watery being stares. The moment stretches on, tension straining to piano wire tautness until the water elemental points past the man, away from the lake, away from danger.

"Vittu," he breathes again, face slack with terror. The torch hits the muddy ground and rubber boots beat a hasty retreat from the shoreline. A car roars to life and tires squeal.

I PULLED MY HAND FROM THE PUDDLE of dirty water, shaking my head. The vision … was as if I stood there with the Finnish man, watching the elemental rise from the lake.

"Father?"

Right. Back to business. "It's okay, Milo." I waved my dripping hand. "This is necessary."

Two days since Fergus died. Two days since Maggie released her inner Valkyrie (although, to be honest, it wasn't so inner. She was all Valkyrie, in and out), coming out of the ordeal with hardly a scratch. She could have killed them all before they entered the limo, but the objective was information, then neutralization.

Hard to believe only forty-eight hours passed since I read the missive Burke sent his number two and so much had to be accomplished. The missive wasn't hard to decipher. I presented the information to my inner circle of Templars in an apartment near Trafalgar Square, above a little pub called The Blade. The owner was a retired Templar, a man named Owen with a large gut and an eyepatch. More than once I had to listen to the story of how he lost the eye to a Dagger Man while preventing the assassination of young Prince Charles. All very hush-hush, need to know stuff. So, need to know, that the prince had no clue how close he came to the other side of the veil.

The inner circle. A dark term considering I could trust most, if not all, the Templars with my life. These people, *sans* His Holiness, were the ones I had to lean on in the thick of the things. Those I could count on to give the correct commands absent my supervision.

"Project Century. That's what Burke teased Hermes about. The endeavor that was near a hundred years in the making." I ran a finger along my rim of my teacup. Oolong. Not my favorite, but I didn't feel like surrendering to something stronger. Too much whisky in the past few weeks and I needed clarity.

Cain sipped his own tea, mirrored shades reflecting the overhead light. "My ears have never encountered the name, my friend. Safe to say I feel foolish for not divining the meaning when you related the conversation with the aforementioned fallen celestial."

"Not much to go on." Maggie snorted. "From what the padre tells me it was barely mentioned in Morgan's translation of the Codex he read."

It was Judas who filled in the empty bits, clarifying the Patron's instructions. "We have a bigger problem than that. Ascension," she stated flatly, eyes flat and dead. "When he extrudes himself into this world through the mortal vessel of his choosing."

Oh, boy. "The Redeemer." My stomach roiled.

"Yes. It appears that Father has chosen his finger puppet."

"You know where it is, don't you? And when."

Her eyes still flat, she focused her gaze on me. "Yes. The location and time are part of the oral history of the Family, never written. The Patron has given this information to every Family head in the hopes of someday witnessing the birth of the Redeemer. From what you have told me, Oliver/Morgan was that man, one who defied his destiny for another path, much like my own decision to forgo the Family in favor of … well, let us say less violent pursuits. This must be quite the irritation to Father, who hates it when His people exert free will."

Great, there were two of them now who couldn't get straight to the point. Cain grinned, no doubt reading my expression like a book in large print. "Mind cluing us in?" I said while giving Cain a good glare. Maggie sniggered.

"Realize that this moment is one two thousand years in the making. The culmination of His dream. If He feels comfortable with Burke as the Redeemer, resurrected or not, He will be among us in the flesh once the ritual of ascension is performed two days hence." Judas sat back, crossing her arms beneath her breasts and smiling without humor at the shock plastered on our faces. "I need a map of England."

Within a few minutes Milo had one spread out upon the kitchen table. Judas stood and considered it carefully. "So much has changed," she muttered.

"Can't find it?" I asked. Maggie and Cain exchanged a look.

"Of course, I can. It is not difficult. The site for the ritual has been there long before Christ walked the earth and will most likely be there long after we are all dust." A hardened finger stabbed the southernmost section of the island. *Thwock!* "Here."

My guts turned to ice and I could hear my pulse in my ears. It was like being in a movie theater watching a thriller and finally understanding the big reveal long after everyone else has. I felt so stupid, yet it was so darn obvious it bordered on the cliché. "You kidding me, Judas? Stonehenge?"

"Almost," she replied as Maggie let loose a goodly amount of cursing. I told the Valkyrie to hush.

Attention back to Judas, I said, "What then?"

"Cain is in position, Father." Milo said, and I dipped my fingers back into the puddle, a warmth suffusing my hand, starting with a tingle not unlike pins-and-needles.

The lake continues to boil as the elemental loses its form, becoming a column of water, a pillar that whirls in place, sucking more and more of the lake into its mass. More water flows into the elemental from the surrounding lakes, from the sea to the south until it tops at well over two hundred feet.

With agonizing slowness, the pillar bent, curving, questing, searching, the terminus hovering over several buildings until it comes to what looks like an unobtrusive office building. Two stories tall, it dominates the city block quietly. A modest business in a modest town in a modest country. It is the kind of building, not glass or steel or fancy, that one would forget two seconds after turning away. The elemental points its liquid senses toward the building and is rewarded with affirmation ... it is guarded by earth.

"You may not trespass, Water," says the earth elemental. A large one by the slow grinding of its voice. "Please leave."

"I cannot, Earth," replies the water elemental. "There is a task I must perform. You must abandon this duty so that it may be completed."

Water receives a tremor by way of reply, a small quake that has the lake waters dancing and the dark pillar of water waving precariously. More lights appear in the homes along the lake.

The Water elemental slowly, with great respect, feels out the dimensions of the not-yet hostile earth elemental and is alarmed. The spirits of earth came in four categories: bits, boulders, mountains and, of course, Prime, that large and singular of elementals that spawns the rest of its kind. This forbidding creature, while not Prime Earth, is nevertheless a mountain, and one of the largest the water elemental has encountered in quite a while.

It feels ... sadness. Battles between the elements is more about dominance games and sport, not in earnest to dissipate the foe. This mountain with its resolve to commit to duty could not be swayed. So, water feels sad, a new emotion it does not care for. The taint of the human Morgan Heart has given it understanding, emotions and a point of view outside of its normal concerns, and that bothers it.

"Please stand aside, brother," water burbles. "for both our sakes."

"You cannot defeat me." The Language of Earth is slow and ponderous, so this reply takes several minutes to form, and water feels the urgency from the mortal it vowed to assist. The human touched by the Creator, the one it owes a boon, can be felt far away on a spot of land surrounded by water. The human summoned the elemental by simply placing a part of itself in water and asking nicely, which water found endearing. The human requested that water destroy this place, this dwelling, with as minimal loss life as possible.

Who knew that it would be such a pain? A thought emerges into water's musings, a phrase that it understands thanks to the unique perspective it now possesses.

Sucks to be you. Water has no face, so it cannot grimace, but there are other outlets for its frustration. Without warning water strikes, using all its elemental magic to focus its being into a tendril, a slender tentacle that contains the fullness of its might. Water thrusts that thread straight at the heart of earth.

Rock explodes, shredded by razor water, torn apart by the rushing force focused at one tiny point. Liquid digs and drills through rock. Where stone fractures, it fills the cracks and expands, breaking the rock even further, turning it to a muddy slurry which is easily pushed aside.

Earth roars, a sound like the shattering of boulders and strikes back, heaving under the lake and opening wide, forcing the waters to drain into the depths. Water grabs at the shore, resisting the pull of gravity, of the draining away, but the ground shudders and gives way beneath the elemental and it drops out of sight, the lakebed now a steaming hole in the ground.

HAND OUT OF THE WATER, BACK in Wiltshire, England, kneeling in the dark with Milo at my back and the end of the world as I knew it a few hours away. It took a few moments for the images of Primal Water's battle with an earth elemental called a mountain to fade. I shook my head. I had no doubt about the Primal's ability, it was the collateral damage that worried me. A few labelled such deaths a tragedy, the fortunes of war and not something that could be avoided. I disagreed. If it was their family that was torn apart by violence I think they'd whistle a different tune.

Stonehenge stood on an almost flat stretch of land in Wiltshire where the grass is so green it almost hurts the eye. Kind of reminded me of Iowa, except a bit chillier and wetter in autumn. We were more than a quarter mile away, hidden behind one of the gentle dips in the land, an earthen ripple frozen in time.

Fifteen feet away a monstrosity rested upon the grass, a stunning figure that upright would dwarf even Cain. A skull made from an anvil's base presented a flat plate to the world. Beautifully articulated hands and feet meshed incongruously with rough rebar and thick rods. I was pretty sure I saw a horse shoe in there somewhere, in the middle. It was a golem, a construct given a sort of quasi-life and subject to its creator's demands. It looked like it could tear a Prius in half. Cain crouched over the giant form, oiling the joints.

He called it Walter.

I stared at the construct for a few moments, not wanting to dip my hand back in the puddle, but knowing I had to. Muddy water enveloped my fingers.

Out in the darkness, something rustled softly, and a faint hoot-hoot of a tawny owl floated on the breeze. I slowly lowered the SMG I didn't remember grabbing. The night sky shone with a thousand stars, but no moon. Not tonight. It was the night of the new moon, which not only, according to Judas, made special in Lucifer's eyes, but added extra meaning and magic to the date. October 31st.

Yeah. *That* day.

Imagine our collective surprise to find we had forty-eight hours to head off the apocalypse. So much to do, so little time. The most important was to personally risk a trip to Italy, to Vatican City. I had seen a man about ultimate evil and how to stop it.

Dante Fischer eeled out of the grass, crouching next to me while staring nervously at the golem resting a few feet away. Cain gave him an evil leer, eyes perfectly adjusted thanks to a Word of Vision.

I turned off my night vision goggles and whispered, "What did you see?"

"A whole assfull of Sicarri, Father." He paused and crossed himself: spectacles, testicles, wallet and watch. "Begging your pardon. But it's just like we thought seeing all them cars parked on side of the road and all."

My lips tried to form a smile, but I bit down on their insides and nodded. "How many?"

"All of them."

PRIMAL WATER FEELS RAGE, A NEW sensation for the old being considering that even when drowning cities, it usually felt only a mild sort of interest. Passions don't run hot in water, it is content to talk and flow. More of the human taint from Morgan Heart. Even now it recalls every instant of the man's life in perfect detail, a side effect of the merging it had undergone a couple of years ago. Even the concept of time feels rather new and contributes to its rage, but, strangely enough, it doesn't want to give up its new perspective. It has come to like these 'feelings', no matter how disconcerting. The rage that grips it, though, feels right, feels appropriate for the situation. It channels that rage into an impetus that utterly shatters the earth elemental, tearing the mountain into pieces no larger than tennis shoe, waters geyser into the hole that earth created, filling it once more.

The resultant release of energy floods the houses along the shore. Lights drown in the deluge before sputtering into darkness. The tiny life-sparks of the people inside begin to flicker as buildings rip from their foundations. As for the mountain, its death cry is a shuddering and heaving, an earthy squeal of pain that results in a large earthquake that, when all was said and done, measured 7.7 on the Richter Scale. The mountain, reduced to much smaller components, gathers what it can of its previous mass and flees deep underground, so deep that not even Primal water can follow because the heat is far too intense.

The people!

Drat that human! Primal Water wants to gnash teeth it doesn't possess. It doesn't mind assisting the human, in fact it has a strange fondness for Michael Engle, but sometimes water had work to do and doesn't want to be disturbed.

-What, Michael Engle? I am busy. -

-The people! Engle says again through their link of water. –In the houses. They're going to die! -

Oh. Humans are so confusing. –No one dies; you know that well enough. They merely transition from one phase of life to the next. Their bodies may crumble, but they will live on. -

-They die before their time. -

-Before their time? What nonsense! Time is irrelevant to an immortal spirit, an artificial structure. Pah! They will transition quickly, their pain minimal, then they can begin the new cycle. -

-Please! - The mental cry holds anguish that pierces the elemental's indifference. -You really are not going to let this go, are you? -

For a moment water wishes it possesses eyes so it could roll them. -They are of no consequence to the mission. -

-Please! - Plaintive, sad.

By the creator! Primal water dithers for a fraction of a second. With a small flick of its will, allows the drowning humans, those sucked into the now re-filling lake, to breathe. Nudging here and there, water gently expels the sputtering people onto shore where they lie in exhausted, if bewildered, piles.

-Happy? -

Inside the building that housed the Century Project, Director Tolonen splashes through three inches of water as he tries to back up all available data on the Family cloud server. Unfortunately, as the lights flicker and pop, the computers do as well. The tall man mutters feverishly as he tries to access the servers. Everything electrical is starting to short out and even the backup generator, ruggedized and built with several redundant features, is starting to fail spectacularly.

An assistant runs up to the distraught doctor, grabbing his arm in a steely grip. "We have to go, Doctor," she hisses, eyes wide with barely restrained panic. "The lower levels are flooded; the pods are destroyed."

Tolonen pulls at his hair, face a mask of grief. "How did this happen?" he screams. "First the earthquake then the flooding. How? How? How?"

The woman raises her hand as if to slap the near hysterical doctor but thinks better of it. "Something, someone defeated the elemental Julian set to guard this facility. Doctor, if someone can do that, what chance do we have?"

For the first time since the earthquake and the flooding, Tolonen's eyes focus on something other than the computer. "Vittu," he breathes. "We have to leave!"

"You think?" The assistant half drags the doctor to the exit. If they are lucky, they could make it to the surface two stories above. The bulk of the complex had been built below a store that specialized in spectrolite, a semi-precious gemstone found almost exclusively in Finland. Of all the places in the world to search for a top-secret laboratory dedicated to the cloning of the world's most sinister assassins, Finland would probably be at the bottom of most people's lists, right after Micronesia and Andorra. It meant that the Family could work in relative peace because the Finns are an easygoing lot whose only real vices are staying overlong in saunas and drinking enough vodka on holidays to kill a normal human being.

The assistant flings the door open, only to be encountered by a wall of water. The liquid fills the opening, cloudy and dense with dirt, but remains static, gently rippling to some unseen current. Dimly seen through the brownish water are a pair of black-clad Dagger men floating, mouths open in the final shock of death.

"Oh, shit," she gasps before the waters take the room, crushing the life from the two like insects beneath a boot.

BACK. WHOA ... I SHOOK MY head and crossed myself. During the ... contact with Primal water, I said nothing about sparing Sicarri lives and I felt a little guilty about that, but they chose their path, so I had to shunt those feelings aside. There was work to do.

"Jammers in place?" I asked.

Nods all around.

"Good. Send out the signal and start 'em up." To Cain. "Let slip the dogs of war and all that."

He slapped Walter on the face plate and gave me a smile that could instantly freeze water. "This, my worthy friend, will be fun indeed."

CHAPTER TWO
MAGGIE

———————

N**O RADIOS, NOTHING THE ENEMY COULD INTERCEPT.** What twigged us to start the radio jammers was a car driving down the road toward Stonehenge. Secreted near a tree and covered by bushes, I peered through my night vision goggles.

Yep, the right front blinker came on, blinked four times, then went out. The signal. I flipped the switch on the black box next to me and waited for the fun to begin.

Radio jamming and cellphone jamming equipment is illegal to use in Great Britain. Good thing we weren't telling Scotland Yard our little secret, although Chief Inspector Darby was one of ours and had supplied us. There were ten cell phone jammers and ten radio jammers all set up around the henge, dug in deep and carefully camouflaged, mated to the master controller I just activated.

Wouldn't want the Sicarii to call for backup, would we?

I still had a hard time believing it. Fucking Stonehenge. Fucking Halloween. Talk about cliché to the max, dude. I wanted to barf.

Judas (can you believe it, *Judas!* I was still geeking out about that one) said that the ritual would start at eleven pm and last for almost an hour.

"There is a reason All Hollow's Eve is special it is not because of goblins and ghosts," she had told us in that little apartment above the pub, which served a stout so fierce you had to chew it before swallowing. "It is because the magic that flows around this planet, the life force of the world expressed in ley lines, is strongest on this date and any rituals performed at the large nexuses where multiple ley lines meet have more efficacy." She paused, taking in the circle of dropped jaws. "This will aid Father's ascension, allow him to extrude a portion of himself into the willing vessel. Much more so than when he possessed me."

So that's why we were there, a quarter of a mile out from the henge and the multitude of SUVs, vans and trucks parked nearby ... the Dagger Man transport brigade.

We had arrived as quickly as we could, only to find the site blocked off for 'archeological reasons', probably relating to the find near there in 2014 that was supposed to be the re-write of British history. If only the archeologists knew, they'd blow a gasket. The Family had other ideas, but we beat the bulk of them, avoiding the casual looking sentries and setting up our equipment. The sentries were looking for people spying on them, but never bothered to look up to see the small dots of RC drones watching *them*. That allowed us to avoid their guards and put our plan into motion.

The rest of the vehicles arrived around 10 pm when it was dark as Hades and the wind carried a chilly bite, disgorging enough men and women to make me blanch. At least three hundred to our seventy-five and it was enough to bring a sweat to my forehead. Long odds and I was on the opposite end from Mike and Cain with only Judas to keep me company, waiting for the sign. I could barely make out the menhirs of Stonehenge from the press of bodies surrounding it.

I didn't have too long to wait.

It started with a *thump, thump, thumping* that shook the air and I began to smile, even though I shouldn't have. Call it a flaw, but sometimes I do so revel in violence.

Walter moved faster than a construct weighing more than Chevy Cavalier should, tromping across the plain, the metal joints clanking and creaking. A quarter mile, thirteen hundred twenty feet, four hundred forty yards ... call it what you will but Walter crossed that distance like the greatest Olympic athlete ever and he (or should I say it?) never faltered, never tired, keeping the same speed from start to finish.

Flashes started up from the Sicarii line of defenders, silenced weapons chuffing away at the charging iron golem, throwing up sparks and letting loose the *spang* of ricochets. The bullets gave the golem no pause, its charging mass too great to be slowed by mere ounces of lead.

One hundred feet. Larger weapons came into play, the Dagger Men no longer caring about noise, about who might hear. A fifty-caliber chattered to life, three-foot tongues of flame erupting from the barrel of the fixed weapon and casings as big as bananas flying everywhere. The finger-long projectiles took some chunks out of Walter and he stumbled ever so slightly as bits of iron began to fly off.

That was *my* cue.

Down and dirty, that's my jam, getting in there with axe, sword and dagger, thrusting for the really meaty parts that go squish. You can't fight in the Valhalla Club and not expect to get covered in sticky red and after a while, the fighting, the blood, the noise and, yes, even the pain become part of you down to the bone. Call it sick, but the feel of steel slamming through flesh in honest combat is a thrill that can't be described, but only felt. I was no slouch with a rifle, more specifically the C14 Timberwolf MRSWS (Medium Range Sniper Weapon System) firing a .338 Lapua Magnum cartridge. A thermal scope rested up top, providing me with fun little Sicarii-shaped blobs to shoot at.

The man at the .50 cal was the first to go, the round turning his head into a canoe and his weapon spun to silence. That single shot, the flash suppressor hiding my location, was the signal for the rest of the Templars to unload hell, pardon the pun, upon the Dagger Men.

With the .50 inert, there was nothing to stop Walter from turning the guards into Dagger Man goulash. At forty miles an hour, the giant golem smashed into the first man with the sound of a sledge hammer hitting a side of beef, not even slowing down as the lifeless body sailed bonelessly over the heads of his compatriots. A long arm swept out and knocked the life out of another while the other arm grabbed a man by the skull and ripped the head off as he raced past.

Bullets peppered my location as I took another Sicarii through the belly, spraying his guts on the grass. I heard Judas curse as one pocked the earth in front of her face. "Keep your head down," I grunted.

Down at the henge, magic began to fly as Sicarii began using their Words seeing how bullets were having so little effect on the golem. Force hammered Walter from the side and nearly knocked him over despite his vast weight and he took a moment after correcting to grab the magus by the skull and squeeze. The Sicarius screamed briefly before his head popped like a zit, sending brains flying high.

One of the pieces of rebar in Walter's chest flew loose and he developed a small tilt to the left, but that didn't stop him from leaping like a gazelle and land on a shouting Sicarius, squishing him flat. The golem spun, tearing up sod with his delicately articulated feet and fists the size of dinner plates crushed chests and skulls.

More Words of Force slammed in to the golem, who immediately turned to the nearest magus and grabbed him by the arms and played make-a-wish, tearing the man in half. Force tore chunks of iron from the golem and it was starting to falter, its flat-faced head a little wobbly, but it still strove to kill, heaving a screaming woman high into the air. She landed on one of the menhirs, cracking her skull on stone.

As for me, I took my shots, punching holes through Sicarii with the Timberwolf, however my shots came slower and slower as I had to take cover from the bullets heading my way. A large knot of Sicarii magi was left to combat Walter, using Strength and Force and Healing to deal with golem, but the rest were coming at the Templars, braving the four hundred forty yards against gunfire to reach us, all while shooting from the hip.

I set the Timberwolf down and drew my axe and a Sig Sauer, adjusting my night-vision googles. Vision wasn't one of the spells in my repertoire. I saw Judas do the same and draw her own weapons, a pair of long knives that could be mistaken for short swords. No idea why she didn't use a pistol, but I guessed she felt comfortable using keen-edged steel.

With a cry, I jumped up and spoke three words in the Language of Air and felt a tug at my hair as the sprites circling above signaled they understood. The charging Sicarii opened up with their weapons and I could almost see the bullets streak toward me and I yelled two Words, one after the other as the sprites batted the bullets aside to the left and right of me and the smell of the Words clogged themselves in my nose, a jumble of scents that had me both hungry and repulsed at the same time and rushed the Dagger Men, firing.

One took a bullet to the nose, a neat hole that suddenly sprouted blood while the other went wide and then we were there, in the thick and up close and personal and it came down to grunts and thrusts and screaming and the smell of blood and shit on my axe as my Strength enhanced muscles cut one man completely in half at the waist. Another Word and I smelled strawberries as Vigor removed fatigue from my muscles and would for quite some time, so I could fight and fight.

A woman with a horrible scar running from left eyebrow, bisecting her nose down to the chin shrieked and thrust with short sword. Cain told me they were always loaded for bear, ready for just about anything, but I knew for damn sure they weren't ready for *me*. I leaned back just in time to avoid sprouting a new mouth and snapped back with the axe, slamming the head against a jaw which caved with an awful crunch and teeth went flying. A gun went off almost in my ear, ringing a bell or two, and the clever sprites around my body stopped the round cold.

As for Judas, well, I thought I was a bad ass, but she was unholy murder on a bloody stick, moving so fast that if I hadn't known she was empty of Words. I would've sworn she used both Grace and Speed. Her knives blurred, flashing, one a mother huge kukri that looked like it could cut down trees. With every stroke blood flew high and men and women were disemboweled, cut to the heart, necks cleaved, and fingers chopped like carrots in a kitchen. I saw two Sicarii women scream and leap at her, only to find themselves dead before they landed.

Blood hit my eyes and I blinked angrily and I realized that my night vision goggles were gone, but I could see as fear drove my muscles and I spun and slashed, hacked and jumped, carving my way through a forest of Dagger Men. Blood coated my axe blade, along with bits of meat and hair. The Sicarii SS teams wore black clothes of ballistic cloth, but that stuff is shit against melee weapons, weapons that cut and crush and pierce so the blood flows free and bones shatter through skin.

A fist, covered in cloth that in turn covered what must have been brass knuckles, came from nowhere to smash into my cheek and I felt a nauseating *giving* as bone lost that fight and I could have sworn I heard an atonal ringing that sounded like the end of my world. My vision became lopsided and I planted my ass in the bloody mud.

A whippet lean man with a heavily scarred face and a porno mustache leaned over, arm cocking back to thrust a large K-bar into my throat. *He doesn't look like a Sicarius*, I thought inanely. *Must be a mercenary. No wonder there are more bodies here, the Family's been recruiting.* That felt like cheating.

I saw my death in his eyes and the only emotion I could feel was fucking *pissed off.* Imagine my surprise when his head suddenly detached from his neck and I found myself covered in his fountaining blood as he fell across my midriff. Gross. Worse than a Tarantino movie, I tell you.

An iron grip pulled me up. Judas tossed me a smile and casually backhanded the Sicarii coming up from behind, her long knife taking the woman through the neck. "You were sloppy," was all she said.

Yeah. Sloppy all over. Suddenly not surrounded by people trying to stick me with long pointy objects. We stood amidst a field of bodies in various stages of disrepair and the ground was slick and black underfoot. My cheek burned, but the broken bone really didn't hurt much because I was still high on Vigor and adrenalin.

"Well, that is something I did not expect to see," Judas remarked, pointing.

I looked to Stonehenge. It was glowing, a deep blue that seemed to emanate from the heart of each menhir and I could almost see through the stone to the origin of the glow, as if they were made of some cloudy glass.

Then things got *really* weird.

CHAPTER THREE

JUDAS

————◆————

"Not quite at Stonehenge, mind you, Michael, but underneath."

When I first met Michael Engle, I was struck by how young he looked. I expected a man in his mid-forties to have a few wrinkles, perhaps a gray hair or two, but he looked as if he saw only a few years into his third decade. Big, as well. A large man with shoulders wide as an axe handle is long, with the scarred knuckles of a fighter and the sloping nose of an aristocrat. This man was a study in contrasts: outwardly rough, but soft spoken … capable of instant violence yet treating others with a gentle respect that disarmed any distrust. If I had not known his vocation, I would have taken him to be an officer in the military or a statesman.

He ran a large hand across his forehead and stared with those intense eyes of his, eyes that seemed to peer into my soul. I could almost feel the Lord's will sh

ine through. "Underneath. I thought archeologists found temple ruins or some such underneath."

"Two miles away there are remains of an ancient arena, and the area around has hidden barrows, henges and pits. Directly beneath Stonehenge is where the Patron shall be reborn into the body of the Redeemer." Only Cain seemed to accept this as boilerplate, nodding slowly. "The henge is the confluence of the ley lines and acts to amplify the magic. The Patron directed the Family to dig deep and prepare the Ascension Chamber. There the ritual will take place in the time of the new moon on the day when the ley runs hot with power.

"Why do you think Stonehenge was put there in the first place? There is magic in this world yet undiscovered by man, magic deep and profound.

Botanical, elemental, Words ... we have but scratched the surface of what the world has to offer. You must realize that complex systems, especially one such as a living planet, are not so easily mapped. We think we are at the pinnacle of what mankind can discover on this world, but there is so much yet to learn."

"How do we access such a remote locale?" asked Cain, leaning back in his chair.

I stabbed a finger at the map. "Here. This menhir on its side, the one near the middle. That is the access point." At their puzzled looks I chuckled. "It is an earth elemental. All you have to do ask it to move in the Language of Earth and it will."

They all stared. Maggie broke the silence. "An earth elemental? It's been lying there for thousands of years."

Cain replied, "Merely the briefest of naps in geologic time, my apprentice. Thousands of years is perceived as the merest tick of a clock to those who measure time in eras bearing names such as Jurassic and Cambrian."

STARLIGHT SHINING ALONG A SHARPENED BLADE told me of the thrust meant for my stomach and the grate of bone across my own knife was my answer as I darted to the side. Twice more my blade licked, creating new mouths that spat blood.

Night vision goggles like the pair Maggie wore irritated the skin around my face, too uncomfortable by half, so I tossed them aside before we charged. My own eyes worked just fine at night without artificial aid. The stars were enough.

Each of the Dagger Men had goggles, a little smaller, more streamlined ... a testament to their access to advanced technology. They huddled around the henge in the dark, keeping a lookout. A quarter mile was too much, I supposed, and that brought a grin to my lips. In my time before I rebelled against Father, such sloppiness, the lack of roaming sentries, would have been cause for a head or two to roll. Centuries of success made them overconfident in the power of numbers. They should have paid attention to the lesson of Agincourt.

I drove a fist into a stomach, followed by a blade across a throat, spinning, spinning, spinning, kukri arcing toward tender flesh, cleaving bone and severing muscles and arteries. A Sicarius managed a shot from a foot away, the sound deafening, the muzzle blast heating my cheeks, but the bullet never made to my face thanks to the sprites. I followed the shot with a stab up under the ribs into a beating heart.

To my left Maggie fought, a force of nature. Where she lacked finesse, she made up with sheer brute force. Every time she swung a fist, a Sicarius fell, jaw broken, neck snapped, and her axe took limbs, sheared skulls and vented guts out onto the ground. The brutality of it almost frightened me, but what took me aback was her blood-spattered grin of genuine pleasure, and that grin gave more than one Dagger Man pause.

I slid through bloody mud under a metal baton and the felt its passing above the crown of my head and flipped to my feet in time to stab the wielder in the kidney with the knife in my off hand. He screamed, and I cut it short with the kukri. From the corner of one eye I saw another charge, thinking to take me unawares, but I planted one foot firmly and hit him in the sternum with a back kick. The force of his charge and the mud underneath knocked me off my feet and we both landed hard. I spun in mud and buried my knife up to the hilt in his left eye before leaping to my feet.

"REALIZE THIS," I SAID. MICHAEL AND the others looked troubled, as well they should be. "Burke will be there as will the few Witnesses, those that are allowed to watch the Ascension. This does not include, however, those who are to be sacrificed."

This tidbit of information drew gasps. "Those that are to be sacrificed?" Michael growled the words, a sound not unlike that of an angry bear. I realized, looking at his muscles bowstring taut under his long-sleeved shirt, how dangerous he was. Here sat a man grown used to violence against God's enemies and who had come to grips morally with that violence. His fury beat against my skin.

"Yes. The willing and unwilling sacrifices. The intricacies of the Ritual were to be delivered to the one who performs the ritual, so I cannot give you a step-by-step, only the broad strokes. Like I said, some things were not written in the Codex."

I rubbed my cheeks with the palms of my hands. "Understand this … my Father is not an imaginative being. His plans are relatively straightforward and lack imagination., but what He lacks in creativity He more than makes up in brutality and violence. You, Michael, having read the Family history, should know that by now."

Michael's glance at the back wall of the small room told me everything I needed to know. His eyes had landed on a rather dismal looking painting of a vase filled with dandelions. A safe behind a boring painting, proving that Michael never traveled without the Codex. I was not sure if it showed distrust in others, extreme paranoia or a desire to reference the material at a moment's notice. The cynical part of my nature informed me to choose the first two, the relatively atrophied optimist in me opted for the third.

ALMOST ABSENTLY I GUTTED A MAN and did not bother to watch the loops of his purple intestines unspool upon the ground as he whimpered. I was in that place, a sort of Zen battle trance where I could think of one thing while performing another. The conversation in the apartment above the pub played out upon the canvas of my mind as my kukri sheared through a wrist while I spun and gutted the woman as she stared at the spurting stump where her hand used to be.

Down below I could see the hulking shadow of Walter as it lumbered among the mass of Dagger Men, crushing several underfoot as it swung with massive arms, sending more flying, broken, into the henge. Black blood splattered ancient menhirs, a sacrifice to imaginary gods.

Sacrifice?

Oh ... shit.

My last opponent died under the kukri, the heavy blade cleaving through the top of his skull to air out his brains and I turned in time to see Maggie fall onto her butt, a man leaning over ready to strike and I moved faster than I thought possible as fear washed through me, the Zen dissipating. For some reason the thought of the brash American dying hurt. I did not even know her well enough to call her a friend, but underneath all that explosive violence was a woman who deserved my respect, one who served Father's enemy and that was friend enough for me.

The man's neck parted under the weight of my kukri and I helped Maggie to her feet, ready to explain what just occurred to me when Stonehenge began to glow, each menhir lit as if from within and I knew my hunch had been correct.

"Well, that is something I did not expect to see."

CHAPTER FOUR
MICHAEL

❖

"**I** CANNOT STAND IDLY BY WISHING FOR a more fortuitous outcome," Cain rumbled, staring at the bedlam surrounding Stonehenge. Thanks to Vision, I could see as well as he, although the colors brought about by the spell were somewhat psychedelic. Okay, a lot. It was like taking a tab of acid before hitting a Pink Floyd laser light show (don't ask, it was a long time ago when I was young and rebellious).

No time for tomfoolery, Cain wasn't running this rodeo. "Easy up there, big guy. Walt is doing just fine."

Those disturbing eyes came my way and he said a couple of Words. Suddenly, I felt as if I could bench press a locomotive and the world all around slowed to a crawl. Two more of those Words and I could see his muscles quiver. "Look, my good friend." He pointed. "Walter finds himself beset by Words and weaponry which is proving to have a detrimental effect on his structure, which I cannot allow. Soon our enemies will cause damage enough to render him inert, then focus their attentions upon us. I say we take the battle forthwith to the Sicarii and render *them* unto their component parts. Sitting here will find us overwhelmed."

While he said that, Walter may have taken ten whole steps, I couldn't quite tell, everything was in slow motion, even the gentle breeze of the sprites circling above my head (every Templar had three sprites courtesy of Cain and ballistic cloth protecting their hides from bullets. For some reason fire and earth did not come when Cain called, no matter how he pleaded. Water was busy elsewhere destroying Project Century in Finland I wondered if he messed with my perceptions, or if I was really that fast.

As for Walter, it was true, the Sicarii were doing him some dirt and I could tell that there would be at least fifty or sixty left to swarm our positions. Their placement bugged me. If I were calling the shots for the bad guys, I would've set the .50 cal and the bulk of the forces *inside* Stonehenge, maybe even dug some earthworks around the monument to provide protection. If they succeeded in calling Lucifer into Burke's body, what did they care about a little landmark desecration?

All that aside, Cain was right. "Okay. Got anything else that could help?"

Two more Words and I felt like I could perform cartwheels in a china shop without disturbing a single teacup. Grace … had to be. I gestured for Milo to stay and cover me and stood. As one, Cain and I ran full tilt toward the battle a few hundred yards away.

The world blurred, and my combat boots kicked up enormous divots as I ran, speeding along faster than I could have dreamt possible. I felt the wind pulling my cheeks and realized that I should have passed out due to acceleration trauma. Whatever magic gave me Speed kept me from leaving my internal organs back with Milo.

As fast as I was, Cain outstripped me. I could barely see his legs as he blurred past, a tall streak of deadly heading for a mass of enemies whose sole purpose in life was to end mine. *I canna tax the engines any more, Cap'n*, I thought inanely.

Then I was among the enemy, firing and laying about with my tonfa, a club with a perpendicular handle attached a third of the way down. Think of the billy clubs the cops use. Doesn't seem like much, but a full swing can kill and kill fast.

I laid it on thick, shattering jaws and teeth and shooting from the hip until my Ruger ran dry, so I tossed it aside and drew a K-bar with a brass knuckle finger grip, the kind they called a trench knife, and thrust into someone's mouth, right through the back of their throat and out the neck. I yanked it out and punched with the tonfa, hitting a yelling man in the eye. It popped like a cherry tomato, flinging him to the ground. Bullets rained down on me, but the sprites kept me safe, along with something else, some sort of invisible barrier in front of me and I realized it was a Shield, one of the Words that only Cain knew because there were twenty-five, not twelve, despite what the other magi in the world thought.

A fist the size of a semi hit me in the kidney and the crippling pain crawled up my back, cramping the muscles along the right side and stars appeared in my vison, momentarily blocking out the rest of the world. I yelled, no I screamed, because the pain nearly knocked me out of my socks. I knew I would pee blood for the next few days. If I lived.

Despite the agony along my side, I whirled, bringing a whole new meaning to the word 'ouch' and laid out with the tonfa, feeling it connect.

Something braced me along my spine, hard and large, and an arm of iron fell in front of my face, smashing *through* the skull of the man who hit me, turning his head into paste, and continued on down into his chest where it flattened his heart and lungs. With his other hand, the one that braced my back, Walter gave gentle pat.

How do you thank a two-ton monster made of iron? Answer, you don't. Might as well thank a retaining wall for holding back the slope. Since people tend to anthropomorphize things, the urge was there.

On the opposite side of Stonehenge, Cain was milling through the Sicarii as if they were standing still. For every meter he traveled, a Sicarius fell, some shrieking, some not. Each movement was augmented by Grace, so his balance, every step and strike, flowed in perfect harmony together as if he danced an intricate ballet of death while the Dagger Men ineptly clogged.

Still, both of us under Speed, Grace and Strength, were not enough because the Sicarii knew exactly what Cain represented … the unholy grail of their ambitions. For centuries he had been off limits to all SS teams except singly, as a test of a Sicarius' abilities, one they always, inevitably lost. Only recently, with the breaking of the Accords, the agreement to leave him alone, all bets were off and, boy, did they ever want a piece of the big guy.

I saw a man manage to stab Cain in the shoulder, the wound closing almost immediately as a Word of Healing took effect. Cain's large hand punched through the assassin's chest and out his back, gripping a segment of bloody spine. Hits were beginning to land on Cain, here and there, and his use of Healing became more and more frequent as he killed, killed, and killed his way through the Family assassins. I could tell that eventually a blow would come that he couldn't parry and that would be it, the oldest living man turned into the oldest dead man. Not on my watch.

Muscles surging, I broke through a mass of Sicarii, taking a few hits, bleeding from cuts that I couldn't cure because I had no Words, no magic, only those spells given by Cain and they would run out and then I would die.

From the corner of my eye I saw a man jump on Walter's back and jam a round something among the rebar cage of his chest and I flashed back to the ending scenes of *Terminator* where the hero Kyle Reese placed a lit pipe bomb in the robot's body. I jumped away.

Speed and Grace allowed me to clear fifteen feet before the grenade cooked off with a noise like semi-on-semi collision. I was glad for every inch because I could feel the concussive force like a big, warm hand on my back *shove* me forward. Even with Grace I almost lost my footing. Something hot and fast pierced my left butt cheek, a blow that didn't really hurt, just felt like someone hauled off with a size thirteen boot and whacked me one.

I stumbled, righting myself amid shrieks of pain, whirling against the tide of moaning, broken Dagger Men and attempted another Speed induced run toward Cain.

I faceplanted heroically, my butt clenched in agony and I felt something hard and jagged buried deep in the muscle as a sticky wetness filled my britches. That was never a good sign.

"Arrrghh!" I grimaced, hand to left cheek. Metal, ragged and sharp, the end of a rebar that sheared clean through my tough trousers to bury deep. Jarring agony raced up my spine and I let go of the metal, hand shaking in horror. My flesh was mortified, and my mind wanted to shy away from the realization. All I could do was wonder what happened to the sprites who were supposed to keep things like this from happening to me.

It was over, some enterprising young Sicarius was about to punch my ticket and all I could do was flail in agony. I prepared for the worst.

It never came. Instead grunts and shouts and moaning greeted my ears, along with the sound of weapons fire. I looked to see the remaining Sicarii engaged in hand-to-hand combat with my Templars. A surge of pride and gratitude washed through me as my boys and girls traded blow for blow, shot for shot with assassins who were better trained than they.

A wash of blue light from behind, rendering the battle in stark relief, illustrating the fact that my guys were getting creamed, unable to fight toe-to-toe with the assassins, who without the benefit of magic flowed like liquid death.

Blue light?

I turned to see Stonehenge glowing, each menhir, an oversized azure night light. As the light grew brighter and brighter, I felt a pressure riding on the air, a palpable thickness that seemed to weigh down upon my body, pushing against my skin, my soul.

Stonehenge became too bright to look at and, as the pressure increased, a sonorous hum filled the air, coming from nowhere, everywhere. The hum increased in volume and during all this I felt a large, gentle hands lift me up, slightly jarring the rebar in my butt and I bit my lip, stifling a scream.

It was Milo, broad face creased in concern. "I thought I told you stay back?" I hollered.

He gave me a look an ex-girlfriend used to when I said something particularly stupid. For a moment I wondered if he was related. I shut up and nodded slightly.

If the world was a bell, then the biggest clapper ever struck the inside and Milo hit the deck, dropping me. Of course, I landed on the rebar and the pain took me to new heights just before I blacked out.

Perhaps a minute or two later I came around to find myself on my stomach and the battle pretty much concluded. A few feet away Cain and Judas put paid to the final Sicarii, hacking them to bits and pieces. The blue glow had faded, but my Vision still worked fine. As for the pressure, it was gone, its absence a sweet clarity that was marred by the pain in my ass.

Milo came into my line of sight, face creased. "I'm okay, big guy," I grunted. Ouch. Even speaking hurt like the blazes.

"I'm sorry I dropped you, Father." Any more doleful and he'd look like the human version of Eeyore from *Winnie the Pooh*. I big, burly, incredibly dangerous Eeyore with a stubborn streak a mile wide with just a touch of insubordination.

"No ... worries," I managed. "The world just happened to choose that time to call. I wonder who answered."

Cain tromped over, and I nearly passed out from the shock of him looking hurt. I mean *hurt*. Both eyes were swelling shut and his nose was broken every which way. Gashes and cuts covered his torso from neck to groin and he listed a bit, favoring his left foot.

"What the heck—*aaaaarrrrhhhh*!!!" I didn't see the hand that pulled the rebar out, but I sure as shooting felt the wet, tearing agony of it. My sight grew white around the edges just as a Word slithered in and out of my ears.

Calling the relief orgasmic would normally be considered strange for a priest to use, but there's nothing else in my vocabulary that came close to the sensation running from butt to neck and back down to my toes. Blessed warmth, lack of pain, knitting flesh and closing wound ... all insufficient to describe the Healing rushing along my nerves. Better than Percocet. I closed my eyes to enjoy the sensation ... only for a moment so I wouldn't cry like a baby.

Puking brought me back to reality. Not mine, but Cain's. He was bent over on hands and knees heaving away as if the lunch he ate in 1964 was swiftly returning to the outside world. After a few moments he finished and wiped the slime from his lips.

"Are you okay, Cain?"

"Far too many Words spoken," he replied much more succinctly than normal. "Backlash has most decidedly set in, so for the foreseeable future no magic shall escape my lips." His normally olive skin was touched with gray and the bruises around his eyes had nearly swelled them shut, hiding their odd whiteness. For the first time since I met him, he looked tired. "The last of my magic Healed you, my friend."

"Your wounds ..."

A large hand waved it off. "Superficial at the worst, injuries that can be easily tended by one who knows the medicinal arts. I fear, however, that dear Walter has traveled to that great scrap heap in the sky. Alas, gone so soon. The poor golem had yet to reach his centennial year upon this earth." He held up the twisted wreck of the horseshoe that used to be welded into Walter's midsection. For a moment I felt a touch of sorrow, but realized that the golem had no soul, that it was merely a hunk of iron animated to serve Cain.

"Sorry to break into this touching emotional back and forth," Judas remarked drily as she crouched between us. "But there are greater concerns."

"Such as?"

Sorry to say I cursed a bit when she threw a hand absent an arm down on the ground at my feet. I scrambled away, suddenly squeamish. "Note the tattoo," she said.

I noted. A black chevron on the back on the knuckles. I looked at Judas for an explanation.

"That tat belongs to a German merc group called The Chosen Ones." Maggie's voice held nothing but scorn. "Real assbags. Got kicked out of Germany, they now operate in Africa selling themselves to whatever warlord has the most money, including Boko Haram. They're aggressive recruiters, but like the WWII SS, they only recruit European or American assbags. A worse bunch of merc dildos you can't find, if you ask me." At my look of surprise, she shrugged. "What? These jerkweeds used to come to the Valhalla Club. Tried to cop a feel every time and every time I kicked them in the junk."

"The majority of the fighters were mercenaries," said Judas mildly, helping me to my feet. Not a twinge from the *gluteus maximus*, for which I was profoundly grateful. "Remember when I said there would be a sacrifice both willing and unwilling?"

Oh, yeah. My stomach dropped several floors and I felt a horrid dread. The only thing I could do was nod dumbly. I knew what her next words would be.

I was proved right. "For a while I wondered why the security on the site was so lax. Why did they not have sweeping patrols of the surrounding area? Not hard to do with ATVs or motorcycles. Why did the majority bunch up around Stonehenge, vulnerable to sniper fire?" Judas turned around and for the first time I saw carnage. Bodies lay strewn about like dolls dropped by a forgetful child. Blood slicked every surface, from grass to stone to clothing. And the smell! In my pain I hadn't noticed, but now...I crossed myself. It reeked like a slaughterhouse, odors of blood and offal and vomit all mixed together in a miasma almost thick enough to cut. "I feel so foolish, Michael. One of the tenants of the Sicarii was to keep our numbers few, easy to manage. The smaller the society, the easier it is to control from a central authority. I let myself be seduced by the idea that the Family had grown large, but I was wrong. I should have known better. These mercenaries were brought here to be the unwilling sacrifices for the ritual and the Sicarii with them were the willing ones, the ones who would be rulers in Hell in reward for their service."

I heard her voice, acknowledged it, but I realized something horrible.

There were only a handful of Templars left and every single one of them bore some wound, suffered some indignity of the flesh from the combat. I crossed myself and fell to my knees, overcome with grief.

It was my fault. I led the Templars, I brought them here and I chose to go with Cain to fight alongside Walter. Of course, the rest of the Templars would charge in like fools once I was wounded, their sense of duty wouldn't allow any other action. They weren't built like normal people ... they were utterly fearless, incredibly loyal and had unshakable faith in God. In me.

Oh, Lord. Please forgive me. There was only one thing to do ... fall back on what I knew best.

"God our Father,
Your power brings us to birth,
Your providence guides our lives,
and by Your command we return to dust.
Lord, those who die still live in Your presence,
their lives change but do not end.
I pray in hope for my family,
relatives and friends,
and for all the dead known to You alone.

In company with Christ,
Who died and now lives,
may they rejoice in Your kingdom,
where all our tears are wiped away.
Unite us together again in one family,
to sing Your praise forever and ever.

Amen."

My voice died down to nothing and I crossed myself, feeling tears slip from beneath my lashes. Warm hands touched my shoulders. I turned, looking into the faces of my friends. My flock. "Forgive me," I whispered.

Maggie took me into a hug that nearly broke my spine. "There's nothing to—"

Rumble!

From behind the menhirs of Stonehenge, silent sentinels for thousands of years, sank into the earth and were gone in a matter of moments.

The profound silence that filled the air was broken a moment later by Judas. "Well, that is something else I did not expect to see."

CHAPTER FIVE
MAGGIE

NOT SURE IF YOU COULD COUNT that as an understatement, but yeah, it sure wasn't something I expected to see, either.

Twenty-four feet of trilithons, about twenty to twenty-five tons each, supporting lintels weighing about half that just don't *melt* into the ground and disappear, leaving enormous holes behind. By the time the last of the bluestones (the smaller stones known for their blue tinge when wet) sank below the grass, only a few seconds had passed.

We all stared. What else could we do? Not like we could stop a bazillion tons of rock from going wherever they wanted to go. It was like reality took a back seat for a moment, leaving us with jaws agape.

Of course, it was Cain who finally broke the silence. "Of course! It had completely slipped my mind that the *entirety* of the henge consisted of earth elementals, an egregious oversight, if I do say so myself."

More staring.

"What?"

Mike. "You *knew*?"

"The past tense is correct, my friend. I did indeed know yet forgot." Another brilliant Cain smile that shone clearly in the night. "An event, although rare, which does occur with the frequency of the Blood Moon."

"Is that all you got to say?" Mike looked *pissed*.

Cain gently rubbed his battered face. "My bad."

I tried not to laugh.

Judas. "This is not information that is germane right now. What is relevant is what happened to the elementals." She tapped her chin. "In fact, what happened to the sprites? They were the first to leave."

Groaning, Mike upended his canteen onto the bloody grass, creating a small puddle, into which he thrust a hand. He squinted. He squirmed. He frowned. Finally, he stood. "I can't get hold of Primal Water."

Mike had told us of Primal Water's agreement to help him when it was needed, and he took the great elemental's offer, sending it to Finland to destroy Project Century. The elemental was our ace-in-the-hole against the Family here, but whatever agency caused Stonehenge to beat its metaphorical feet seemed to be interfering with contact with the Primal. A cold shiver ran down my spine.

Judas put the kibosh on any possible blossoming hope. "I think ..." she began haltingly. "I think we are too late."

Oh, shit and fried eggs. The horror of the moment really began to sink in. The incompetence of the Sicarii, our ability to kill them all despite being outnumbered three-to-one and the presence of the mercs as unwilling sacrifices for the Ritual of Ascension ... all pointed to one thing. The success of Burke to summon the big daddy bad guy. That realization passed from face to face and a few of the remaining Templars (it broke my heart to see how few, how wounded and tired and downright *beat* they looked) to groan in misery.

Milo piped in, one of the only times I heard the big guy speak. "I think we should go to the ascension chamber and find out."

You could see Mike screw up his resolve. That was the thing that drew me to the guy in the first place ... he had an unshakable moral compass, the resolve to do what was right no matter the cost. I think that's the reason Morgan finally became the man he was meant to be, because of the example this priest set for him.

The image that comes to mind of a Catholic priest is one of a pasty, skinny, inexperienced virgin who will eventually commit some horrible sin against an altar boy. One look at Mike put paid to that stereotype. Tall (of course he looked kinda puny next to Cain), muscular and utterly *capable*. This was a man who had seen the horrors of war, fought hand-to-hand against the agents of Lucifer and emerged from the fray with his faith intact, despite having his eyes opened to the world as it really was. Most of us would run home screaming and hide in the broom cupboard for a few decades.

What is it with the guys I find myself attracted to? The first was a failed antichrist, the second a fucking Catholic priest? I began to wonder about my judgement and whether I should chuck it all and become a hermit. Beats working for a living.

"We go," Mike said with a frown. "Maggie, me, Cain, Judas, and Milo." He looked at the handful of Templars still standing. It looked like a stiff breeze would knock them sideways. "You guys look beat. Stay here." When it looked like they would protest, he adopted what I called his 'command voice'. "No arguments." None were given.

At the hole that lay beneath the elemental that comprised the giant slab of rock in the middle of Stonehenge, Mike stopped us all, staring at what appeared to be a set of steep stairs descending into darkness. "You know, it would be a comfort if these missions didn't end with the assailing of a secret lair. Yeah, I could get used to a cozy little cottage in Colorado somewhere. A place where all we had to do was drink some wine and have a chat with the bad guy, convince him to leave the world alone."

That earned a few tired chuckles and Cain said, "I have in my possession a rather nice domicile in that very state you mentioned. Despite rampant loneliness and the bitter cold of winter, I found myself a modicum of peace until our mutual former Sicarii friend stumbled through my threshold."

I licked lips suddenly gone dry. "Is it me, or are we just procrastinating? Because I'm perfectly good not finding out what lies at the bottom of this hole."

Judas chimed in. "The ritual could only be attended by a few chosen individuals, so I do not expect much resistance. Except for Father, of course." She sounded like squaring off against the Devil was as common as pancakes at IHOP.

We stared at each other and even Cain looked a little put off, which sent more cold shivers across my skin. If he was nervous, then we were closer to The End than I thought.

Without a word, Mike slowly started down the steps, unclipping the flashlight from his belt. I figured his Vision must've worn off and decided to add to whatever lumens his LED light could provide by unclipping and shining my own down as I followed. Judas and Milo followed with Cain bringing up the rear ... which begs a whole slew of jokes right there.

"Ring around the rosies, pockets full of posies, ashes, ashes, we all fall down."

It took a second, but I realized that Mike was *singing*. Quietly, a little out of tune, but singing. He had a pleasant baritone that wouldn't turn a chair on *The Voice*. "Uh, Mike?" I whispered.

"Sorry. Seems to be a habit I've developed."

"Your habit is freaking me out, dude."

There was no humor in his chuckle.

Down, down, down we went, the stairs, made of rough gray stone, passing through a thick layer of chalk, then bedrock and further. Condensation built along the steps, making them slick underfoot and if it hadn't been for the hard rubber of my boot soles, I would have fallen ass over teakettle, bouncy, bouncy, bouncy, all the way down until I wound up at the bottom a shattered mess of a former magus. "Who the heck built—" I began quietly to have something to do besides trundle down stairs.

"Earth elementals," Judas cut in. "When you ask nicely, and if they are in the mind to, earth elementals could build a full-scale replica of the Colosseum at Rome in less than a day."

Wow.

Within minutes, as my calves and thighs were starting to feel the burn, we saw a rectangle of light below. Not bright, more like a gray, flickering illumination that reminded me of torchlight. Torchlight filtered through frosted glass. It didn't look inviting.

We all readied our weapons, although when I checked I only had about twenty rounds or so left. Not much if there were more Sicarii assbags waiting for us, but if what I think happened, happened ... than no amount, of bullets would help. We would need a steaming pile of divine intervention to carry us through and, sorry to say, I didn't have near the faith Mike possessed.

At the bottom, nowhere to hide, no landing, the stairs simply dumped us right into a room that took a few moments to comprehend. All of us gasped at the same time.

Mike crossed himself.

Cain whistled low and slow.

Milo ... was Milo, not saying a word, but his eyes sure got big.

Judas muttered, "Not what I would have ordered. This is excessive even for *my* Family."

As for me, I tried not to cringe. The ceiling must've hit the fifty-foot mark and was supported by what looked like hundreds of intricately carved cylindrical pillars, four-foot thick solid pieces of blue stone like some of the menhirs above, but smooth and artistically rendered. We were too far away to see the carvings on the closest, but even from our vantage point they looked ... disturbing.

And the light, that icy gray light that I said seemed filtered through frosted glass came from far ahead through the forest of carved stone. There was no rhyme or reason to the placement of the pillars except they were no closer than five yards apart, but there were enough of them to block from our sight what lay ahead.

"This ain't good." I didn't realize I spoke until the last word crossed my lips.

"It has not been good for quite some time," Judas remarked. Nods all around.

To the left and right the walls curved inward and a quick think had me estimating that the room, if it was indeed a room, was bigger than Yankee Stadium. Beneath Stonehenge. Just when I thought things couldn't get much weirder.

Without waiting, Mike started forward at a good clip. Milo tried to hold him back, but a stony glare from priest stilled him quick. Mike was all done fooling around and he wanted to do some dirt with that SMG clutched tightly in his big paws. As for me, I unlimbered my axe and got ready to go full-on Valkyrie. I didn't know much, but I knew mayhem.

Sweat rolled down my forehead and back. I blinked furiously and wiped my eyes and tried not to let the butterflies in my stomach fly outta my mouth. I had a feeling that by the time this was over I'd either be dead or ... hell, the way things were going the best I could hope for was a quick, clean death.

Besides, in front and behind I could hear breathing. Heavy, anxious breathing. Even Cain, who was as cool as a cucumber even at the worst of times (to hear him talk about it, he was positively serene when he helped Ike plan D-day) sounded like Darth Vader with a faulty iron lung. If I didn't know him better, I'd say he was scared shitless, which didn't do me any favors in the anxiety department.

A few minutes later we were through the forest of pillars into a clearing in the middle of the ... well. Room.

Up close I could see the pillars were carved with scenes from Dante's *Inferno*, which added to the tension when Judas pointed that out. From our vantage point I could see the place had been created to be perfectly circular, just as the pillars perfectly circled the center where lay a circular dais atop a pair of steps some twenty feet away. On that dais was a throne.

If God had a throne, then this was an attempt to copy it. The back rose fifteen feet in the air. The arms and feet were smooth and unadorned, yet elegant in their simple perfection. The thing would have been almost ordinary if it hadn't been carved out of a single, giant diamond. My mind couldn't come up with an approximation of the carat weight.

The cold, gray light shone from behind the throne, which split the light into thousands of beams, most of which bypassed the first few pillars in their journey to the curving wall. For some reason, the light refused to be rendered into its component colors, instead remaining a uniform gray through every small facet of the great crystal. Overall, it was an attempt to shock and awe that succeeded quite nicely. I was plenty awed and had enough shock for two.

However, it was Burke who commanded our attention. He sat on the throne in jeans, Timberline boots and a dark gray sport coat over a light blue henley shirt. A nice outfit if you like villain casual. One leg was draped over an arm of the throne as he slouched in total ease and comfort, as if he hadn't a care in the world. Judging by the people at the foot of steps, he didn't have to worry about a damn thing.

A big guy, the sort of big you created by CGI in movies about dragons and horse riding, savage nomads and their platinum-blonde queen stood to his left. A black XXXXXL t-shirt strained to hold back his immense musculature.

I was kinda surprised that the shoulder holster rig came in a size large enough to accommodate his torso. It was as if the Incredible Hulk had a Viking cousin with a fetish for rust-colored tattoos that covered both arms and his neck. I reckoned that if he peeled off his shirt his entire torso would be like an M. Escher painting. One enormous hand held a .44 revolver that looked ridiculously tiny by comparison. Next to him, one step up, stood a youngish man who resembled Burke a little too much ... same shit-eating smile, same light-drinking black hair and the same eagle beak nose. They even shared the same eyes, piercing and contemptuous as well as the same fashion sense. Despite the resemblance, there was something else very familiar about him. Next to him stood a beautiful, raven-haired woman in standard black SS garb. The light of madness shone from her almond eyes.

Mike gave a slight nod. "Burke."

The new Family leader raised a finger, wagging it at us. "Not ... exactly."

It was Cain who clarified it for us. "Lucifer."

The smile the Burke body gave us, pardon the pun, was Hellish.

CHAPTER SIX
JUDAS

———— ∼∼∼ ————

FATHER WAS IN THE HOUSE, so to speak, and I felt a terror more intense, more gut-wrenchingly horrible than ever before. It eclipsed the emotions felt when I finally understood the enormity of betraying my best friend so long ago. My bladder felt hot and full and I desperately wanted to sneak off behind a pillar to relieve myself.

For decades I hid from His awful gaze, protected by a bible blessed by a truly pious priest (supplied to me after my rescue by the Templars) and a copy of the Torah (old habits die hard). With those copies secreted on my person, Father's gaze was averted, and I found myself safe from Him for the first time. Ever. The relief of it nearly had me in a weepy puddle on the floor, but I learned never to cry in front of others. Especially Templars. But now they were of no use because there he sat, casual and contemptuous, at ease in his assumption of Burke Deschamps body, looking out through eyes I would normally categorize as velvety brown, but now were hard and cold as chips of flint, shiny like oiled marbles. What I had hoped for, and feared, for two-thousand years finally came to pass and it felt worse than anything.

It was the man standing next to the giant who grabbed my attention after I pulled it away from Father. "Julian."

I heard Michael draw a large breath, hissing between his teeth. I guess he finally recognized him as well.

"Judas." Project Century had returned youth to Julian, restoring him to the man I knew, the man who raped me over and over, so I would bear his offspring.

The familiar feeling of tearing violation came over me as Julian gave me a knowing smirk. I bet it tickled him to no end to rape the Founder, his distant ancestor who created the Deschamps dynasty. Not the act of intercourse, but the violence, and when not violence, the degradation and humiliation as I had to lie there and take his awful seed. Dozens of men over the long years raped me and Father was amused. Laughing His ass off in Hell, enjoying every moment of my pain, every second of torture. Those feelings came upon me again in an instant and my knees weakened, near spilling me to the floor. A strong hand, a large one, gently took my elbow, steadying me and I was grateful to Cain for the assist, but his touch, although meant to be supportive, made my skin crawl.

Julian, of course, caught everything, not missing a beat. "Hello, lovely Judas," he purred, his smooth, buttery voice echoing slightly among the pillars. "Good to see you again. You have aged well."

Fortunately, Michael cut in, anger coloring his voice. "Last time I saw you, Julian, you were gray and possessed."

"Not so gray anymore."

"Enough." Burke's voice, Father's undertone of shit. It shut everyone up. We made ready with our weapons, and I for once, was eager to die. "Hans, kill them."

To my surprise, and I think everyone else's, the giant nodded and holstered his revolver. Cain cocked his head to the side and pulled the trigger on the H&K .45 ACP leveled at the giant.

Click.

What?

Father smiled. Maggie swore, and Michael quickly crossed himself.

This was no surprise to me. The laws of physics tend not to work in the most convenient fashion when Father was around. It was the reason that all the elementals, from the sprites to the menhirs of Stonehenge, departed. It was written in the Family history that when He returns, no forces of nature would abide his presence. I did not tell the others because of the fear that threatened to tear me apart and leave me in a quivering, mewling heap on the ground, a fact of which I am not proud.

Faster than I thought possible, the giant was among us, massive tree branch arms swinging. Cain flew backward, while Maggie grunted, falling, and I scrambled back with Michael, trying to avoid the fray while drawing my knives.

I did not have to deal with the giant, however, because the woman, the pretty one with the crazy eyes, was right *there*, slashing at my midsection with a machete that looked big enough to decapitate a rhinoceros with a single blow.

Whoever she was, she had (and I am quoting from American television, which is a cornucopia of both wisdom and trivial horse shite) mad skills. The machete, instead of slicing my nose off, merely parted the skin on my left cheek in a stinging, paper-thin line. Spinning, I dodged a surprise thrust and slammed an elbow into the meat of her triceps, momentarily paralyzing her arm. The machete dropped to the floor.

"Not bad for a bitch," snarled the madwoman, pulling a long knife from the small of her back.

Why bother talking when someone is trying to perforate your skin? I whipped around, slashing with the kukri, but only managed to slice air. My follow-up thrust hit more air, as did the next and the next.

Pain along my thigh and I hit the floor, one of my knives skittering away to come to a rest at the base of a pillar. Crazy lady came at me in a whirl of razor death.

CHAPTER SEVEN
MICHAEL

———

Two days ago:

"BLESS ME, FATHER, FOR I HAVE SINNED."

"You need no confession, my son."

"I beg to differ."

His Holiness smiled, face a topographic map of wrinkles. He patted the couch next to him and I dutifully sat.

My mind was operating at half-speed because of jet lag and zero sleep for the past day or so. Good thing His Holiness was able to sneak off for a meet-and-greet at Cardinal Meccio's brother's place in Rome. The cardinal was one of the few in the Vatican His Holiness could trust and the little apartment I found myself in, very similar to the one in Bruges, was crowded with trusted guardians. The Swiss Guard, great big men with large muscles, weapons and no sense of humor, were giving me the eye from across the room while I talked to their boss and nothing he said would change their watchful stance. Both looked like they wanted to take a chunk out of my hide while Milo, who would not be left behind, watched them with equal distrust. It was hard to imagine we were all friends here.

"Tell me, my son, what brought you here with your tail on fire? What do you have to tell me in person what you could not over a tablet?"

Those kind eyes behind their wire rims twinkled merrily, as if he knew a joke the world needed to hear. It was those eyes which enchanted Catholics and non-Catholics the world over. It was his air of simple piety that disarmed the villains in the Vatican, had them thinking he would be a high pontiff they could control. Once the pope hat (the mitre hit his brow, they found out just how wrong they were. His keen, piercing intelligence coupled with indomitable faith and iron will proved to be a perfect brew for a man no one could buy.

"Your Holiness, I think in a little less than two days our great enemy will finally realize his plan to enter our world. This could be the End of Days."

That twinkle in his eye became a shining, diamond hardness. No, no messing with *this* guy. The Sicarii hidden like snakes in the grass of the Vatican made a huge mistake when they voted him in. "My son, are you sure?"

"As sure as I can be given the circumstances."

The old man crossed himself and sat in silence for a moment while he gathered his thoughts. It struck me again how old he was. The vibrancy with which he approached the world belied the time hung around his shoulders. Just as the joyous smile on his face belied the razor intelligence that lurked behind his wire rims. "What do you need from me?"

"The thing I asked you about, you know ... the artifact. Did you find anything in the archives?" The Vatican Secret Archives (or as we were discussing it, the *Archivum Secretum Apostolicum Vaticanum*) was the repository of knowledge for all the acts promulgated by the Holy See. It also houses correspondence, papal account books, and state papers as well as all documentation relative to the Catholic Church over the centuries. These documents included everything worth knowing about artifacts, up to and including the Holy Grail and the Arc of the Covenant, where these artifacts were located and their reported abilities. Not too long ago I asked His Holiness to perform a small bit of research for me on a specific item.

Inquiring minds wanted to know.

He smiled.

NOW:

"Join Me, won't you?"

The words didn't register because I was watching the giant fight and man, he was a blur. Literally, not a figure of speech, but an actual blur of motion as he took Cain to task while easily fending off Maggie as if she was a six-year-old. Not too long ago a big serial killer called The Atheist came calling to my church, killing Father Paul and darn near doing away with my mortal coil. This guy was bigger by half, at least seven feet tall and twice as wide as me. It looked like his existence violated the known physical laws of the universe.

I holstered my pistol and made ready to join in the fray when a movement at the corner of my eye brought my attention around.

Julian rushed me, swinging for the cheap seats with a telescoping baton. I ducked and punched, catching him in the ribs and he spun away, the baton smacking my shoulder lightly. It stung.

Then Milo was there.

Big Milo, my bodyguard, a savage look, on his face and resolute purpose in his eye. Julian, wincing slightly and favoring his bruised ribs, smiled and, with snakelike grace, struck at the larger man.

"Leave them to it."

This time the words penetrated. I turned. Burke ... wait, no ... not Burke. I had to get it through my thick skull that the man seated on the crystal throne was no longer human, but a skin suit for the evilest creature in the universe. I wanted to spit.

He seemed amused, gesturing me forward. "Come, let's talk like adults." His voice carried quite well, almost intimately despite the ruckus all around and I moved forward until he motioned for me to stop at the first step. "Thank you. Let us let the others have their fun. We have business, you and I." The Patron smiled, a surprisingly warm gesture and seemingly sincere. I, of course, wasn't having it.

For the moment it looked like the giant had his hands full with a pissed-off Valkyrie and a man with more combat experience than anyone. Still, I would keep an eye on the ball and dive in when needed. "What do you want, Lucifer?"

Again, that smile. "I want what you want."

"You to go back to Hell where you belong?"

He shook his head before I even finished. "No, son, I want *peace*."

"My ability to accept that statement seems to be malfunctioning."

Lucifer maintained his casual pose, but his words became insistent. "Droll, but you have to realize that mankind has been in a state of war for as long as there's been a mankind. War. A constant throughout history because at every moment when humanity reached a technological milestone or achieved some great feat of social cooperation, God, our daddy on high, comes along with one of his winged party boys and does humanity a dirty, reversing the clock, driving mankind back to the stone age." His voice smoothed out, becoming seductive. "Think about it, thousands of years ago a civilization based in the Mediterranean basin achieved a level of advancement equal to the 11th Century and was wiped out except for a dude called Noah and his brood. An entire civilization! Then comes the Tower of Babel incident where unparalleled cooperation creates the world's largest structure, one so tall that by the time you reached the top the air is thin enough that you're gasping desperately for breath. What happened? The big guy flippped a switch in mankind's mind and suddenly we have language problems. 'What we have here is a failure to communicate,'" he quoted. "Look at the fucking Roman Empire, practically brought down to its knees by Christianity. Oh, sure, there was some problem with corruption and inbreeding, but the Romans set a standard for discipline and the single-minded devotion to a vision that hasn't been matched since."

"And the wars you propagate? What about them?" I crossed my arms, keeping an eye on Judas and Annabeth. Yes, *that* Annabeth, the one who captured me after I destroyed the Silver and beat the ever-loving stuffing out of me. It sure looked like being reborn only accentuated the molten crazy that ran through her veins. It looked the Sicarii woman had a handy way with that machete of hers.

"On the contrary! I've been a great supporter of mankind from the beginning!" Lucifer lost his casual pose, planting both feet on the dais and leaning forward, his body straining with the force of his sincerity. "Every war I've ever had a hand in *launched* man forward technologically and culturally. The Civil War saw great advances in medicine and weaponry, the First World War brought airplanes to the forefront of combat. World War Two advanced aeronautics even further, as well as rocketry and physics and gave birth to the computer age! That's all Me, My works, My contribution to mankind under the rules set by dad. If I hadn't meddled, you all would be still be using black powder weapons and dreaming of flying to the moon."

"And Korea? Vietnam? Iraq?"

He threw up his hands. "Hey, don't blame Me for *everything*. That's all you guys. Humans don't need Me to start crap for their own greed and self-interest, they've been programmed by God to kill each other off. What I want to do is end all that. I want to *help* mankind."

Chapter Eight
Maggie

———

THE BIG DUDE KNOCKED ME SIDEWAYS and I thought my guts would spurt out through my nose. I mean, he hit *hard*. Cain once hit me with full strength and that put paid to what would've been a great weekend, but this tattooed giant dick took it to the next level and beyond.

My lungs decided to take a nap and for the next few minutes all I could do was try to breathe around the cramping knot in my chest while blood rushed to my cheeks. I knew that in a few seconds, if I didn't pass out, the first breath to hit my lungs would hurt almost as much as the punch.

Oh, Lord, it knifed through my heart and I thought it would burst in agony as my back arched backward to draw in more air. All I could do was gasp and gag and try not to puke because my stomach felt like throwing out the leftover shepherd's pie I had for lunch.

Years, decades, later my stomach muscles contracted enough to draw me into a fetal position and eventually I made it to my feet in time to watch the battle royal happening a few feet away.

Cain jabbed and kicked, but the giant was faster, which threw me for a fucking loop because that never happened before, at least not since I've known him. Blows that would've shattered bone and torn flesh bounced off the giant like raindrops, but that didn't stop Cain from trying.

Hans lunged forward and enveloped Cain in a bear hug, insanely thick arms tightening, muscles moving like pythons under the skin. Cain shrieked, arms trapped at his side and back arched in agony. I heard bone creak, then more begin to pop. Blood drooled from the corner of Cain's mouth.

Maybe it was muscle memory, or adrenalin or whatever, but the next thing I knew my axe was buried in Hans' side all the way to the handle, at least five inches deep. He dropped Cain, who sprawled on the floor, writhing and puking blood. The giant turned a glare my way, slapping my hand away from the axe handle. He pulled, the flesh of his side deforming around the blade until it came free in a squelch of blood.

And my brain went for a walk as the gash, no doubt cleaving organs and bone, instantly began to heal, flesh knitting so fast that within seconds not even a scar was visible beneath the hole in his t-shirt.

"Oh, shit," I breathed before a fist the size of New York filled my vision. First, I saw red, then black, then red again, then stars when I hit the floor hard enough to rattle my teeth. No pain, what happened to me was too big for something like pain, my mind couldn't grasp it, couldn't understand the sensation that flooded my skull. Smooth, warm marbles filled my mouth along with the coppery taste of blood. I wanted to scream because I knew I was hurt badly, knew that Hans' big fist did something serious to me, but everything was spinning and tilting. I drooled blood onto the floor and tried not to scream.

From my vantage point, both Cain and Hans were immeasurably tall, ten-foot giants battling over the city that was my body and they hammered at each other relentlessly. Somehow, Cain got himself a knife, a brutal looking thing with serrations on the back end and was trying to put it to good use, but the giant kept his distance and any damage he did take healed so fast he hardly bled a drop.

Something fell from my mouth, clattering. Somehow my vision was all kerfuddled and brumbly, but I made out a squarish pebble with two stalks lying in a pool of red. Another pebble fell from my mouth and I saw it was a tooth and more followed, some shattered, some whole but all part of my dental history.

"Blahh," I cried, horrified ... mortified at what I saw.

The mind is generally not used to sight of damaged flesh, to the sheer, unnerving knowledge that what was right is now wrong, malformed and broken. Sure, I suffered before ... cuts, bruises and the occasional broken bone, but the enormity of my jaw hanging at an appalling angle, dislocated from its perch, didn't quite fit into the space between my ears. How could this be? Why did the flesh hold misaligned bone in place so poorly? There was no pain, none, really, only a sort of enormous pressure where my teeth used to be as if someone stuck an air hose in my face and was blasting away until my head reached 32 psi.

I moved my neck, scrabbling to my hands and knees and that's when the pain hit, ruining me for a few seconds as my eyes screwed shut against the lightning bolt that slammed through my jaw into my brain. My body went numb, the only thing I could feel was the electric agony that had become my entire world. I gently touched my jaw, butterfly light, and nearly fell unconscious.

Once when fighting a gladiator named Miles Champion, (really, that was his name. I blamed his parents and so did he) I took a cestus to the ribs that my chain mail did little to soften. My ribs broke like matchsticks and one punctured a lung, filling it with blood. I won the bout, hacking two fingers off Champion's left hand while I coughed up red. This hurt worse.

Words didn't work. For some reason when I whispered Strength when the battle began, nothing happened and that was scary enough for any magus. Had to be Blood Magic, the kind that Morgan wrote about in his letter to Mike, so it looked like I was shit out of luck in the Healing department. That sucked three kinds of dick.

When I pried my eyes open, it was to see Judas on her ass, about to be carved into cutlets by Ms. Psychopath, one of Burke's trusty SS people, no doubt.

Through the haze that clouded my eyes I stumbled forward, not sure what to do, only knowing I had to do *something*. I shifted my body to autopilot and lashed out with a foot, catching crazy lady at the knee, bending it sideways. It *crunched*. Boy, was I familiar with that sound. I smiled slightly and the pain of it took me away again.

CHAPTER NINE
JUDAS

A BIG BOOT APPEARED FROM NOWHERE, catching the crazy lady at the knee, popping her leg sideways. She fell with a teakettle shriek that tore at my ears as it rose higher and higher. Only when one of my knives entered the soft tissues of her throat did it cut off and she gave me a slightly puzzled looked before her eyes rolled up into her skull.

Maggie!

I was fond of the big woman and spying her crumpled in a heap, drawn up in a fetal position sent fear racing through me. I checked her pulse. She had one.

Cain and his giant opponent danced amongst the pillars, bouncing off them like billiard balls, leaving smears of blood behind like obscene punctuation marks. All I could do was get in Cain's way. There had to be something else.

Then I spied Julian.

Emotions like leaves falling from autumn trees fluttered through my mind, the chief of which was rage. Julian was young again, younger than me, an old soul brought out of Hell by Father and stuffed in a new body created for a new cadre of Sicarii. One that could come back again and again, sweeping their enemies away in a tide of blood. Oh, how vibrant he was, handsome and utterly without morals, without a sense of right and wrong, of good and evil. A fully functioning sociopath.

It was my fault. All the decisions, the choices in my life led to his creation. Led to him becoming one of the world's most powerful men with an unshakable ambition to control it all. He meant to bend the earth to his will, to break it and shape man in Father's image. Lucifer's image.

The thought of those nights so long ago, him sweating and heaving above me as I lay passive and devoid of hope. Forced to take his seed, nurture it within my womb so I could gestate a new generation for his enjoyment, to fulfill an awful purpose I was so instrumental in bringing about.

Guilt, rage and shame racked me, whited out my mind. I wanted, for the first time in decades, to really *kill* for sheer enjoyment. With that in mind I gathered up my fallen kukri and made my way to the two men as they struggled.

I could see the damage Julian had already sustained, the little finger on his left hand bent the wrong way and the swelling around his right eye that would soon purple and obscure his vision. As for Milo, Michael's doughty bodyguard, he looked a little worse for wear. His left arm hung at an awkward angle and I knew from centuries of experience that it had been dislocated. The gray light flickered over their faces, adding to the air of violence.

What happened next, I caught only because I was looking as well as being only a few short feet away and closing. Julian's right arm moved as if the intervening space from where it started to where it ended had been edited from reality. One second the knife in his right hand shone with keen potential, the next it dripped slickly red.

Milo looked down, face troubled, his large hands to his stomach. The black shirt covering his torso suddenly split and loops of gray and purple fell through his suddenly clumsy fingers to land *plopping* onto the floor. Blood splattered and drooled, and Julian stepped back, a quirky smile of arrogance on his handsome features.

Slowly, ponderously, Milo fell to his knees, then onto his face, obscuring the coils of his guts with his body. He twitched once, twice, then lay still.

Then I was *there*, in the fray, attacking Julian with all the speed I could muster, with my centuries of training. Me, the first Sicarii of the Family, the Founder, hacking away blindly at my many-times great grandson with knives barely seen as my hands arced toward his body, his neck, his face and he danced, danced, danced away from my blades, my anger, my hatred.

Back and forth, not wasting breath on taunting, not wasting breath to vent the fury in my soul. I let my knives speak for me, my kukri was my tongue, the other dagger the words that delivered my meaning. A pang on my shoulder as his blade pierced my defenses. Not a deep wound, but it bled, and it hurt, slowing that arm just enough that another edge found the skin over my left breast and that bled, too. Despite the fact he had only one blade to my two, he was better, younger, faster.

Slowly I realized that he was slicing me to death, letting me bleed from cut after shallow cut until I would run out of strength and my speed would fade and I would finally fall to his knife as he grinned down upon me in delight and that thought drove all else from my mind, drove away any desire to confront Father, any fear of being reborn into a world where I was raped again and again, totally at the mercy of the Family because at that moment I thought, *fuck him*.

Only a little skill is needed to win a fight. True victory depends on what someone is willing to sacrifice to achieve it. For most, the price for success is too high and might be counterproductive. For me, price was no object and I was highly skilled indeed.

My plan came into play without a second thought … and hardly a first thought at that. I shifted my shoulders ever so slightly, telegraphing my intent to Julian who was learned enough to understand such subtle cues. My right hand darted forward only to be met by his blade, which chopped through the index finger, cutting it away with almost surgical precision and damn that hurt, but the pain was nothing compared to what was to come.

The knife hit the floor the same moment Julian's entered my gut just below the sternum, his move fluid and fast. I wasted no time lunging toward him, enveloping him in a hug that dug his knife deeper, tearing at my internals just as the one in my off hand dug into his back over and over, blood spurting. His hand was trapped between our bodies as I gripped him tighter and tighter with my damaged arm, not caring about the pain that flooded my torso, only wanting him dead. I embraced him with my legs, pulling him off balance as I stabbed, and we fell to the floor, once again with Julian on top, but this time I assaulted him, this time I caused the most pain and horror. This time I won.

CHAPTER TEN
MIKE

Two Days Ago:

"AH, MY SON. I DID INDEED learn some things that you might find very interesting." His Holiness' face was beatific. He took one of my scarred hands in his soft ones. His touch was warm. "May I see it?"

"Of course, Your Holiness." I opened at briefcase that lay at my feet and removed the item, handing it to him so he could inspect it.

The Pope crossed himself, tears welling behind his wire rims. "This has been touched by the blood of the Christ."

"Yes, Your Holiness."

He removed his glasses and bowed his head over the object. Tears pattered down upon the dull metal

I hated to butt in on his moment, but time was of the essence. "Your Holiness, what did you find?"

"There is an old scroll," he began. "Written by St. Ignatius of Antioch. It concerned the great artifacts of Christ, the greatest of all, of course, is the Holy Grail." He licked his lips while the tears continued to fall. His voice had become husky with great emotion. "He postulated what he called the Powers and Intents of each of the artifacts, what miracles they wrought, what might be their divine purposes."

"It mentioned this?" I pointed.

"Yes, my son. It went into great detail about it, as it did with all the artifacts."

"And?"

He put my hand on the hilt of the dagger, then plunged it into his chest.

NOW:

Help mankind. Right. Easy to say when others fight and die for you. I watched Milo fall, his death coming so quick I could barely move before his intestines hit the floor. Then Judas came in and she became a blur while Julian matched her strike for strike and then they hugged, but it wasn't a hug, it was a death … and they fell.

"I know you want to help them," said Lucifer with what sounded like real sorrow in his fecal infested voice. "Hans is tattooed in Blood Magic, so Cain's Words will have no effect. As for the rest, they fight as they will, with skill and boldness. Not even their guns will work as long as the magic of the Ritual of Ascension is active. But they fight that you and I might talk, so we can reach an agreement."

"An agreement," I muttered, looking at Maggie's crumpled form. She looked so small, so broken.

"Yes, of course. It's always come down to this. Two sides, two labels."

"Good and Evil."

"A matter of perspective."

"Opposites, then." Why was I having this conversation? Why wasn't I trying to kill this...person?

"Yes. We are defined by our opposites. What is up without down? Dark without light? God and Lucifer, two sides of the same coin."

"You want to enslave us."

Laughter, loud and surprisingly musical. "I am trying to uplift mankind. Make them perfect."

"Make them ants."

The Burke body spread his hands. "And what is wrong with that? Ants are possibly the most amazing creatures ever. They build colonies that rival, in scale, to any city on the face of the earth. They have total cooperation, every ant knows its place, contributes to the whole without violence or shame or regret. There are no ant politicians, no ant lawyers, only the collective which has a singular mission … to serve the queen and make their society greater."

My mind felt fuzzy. "But they have no … consciousness. No sense of self."

"What has a sense of self done for man? War? Ego? Vanity? Murder? Porn? All that and more. Overrated, I tell you, and unnecessary."

"No art. No love. No appreciation for beauty." My hands tingled, and I dimly noticed that the icy gray light was starting to fade.

"They don't need it. They create beauty every day, their art is in their colony and they love their queen unconditionally. Utter devotion that aids them in their efforts. All mankind needs is a guiding hand that can get them there. Once that is achieved, there will be cooperation on a scale not seen since Babel, advancements in medicine and technology that boggles the mind. In less than twenty years mankind can develop interstellar flight and the ability to colonize new worlds, see new suns and horizons. Mankind can populate the galaxy and insure its survival for another thousand plus years."

I wanted to argue. I needed to, but I couldn't really find the energy to refute his claim. It all seemed so sensible, so rational. Uplift mankind, stop wars, stop murder and strife, envy and sloth. Do away with all seven of the deadly sins.

Would that be so bad? My mind spun in a thousand directions, thinking of all possible futures where mankind could excel if it wasn't bothered by jealousy or hate. A world where peace would ultimately reign.

My eyes wandered to where Judas lay under Julian's corpse while the Patron kept up his talk of a perfect society that would touch the stars, bend the laws of physics to its will and reach immortality. She twitched. Once. Twice. My eyes narrowed as she slowly pushed the now young-but-dead Julian aside. Her deep eyes found mine as her hands clutched her midriff, red and sticky with blood. From between her fingers a hilt of a knife bobbed with every labored breath and I wanted to go to her, I did, but a curious lethargy gripped my limbs and I couldn't move.

"*Michael.*" I didn't hear the word, but I could read her lips. My name. Michael. Yes. "*Michael,*" she continued. "*The gray light.*"

Yes. The gray light. Kind of pretty. Hypnotic, although not as bright as it used to be. Strange.

"The gray light."

She said that already.

"When it is gone ..."

What?

The Patron's voice slithered over my skin, almost soothing in a way. "Relax, Michael Engle. All you have to do is take My hand and we can do this together, you and I?'

That's it? Sounded easy. I almost turned back, and I knew when I did he would be right there, waiting for me with a smile on his face and a hand out to take mine so we could start a new venture in the next phase of humanity.

Judas' lips were still moving. I tried to concentrate. So hard. So very hard. "*When it is gone ...*" she continued, blood dripping from her lips. "*Then the ritual will be complete.*"

Ah, the ritual. The one that brought him here.

"Turn around, Michael."

Sure, what a good idea.

"*When that happens, he wins.*"

Wins? Wins what? Man, I had the biggest case of medicine head in the world, like someone rubbed Vick's Vape-O-Rub on my brain. Win? Did she say win?

"Michael. Turn around please."

A single thought took root in the cotton surrounding my brain. A single word planted by the betrayer of Christ and from that seed sprouted a thought that sent tendrils through my mind. Win. She said he would win.

Win.

Not on my watch.

What happened next started as a thought, words that never left my lips, but I knew them by heart and when they began to unspool, I felt a strengthening.

Lord, you are Holy above all others, and all the strength that I need is in your hands.

I am not asking, Lord, that you take this trial away. Instead, I simply ask that Your will be done in my life. Whatever that means, that is what I want.

I admit that it's hard, Lord.

My limbs began to tingle, the malaise gripping them leeching away as the thought words finally reached my mouth and I began to whisper:

Sometimes I feel like I can't go on. The pain and the fear are too much for me. I know that I don't have the strength on my own to get through this.

I know that I can come to you, Jesus, and that you will hear my prayer. I know that it is not your intent to bring me to this point just to leave me in the wilderness alone.

Please, Lord, give me the strength that I need to face today. I don't have to worry about tomorrow.

That was the stuff. Clarity invaded my mind and I felt the strength rush back into my body as the words flew loud and true from my mouth, unstoppable, a prayer for strength, a supplication to the Lord not to lift a burden, but for guidance so one could shoulder it. My heart soared.

If you just give me the strength that I need today that is all I need.

Keep me from sinning during this trial. Instead, help me to keep my eyes on you. You are the Holy Lord, and all my hope rests in you.

Thank you for hearing my prayer.

In Jesus' name. Amen.

The last was a shout of defiance and I turned, ready to face what may come because the Lord was with me, filling me with His might and His glory.

Lucifer was indeed standing only a couple of feet away on the dais, a resigned look on his face. "Oh, well," he drawled. "Going to have to do this hard way, I guess."

He said a Word.

Pain was one of the Words in the magi lexicon, but what Lucifer said was to Pain what an Abrams tank was to a Smart Car. The Words magi used didn't stay in the mind of non-magi, but this one did. This one settled in for the long haul and began to dig through my soul with claws made of rusty iron and electricity.

The Word was Excoriate.

I knew that as pain that flensed every nerve ending, every cell in my body, pain that made burning to death at the stake look like toasting marshmallows, in a few seconds my eyeballs would literally explode. The blood vessels in my head would pop like a champagne corks and flood my brain with blood and the heck of it, the sick and wrong part here was I would still be alive. It wouldn't kill me, nope, no siree. What would happen is the Word would keep me alive and conscious and sane as my cells slowly disintegrated and my organs painfully liquefied. My bones would be eaten by cancers and my muscles turn into lumps of gangrenous flesh. Only when I was reduced to a smelly puddle would I die. Only then would peace descend.

I don't know how I did it, but I began to speak through the red haze that clouded my vision. "The Lord is my shepherd; I shall not want. He maketh me to lie down in green pastures: he leadeth me beside the still waters." Mushy and barely comprehensible, they still emerged from lips coated with fire. "He restoreth my soul: he leadeth me in the paths of righteousness for his name's sake. Yea, though I walk through the valley of the shadow of death, I will fear no evil: for thou art with me; thy rod and thy staff they comfort me." The pain began to recede, and my flesh became calm, my mind more focused and centered. "Thou preparest a table before me in the presence of mine enemies: thou anointest my head with oil; my cup runneth over." Lucifer was not looking like a happy camper and that gave more power to my prayer. Thank you Psalm 23. Thank you, Lord. "Surely goodness and mercy shall follow me all the days of my life: and I will dwell in the house of the Lord forever."

"Ugh," snarled the Beast, face lit from within by some light that had no familial tie to our color spectrum. "I guess I'll speed things up." He used Insanity.

The walls of my mind started to cave as if they were constructed of wet cardboard. I expected this and had my defense ready. "The earth is the Lord's, and the fullness thereof; the world, and they that dwell within. For he hath founded it upon the seas and established it upon the floods. Who shall ascend into the hill of the LORD? Or who shall stand in his holy place? He that hath clean hands, and a pure heart; who hath not lifted up his soul unto vanity or sworn deceitfully. He shall receive the blessing form the LORD, and righteousness from the God of his salvation. This the generation of them that seek him, that seek they face, O Jacob. Selah. Lift up your heads, O ye gates; and be ye lift up ye everlasting doors; and the King of glory shall come in. Who is this King of glory? The LORD of hosts, he is the King of Glory."

Then Lucifer tried Immolate, but Psalm 25 shielded me from the flames that burned but did not consume. "Unto thee, O LORD, do I lift up my soul ..."

Enslave ... Psalm 26. "Judge me, O LORD; for I have walked in mine integrity: I have trusted also in the LORD; therefore, I shall not slide."

Rend ... Psalm 27. "The LORD is my might and salvation ..."

By the time I reached Psalm 29, Burke's nose began to bleed and the light behind the crystal throne began to dim. He was almost at full ascension.

"Fuck this," Lucifer said, wiping the mortal blood from his lips. "My flesh is proof against your mortal weapons, priest, and in a few moments, I will be at full strength. If the Terrible Words won't hurt you, then I guess I'll have to rend you limb from limb."

The Glory of the Lord was in my eyes and he winced slightly when he met my gaze. "True," I said with a smile. "But then again, you were never all that bright, were you?" I reached behind my back and drew Ablewand from the sheath strapped beneath my shirt.

Eyes filled with hate grew round with sudden fear, but before he could move I plunged the weapon into his heart.

EPILOGUE
ENDINGS

———

"Was it not in your power to inform me of your rather fiendishly clever plan?' Cain held the umbrella, the rain pattering on the waterproof canvas.

Fat, gray clouds let loose their burden attempting to soak everyone at the funeral, but there were plenty of umbrellas to go around, especially considering how few of the Templars there were left.

I looked around. "A good spot isn't it?"

A wry look and a nod answered me.

There was no tombstone, only a largish black rock on which the words A FRIEND were carved. I knelt and ran my gloved hand across the words. Even through the thick leather they felt cold.

All around the few mourners that showed slowly dispersed, moving far enough away to let me deal with my grief. They needn't have bothered; I wasn't grieving … exactly. Only Cain remained, standing over me with the umbrella.

"You never told me what she said," he remarked, face inscrutable behind his mirrored shades.

What she said. For some reason I held her final words to me like precious gems and they provided sadness and hope.

Her blood had slicked my hands and her grip on them turned the flesh underneath white. Her eyes bored into mine with a feral intensity.

"Is it done?" she'd asked in a rasping tone.

I nodded.

"How bad do you think He will torture me this time?"

Racking my brain, I couldn't really provide an answer. When she died, her soul would depart and be placed into the body of a newborn descendent, like it had for the past few hundred years. That made me angry.

Her soul.

Her *soul*.

Hope blossomed, and I stared into Judas' face which was heavy with the knowledge of what lay before her. "Judas ... I have a couple of questions."

Puzzlement and a small nod. She coughed a little blood and spasm marred a cheek.

Good. "Do you seek forgiveness? Do you want to be forgiven?"

Realization dawned, but quickly died. "How can the Lord forgive me? I am a betrayer."

"Judas, those that truly accept Christ into their hearts can earn forgiveness. I am the instrument of His will." I took a deep breath. "Now, do you accept Christ as your savior? Do you accept Him in your heart and seek forgiveness for your transgressions against Him?"

Her grip became painful. "I miss my friend. I want to say I am sorry." Tears rippled across her eyes as she nodded. "So *sorry*," she wailed, a long lifetime of misery expressed in two words.

A warm assurance filled me, and the words slipped out without my mind producing them, "Then repeat after me, my friend."

"O Lord, Jesus Christ, Redeemer and Savior, forgive my sins just as You forgave Peter's denial and those who crucified You. Count not my transgressions, but, rather, my tears of repentance. Remember not my iniquities, but, more especially, my sorrow for the offenses I have committed against You. I long to be true to Your Word and pray that You will love me and come to make Your dwelling place within me. I promise to give You praise and glory in love and in service all the days of my life."

The Prayer of Forgiveness slid away like the life that slid from her body and I held only cooling flesh on a stone floor.

I looked from the grave to Cain and said, "She said she missed her friend and was sorry." Dusting off trousers, I stood and stared at A FRIEND.

A large hand clasped my shoulder. "I never thanked you for saving me."

Ah, that. When Judas died, I turned my attention to the fight between Cain and Hans. The giant had Cain on the ropes, pummeling away at the swiftly tiring ancient, but fortunately for me Lucifer's defeat allowed my firearm to work again. I put two through the giant's skull from behind. I could almost hear Morgan saying, 'Hey, that's kinda rude, man.'" I wasn't in any mood to play nice.

"You never have to thank me, buddy," I replied. "You stood by me until the end and for that I'm grateful."

"Should we go?"

I stared at the little village Judas called home for so long. Yeah,

I thought she wouldn't mind resting here at all. "A few minutes longer."

Peace settled on me like a warm blanket, soft and comforting and reflected upon the real tragedy of the past few days.

Sure, losing Judas hurt, but losing the Holy Father hurt more. Oh, I wasn't sad for him because I knew he rested in the Kingdom of Heaven ... no, I was sad for me and for the world. His influence was still sorely needed, and his rock steady faith and kindness would be missed by all. If it wasn't for him, Lucifer would be striding the world like a colossus.

It was Ablewand, you know. That was the key. For centuries the Family thought that the artifact drank in souls, providing vitality to the wielder and it was easy to see why they would think that. When it took a life, the bearer experienced an influx of energy that provided everything from healing to a relief from Backlash, the sickness caused by too much magic use. The same energy that restored a bit more of Hermiel's angelic might.

That was not its purpose, though. Its true power lay in the concept of willingly sacrificing yourself for others. Like Christ ... He sacrificed Himself for our sins and a portion of that Grace was endowed upon the nail that pierced his right palm. The Holy Father found this out in the writings of St. Ignatius, a bit of research the Family never bothered with because, I believe, they thought they already had the measure of the weapon.

When a person willingly impaled themselves upon Ablewand, naturally their soul departed, but their life's energy transferred to the weapon for the purpose of fighting evil. When His Holiness rammed the dagger into his chest, his goodness, nobility of spirit and kindness stayed with the dagger, I could feel it. I could feel His Holiness' divine impression, his love. As the blade slid from the body leaving no mark on His Holiness' skin, I felt the purpose and the will inside the weapon. I knew it like I knew the shape of my face, like I knew the goodness that lurked in the heart of my friend, Morgan.

Lucifer couldn't stand up to the sheer decency and goodness that flooded his body when I stabbed him ... it was anathema to his very being and it forced him from Burke's flesh like toothpaste from a tube. By the time he had finished screaming, Burke's flesh was a mottled gray and purple, as if he'd died from some horrible infection, which, I guessed, was not far off the mark.

As for Stonehenge, it was back to normal, or as normal as it ever was. Cain called the earth elementals to resume their slumber as menhirs and if anyone noticed that one or two didn't seem to be sitting at the precise angle as before, they sure weren't talking. Earth, at Cain's request, completely obliterated and filled in the enormous underground chamber, erasing all evidence of how close we came to becoming an ant colony.

It was the good people, those willing to sacrifice themselves like His Holiness and Milo (whose absence still ate at me) that made the difference.

All the little things, the kindnesses, the noble deeds, the small charitable acts and the plain old decency of those who wished to stave off the darkness added to the scales that tipped them our way.

A strange end to this story.

After a while I looked at the darkening sky. It was a long way back to Kathmandu and the helicopter pilot was probably getting antsy. "Let's go," I said.

Cain nodded, and we strolled across browning grass. Maggie saw us coming and started warming up the helo.

"All in all, my clerical friend, I feel the circumstances of our victory constitutes a miracle."

"That's my jam, Cain good buddy," I replied with a smile as the wind from the rotors tore at my hair and I had to raise voice to a shout. "But I think it was more of Lucifer's sins. Those of arrogance and pride."

He raised an eyebrow.

"Think about it ... he thought that with all the Blood Runes tattooed on Hans' body giving the bodyguard superior strength, vigor and speed he had us by the short and curlies. Add to that his either intentional or unintentional affect, on our firearms and it seemed like the win was in the bag. He didn't count on one thing, though."

"Ablewand."

"Ablewand," I agreed. "It seems to me that Burke held back on telling the boss that he bargained it away to Hermiel. An artifact anointed with the blood of Christ kind of trumps the Lord of Hell not yet fully ascended into a mortal body. Gave us the win. That and His Holiness' sacrifice to the cause."

"I sense a certain irony when it comes to sacrifices both willing and unwilling, my friend."

A sigh blew through my lips, stolen by the wind. "Yeah, but I think that when a man sacrifices himself in the name of God it's done out of love and faith, not attributes high on the infernal pay scale."

Cain nodded. "What plans have you thoughtfully considered for your future, my friend?" He smiled down at me. "Now that the war of the ages has come to a fateful conclusion."

I laughed, but without much humor. "Sorry, Cain, but the war isn't over, just one small chapter, one battle. As long as there is Good and Evil, there will always be struggle. Lucifer still sits on his throne of bones and blood, weakened and hurt, but still plotting." I drew in a goodly lungful of Himalayan air. Tasted a lot different than Paris or Omaha. "My part isn't done by a long shot. The Family is still out there, their Board still plotting, still raising little Sicarii weapons, still fomenting war and death. Like their master, they're down, but not out and the Templars need some serious rebuilding. That's my job. I have a feeling it's gonna take the rest of my life." I raised my voice above the helos whine. "What do you have planned."

Darkness had begun to settle, and Cain removed his sunglass to reveal eyes so brown they almost appeared black. "For the first time in my long life, I have no clue."

I laughed. "Good for you. Go be spontaneous, it'll make you feel great. Perhaps start using sentences with as few words as possible. For me, the College of Cardinals will pick a new Pope anytime now and after that the Vatican needs to be weeded some ... the Sicarii have had way too much influence there and it's time to put things to right now that the Family has bigger fish to fry. Besides, it's not like I'm heading back to Omaha anytime soon."

"And how, my goodly and godly friend, do you know this new High Pontiff will be of a caliber and quality to join the crusade against the evil that still threatens our fair world?"

"I don't, but I have faith."

An End

AUTHOR BIO

B ORN IN HELSINKI, FINLAND, MARK EVERETT STONE arrived in the U.S. at a young age and promptly dove into the world of the fantastic. Starting at age seven with the Iliad and the Odyssey, he went on to consume every scrap of Norse Mythology he could get his grubby little paws on. At age thirteen he graduated to Tolkien and Heinlein, building up a book collection that soon rivaled the local public library's. In college Mark majored in Journalism and minored in English. Mark is feverishly working on his next book while his amazingly patient wife, Brandie, keeps him and their two sons, Aeden and Gabriel, in check.

www.ingramcontent.com/pod-product-compliance
Lightning Source LLC
Chambersburg PA
CBHW011116100726
47898CB00011B/3104